Enjoy the enchanting
Rachelle Edwards
in this special volume
of two fabulous romances . . .

"Ms. Edwards is an impeccable craftsman who
imbues her tale with both wit and charm."
—*Romantic Times Magazine*

By Rachelle Edwards
Published by Fawcett Crest:

THE HIGHWAYMAN AND THE LADY

♥

LOVE FINDS A WAY

Rachelle Edwards

FAWCETT CREST • NEW YORK

A Fawcett Crest Book
Published by Ballantine Books
The Highwayman and the Lady copyright © 1989
by Rachelle Edwards
Love Finds a Way copyright © 1990 by Rachelle Edwards

http://www.randomhouse.com

Library of Congress Catalog Card Number: 96-91022

ISBN 0-449-28795-5

Manufactured in the United States of America

First Edition: June 1997

10   9   8   7   6   5   4   3   2   1

Contents

The Highwayman
and the Lady

Chapter One

The post chaise had been on the road for some time, pounding along at a spanking pace. Inside it sat the two occupants, Sir Hector Hamilton and his younger daughter, Leonora.

Sir Hector occupied his time reading as best he could whilst the carriage swayed from side to side, and his daughter eased her tedium by gazing out at the endless hedgerows that flashed past the window. When at last a sigh escaped her lips, Sir Hector looked up from his book.

"Leonora, my dear, is something troubling you?"

The girl turned to smile at her father, and it transformed her face, which was naturally pale. Her eyes were of the clearest blue, fringed by long, dark lashes, and they always sparkled with liveliness. Her fair hair, dressed in a profusion of fashionable curls, formed a frame for the perfect oval of her face.

"It is nothing, Papa," she answered.

"If the journey is becoming onerous to you, I must point out we still have a fair way to go."

"No, it is not that," she answered, smiling faintly.

"Then what is it that teases you?"

"I simply wish I did not have to leave Mama just now. I really would have preferred to stay at Talworth to be at her side."

Sir Hector closed his book. "Your desire to stay close to your mama does you great credit, my dear. Indeed, you have always been the most conscientious of daughters since your mother became an invalid, but you know full well it is her dearest wish that you enjoy a Season in London."

"I daresay it will be very diverting after rusticating for so long . . ."

"Your mama will be well looked after by the servants, never you fear. They are all devoted to her. Naturally, as soon as I

3

see you safely ensconced in your sister's house, I will return to her."

"I shall certainly miss you both," Leonora told him in heartfelt tones. "I shall even miss Edmund, and look upon his tiresome ways with more fondness than I do when I am at home."

"The house will certainly seem empty without you, even with your brother at home. He will be going to Eton soon enough in any event."

Suddenly Leonora chuckled. "Aunt Eudoria was bound to be mortified when she discovered it is Christobel who is bringing me out."

"That was your sister's choice, even though she is much occupied with domestic matters. I have it in mind you will deal better with your sister than mine."

Leonora laughed. "Aunt Eudoria only appears daunting, and I am exceedingly fond of Freddie."

"You must know, Leonora, it will please us all when you are well settled with an establishment of your own. We only hope you eventually make as good a match as your sister."

Once again Leonora's pale cheeks became tinged with pink. "She and Sir Philip are very happy, I daresay, and it will be good to become reacquainted with the children again. After some months they always seem to have grown so much. To spend an entire Season with them will be most enjoyable."

"Not to mention all the balls, routs, and assemblies your sister will be arranging for you to attend," he added slyly.

Although Leonora's cheeks dimpled, she said, "My enjoyment of them will be tinged by my thoughts of Mama."

"Naturally she will miss you, and so shall I, but it is our wish you go to London." Leonora sighed again, and her father brought out his gold hunter, which he glanced at before returning to his pocket. "We should soon be arriving at the Crown and Anchor for our supper," he remarked. "Traveling is always tedious, I find."

Leonora pushed her hands farther into her muff. "Fortunately it is not too long a journey. We shall be in London on the morrow."

"I own I shall be glad when we are nearer town."

"The thought of supper is an inviting one."

He frowned. "It is not for that reason I mentioned it. This

4

stretch of road is a known haunt of highwaymen, and the delay we had in leaving our last stop has made us later than I would have wished. I did hope to reach the Crown before dark. It was always intended that we should."

His daughter, who was renowned for her spirit, turned to look at her father in alarm. "Highwaymen! Oh do not say there is a danger of being held up. I had it in mind that patrols had all but put an end to that peril."

Sir Hector smiled slightly. "Forgive me, my dear. I would not for anything alarm you. I was, in a sense, thinking aloud. It is, of course, true horse patrols have put these cursed tobymen to flight, but only nearer London. Here in the country, there are still a few isolated incidents, but do not fear, I have a few guineas in a purse to satisfy any tobyman who has the temerity to accost us."

"I hope you have also brought your pistols, which are more like to protect us." Sir Hector sighed. "Papa, you did bring your pistols?" Leonora insisted, feeling a sudden rush of alarm.

"I intended to, I own, but your brother at the very last minute diverted me just when I was about to fetch them from the gun room." His daughter gasped and fell back against the squabs, and he went on to assure her, "The driver has a shotgun, so you may have no fear. In any event it is most unlikely that we'll encounter any villains."

"I hadn't given much thought to the matter, but now I recall that I have heard tell of a tobyman by the name of Captain Starlight. Mayhap he robs carriages on this stretch of road. Do you know of that, too, Papa?"

Sir Hector smiled faintly. "I cannot be certain."

"They say he is totally ruthless and has an enormous price upon his head. It would be terrifying to be held up by such a criminal."

"Oh dear," murmured Sir Hector. "I do wish I hadn't spoken. I daresay, I have alarmed you unduly."

It was Leonora's turn to be reassuring. "I am being foolish, Papa. As you say, we should reach the Crown safely before long now."

When the coach began to slow down, Sir Hector smiled. "I daresay, we are approaching the hostelry now, so you may rest assured, my dear. We are quite safe."

5

"Christobel must be eagerly awaiting our arrival so we can begin to shop. Mama would have enjoyed that. I have resolved to write to her often, to tell her of all my news. I recall Christobel writing to us when she had her Season, and we so enjoyed hearing of her pursuits around Town."

Just as the carriage jolted to a complete stop, Sir Hector frowned and put his head out of the window. He looked no less worried when he looked at his daughter again.

"This is not the inn. I wonder why we have stopped here."

Before Leonora could vent her own anxiety, the sound of shouting could be heard and then the noise of a thud. Just as Sir Hector was about to open the door, a face loomed in the aperture, causing Leonora to scream and to shrink back into the squabs.

"Out yer get, the both of yer," the man called, pulling open the carriage door. "We've got a pair o' the Quality 'ere and no mistake."

As the door opened, the occupants could see he was brandishing a pistol in a most threatening manner.

"I have a purse you can gladly have if you let us be on our way," Sir Hector told him.

"Out!" the ruffian repeated, and then, looking across at Leonora, "Yer can leave the muff in there, if yer please, and move very slowly the both of yer if yer value yer lives."

Leonora was about to utter a protest, but when her father flashed her a warning look, she complied with the villain's instructions. Sir Hector climbed down under the watchful eye of the ruffian, and then he gave his hand to Leonora. When she stepped into the road, she saw the driver and postilion standing with their hands in the air, the shotgun lying some distance away on the verge. The highwayman who had ordered them out was a small fellow made bold by his pistol, which he kept pointed at them all the while. Since his hat was pulled low over his brow and a muffler was tied around the lower part of his face, it was impossible to see his features, although his speech was not that of a gentleman.

However, it was immediately apparent he was not alone. Another highwayman was seated astride a coal black mare, and he, too, pointed a pistol in their direction. As soon as they had alighted from the carriage, the small man climbed inside, and they could hear noises that indicated he was searching it most thoroughly.

"You may have our money," Sir Hector told the horseman. "Just let us be on our way. We have an unconscionable distance to travel before we reach our destination."

The rider was enveloped in a frieze coat and a beaver hat that was pulled low. Like his accomplice he wore a muffler to hide the lower part of his face. Leonora looked up at him and involuntarily shuddered, for he seemed so large, so black, and very sinister, outlined against the darkening sky.

"How dare you stop Sir Hector Hamilton going about his lawful business," she protested, her fear making her bold.

The highwayman merely laughed behind his muffler. "I admire your spirit, ma'am, but do not, I beg of you, seek to hinder Captain Starlight, going about his unlawful business."

"You are brave behind your pistol and muffler, sir!"

"My daughter is young, sir," Sir Hector hastily explained. "She means no disrespect."

"Your daughter, sir? By gad."

The other man came out of the carriage saying, "Nothing there, Cap'n."

"There must be," the rider snapped.

"Ripped out the squabs, and I vow if there was anything to find, I'd be the one to uncover it."

"We have no valuables," Leonora protested. "Why won't you believe us and let us be on our way?"

"Here," Sir Hector offered, passing his purse to the highwayman. "This is all I have with me, but you are welcome to it."

"You'll regret hiding anything from Captain Starlight," the rider warned them. "Hand them over now, and you can be on your way with no further hindrance."

"I assure you we have nothing more with us," Sir Hector pleaded. "I have given you all I have with me."

At this point Captain Starlight turned his attention to Leonora. She could see only the dark intensity of his eyes, which made her shiver.

"Come here," he ordered.

When she appeared disinclined to obey, the other man pushed the pistol in her back and edged her forward.

7

"No!" Sir Hector protested, his eyes wide with fear. "Leave her alone, I beg of you! She is but a child. Can you not see that?"

When he rushed forward to his daughter's aid, the rider edged his horse between them. "Stay where you are, sir, and all will be well."

"Papa, don't give him any reason to harm you," Leonora begged, distressed more by the look of fear on her father's face than any threatened danger to herself.

"Good grief, sir, what do you want from us?"

"If you have valuables with you, I want you to hand them to me now," Captain Starlight answered.

"There are none, else I would gladly hand them over to you."

"In that event you may well pay a fine ransom for the chit. If not, I may have a fancy to keep her for myself."

Leonora gasped, but before she fully understood what was happening, Captain Starlight had reached down and pulled her up in front of him. She began to struggle, but one arm pinned her against him—a viselike grip—while his other hand expertly handled the horse's reins.

"Leonora!" Sir Hector cried in anguish. "In the name of pity, set her down! Take me in her stead."

"Papa!" she called to him, but her cry was lost as Captain Starlight dug his spurs in the horse's flanks and galloped away.

Still she struggled in his steely grasp. Even through her panic she could still be nauseated by the smell of the stable that clung to his frieze coat. She jabbed at him constantly with her elbows until at last he slowed his horse to a trot.

"Madam, if you do not cease to struggle, I shall be obliged to render you senseless."

The note of resolve in his voice was not lost on Leonora, and after that she contrived to hold herself stiffly in an attempt to have as little contact with the vile creature as possible.

"That's better," she heard him mutter as the horse took up speed again. "I do like an obedient wench."

Normally, riding her own horse through the land adjacent to Talworth House, Leonora loved to feel the wind in her face. Today, however, as a damp dusk began to fall, she could feel only the stinging of her tears on her cheeks.

8

Although the highwayman's words were muffled, she had the distinct feeling he was not the ruffian his accomplice had appeared to be. This did not surprise her, since so many officers had returned from the war penniless and disaffected only to turn to crime. The fact that this particular villain enjoyed the title of captain seemed to indicate that he was one of this breed, but that did not reassure her. Ex-officer or not, he could be as ruthless as the lowest creature, and she was afraid as she had never been in her life before. The sheltered environs of Talworth House had not prepared her for the unsavory side of life.

They seemed to have been riding for a long time, but she could not be sure. Her fear only served to nullify most of her other senses. Leonora was aware that they had left the road and were traveling cross-country now. It was almost totally dark except when the moon came out from behind a cloud, but the highwayman seemed to know where he was going and his horse was surefooted. Indeed, Leonora knew he must have a safe hiding place, or else he would have been apprehended long ago. Captain Starlight had a reputation not only for being dangerous but also for his cunning in evading all attempts at capture. Concerted efforts throughout the county had failed to effect his capture over a long period of time.

The narrow path they had taken widened suddenly, and there, in a clearing, stood a cottage that Leonora knew was their destination. Its very isolation and air of desolation filled her with fear anew. As they came closer, she could see it was no more than a hovel, but there appeared to be a light in the window. Evidently it was remote enough for the highwayman not to concern himself about discovery. In the depths of her despair Leonora acknowledged he could hold her here for as long as he wished.

When the mare came to a halt outside the cottage to Captain Starlight's soft "Whoa!" he dismounted.

"This is an abomination!" she declared, determined not to show her fear. "You will answer for this to the highest authority."

"Come along down now, ma'am," he ordered, apparently unmoved by her threat. "You will be much more comfortable inside."

"Comfortable! Do you truly believe that Sir Hector Hamilton's daughter would find anything remotely resembling comfort in such a hovel?"

"I truly regret that a palace was not available tonight, your highness," he scoffed, something that could only increase her rage and frustration.

"What will you do with my father?" she demanded.

"It is what I shall do with you that should concern you." When a strangled gasp escaped her, the highwayman went on quickly, "I don't doubt he is, at this moment, making arrangements for a ransom to be paid. At least that is what he will do if he is the sensible cove I believe him to be."

"I may as well warn you that he is not a rich man."

"Richer than I" came the reply.

"My mother is an invalid. If news of my abduction reaches her, I dare not contemplate the result."

"Then it is all the more imperative for the ransom to be paid, but that, I assure you, is the least of your concerns just now, madam."

"Have you no pity?"

"Come along now," he said abruptly. "You will grow chilled sitting there."

"Your concern for my welfare is quite overwhelming," she muttered sarcastically as she climbed down at last, avoiding any assistance from him.

It was not until her feet actually reached the ground that Leonora realized she was none too steady on her feet. The highwayman reached out to steady her, and she recoiled from his touch. Up until that moment she had been too angry to know a very real fear, but out there in the middle of nowhere, at this man's mercy, she realized at last what a situation she was in, and she shuddered involuntarily.

"What is going to happen to me?" she asked in an unsteady whisper, allowing fear to show through her bravado at last.

"Now, just what do you think is going to happen to you?"

Although his face remained obscured and his voice muffled, Leonora gained the distinct impression he was teasing her, but she was not at all reassured. Once again she shivered, and he took her arm and propelled her into the hovel, slamming the door shut behind them.

The tiny room was cold and filthy despite the meager fire in the hearth, and some evident, but not very effective, attempts to clean it. As Leonora stumbled inside, the unmistakable smell of tallow candle assailed her. It was murky in there despite the one lighted candle, and it was a moment or two before she realized that someone else was present. Near the fire sat a woman who seemed not in the least surprised to see the highwayman return with a woman.

"You're back sooner than expected," she told him, eyeing Leonora coldly as she got to her feet.

"Dame Fortune was with us this night," he explained. "It was surprisingly easy. Take her upstairs, but be careful, Meggy. She's got spirit."

The woman smiled grimly. "No more than I'd expect, but she'll not escape me, you may be certain, Cap'n."

All the while they conversed Leonora's mind had been working on the possibility of escape. Captain Starlight blocked the way back to the door, so she knew there was no way out there. In any event she had the oddest feeling he expected her to attempt an escape in that manner and was ready to stop her. The only other thing she could do was feign weakness until an opportunity for escape presented itself.

"Have mercy upon me," she begged in a voice she scarce recognized as her own.

When she put one hand to her head and swayed, the woman warned, "Watch her! She is going to swoon."

As she went limp, Leonora felt herself being caught and held tightly. From the strength of the arms that went around her and the smell of his coat, Leonora knew that Captain Starlight stopped her falling to the floor. A moment later she felt herself being swept up into his arms and carried up some rickety steps. Leonora did not dare open her eyes, and it was difficult for her not to cry out in fear and alarm at being held so close to this vile creature, but she contrived to continue her swoon.

The woman he'd called Meggy must have followed with a candle, for the upstairs room grew lighter when they got to the top of the stairs.

"She looks too young," the woman murmured as Leonora

was being carried across the room. "This might well be a mistake after all."

"The thought has occurred to me, but we must not underestimate our enemy," he replied. "That would be an even greater mistake."

He placed her with surprising gentleness on what seemed to be a pallet. Leonora squinted through her lashes and saw him looming over her very close. Swiftly she reached out to pull the concealing muffler away from his face, but his hand clamped about her wrist, holding it in a vise. She gasped in pain and was close enough to see the menace glittering in his eyes. She knew then what a foolish gesture she had made. Her only hope of salvation was if he remained unrecognizable.

"Have a care, madam," he warned. "My patience is not endless and you might regret crossing Captain Starlight."

The woman sniggered and in exasperation Leonora sat up, just as he let go of her wrist. "How I will rejoice when I see you swing from the gibbet, sir, and enjoy every journey that takes me past Hevening Hill, where you'll hang in chains for all eternity. Children will be brought to see you as an awful warning. The thought of that day will sustain me until I am back with my loved ones."

He was staring at her, which was a disconcerting experience, and then he said, "Who'd have thought you such a chatterbox?" before turning on his heel and striding across the room toward the stairs.

As soon as his footsteps had died away, Leonora pushed off her bonnet, which had become askew, and swung her legs over the edge of the pallet. As she took her bonnet off, her hair came free of most of its pins and fell to her shoulders in a golden cloud.

"How long do you intend to keep me here?" she asked, feeling utterly dejected now.

"As long as it takes, dearie."

After considering the woman for a moment or two, Leonora said, "If you are seeking wealth, I know where it is to be found."

The woman looked satisfied. "I knew you'd see it our way in the end. Where is it, then? You can tell me."

"There is a reward for the capture of the tobyman. If you help me escape, the reward will be yours, and my father will, no doubt, add his own gratitude."

12

The woman laughed. "If I cross the captain, I might as well be dead."

Leonora eyed her coldly. "What kind of creature are you to consort with such an evil man?"

"Evil is a matter of perspective. It's how you look at it that matters in the end."

Leonora looked up in surprise, her eyes narrowing. "Perspective is a fine word for a tobyman's doxy to use."

The woman's face twisted into an ugly grimace, and then she reached out and pulled Leonora to her feet. The girl gasped with pain, but immediately recovered her wits to say:

"If you harm me, there would be no point in my father paying any ransom, so be pleased to desist."

"Mayhap there's ransom enough here already. We've just got to find it. Take off your gown and hand it to me with your cloak."

Leonora's eyes grew wide. "What did you say?"

"You heard me well enough, I fancy. Take it off and give it to me."

"Certainly not," Leonora retorted, her head thrown back in a defiant gesture.

"If you don't, missy, I can easily do it for you, but let me warn you, Captain Starlight is an expert in that line. Would you like me to call him back to assist? He'd be obliged to me if I did."

Once again Leonora felt tears of frustration pricking at her eyes, but she fought them back as she handed over her fur-lined traveling cloak to the woman.

"Now, don't try to be facy with me," she warned. "You can't escape, so don't make any attempt."

"I never imagined anyone could be as depraved as you and that creature who calls himself Captain Starlight. What an insult to all our brave fighting men." The woman smiled oddly as she searched the cloak's lining carefully. "What do you think you'll find? There is nothing concealed, I tell you, nothing."

Leonora shivered in her lawn shift as she handed over her gown at last. The woman searched every inch of it before muttering, "Nothing. Nothing. But there must be—somewhere."

When she heard heavy footsteps on the stairs, Leonora's head snapped up in alarm. Then the highwayman appeared at the top of the stairs. He stopped, staring across at her as she stood in her

13

shift in the half-light, unaware that the position of the solitary candle rendered her thin garment almost transparent.

"There's nothing here. Nothing at all," Meggy cried in desperation. "I don't understand."

Captain Starlight came across the room then, and Leonora flinched away from him. He seemed suddenly even more dark and menacing than before. Before he reached her, he snatched the gown from Meggy, thrusting it toward Leonora.

"Put it on," he ordered in a terse voice.

Somewhere through her fear a sound registered in her mind. A horse was approaching. As the highwayman moved back toward the stairs, Leonora slipped on her gown, sensing a reprieve of sorts. The door to the cottage banged shut, and footsteps thundered across the flags and up the stairs. The other highwayman appeared at the top. He looked across at Leonora for a long moment, and then he turned to Captain Starlight and began to whisper in an agitated way. Much of his excitement conveyed itself to Leonora, who could not hear what was being said. Her spirits rose a little when she wondered if the ransom had been paid, although it seemed unlikely so soon after the abduction.

However, a moment later, she started when Captain Starlight cried, "Hell and damnation!" and thumped his fist against the wall, making her fearful once more, and then he stared across at her again for a moment, which seemed to last forever, before turning on his heel and hurrying down the steps. He was followed by his two accomplices. Seconds later the door slammed again. Leonora could hear the whickering of the horses and then the sound of them galloping away. After that there was silence, broken only occasionally by the hooting of an owl or the cry of some wild creature in the fields.

As she listened to the silence, Leonora began to shiver uncontrollably. The fear that pride had kept at bay in the presence of her captors now took hold of her in their absence. After a moment she reached out for her cloak and wrapped it around her. Presently the trembling ceased, and her thoughts began to take form again. That someone had left was not in doubt, but she had no way of knowing if one of them remained downstairs to guard her. Meggy and the other man were loathsome enough, but she

14

shuddered at the thought that Captain Starlight might be lurking in the room below, just waiting for her to try to escape.

After a while she walked over to the tiny window, but could see nothing save the trees a few yards from the building. She still had no notion where she could be, and she really couldn't fathom how long she had been left alone there.

As she reached out for the window catch, she saw that her hand was trembling. Despite that, she pulled at the catch. It was rusty and looked as if it hadn't been used for years, but Leonora persisted, pushing harder and at the same time desperately trying not to make any sound. Her feelings were made even more tense by the knowledge that her captors might return at any moment and catch her trying to escape. At the thought of that, as she struggled to move the catch, beads of perspiration broke out on her brow, and she discarded the cloak. After what seemed to be an age, and with Herculean effort, the rusty catch did begin to move. When she made one final effort, the catch gave way and the window creaked open. In the silence it sounded exceedingly loud. Leonora froze and listened intently, but to her great relief, the silence remained unbroken.

Breathing a little easier, she rested her head against the wall for a moment or two, her eyes closed. Then she rallied to push the casement open as wide as it would go. The cool night air felt good on her cheeks, and when she put her head out the window, she experienced a great surge of excitement, for she could see a creeper was growing up the wall very close to the window.

She reached out and tugged at it as best she could. It appeared firm enough, but she knew there was only one way to test it properly. Taking only enough time to glance back toward the stairs, Leonora sat on the window ledge and swung her legs out. Although she urged herself to go slowly for safety's sake, every nerve in her body impelled her to hurry. Tentatively she gripped the creeper, found a foothold, and then carefully began to climb down.

When her foot encountered the ground at last, Leonora could scarcely believe she had gained her freedom. Glancing around, she saw the lane from which she and Captain Starlight had approached the clearing, so it seemed to be the route to avoid, and she turned and began to run in the opposite direction, plunging into a newly plowed field. Her prime objective was to put as many miles as possible between her and the cottage.

At the other side of the field she plunged into a wood that afforded some concealment, but in the dark, with only the intermittent light of the moon filtering through the branches, it was a terrifying place. Every so often she stumbled on a tree root, grazing her legs, tearing at the hem of her gown and her stockings, and on one occasion scratching her cheek on a low branch when it whipped against her.

When she eventually came out of the wood, Leonora was close to exhaustion, but she did find herself on what appeared to be a main road. It was, she realized, the only place she might find help. It was also the most likely place Captain Starlight would come across her.

Whatever the risks, however, Leonora knew she must rest for a while, and she sat down on a milestone, burying her head in her hands, wondering how she had come to this sorry state. That very morning she and her father had set out on an exciting journey to London with only the fact of her mother's chronic ill health to tease her mind. At the time that matter was concern enough. It seemed inconceivable then that the day could have turned into such a nightmare.

As she sat there on the point of exhaustion, the distant sound of pounding hooves could be heard. As the sound came closer, a wave of hope surged through her. Help was on its way. But then, as she got to her feet, she caught sight of a rider in the distance, outlined against the moonlit sky. The hope died and she was filled with dread once more. It could be Captain Starlight. Who else but a highwayman would be abroad at night on the King's highway?

In desperation she looked around for a place of concealment, and for the first time she saw that a pair of gates at the opposite side of the road appeared to lead to a driveway. Leonora rushed across the road and through the gates just as the horseman thundered by. She ran as fast as she could in her exhausted state, but was tempted simply to lie down and give in to her utter fatigue. Just when she had decided to do that, she saw ahead of her the lights of a house. Somewhere not far away a dog barked. She was reminded of her own home, a haven, which now seemed so far away. What of Papa? she thought as she pressed on. Was he out of his mind with worry by now? Had Captain Starlight's accomplice harmed him in any way? She had come a long way since leaving the hovel, but the house ahead of her seemed just as far distant now.

The barking of the dog seemed louder, however, and she thought she could see a flickering light coming closer. When a large dog bounded at her out of the darkness, Leonora screamed, then stumbled, and fell in front of it.

"Hold hard!" a voice ordered.

"Help me!" she cried, raising her head from the gravel. "Please help me."

As she looked up, it was to see a lantern being held over her while the dog pranced and snarled about her. She couldn't see who bore the lantern, but she implored, "I have just escaped an abductor. Leonora Hamilton, daughter of Sir Hector Hamilton of Talworth. Please . . . help . . . me . . ."

"Good grief!"

"It's a lady, sir."

"Yes, indeed, I can see it is" was the brusque reply. "Here, Simmonds, hold the lantern while I assist her. Down, Jemma! Heel, I say!"

The dog grew silent, and withdrew a few paces, and Leonora almost fainted with relief. The creature had looked quite fearsome in the lantern light. Strong hands were helping her to her feet and she was glad enough to allow herself to be assisted. The strength that had aided her escape now seemed to have deserted her. She felt a coat being wrapped around her frozen shoulders, and the warmth it afforded was very welcome in the chill of the night.

"My God, she's as light as a feather," the gentleman declared. "Simmonds, I can manage myself. Go ahead and warn Mrs. Torrington of our coming."

After being helped along a short way, Leonora felt herself being lifted into someone's arms. The odor of his cologne made her senses swim, but she did feel safe at last.

Moments later Leonora was aware of being carried into a large hall so bright that she was dazzled. What seemed to be a great many people were milling around her, exclaiming loudly.

17

"The poor child is in such a state," a lady's voice proclaimed. "What can have befallen her?"

"She says she was abducted," a man replied.

"How shocking. Do you think it's true?"

"Does it matter? She needs our help."

"She is in a pitiable condition. We might be obliged to burn feathers."

"Do what you can for her. Shall I send for a physician?"

"I will let you know presently. Come along, my dear," she addressed Leonora. "Let us make you more comfortable."

Suddenly Leonora felt herself being bundled up a wide flight of stairs and into a wonderfully warm room. When she opened her eyes, it was to see women scurrying about what appeared to be a bedchamber. There was a four-poster bed at the far side of the room, and she could feel the welcome warmth of a roaring fire.

Hands were undressing her, and Leonora found that she had no will either to resist or assist them. Moments later she was being immersed in a warm, perfumed bath. As the grime was washed away, she found herself hoping that the taint of Captain Starlight would also be removed. Gentle hands wrapped her in a towel, and then a soft lawn bed gown was passed over her head. Leonora sank gladly into the soft folds of the bed, but before she could put her head on the pillow, some liquid was forced between her lips. Then she knew no more.

Chapter Two

A large black figure loomed up before her. Leonora choked back a scream and then opened her eyes. Memory rushed back in that instant. She recalled everything that had happened to her, even falling asleep in the huge four-poster the previous evening. Now she could see its hangings of pretty chintz that matched the curtains at the windows. Everywhere there seemed to be the fresh smell of beeswax, and each piece of fine furniture gleamed as if new.

It was immediately evident that she had fallen into the hands of respectable gentlefolk. In her distress the night before, she hadn't even given a thought to the possibility that she might have become embroiled with those as evil as Captain Starlight and his cohorts.

When Leonora heard the scrape of a coal scuttle, she turned to see a maid moving away from the fire, and then another figure came into her line of vision, a woman who was smiling. She had a plain face but it was a kind one. Her clothes were not in the least modish, but Leonora was glad to see her.

"Miss Hamilton? It is Miss Hamilton, is it not?"

"Yes. Where am I?"

The woman put the tray she was carrying onto the bedside table. "Hevening House."

Leonora shook her head perplexedly. "I do beg your pardon, ma'am, but who are you?"

Again the woman smiled. "I am Anne Torrington. I live here with my brother, Sir Ashley Warrender. It was he who found you last night."

"I am most obliged to him, and to you."

When she attempted to move, her bones felt sore and stiff, and the woman asked, looking suddenly anxious, "Do you remember coming here last night?"

Momentarily Leonora closed her eyes before nodding. Then she begged, "Please, Mrs. Torrington, I must send word to my father . . ."

Anne Torrington smiled once again. "Don't let it trouble your head, my dear. My brother has the matter in hand. You did tell him all he needed to know to contact your relatives. In the meantime you must rest. You were quite overset when you arrived."

"I cannot thank you enough."

"Tush. Anyone would have done the same. Here, take some chocolate and bread and butter. It will make you feel better."

It had been more than four and twenty hours since she had last eaten, and Leonora did find she was hungry. She quickly devoured the food under the watchful eye of Anne Torrington.

19

When she had finished, Leonora said, a little shyly, "I really am most obliged to you and your brother for your kindness to me."

"You must not mention it again, I entreat you. It was no more than any right-thinking folk would have done in the circumstances. Tell me, is it true you were abducted by a highwayman?"

At the reminder Leonora's eyes immediately filled with tears. "Yes."

"Such an experience is like to unhinge a less stoic person than yourself, ma'am."

Leonora stared past her into the distance. "It was truly dreadful. I feared for my life, but what Papa must have experienced, not knowing my fate, I cannot conceive."

"My dear, your concern for Sir Hector is laudable, but it must have been far worse for you." She frowned slightly. "Now that you are safe, you will naturally wish to put the wretched matter behind you, but my brother happens to be the magistrate for this parish and would wish to question you. Do you feel able to face that? If you do not, I assure you, I shall inform him of the fact, and you will not be troubled."

Leonora struggled to sit up in the pillows. "If I can contribute anything, anything whatsoever, to the apprehension of that fiend, I am willing to do so. What happened to me must not be allowed to occur to any other female."

Once again the woman smiled as she got up from her chair. "I do admire your spirit, and I know my brother will be most obliged to you for your fortitude, Miss Hamilton."

"It is my bounden duty, Mrs. Torrington. I can do no less."

"Captain Starlight, as he calls himself, has become quite dangerous, and Ashe is determined to oversee his apprehension. It has become something of a crusade for him. When you feel well enough to get out of bed, and I entreat you not to hurry yourself, I will send one of the maids to assist you."

Even before Mrs. Torrington had finished speaking, Leonora was swinging her legs over the side of the bed. "I am ready now."

Again Anne Torrington looked concerned. "Miss Hamilton, do have a care. I would not have you succumb to a chill after being exposed to the elements for so long."

"Oh, I am quite recovered," Leonora replied, casting her a

grateful smile, "and I would not wish to impose upon you a moment longer than is absolutely necessary, ma'am."

"Oh, my dear, it is no imposition, I assure you. Much as I deplore the dreadful ordeal you have undergone, I assure you life here is never out of the ordinary, and a visitor is always very welcome. Since my brother inherited this estate, he has been so engrossed in its running, he has had little time for social intercourse; and I have lived here only a short while, during which the interior needed a good deal of attention."

"I did wonder why we did not know you. From the little I have yet seen, the house does you great credit, Mrs. Torrington."

When the woman smiled, she looked almost beautiful, possessing wide brown eyes and clear skin. Leonora wondered if there was a Mr. Torrington. "Thank you, my dear, but the great burden of work has fallen upon Ashe. On my shoulders has fallen the pleasurable task of spending his money."

"You have done it with great taste, ma'am," Leonora assured her.

Again Anne Torrington frowned. "Your gown has been cleaned and mended as best we could contrive, my dear, but it is still a sorry sight."

"I don't doubt it will suffice until I return home."

"Take all the time you need to dress, and I shall see you downstairs when you are ready."

When Leonora began to dress, it was clear that Anne Torrington had not exaggerated the state of her clothing, but it merely served to remind her of her fortunate escape. As the maid helped her style her hair, she reflected that she had been equally fortunate in finding herself at Hevening House. Soon she would be reunited with Papa, and the incident could be put behind them both. But she wondered how quickly the memory of it would fade from her. It seemed certain that the recollection of Captain Starlight's dark menace would return to haunt her for some time to come. Even now the memory caused her to shiver, but the sight of the sunshine streaming in through the window soon dismissed the thoughts that alarmed her.

Eventually she emerged from the bedchamber, feeling shy and uncertain again, for she had no real knowledge of those who lived here. Mrs. Torrington had proved herself to be kindness itself, but Leonora was very conscious that she had burst into the lives of these people and they must be somewhat bemused.

Her memory of arriving was only a mass of jumbled images, but now, in the light of late morning, she could see she was in a most handsome house. A wide staircase curved downward into a hall, which had a splendid marble floor. Niches and alcoves were filled with busts, and paintings of ladies and gentlemen in the dress of various bygone ages adorned the walls. All those depicted bore a faint resemblance to the others. The family War-render, no doubt, Leonora decided, and from what she could see, it must be a very old one. She wondered if her father knew of them. It would be odd if he did not, for they could not live so very far from her own home at Talworth. The problem was that since her mother had been an invalid for so long, they did not go visiting, and only those friends of long-standing troubled to call upon them.

As she contemplated her surroundings, a noise made her start and look at an upper gallery to see two small children peering down at her through the banister rails. Leonora's face relaxed into a smile, and she called out a greeting to them, whereupon they began to giggle and then ran away to the upper floor of the house.

When they had gone, Leonora started down the stairs, not at all looking forward to answering Sir Ashley Warrender's questions, which would bring back all manner of unwelcome memories. Even now she could scarcely believe she was safe with the nightmare behind her. All at once she was angry. Captain Starlight had infested the roads in the area for some considerable time, so why had he not been apprehended? she asked herself. It seemed evident not enough effort was being made to bring the villain to book.

She was halfway down the stairs when the front door opened and a man strode in. Leonora immediately stopped on the stairs and watched, as he took off his high-crowned beaver and threw his gloves and riding whip into it before handing them to the house steward.

As he shrugged out of his many-caped driving coat, Leonora heard him ask, "How is our visitor today?"

"I believe she is much recovered, sir," the lackey replied.

22

Just then Leonora could see only the back of the man's head, which was a mass of glossy black hair. He appeared to be dressed more fashionably than she had expected here in the depths of the country. Mrs. Torrington was quite old-fashioned in her mode of apparel, but her brother's brown riding coat was of an excellent cut, his shoulders broad, his waist slim. Leonora was certain Beau Brummel himself would find no fault with this man's appearance, and she was, for some reason, taken aback.

She must have made some noise, for he turned on his heel and then looked up to where she was standing, one hand resting on the banister rail. For a moment he stared at her, and she was once again surprised, for she had somehow expected a man much older. However, it appeared he was younger than his sister. There was no expression on his face as his dark eyes surveyed her, but that in itself was disconcerting. Momentarily she was reminded of the way Captain Starlight had gazed at her, and she shivered and looked away from him.

"Miss Hamilton, good day to you," he greeted her. "Ashley Warrender at your service."

For a moment she was tempted to run back upstairs, but decided prosaically she was allowing her escapade to make her too fanciful. She began to come down the stairs again, forcing a smile to her lips, although she wasn't sure why she felt so distant. Ashley Warrender was a handsome man, but there was something very daunting about him, too.

"It appears that you already have been, Sir Ashley. I am entirely in your debt for your assistance last night."

The ghost of a smile passed his lips, softening his severe expression, but Leonora gained the distinct impression that did not happen very often. "It is an honor, ma'am."

"I must beg your pardon most heartily for intruding on your privacy."

"I entreat you do not, ma'am. You would do me an honor if you accepted my apology." As Leonora looked perplexed, he explained, "For my inability to bring this villain to justice before you were so ill-used."

"No one could possibly lay the blame with you, sir, but I do trust that the omission will soon be mended."

"You may rest assured that every effort is being made. The

23

countryside is now being scoured for any trace of the black-guard."

"I am glad to hear you say so. I am anxious for my father to be told of my safety, Sir Ashley."

Once again that elusive smile softened the severity of his expression. "Be assured, Miss Hamilton, a note was dispatched at first light this morning. I am certain he is on his way here now."

Momentarily Leonora looked surprised. "I am increasingly indebted to you." Even as she spoke, Leonora was unable to inject any warmth into her manner, despite having such great cause to be grateful to him.

"You did tell us a little about yourself last night before you were overcome by exhaustion, which I am glad to say is all that ailed you."

A door opened and a large dog came bounding into the hall and up to Sir Ashley. He bent and patted the dog whom Leonora believed was the one that had knocked her over the night before.

"Jemma can be a little overzealous on occasions," her master explained. Then he looked up at Leonora again. "Miss Hamilton, I appreciate the horror of the ordeal you endured yesterday, and I know full well you only wish to put it behind you, but there are so few witnesses who have actually seen Captain Starlight, and none, apart from yourself, who has been in such close proximity to him . . ."

"You wish me to answer your questions, sir," she said, taking in a deep breath.

"Only if you are certain it will not overset your sensibilities in doing so."

Leonora managed to smile at last, although it was a grim one. "I am made of sterner stuff, sir."

He regarded her carefully for a moment or two before he said, "So it would seem. I am bound to confess I am full of admiration for you, ma'am. Moreover, I am as anxious as you that this tobyman be apprehended and hanged." Ashley Warrender hesitated a moment before asking, "The weather today is clement, so would you like to take a turn about the garden while we talk?" When she hesitated, he added, "I assure you, Miss Hamilton, you are entirely safe now."

"I daresay a breath of air will be welcome," she agreed at last, feeling foolish.

"You arrived last night without any outdoor clothes . . ."

"In my haste to escape, I left my cloak behind."

He nodded his understanding. "If you care to wait here for a few moments, I will fetch one of my sister's cloaks."

She watched him as he took the stairs two at a time, and then when he had gone, she noticed that the house steward and a footman were eyeing her curiously. In some confusion she turned her attention to the dog, whose dark brown eyes studied her hopefully.

"Shall you and I be friends now, Jemma?" Leonora asked, and the dog came and sniffed at her suspiciously.

By the time Sir Ashley came back down the stairs, followed by his sister, Leonora and Jemma were firm friends, the dog wagging her tail happily.

"Now, Ashe," Mrs. Torrington fussed, "I entreat you not to tire Miss Hamilton unduly with your questions. Have a thought for her sensibilities."

"Now, don't fuss, Anne. Miss Hamilton assures me she is made of stern stuff, and I can well believe it is so."

In his bantering Leonora saw him unbend for the first time, and it was something of a revelation. He held out the cloak, and when he enfolded it around her shoulders, she could not help but shiver slightly, recalling the feel of Captain Starlight's arms around her. Would she ever rid herself of his odious influence over her thoughts? she wondered.

"Are you certain you will be warm enough?" Mrs. Torrington asked, noting the shudder but mistaking its origin.

"I'll be fine," Leonora assured her, but as she left the house with Sir Ashley at her side and Jemma trotting at his heels, she couldn't help but wish Anne Torrington was coming with them instead of leaving her in the sole company of her enigmatic brother who, for some reason, disturbed her.

Leonora reasoned it was because he was dark and of a similar height to Captain Starlight, and for the foreseeable future all men were likely to remind her, if only vaguely, of her experience.

"Mrs. Torrington is very kind," Leonora heard herself saying as they left the house.

"Yes, indeed. A man could not wish for a finer sister."

"She did tell me she lives here with you . . ."

"She is, alas, a widow, but her misfortune has been a blessing to me. As I am unmarried, she is an ideal hostess, and I enjoy the company of my nephews."

"I too have nieces and nephews whom I adore," Leonora told him, glad of the neutral topic of conversation.

He looked at her with interest as they walked down a path in the formal garden. Gardeners were working everywhere, preparing for the coming Season.

"My sister is Lady Christobel Langridge, wife of Sir Philip Langridge," she felt bound to add as the gardeners acknowledged them respectfully as they passed by.

His eyebrows rose slightly. "I am acquainted with them even though it is some years since I last saw them."

Leonora was somewhat taken aback by the confession, for it seemed most unlikely that he knew her sister and brother-in-law, who were prominent in London Society. "I am—I was about to join them when . . ."

She glanced back to look at the house from a distance. It was not so large but quite exquisite, for the Queen Anne house was perfectly proportioned and much to her taste. "Your house is beautiful, Sir Ashley," she told him.

"How kind of you to say so, ma'am." He was hatless and his dark curls were being gently ruffled by the breeze. "A few years ago, when I inherited the place, you would not have thought so. It was all but derelict. Putting it to rights seemed a hopeless task to me then."

"Its restoration is even more to your credit than I had at first supposed."

"It has been hard work restoring the place to its former glory, I must own, but a most satisfying task now that I can look back upon it."

Coming out of the formal garden there was a gentle slope down to a small lake, its surface gently rippling in the breeze. Involuntarily Leonora's eyes misted, for there had been moments during her captivity when she had wondered if she would survive to enjoy such beauty again. Exposed, the wind now whipped at her cloak, which she clasped around her. The wind did feel good, though. It signified her freedom, and she could not help but rejoice in it, turning her face up to the sky in a gesture of gratitude for her deliverance from danger.

Leonora wasn't certain if Sir Ashley was aware of her gesture, but a moment later he touched her arm gently and then guided her toward a folly on the hillside that enjoyed an uninterrupted view of the lake and the countryside beyond. Inside, he gestured toward a bench, and when she was seated, he sat down beside her. At that moment she couldn't help but wish he had put more space between them.

"Now, Miss Hamilton, do you feel able to tell me what happened to you yesterday? You were, quite understandably, less than lucid when you arrived here, although you did manage to convey the bare bones of the matter."

Knowing he was watching her so carefully did nothing to ease her disquiet, but slowly and haltingly she told him what had occurred from the moment the carriage was held up. It seemed so odd talking about those awful events while gazing out at the peaceful scene outside the folly. She finished the tale with her discovery of the gates of Hevening House.

When her voice faded away, there was a moment's silence before he said, "How dreadful it must have been for you, Miss Hamilton. I have never before regretted not apprehending the fiend more than I do now."

"It is not your fault, sir," she said in a whisper.

"You are being uncommonly generous, ma'am."

"You are not dealing with any tobyman. This one is exceedingly cunning."

Sir Ashley chuckled mirthlessly. "Oh, indeed he is. So many others have been apprehended and brought to book, but he seems to have the ability to melt into the countryside at will."

"If you discover his cottage you will, no doubt, find the culprit."

He drew a deep sigh. "Indeed, but have you any notion how many laborers' cottages there are in this county?"

"A great many, I daresay. Do you think Captain Starlight is a laborer?"

"He could be anyone or anything," came the reply, and she

27

shuddered at the truth of that statement. Quickly he added, "I did not wish to alarm you unduly."

"It is of no matter," she replied, staring down at her hands. "The memory is still fresh in my mind, but it will grow less in time, I fancy."

Suddenly his eyes narrowed. "What exactly did he steal from you, Miss Hamilton?"

"A few guineas only, I believe. We were not foolish enough to carry more. My jewelry is with my sister in London."

"Tell me, Miss Hamilton, would you recognize him if you were to see him again?"

Leonora looked at him in alarm and then was forced to avert her gaze. "I do pray I shall not clap eyes upon him again, but if I do, I consider it unlikely I would recognize him. He took great care to keep his face covered, as did his accomplice, which leads me to suspect he is no low ruffian, but mayhap a gentleman of some kind."

Sir Ashley looked surprised. "Perchance that is why we have failed to apprehend him, but make no mistake, his days of liberty are numbered. I am determined upon that."

"Oh, I do so pray you are correct," she answered, displaying rare passion. All at once she turned to look at him. Although he still disturbed her, excitement now assailed her more forcefully. "It is true I would not recognize him, but I would certainly know his doxy, Meggy, if I were to encounter her again."

He exhibited no obvious delight at the information, merely saying, "That may be of some help. We shall see. What can you tell me about the hovel they took you to? Is there anything about it you can recall that might aid its discovery?"

"We approached in near darkness. It could have been any cottage, anywhere. Certainly I gained the impression that no one was actually living there." She hesitated for a moment before adding, "One thing I did notice was his horse." Sir Ashley looked at her curiously as she went on, "It was a fine mare, no daisy cutter. Is it likely a common tobyman would ride a piece of prime blood?"

He considered for a moment or two before saying, "Mayhap some other pieces of relevant information will return to your memory in due course."

28

"There can be nothing else, I fear, for I shall endeavor to erase the memory of it from my mind from this day onward."

"For that I cannot blame you, Miss Hamilton."

When she looked at him again, it was he who was staring out at the lake as if deep in thought. "Tell me, Sir Ashley, in your experience has Captain Starlight ever abducted anyone for ransom before?"

Slowly he withdrew his gaze away from the lake and back to her. "Not as far as I am aware."

"Then why do you think he abducted me?"

"He might have been desperate for funds or, simply," he added, getting to his feet, "enchanted by you."

Her eyes opened wide with shock when she met his brooding gaze. "Oh, that cannot be!" she gasped.

"You did make mention that he said something about keeping you for himself if no ransom was forthcoming."

The reminder caused her to shudder. She recalled Captain Starlight's mockery of her fear of him, and the way he had stared at her in her shift. It was something she had not revealed to Sir Ashley, nor would she ever divulge it to another living being.

"He was merely attempting to frighten Papa," she answered at last.

"Perchance that was so, but even the direst villain is likely to be moved by a fetching female."

Leonora jumped to her feet and preceded him out of the folly, her mind somewhat troubled by what could only be his way of trying to soothe her sensibilities, although it could only have an opposite effect.

"Tell me, Miss Hamilton, do you intend to go to London now?"

Surprised by the question, she answered, "Oh yes, I daresay we shall. My sister is most anxious to oversee my debut."

"That, at least, is certain to divert you."

"I do trust that you are correct, Sir Ashley, for in all truth I was not at all anxious to go."

He looked at her in some surprise. "That is most uncommon of you, Miss Hamilton."

"Mama is an invalid. I would as lief remain to bear her company as go to London."

29

"You are entitled to a Season, I would think, and I can fully understand Lady Langridge's anxiety to see you in Town."

"Oh indeed. Married people are always in a fidge to see others suitably legshackled."

To her surprise he laughed. "Oh yes, Miss Hamilton, I had noticed it was so!" After a moment he glanced at her curiously. "You seem uncommonly reluctant, though."

"I daresay I shall grow accustomed to the idea."

"I believe the debutantes like nothing better than for beaux to pay court to them." When she made no reply, he went on, "No doubt when you next embark upon your journey, Sir Hector will take more stringent precautions for your safety."

"I will ensure that he does," she answered grimly. "Our driver was armed, but the highwayman contrived to disarm him."

"Captain Starlight has ridden the high toby for many years. He is experienced enough to best most drivers. Outriders make a journey safer. There are those who say Starlight is an ex–navy officer, hence his title. Who knows? One day we will know all about him, that much is certain. More likely he is a seaman who has conjured up his elevated title." After a moment's pause he went on, "You were remarkably deft in climbing from that window, Miss Hamilton. It was incredibly brave of you, and yet rather foolhardy."

For the first time Leonora smiled with natural pleasure. "Not really. You see, I have a younger brother, Edmund, and climbing out of windows is one of the skills he endowed upon me." Sir Ashley looked astounded and Leonora went on, "It is one of those pursuits frowned upon by parents and nursemaids alike, and I have often been chastised for acting the hoyden, but in this instance it undoubtedly gave me an advantage."

It was his turn to smile. "How odd. When Anne and I were children I never thought to teach her to climb. I think it is too late now, don't you?"

Leonora laughed again and felt that the unhappy episode would indeed fade in time. Having unburdened herself to a virtual stranger whom she was unlikely to encounter again, she was beginning to feel better already.

As they approached the house, she hesitated a moment before saying in a thoughtful tone, "One other thing I do recall . . . when they thought I had swooned, the woman, Meggy, said I looked too young, and he, Captain Starlight, answered, 'We must not underestimate the enemy.' It seemed a trifle odd to me at the time. What do you think it meant, Sir Ashley?"

For a moment he said nothing. He just kicked at the gravel with the toe of his riding boot, making the tassel swing from side to side. Then he smiled up at her and answered, "I think we need not put too much emphasis on a remark such as that, Miss Hamilton. You may not have heard correctly . . ."

"Oh, I did," she insisted and he straightened up, looking grim once again.

"To creatures such as Starlight the whole of Society is the enemy. You, being a member of the ton, would certainly be regarded as such."

When they walked around the side of the house, it was to see a chaise drawing up in front of it. For a moment Leonora hesitated and then ran forward crying, "Papa!"

Sir Hector was just climbing down when he looked up, and she could see how gray and pinched he looked. All her own suffering seemed of no account. When he saw her running toward him, his face broke into a smile of pure delight, and she flung herself headlong into his arms.

"Oh, Papa, I am so glad to see you!" she cried.

He clung on to her tightly as Sir Ashley walked slowly toward them, Jemma barking and jumping at his heels.

At last Sir Hector held her away, and she could see that despite his outward joy, his eyes were full of pain. "My dearest girl, this is the happiest day of my life. You're safe and I can only thank God for it." He frowned suddenly. "Did that fiend hurt you?" She shook her head. "You have a graze upon your cheek."

"It was sustained during my escape. It is nothing I assure you, Papa, but does Mama know of what has happened?"

"She knows nothing," he answered much to his daughter's relief. Suddenly Sir Hector's hands tightened on her shoulders. "Are you quite certain he did not harm you?"

Leonora averted her eyes as she replied, "Yes, Papa. I am quite unharmed, you may be sure." After a moment she forced herself to ask, "Were you obliged to pay the ransom?"

"I never received a demand for one," Sir Hector replied.

31

"When the message arrived from Sir Ashley this morning, I thought that must be the demand at last instead of the blessed news that you were safe and awaiting me here. The rapscallion is too tardy, I am glad to say. Oh, Leonora, my dearest girl, I am so relieved at this outcome. You must tell me exactly how you contrived to escape."

"Later, Papa, later."

Once again she allowed herself to be enveloped in the safe haven of his arms, but a moment later Sir Hector moved away and said, when Sir Ashley joined them, "I owe you, sir, an enormous debt of gratitude. How can I ever repay you for your kindness to my daughter, and your consideration of me?"

"I did nothing, Sir Hector, I assure you. Miss Hamilton found her own way here and displayed great enterprise and fortitude. We merely gave her shelter. Do come inside and take some refreshment with us, even though you must be in a fidge to take Miss Hamilton home. Before you leave, I would very much like you to meet my sister . . ."

Once again Sir Hector put his arm around his daughter's shoulders, and together the three of them walked up the wide flight of steps into Hevening House, the two men already forging a firm friendship.

Leonora only regretted that she could not like Sir Ashley Warrender more.

Chapter Three

"You have no notion how long I have been relishing the thought of having you here with us in London," enthused Lady Langridge as she gazed across at her sister.

The two young ladies were ensconced in Lady Langridge's sitting room in her Mount Street house. Christobel Langridge bore a striking resemblance to her younger sister, with similar coloring and appealing blue eyes. On the occasion of her social debut she had caused quite a stir among the eligible young men, and now that her sister was about to come out, she looked forward to it with relish.

Leonora sipped at her tea thoughtfully before replying. "I believe it is true to say, Christobel, that there was a time when I feared it would not happen."

Lady Langridge's smile faded somewhat. "My dear, what an ordeal you endured. I still cannot credit it has happened."

"Nor I. It seems no more than a particularly vivid dream."

"I am ever thankful you escaped with no real injury. You might have fallen from that window and broken a limb. Well, you came to no actual harm, but I do hope the experience does not have any lasting effect upon you. That would be too awful to contemplate."

"No, I think not. You need not trouble your head about it."

Lady Langridge still looked unconvinced. "I do trust you are correct, my dear. I recall a few Seasons ago Lady Denway was accosted by footpads who stole her purse. You may have heard tell of it."

"I trust she suffered no ill effects."

"The poor dear was unhinged entirely and to this day has failed to recover her spirits. Moreover, she was not . . . abducted."

"Christobel! What a dismal picture you paint," Leonora scoffed, feeling uncomfortable at the constant reminders of her ordeal. "I did hope, once I arrived in London, I would be allowed to forget about it and enjoy the diversions."

Christobel Langridge sighed deeply. "I have to warn you, dearest, that I do not believe you will be allowed to forget about it so readily. The tattle-baskets have talked about little else for almost a sen'night."

Leonora put down her cup, looking shocked. "How can that be?"

"It is a matter of great interest."

"I cannot conceive how that may be."

Christobel Langridge looked irritated by what she deemed her sister's obtuseness. "How many females do you know who have been abducted by a highwayman, and escaped his clutches in such a dramatic way? None other, I'll warrant. You are my sister,

Leonora, I cannot ignore what has happened to you if it can be turned to advantage."

Leonora sank back into her chair and closed her eyes. "Oh, you cannot have told everyone."

"Only those I could trust entirely to turn it into the most interesting *on dit* of the Season."

"No, no, no," her sister moaned.

"Yes, yes, yes," Lady Langridge mocked. "Oh, dearest, do not scold me, for I am not entirely to blame."

"Aunt Eudoria."

"Oh, indeed, but there was mention of it in the *Morning Post* for everyone to see, so you could not hope to keep the matter secret, and why should you? Only think, dearest, this Season sees the debut of so many young ladies, many of them with greater fortunes even if they are not more handsome than you. You need an advantage over them to launch yourself successfully, and this is most certainly it! Everyone is in a fidge to make your acquaintance. You, my dear, will become all the crack this Season. I tell you it is going to be *brilliant*!"

Despite her annoyance and disquiet, Leonora could not help but smile at her sister's enthusiasm. So much for her wish to put the wretched affair behind her.

"Christobel, dearest, I still cannot help but wish you had not. I am already heartily tired of recounting the tale at every turn."

Ignoring her protests, Lady Langridge poured more tea and selected a morsel of plum cake before going on, "How did you contrive to keep the awful news from Mama?"

"Papa explained that there was some problem with the carriage, which made it necessary for us to turn back."

"I am heartily relieved to learn she is unaware of your little adventure."

"Adventure! So that is what you are calling it. It was an encounter with fear. I do not believe you fully recognize that, Christobel."

"Oh, be assured, that I do. I am not so unfeeling as you suppose, but you do not seem to realize you should be crying roast meat over this. It has happened. It cannot be undone, so, my dear girl, make the most of it. Any other female of my acquaintance

34

would be as gay as a goose in a gutter over the adulation you will receive."

"I am not such a goosecap," came her sister's uncompromising reply.

"Faddle! You're as melancholy as a gib cat and I cannot credit it in you."

"If everyone I encounter insists upon quizzing me about Captain Starlight, as if I'd had an audience with the Prince Regent, then I daresay I shall stay Friday-faced for the remainder of my sojourn in town."

Realizing the wisdom of changing the subject, Christobel said a moment later, "Aunt Eudoria was miffed when I informed her I was bringing you out, but now you have become all the crack, she is as mad as a weaver. In all honesty, Leonora, I cannot find it in my heart to blame her."

"Aunt Eudoria is not a lady I should like to cross, Christobel."

"In view of your fame you need not fear that is so. You are her niece, and she will be proclaiming that fact loud and clear to all her cronies, which is just as well, for you need her kind offices to gain access to Almack's. That is the one thing I cannot contrive, so we must tolerate her condescension and toplofty ways in order to gain some further advantage over all your rivals. Maria Tresco comes out this Season, and she has a fair fortune, not to say the sweetest disposition. Tush! I am persuaded no one can hold a candle to you, my dear. Oh, it is going to be quite, quite splendid. Good Fortune has ensured I am not increasing this Season, the children have an excellent nursemaid and governess, so I am going to be able to devote myself to see you well settled."

Leonora looked at her askance. "Christobel, you have more in common with Aunt Eudoria than you know."

Lady Langridge laughed merrily. "Oh, do not say so! If Philip hears you, he will institute an act of divorce, no question of it. He cannot abide our Aunt Eudoria."

"I vow you are displaying distinct signs of imitating her."

"If I were not so delighted at having my dearest sister here with me, I should take the gravest exception to that. Aunt Eudoria has grown more toplofty with age. I have seen grown men tremble in their breeches in her presence."

Leonora could not help but laugh. "What taradiddle." And then

35

a moment later, in an attempt to change the subject of the conversation, she ventured, "How little Cyrus has changed since I last saw him." Christobel was always eager to discuss the merits of her various offspring. "Babies, I find, change so much in such a short time."

"They are all growing at a fast rate," their mother agreed. "I do hope you will soon be settled, and then our children can grow up together." She beamed at the thought. "You have no notion how I miss you and all our little confidences. Acquaintances just cannot do as well." She looked at Leonora with earnestness. "When all those beaux are paying court to you, I do hope you will confide in me."

Leonora began to look uncomfortable. Prior to her departure for London she had scarcely thought of choosing a husband. She couldn't imagine what it would be like to fall in love. Now, unaccountably, she was even more confused.

Christobel suddenly sat forward in her chair, looking all at once concerned. "Oh, dearest, I have it in mind, you have been more affected by this dreadful experience than you are willing to admit to me. You have made a valiant attempt to hide your sensibilities from me, but I do know you better than anyone else, and I fear you have been roundly overset more profoundly than we have realized."

Leonora forced a smile to her lips. "I confess the memory of it still haunts me, but I vow that when the Season begins, I will lose the megrims."

"I will ensure that you do," her sister vowed.

"I would be a chucklehead indeed if I were to allow that creature to taint my life."

"Have no fear, dearest, I shall keep you so busy, you will have no time to be out of humor on any account."

A knock at the door heralded a footman, who announced, "The Marchioness of Clayborne awaits below, ma'am."

Both young ladies gasped in unison, "Aunt Eudoria!"

Christobel looked wide-eyed at her sister. "A visit from our aunt is certain to ensure your sensibilities are totally overset. Shall I send word that you are indisposed?"

"Good grief, no!" Leonora protested. "She will think me

nursed in cotton. In any event I shall be obliged to see her eventually, so it might as well be now."

"Oh, you show true Hamilton spirit." At the sight of her sister's dismay she asked, "Leonora, what did I say to put you out of countenance?"

"Nothing of any consequence, dearest." When her sister continued to look at her worriedly Leonora drew a deep sigh. "It is only that he, Captain Starlight, said I was spirited."

Christobel Langridge nodded to the footman. "Remove the tea kettle and show her ladyship up." When the lackey left the room, Christobel turned to address her sister in a firm tone. "A coze with Aunt Eudoria will soon cast all thoughts of that creature from your mind."

Leonora could not help but laugh, and a few moments later Lady Clayborne swept into the room, dominating it immediately. "My dears. How fortunate I have caught you both at home."

The two sisters exchanged wry looks as their aunt seated herself on a sofa near the fire. She always dressed in the height of fashion and today was no exception. She was a large lady, and the cerise heavy satin gown and pelisse emphasized her size in no small measure. Everyone was in awe of her, including her husband, Lord Clayborne, and her son, Freddie Littleborough.

"Leonora, how good it is to see you looking so fetching after your terrible ordeal. When news of it reached me, I could scarce believe my ears. My niece abducted by a tobyman! Tompkins was obliged to burn feathers, so great was my shock."

Leonora drew a deep sigh before smiling. "Thank you, Aunt, for your concern, and I can only regret the adverse effect it has had on you."

"Tush! That is of no account. You appear recovered I am glad to see. It would not do for you to appear hag-faced when you make your debut. Ah, but you are not in the normal way of being vaporish. I told Lady Sefton only this morning: Leonora will endure, I told her, and it is so. Now, tell me, how is your poor dear mama?"

"She is in good spirits, although her health is as indifferent as ever it was."

"She need not concern herself on your behalf. I will certainly look out for you while you are in London." Leonora dared not

37

look at her sister. "It really is the greatest pity you did not consent to allow me to bring you out, my dear."

"Aunt Eudoria, Christobel . . ."

Lady Clayborne put up one hand, and as she did so, the splendid osprey feathers adorning her bonnet trembled violently. "Yes, I have heard the arguments. Fortunately with your looks and portion there will be no difficulty in seeing you settled. Now that you are looked upon as a heroine, you are set to be the great success of this Season. In all truth, dear, there will be little work for your sister to do."

Ignoring this slight on Christobel, Leonora replied, "Let us be plain, Aunt, I am no heroine. I was at all times exceedingly fearful, if the truth be known."

"Nevertheless, you are being looked upon as a heroine. You can be no other, for you escaped from that fiend. You do know how the ton loves heroics of any description." She paused for a moment before going on, "Leonora, my dear, you must tell me what transpired."

"You must have heard," Leonora replied wryly, "to the point of boredom."

"Not from your own lips. *On dits* are not always accurate. Do tell me exactly what occurred."

Her eyes were bright with anticipation, and Leonora had the awful premonition that she would be called upon to recount her ordeal many times in the weeks to come to ladies eager to hear any lurid details. Once again Leonora took a deep breath, and in as few words as was possible recounted the story to her aunt.

Lady Clayborne looked shocked and clucked her tongue. "How astonishing to think that you actually saw Captain Starlight and lived to tell!"

"No, Aunt, I did not see him. His face was obscured. If I had seen him, I believe I would not be here to tell the tale."

Once again Lady Clayborne clucked her tongue. "You are making me shiver, Leonora."

"You did want to hear me tell the truth, Aunt."

Christobel murmured, "I have heard tell he is very handsome."

"I couldn't say," Leonora answered, feeling uncomfortable again. She remembered only his dark menace and the feeling of his eyes burning deep into her. "You would oblige me by telling the tattle-baskets I am wounded by the memory and find it difficult to talk about."

"You do yourself an injustice, and to me also if you think I have the ear of every tattle-box in town."

Out of the corner of her eye, Leonora could see her sister stifling her laughter. "I meant no disrespect, you may be sure," Leonora murmured contritely.

"You can rely upon me to attempt to circulate an *on dit*, but you must be prepared for a good deal of interest. Emily Castlereagh herself approached me at Almack's the other evening, inquiring as to your well-being, and your name cannot be elevated higher than that."

"The sorry matter would have been of interest to no one but myself if the news had not been broadcast around Town," Leonora said resentfully, not at all impressed by this news.

Lady Clayborne laughed. "My dear, you cannot keep a matter of such great interest entirely to yourself. No harm ensued. Indeed, it can do you nothing but good in the haut monde. It was of the greatest good fortune you were found by some good fellow."

"Ah yes," Leonora replied, relaxing a little more now. "I am more than obliged to Sir Ashley Warrender and his sister for their kindness to me."

Christobel sat forward in her chair. "Did you say . . . Sir Ashley Warrender?"

"Ah yes," Leonora answered, looking at her with interest. "You do know the gentleman, I believe."

Lady Clayborne cast her niece a curious look. "That name has a familiar ring to it. Should I know these people? I confess I cannot immediately place them."

To Leonora's surprise her sister's cheeks turned quite pink. "You may recall Sir Ashley, or Mr. Warrender as he was then, paying court to me when I had my Season, even though it was several years ago."

Once again Leonora was startled. Sir Ashley had spoken of knowing her sister, but he had made no mention of being one of her suitors. Indeed, she could not imagine the somber Ashley Warrender paying court to someone who had always been as giddy as Christobel.

Lady Clayborne's eyes narrowed thoughtfully. "Indeed, I do recall him now. He's a member of the Kirby family, which is a totally dissolute clan, if my memory serves me right, and it usually does. He had not a title then."

Just at that moment the clock on the mantel struck the hour, and the marchioness got to her feet, at the same time picking up her fur-lined muff and her dainty reticule.

"This is, of necessity, a fleeting visit, for I am engaged to call upon Lady Sefton, so I am obliged to leave you now. Christobel, I trust you will endeavor to provide your sister with more modish apparel before her Season commences."

"This gown is exceedingly modish," Leonora protested, looking down at the white muslin which she liked so much.

"No, it is not," Lady Clayborne contradicted. "Your sister knows full well that the style is several months out of mode."

"That is because I sent the plates to Talworth several months ago," Lady Langridge explained as her aunt swept out of the room.

Leonora let out a long breath. "I am persuaded being presented to Her Majesty cannot be such an ordeal as a coze with Aunt Eudoria."

Christobel laughed. "Imagine what it was like to be brought out by her, my dear. I lived beneath her roof until the day of my wedding."

"No disrespect to dear Philip, but I should have wed the first man who came up to scratch. Indeed, 'tis amazing any man dare to come up to scratch." After a moment Leonora looked at her sister curiously. "Is it true Sir Ashley paid court to you?" ·

"Oh, yes, indeed."

"That is truly amazing. Was he . . . did you . . . were you in the least partial to him?"

Christobel's eyes took on a faraway look. "I have not thought of him for years, but yes, for a while I did favor him above all others."

"Did he come up to scratch?" Leonora asked breathlessly, wondering how she would feel if Sir Ashley Warrender were her brother-in-law instead of the more prosaic Sir Philip Langridge.

"No . . . Aunt Eudoria favored him rather less than I. When Philip made an offer, it was accepted, and I scarce saw Mr. Warrender after that. I believe he left Town. He had at that time no title and no fortune. Aunt Eudoria would have had an attack of the vapors if I'd as much as mentioned him making an offer."

"No fortune, you say? Christobel, he appears to be very well breeched now."

"I recall he had just inherited a bankrupt estate from an uncle, and he had come to Town in search of a fortune to wed. In all truth, Leonora, my portion was not large enough for his needs, but I do know, I found favor in his eyes. He must have been in some torment on that score."

"He has certainly found his fortune, if appearances are anything to show, and he has not married one."

"I believe I have heard he has made his fortune, but I did not know he was still unwed. I confess that surprises me. The poor dear was always a trifle uncomfortable that his pockets were to let. Naturally, most of us coming out that Season would have little to do with him because of that. I recall he often consoled himself with a Cyprian called Clara Moresby. She is much in demand today and not obliged to consort with those who are dished up. He was always so reckless, trying to prove himself. I recall one curricle race in Hyde Park . . . well, suffice to say he won." She frowned suddenly. "He used to belong to White's and Boodle's and enjoyed a rubber of whist. Mayhap he found good fortune there."

Leonora laughed. "Christobel! I doubt if you can look to that for an explanation. Gaming is more like to lose him a fortune as make him one, I fancy."

Christobel nodded sagely. "Indeed, it is usually so. Tell me," she mused, "is he as devilishly handsome as I recall?"

Having to ponder that made Leonora feel distinctly uncomfortable. "Oh, that is very much a matter of opinion, so I cannot say," she replied airily. "He has a fine countenance, I daresay. Does he," she ventured a moment later, "ever come up to Town nowadays?"

"I have seen him on one or two occasions since my marriage, but I fancy he does not come up very often. No doubt he has been well occupied mending the estate's affairs. Moreover, he has no house here." Christobel looked wistful. "I own I should not be averse to seeing him again."

"I cannot believe you wear the willow for him."

It was Christobel's turn to laugh. "Indeed, I do not. There is no doubt I made the correct choice in dear Philip. In Mr. Warrender's company I always felt a trifle uncomfortable, if you can understand my meaning. Philip is entirely comfortable." Leonora understood all too well what her sister meant. "But it would be nice to think he might be wearing the willow for me." A moment later Christobel got to her feet. "We have so much to do, Leonora. If you have recovered from the journey, as I am certain you have, we shall be obliged to begin our preparations for your come-out. The first thing we must do is make lists. Let us begin with no further delay."

Leonora steeled herself for a hectic time, but she did acknowledge that to be diverted from most of her uncomfortable thoughts was no bad thing, and she could rely upon her sister to help her do so.

Chapter Four

When Sir Philip Langridge's liveried footman handed the two young ladies from the carriage, they were both laughing merrily.

"How could Lady Swaffen wear such an ugly bonnet?" Christobel asked. "And in Oxford Street for all to see!"

As Leonora stepped into the hall, she tugged at the ribbons of her own bonnet. "I could not credit seeing Sir Humphrey Dutton becoming entangled in the lead of his little pug. I thought I would die laughing when he fell flat in all that mud on the roadside. This morning's outing was as good as a visit to the circus."

"Yes, it was great fun," Lady Langridge agreed. "I have not enjoyed myself so much since I prepared for my own come-out, and this was just visiting mercers' emporiums. When the Season begins in earnest, it will be even better."

"I own that it is a great lark," Leonora replied, swinging her bonnet from her fingers, "but if I am obliged to recount the story of my abduction one more time to any more females of Aunt Eudoria's acquaintance, I vow I shall have an attack of the vapors!"

"Tush! You are not in the least vaporish."

"I could so easily learn to be," Leonora teased.

"I do declare the story is becoming a trifle tedious to me, too. You really will have to embellish it the next time, dearest. Make it sound far more fearsome. It will be well received, I assure you. Moreover, our aunt will be delighted at the renewed interest."

"Some people can lie faster than a dog trots, but for me the reality was fearsome enough."

As they walked up the stairs together, Christobel mused, "I adored the striped poplin you chose today, and the sprigged muslin also. They will both suit you admirably, I fancy. I confess, I am in a fidge to see them made up into modish gowns. When Madame Yvette has done her best, as she is bound to do, you will look exquisite every time you venture forth from the house."

"I do think I have chosen sufficient material to last for three Seasons, not to mention all the bonnets, shawls, and endless ribbons you have insisted that I purchase. I cannot need another gewgaw."

"A lady cannot have too many gowns or accessories. You would not wish to be a dowd, and I will not have Aunt Eudoria, or anyone else, call us cheeseparing."

"I don't give a fig for what Aunt Eudoria does or does not think."

Christobel laughed. "Oh, how spirited of you to say so, but do, I beg of you, bear in mind the sphere of her influence. All doors will be open to you, mainly due to her good offices. Her closest cronies are Lady Sefton, Lady Jersey, and Madame de Lieven, all of them patronesses of Almack's. La! I must go through our guest list for your ball and ensure their names are at the very top."

"I did hope to join the children for a while. It will give Miss Farrow a rest from them for an hour or two."

Christobel cast her sister a wry look. "How kind of you to think of Miss Farrow, who is well paid for her trouble. I'd as lief believe you just wish to play with the children." Leonora responded with a mischievous grin that reduced her to little more than a child herself. A moment later her sister went on, "Marriage will suit you, Leonora, and I fancy you will enjoy your own brood very well."

Leonora drew a heartfelt sigh. "First of all, I must marry."

"That thought should not tease you, my dear. Your real problem will be which one of your suitors to choose."

As she hesitated on the landing, Leonora continued to look troubled. "I cannot imagine choosing a husband, Christobel. All the young men I have so far encountered are pleasant enough, but marriage . . . It must be devilish difficult to decide."

At this pronouncement Christobel laughed. "It is not in the least difficult, I assure you." All at once she frowned. "Since you arrived, I have harbored the distinct feeling there is something you have not yet told me."

Leonora's eyes grew wide. "I cannot conceive what that might be."

For a moment Christobel bit her lip thoughtfully before venturing, "Forgive me for mentioning this, dearest, but is there something that passed between you and . . . Captain Starlight that you did not tell us?"

Leonora looked horrified. "Indeed not! What else could there be?"

"You do not . . . harbor a . . . fondness for the rogue, perchance?"

"Christobel!" Leonora protested in outraged tones, but her cheeks grew pink all the same.

Lady Langridge shook her head. "I do beg your pardon, my dear, if I have outraged your sensibilities. I do not believe you would be such a chucklehead, even though there are those who would turn the ordeal into a romantic adventure and expect everyone to believe the Banbury Tale. There are those who find it difficult to conceive that it was such an ordeal for you."

Leonora smiled faintly. "Thank you for understanding, Christobel. There have been occasions of late when I have wondered if you realized how disagreeable an experience it was. You must recall, for a while at least, I was in considerable fear for my life."

"You may find consolation in knowing it is well and truly over now, my dear. You are safe with us and destined for a brilliant future. Captain Starlight can go to the devil, and will no doubt do so before long. Do go along and divert yourself with the children if you wish, but I beg you to recall that Madame Yvette is calling later to discuss the making of some of your gowns."

"I am persuaded you will remind me if I happen to forget," Leonora answered pertly as she ran up the rest of the stairs to change from her outdoor clothes to something suited to the nursery.

Some time later she was running down the corridors and stairs only just ahead of her nephew and nieces—the baby being too young to leave the nursery. The children were shrieking with delight, for Hunt the Slipper was a favorite game, and Leonora entered into the spirit of the game with as much relish as the children. Even though they were young, she had no intention of allowing them an easy win. She always enjoyed their games together and laughed delightedly as she ran ahead of them down the stairs, resisting the impulse to slide down the banister rail. She reckoned she had almost evaded the children as she came to the bottom of the stairs, when the heel of her slipper caught in the hem of her gown, and she fell headlong down the last two steps to land in an ungracious heap on the floor of the hall.

She heard the children scream in alarm, sensed that the footmen were coming to her assistance, and then just as she caught her breath, an unfamiliar voice said, "Do allow me to assist you."

A moment later Leonora felt herself being raised from the cold, tesselated floor. A pair of polished Hessians, buckskin breeches, and a fine coat of broadcloth passed her eyes in quick succession before she heard her brother-in-law ask:

"Good grief, Leonora, what *are* you about?"

The children were jumping up and down and all talking at once in high-pitched voices. Sir Philip snapped, "That is enough, children! Go back to the nursery at once."

Their excited chattering died away abruptly, and moments later Leonora heard them running back up the stairs.

"Here, take a seat," the unfamiliar voiced invited, and she found herself seated before she had a chance to protest, realizing belatedly that she was, after all, considerably shaken by the fall.

45

"Really, Leonora, this will not do," Sir Philip admonished. "You must take more care and not act the hoyden."

"Tush, Langridge," the other man said. "You cannot scold Miss Hamilton on that score. I will not have it."

When her breathing returned to almost normal, Leonora looked up at last, but then her heart began to beat unevenly once again as she set eyes on her champion. Dark haired and foppishly dressed, his dark eyes studied her worriedly from beneath thick, dark lashes. He looked so very familiar that seeing him was a great shock, but then she realized he was, after all, a complete stranger, and she had never set eyes upon him before in her life. However, for one very short moment she had thought . . .

"Leonora, my dear," Sir Philip said in a more conciliatory manner, "how do you feel now? No strains or sprains, I take it?"

She managed to convey a reassuring smile while casting a curious look at the stranger. "Oh, I am perfectly recovered now, I thank you. I own, I do become a trifle foolish when I am playing with your children."

"You could never, ever, be considered foolish," her rescuer said, looking upon her with a degree of admiration that made her cheeks grow pink.

"Allow me to present to you Captain Dermot Symington, late of the King's Royal Hussars and now gentleman about town," Sir Philip intoned.

Captain Symington raised her hand to his lips, but his gaze did not leave her face. "I am delighted to make your acquaintance at long last, Miss Hamilton."

"And I yours you may be sure, sir, but why do you say 'at last'?"

He smiled, reinforcing her earlier feeling that they had met before, but she could not for anything think where that might have been. Indeed, if she had encountered him before, Leonora was quite certain she would not have forgotten someone as handsome and personable as Captain Symington.

"You must be aware, ma'am, that you have achieved some modicum of notoriety of late." Leonora could not help but groan as he went on. "Everyone is in a fidge to make the acquaintance of one who has braved a desperate highwayman. You cannot blame us for making much of you."

Leonora's laugh had a strangled sound to it. "I wonder if everyone will still be speaking of it when I am in my dotage."

"Take heart, Miss Hamilton, I vow no one—no gentleman certainly—would wish to make your acquaintance on that score alone."

"Captain Symington insisted upon being brought here to meet you," Sir Philip told her.

"And I was never more glad to make anyone's acquaintance. My sainted cousin always has Dame Fortune at his side, and never more than on his encounter with you, ma'am."

"Your cousin, sir?" Leonora asked with a frown.

"Sir Ashley Warrender. I have heard tell of the circumstances of your meeting, and as I said, he is always deuced lucky."

At the mention of the name Leonora gasped. So that was why he had seemed so familiar. They were very much alike except that the sparkle in Captain Symington's eyes showed him to be considerably less inscrutable than his cousin and instantly more likable.

"You have a decided likeness," Leonora told him, for she was somewhat at a loss what to say. She had gained the immediate impression that Dermot Symington was not the greatest admirer of his cousin.

"Our likeness, you may be certain, is restricted to our looks. I, I am bound to confess, come from the reprobate side of the family."

Sir Philip laughed. "You do yourself a disservice, sir." Then he looked at his sister-in-law. "Captain Symington, I may tell you, acted with great bravery at Salamanca, and was wounded for his trouble."

"Foolhardy rather than brave," countered the other man.

"Bravery is always to be applauded, sir," Leonora assured him. "You must not deprecate yourself. Indeed, I shall not allow it in my presence at least."

He subjected her to a dazzling smile. "It is kind of you to say so, ma'am, but my uncle must also have believed it, for he left all his possessions to Cousin Ashley. In retrospect I suppose it was a wise move to make. My cousin has certainly made the estate thrive again although," he added with a laugh, "I have no notion how he has contrived to do so."

47

Still at a loss for suitable conversation Leonora murmured, "I trust that your injury causes you no lasting discomfort, sir."

He smiled deprecatingly. "Only on occasions, ma'am, and then it merely reminds me of my rashness. It is nothing, I assure you."

"Well, it is good news, indeed, that Boney is at last on the retreat," she went on. "I do believe we might soon see the end of this wretched war."

"Let us hope so. It would be a great blessing for us all. The Frenchies themselves, I am persuaded, are heartily sick of the fighting." He gazed down at her in a way that made Leonora feel decidedly uncomfortable. "I am bound to confess, Miss Hamilton, for the first time I do not regret being obliged to leave my regiment and return home. For so long I wished myself back with my comrades, but for this Season at least I shall enjoy being in Town."

Under his intense scrutiny Leonora found her cheeks growing pink again and was somewhat relieved when Christobel came hurrying down the stairs, looking to be a trifle perturbed.

"Oh, how glad I am to see you unharmed!" she exclaimed. "Hubert has just told me of your fall."

"You need have no fear, dearest, I am unharmed as you can see."

"Oh, indeed, but dear Hubert did not deem to tell me how many stairs you had fallen down. It could have been all of them for all I knew." She looked at her husband and smiled, then to Captain Symington. "I see you have been making my sister's acquaintance, sir."

"Indeed I have, ma'am, and displaying traits of the resource-fulness for which my family is renowned."

Christobel laughed. "You certainly cannot be considered tardy, Captain Symington. Well, now that you have contrived to make my sister's acquaintance, I do hope you find her as delightful as we do."

"I could not admire her more, ma'am." He glanced at Leonora and added, "Very soon now Miss Hamilton will be subjected to an inundation of admirers. Being one of the first must stand me in good stead, don't you think?"

"Your charm will achieve that objective, sir. There is no doubt of it." She transferred her attention to her sister. "Madame Yvette has arrived and we have a deal of work to do."

"How unkind of you, ma'am, to deny me Miss Hamilton's delightful company now that we have made acquaintance."

"I do not doubt you will have many further opportunities" was Christobel's reply.

"You may rely upon it," Captain Symington assured her, smiling at the younger woman in his disconcerting way.

"Let us take a glass of Madeira, Symington," Sir Philip suggested and then, "Ladies."

Captain Symington bowed, and Leonora and her sister watched them go to Sir Philip's study. Christobel looked at Leonora as if she wished to question her, but there was no opportunity because Lady Clayborne entered at that moment, accompanied by two other females.

"How opportune," she declared, beaming at the two young women.

"Aunt Eudoria, delighted as we always are to see you, the mantua maker is awaiting us upstairs," Christobel told her, exhibiting considerable dismay.

"Splendid! This visit is exceedingly well timed. This is Miss Fulford, *my* mantua maker, and this is Mademoiselle Duvalle, my milliner. There are none better, and I insist they dress Leonora as she deserves. Both Miss Fulford and Madame Duvalle are possessed of the latest fashion plates from the court of Empress Josephine herself."

"So has Madame Yvette," Christobel retorted, looking for once annoyed.

Leonora looked from her sister to her aunt and after a moment declared, "I have so much material to be made up, I am persuaded it would take the skills of more than one mantua maker. Mayhap Miss Fulford and Madame Yvette could share the task between them. It would be altogether too much for one person at this late date."

The other ladies stared at her in astonishment for a moment or two before Lady Clayborne declared, "That is a splendid notion. Let us begin the task with no further delay. In all honesty Leonora should have been here a month ago to allow far more time for preparation. However, we must make do as best we can . . ."

Both Leonora and Christobel exchanged looks of pure relief as they began to follow Lady Clayborne up the stairs. For once, however, pleasing her aunt had not been in the forefront of Leonora's mind. Despite his charm and good looks she had been glad enough to take her leave of Captain Symington, although she wasn't sure why.

Prior to coming to London, she had always been able to conduct herself perfectly well in any gentleman's company. Now she found them discomforting especially when they admired her, and she wondered if that might be because she would be obliged to look upon them as possible husbands. Somehow it did not seem to be the entire answer, although secretly Leonora did feel she had changed in a subtle but unspecified manner since her encounter with Captain Starlight and the ensuing events. Leonora knew that her life could never settle into its previous tranquil manner again.

The wind was stinging her face, strands of hair fought to free themselves from the pins that were restraining them, and her elegantly tailored habit flapped against her legs in a punishing tattoo. Leonora's mare thundered through the peaceful fields of Hyde Park, startling grazing cattle and making it decidedly difficult for Sir Philip Langridge's groom to keep up with her.

Leonora gloried in the speed and the feel of the cool air against her cheeks, which took on a healthy glow absent since leaving Talworth House. The ride was reminiscent of the days she galloped unfettered over her beloved countryside. Not that she truly minded her move to London. Town had its own attractions, and she was discovering more and more of them every day.

Whenever she walked into a room, she caused an immediate stir, and being obliged to recount her meeting with Captain Starlight was no longer such a painful experience for her, especially when it prompted such unanimous admiration. It would have been inhuman of her to resent it. Gentlemen had begun to shower her with little gifts, and at routs she was never left on her own for a moment, nor obliged to sit out a dance. Of all her would-be suitors Captain Symington was the most persistent. Leonora was not certain of her feelings toward him. He was undoubtedly handsome, possessed an attractive wit, but despite that Leonora harbored a certain reserve toward him that time had failed to dissipate.

She was riding hard, deep in her thoughts, when she saw a horseman approaching. He was galloping as fast as she, and Leonora was obliged to swerve sharply to evade him. She reined in her mare sharply, causing the animal to whinny in protest. The other rider came to a halt a few yards away, turned around, and cantered back toward her.

"Miss Hamilton, you're an excellent horsewoman."

Having calmed her horse, Leonora straightened up in the saddle and looked at him in alarm. "Sir Ashley!"

He doffed his high-crowned beaver. "How agreeable to meet you again, and in much more felicitous circumstances than our last encounter."

Leonora's face became set into an expressionless mask. "Any circumstance is likely to be better than that."

"Quite so. It is obvious you do not suffer any ill effects. I hear you are the toast of the Town this Season."

Suddenly Leonora's high color bore no relation to the excess of fresh air she had been enjoying. "You are remarkably well informed at Hevening, sir."

He subjected her to one of his restrained smiles, and Leonora was bound to observe how different he was than his more out-going cousin despite the physical likeness. "I confess to have been in London for several days. In fact, I called earlier at Sir Philip's house to pay my respects, but you and Lady Langridge were not at home."

"We lead a hectic social life of late."

"I would be astonished to hear you say you did not."

All at once Leonora felt oddly annoyed with him, almost resentful, as if his arrival in London was an unwarranted intrusion upon her life and done expressly to irritate her, which she knew to be nonsense.

Nevertheless she said, "Sir Ashley, I did not look to see you in Town. I was given to understand you eschewed the Season."

"I am bound to confess, I have been absent for several years past, but it was not entirely out of choice, I assure you. This is the first time I have been able to leave my estate for any length of

51

time. It is, I own, good to be back. I had all but forgotten the delights of London."

"How does Mrs. Torrington?" Leonora asked, unable to dismiss the coldness in her manner.

"She is in fine health, I thank you. Before I left, she charged me to convey her good wishes to you."

"So she has not accompanied you?"

"I regret not on this occasion, but I do hope to persuade her to join me here in due course."

"I should be glad to reacquaint myself with her."

"I am persuaded Anne is just as anxious to see you again. She speaks of you often."

As Leonora averted her gaze from his altogether more disconcerting one, she noted that his horse was a fine one, coal black, reminding her painfully of the one Captain Starlight had been riding on that fateful evening. Indeed, seeing Sir Ashley astride the mare caused her to be reminded that they might have been of a similar build if she discounted Captain Starlight's all-concealing frieze coat.

"Your horse is a fine one," she retorted, almost accusingly, something she regretted but could not help.

He patted the mare's neck and was rewarded by a friendly snicker from the animal. "This splendid creature is not mine, I regret to say. I have no house in London and, therefore, no stables in which to keep one. This one is a hired hack from the livery stable at Park Gate."

"I have heard of it."

Suddenly something sparked in his dark eyes, a rare revelation of his thoughts. "I doubt if sweet Merinda here can be the same animal the tobyman was using that night."

Leonora was no longer annoyed. She was furious with herself and with him that her thoughts had been so accurately interpreted.

A moment later he replaced his high-crowned beaver. "We seem to have developed a habit of running full tilt into each other, Miss Hamilton, so no doubt our paths will cross on other occasions, but for now I must reluctantly take my leave of you. I am persuaded you, too, must have pressing engagements to fulfill."

At last she was able to laugh. "Sometimes I believe there are too many of them."

"No debutante truly believes that," he chided, and when she spurred on her horse, he asked, "Do allow me to ride with you to the gate."

"As you wish, sir," she murmured.

They rode on in silence until they reached the paths that were teeming with riders and pedestrians, and Leonora felt happier to be in the company of others. Christobel always liked to ride in her carriage when she came into the park on an afternoon, but Leonora had eschewed that to ride as she so enjoyed on one of Sir Philip's prime bloods. As soon as her presence was spotted, she began to be addressed from all sides, a most satisfactory state of affairs, especially as it was witnessed by Sir Ashley Warrender.

"I believe I may safely leave you to your acquaintances," he said wryly. "Good day, Miss Hamilton."

She inclined her head in dismissal of him, but just as he was about to ride away, she called, "Sir Ashley, my come-out ball is to be held tomorrow evening. May I send you an invitation?"

He looked for a moment surprised and then pleased. Leonora couldn't explain why she had given in to that impulse, but she immediately regretted it. She didn't really want him to be there, for he was a tangible reminder of one of the most awful times of her life, and his presence in Town could do her composure no good at all. He had seen her in the most pitiable circumstances, which boded ill for her pride, but she had spoken and it was too late to retract her words.

"Miss Hamilton, I would be delighted to receive an invitation."

"Where am I to send it?" she asked, disappointed in his quick acceptance. As it was such short notice, she might have hoped he had made prior arrangements for his evening's entertainment.

"I am most obliged to you. At present I am lodging at 17 Conduit Street. Until the morrow then."

Leonora watched him ride away into the crowds, a fine figure of a man, she reluctantly admitted to herself. Recalling he had paid court to her sister, she could not in all honesty understand Christobel's voluntary choice of Sir Philip, who tended to plumpness rather like his crony, the Prince of Wales, and did not even possess a very lively wit.

However, Leonora could readily understand her sister being

53

more comfortable with Sir Philip. One thing Sir Ashley Warrender could never be—and that was a comfortable companion.

Chapter Five

The ballroom of Sir Philip Langridge's house was ablaze with lights that reflected on the magnificent jewels of the guests at Leonora Hamilton's coming-out ball.

Christobel had done her sister proud in inviting the cream of the haut monde to the function. Dukes, duchesses, marquises, and mere baronets mingled happily with army and naval officers in the colorful uniforms of their various regiments. All civilian gentlemen were in evening dress, but naturally they were outshone by the ladies in wonderful gowns of myriad colors that were sequined and bejeweled as were their throats and wrists, too.

Leonora had chosen a fine muslin lawn that had been embroidered with crystal beads. Combs adorned with crystal decorated her hair, and one glance in the cheval mirror before coming down for dinner told her she looked splendid, but she was nervous all the same. All eyes would be upon her during the evening. Everyone with whom she conversed would be noted and possible husbands discussed by the many gossips present. It was all a far cry from Leonora's quiet country life at Talworth.

However, as soon as the ball commenced, she relaxed considerably, for young men jostled one another in their anxiety to engage her for dances, to bring her champagne, or do her any little favor. She could not help but be flattered and pleased, even when she was irritated by them. Soon after the ball had begun, the Prince of Wales had arrived, accompanied by his current favorite, Lady Hertford, and his presence set the seal on the evening's success.

His Royal Highness condescended to speak briefly to Leonora before taking to the dance floor with Lady Hertford. Leonora was flattered by his attention, quite naturally, but could not like him. She knew how badly he treated poor Princess Caroline, although Lord Hertford did not seem to mind his wife's liaison with the prince. Leonora supposed when one is the future king, anything is permissible, but in her heart she did not blame the populace's dislike of him. They booed him frequently when he was seen abroad.

As Leonora gazed across the ballroom at the prince, a voice said in her ear, "How useful it must be to have a relative who is one of the Carlton House set."

Leonora turned her attention to the speaker, another debutante, Lady Henrietta Drewe, daughter of the Earl of Tarlton. The girl was tall and thin with an acidic air that convinced Leonora she would not care to make a bosom friend of her.

"I own I must be," Leonora replied with a smile, aware that Lady Henrietta appeared resentful of her popularity.

"What a hurricane this is, to be sure. I have never witnessed such a crush."

"Your own come-out ball was a fine success, I recall," Leonora assured her.

The girl's lips formed into the semblance of a smile. "None of us can possibly compete, Miss Hamilton. You seem to have been endowed with an uncommon amount of good fortune to herald your come-out."

"I am not certain I understand your meaning, ma'am."

"You cannot be unaware that the news of your adventure did not harm your social success."

"I'd as lief have less interest in me on that score as endure such an ordeal," Leonora replied, her manner becoming considerably cooler now.

"You must own that the timing was a . . . trifle . . . convenient."

Ignoring the insinuation, Leonora replied tartly, "If I had not been on my way to London for my come-out, I would not have encountered that rogue, so the timing could not have been different."

"It was great good fortune that you contrived to escape before you were harmed or robbed." Leonora was beginning to become indignant when Lady Henrietta went on, "They do say Captain Starlight is a gentleman who returned penniless from the war."

"It is possible . . ."

"Imagine," the girl added, her eyes growing bright, "it is not beyond the bounds of reason that he is here tonight."

"Lady Henrietta, I sincerely trust he is not!" Leonora responded, affecting an uncomfortable laugh.

"Ah, so here you are!"

Leonora had never been so glad to see Captain Symington, who approached, bearing two glasses of champagne. She was aware she was engaged to stand up for the next dance with him. Gallantly, although he had obviously brought the champagne for himself and Leonora, he gave his glass to Lady Henrietta, who blushed and simpered. Although he was no longer in the army, he wore the dress uniform of his regiment, and he looked very handsome in it.

"I have been waiting an unconscionable time to stand up with you," he confided.

"Tush, Captain Symington, this will be your second time, and on this occasion we are engaged to lead the set."

"A double honor, but does that signify you'll look upon me with special favor, ma'am?" he asked mischievously.

"It signifies, sir, that you are by far the most persistent of my partners."

"Then it is evident that persistence has its own reward."

"You are acquainted with Lady Henrietta Drewe, I take it," Leonora asked in an effort to divert his rather overpowering attention from herself.

"Oh, indeed I am," he replied, switching his abundant charm to the young woman, who responded by smiling foolishly.

A moment later Lady Henrietta asked slyly, "Did you know that Sir Ashley Warrender is in town?"

"I have heard it is so." He glanced briefly at Leonora. "If anyone expects me to hurrah on that account, they are bound for disappointment. Ashe Warrender and I have little in common save our kinship, and I wish even that were not so."

"I had noticed," Leonora answered wryly.

"Such a cavalier attitude to one's kinsman is quite shocking," declared the other young lady in a haughty manner.

Captain Symington cast her a smile designed to melt the

stoniest of hearts. "I am shocked by it myself, ma'am. No one wishes it were not true more than I, but the fact remains, kinsman or not, I do not like the fellow."

Leonora was eager to question him about his reasons when Sir Ashley approached. His elegant dark-blue evening coat fitted his broad shoulders perfectly, and his breeches displayed a fine leg. There was no doubt he employed only the finest tailor.

As he made his way through the crowds, it was evident other ladies thought well of him, too. It was clear by the purposeful manner in which he moved, he was approaching Leonora, and to cover her confusion, she sipped at the champagne with rather more relish than she usually employed.

"Miss Hamilton, how glad I am to be present at such a successful debut," he said, raising her hand to his lips.

"I am honored you could be here at such short notice."

"As I am in Town, nothing would have kept me away." He smiled suddenly. "Nothing save the lack of an invitation, naturally." He bowed toward Lady Henrietta, and her cheeks flushed so furiously, she was obliged to conceal them behind her fan. Sir Ashley looked very pleased with himself as he added, "I truly feel as if I have never been away."

"Which indicates that you are likely to stay," remarked his cousin.

After a moment's consideration Sir Ashley agreed, "I believe that I will. After the welcome I have been afforded and the hospitality extended to me, it would be churlish to do otherwise. Miss Hamilton, do I dare to ask if I may stand up with you?"

"Miss Hamilton is engaged to lead the next set with me," his cousin answered before Leonora could reply.

Sir Ashley was not taken aback as he eyed his cousin coldly. "You could stand down."

Captain Symington smiled maddeningly. "You must know that I will not."

"Then if I am to be denied that honor, I must beg Miss Hamilton to allow me the pleasure of taking her into supper, unless, of course, you have bespoken that privilege too, Symington."

Leonora hesitated a moment before hearing herself say, "Thank you, Sir Ashley, I believe you have earned the right.

Without your kind assistance I acknowledge I might not be here."

He smiled ironically. "In truth, I had not expected so great a reward, Miss Hamilton."

Captain Symington looked annoyed as he asked, "What brings you up to Town after all this time as a rustic?"

Sir Ashley transferred his attention from Leonora to his cousin, losing none of his aplomb. "The same that brings everyone here—a desire to enjoy good company and as many diversions as is possible."

Captain Symington frowned darkly as he swallowed his champagne. "I had it in mind you disliked the Season."

"You are mistaken. I merely stayed away until I was able to pay my way. Now, if everyone was of a like mind, a good deal of grief would be spared."

Captain Symington burst out laughing. "If everyone was of a like mind, the Season would be devilishly dull."

Lady Henrietta laughed, too, but with Sir Ashley returning his dark, brooding gaze to her, Leonora could only smile faintly and then turn away in the guise of discarding her glass.

"You will discover things are not as they were when you were last here," Captain Symington warned.

His cousin's eyebrows rose slightly. "In what way? London looks—and smells—as it always did. There are more gaslights in the streets than I recall, but nothing untoward, I fancy."

"There is a rift between Prinny and Brummel. You may be obliged to choose between them."

"I have just spoken with His Royal Highness to renew our acquaintance, which is both an honor and a pleasure. I don't believe there will be any difficulty."

"So that is where your allegiance lies," Captain Symington remarked, looking satisfied.

"My allegiance has always been with the Crown."

Captain Symington's lips formed into a sly smile. "Princess Caroline is not in favor either, and I recall you were a particular favorite of *hers*." Just as the music struck up, he transferred his attention to Leonora. "Miss Hamilton, our set, I fancy."

Sir Ashley bowed, apparently not at all put out by his cousin's scarcely concealed barbs. "Until later, then, Miss Hamilton."

58

"I wonder why he has come to London now, after all this time away," Captain Symington murmured as he led Leonora onto the dance floor.

"He did explain quite fulsomely."

The young man smiled without mirth. "Surely you cannot believe that taradiddle."

"Naturally," Leonora replied, her eyes wide with candor.

"You may come to learn, Miss Hamilton, that nothing concerned with my cousin is ever so straightforward."

Leonora could not help but glance back to where they had left him, only to see he was leading the hapless Lady Henrietta onto the floor and behaving toward her as if she were the most alluring female in the room.

"Your encounter with the tobyman appears to be attracting a good deal of interest."

Sir Ashley was carrying two plates piled high with morsels of delicious food from the buffet table. The moment she had agreed to allow him to escort her into supper, Leonora had again regretted the impulse. She regretted it even more now, for their entry into the supper room had excited no small amount of interest. Any gentleman in whose company she was seen, attracted attention now, but this one in particular, for it was well known it was into the arms of Sir Ashley Warrender that she fell after escaping the evil clutches of Captain Starlight. As far as the tattle-baskets were concerned, the situation could not be more intriguing.

"I really do not like talking of it," she replied as she took the proffered plate from him.

His smile was a sardonic one. As he drew up a chair next to hers, she could not help but note that the pristine whiteness of his neckcloth contrasted starkly with his dark coloring.

"You must be the only female in London who does not."

"That is only because they did not experience it. Someone has had the temerity to suggest he might be encountered socially, which I own, I find a horrendous thought."

Sir Ashley looked shocked for a moment, and then he regained his self-possession. "My dear Miss Hamilton, I think it unlikely . . ."

"It is not such an outrageous possibility, sir. He could be a member of Society. I am persuaded he was no low felon."

"Mayhap, but you may console yourself that even if you were to encounter him socially, you would not know. As to his social standing, not until he is captured will we know for certain. In the meantime I beg you not to let it tease you. You must own that the *on dits* have done your social standing no harm at all."

"I own only that my Aunt Clayborne and my sister are tattle-boxes. Not everyone is impressed by my escape, I may tell you, sir. Some suggest it was a ruse to enhance my social standing."

For only the second time she heard him laugh. "Miss Hamilton, you must accept that there are those who are bound to envy you."

"Oh, indeed. How I wish it had been one of them who had feared for their lives."

"One thing is certain, no one else could have acquitted themselves so admirably. You may find comfort in the fact that as far as I am aware, the felon who calls himself Captain Starlight has not resorted to violence against any female."

"I did not know that."

He looked at her and she was unable to meet his dark gaze. "In any event, there are a great many things about you that are likely to excite envy in the hearts of others."

At such praise Leonora felt her cheeks growing hot, and murmured, "It is kind of you to say so."

"You must be by now accustomed to admiration. From all I have observed, there is a great crush of those wishing to grease your boots."

"I have it in mind, you are not a man to curry a lady's favor with moonshine."

He cast her a wry smile. "It is certainly true to say I am out of practice, and no gentleman should be so foolish in any event. You have far too much common sense to be swayed by flummery." He glanced across the room, where Dermot Symington was in conversation with several young ladies who appeared to be enjoying his company. "Speaking of flummery, I am glad to see my cousin enjoying the excellent diversion tonight. It is beginning to look as if he is preparing to settle down at last, after many years spent in dissipation. Becoming legshackled to some suitable female would be good for him, I fancy."

"In that respect you do not speak from personal experience, Sir Ashley."

"That is a matter of deep regret to me. My cousin, however, has not experienced as much good fortune as I in other respects in the past few years, so an advantageous marriage would benefit him greatly."

"I gained the distinct impression that you and he were not on good terms."

Sir Ashley was not in the least dismayed by her observation. "His resentment of me is well founded. The title became mine from a relative who had no property, so I fancy he did not resent that, but our other uncle chose to leave his possessions to me, which Captain Symington naturally took amiss. Ironically, at the time I came into my inheritance—Hevening House—I'd as lief it had been left to him."

"I have heard tell how magnificently you have transformed a derelict estate to one that is thriving. I am full of admiration for you."

His lips curved into one of his ironic smiles. "It is my turn to be flattered, Miss Hamilton."

"Knowing him as I do, I doubt if Captain Symington could have done as well."

"You and I are in total agreement upon that. My cousin is too fond of his pleasures, but I have observed that you and he appear to be on exceedingly good terms."

"He is diverting," she affirmed, smiling across at the gentleman in question, who glanced at her, too, at that moment.

He returned her smile, but when he looked at his cousin, he began to frown. Despite Sir Ashley's bland comments Leonora was convinced the acrimony between them was mutual.

When Leonora espied her aunt approaching, she did not know whether to be glad of it or not. Aunt Eudoria in her magenta gown and jeweled turban was cutting a swathe through the crowds, even though her acquaintances strived to arrest her at intervals.

Leonora heard Sir Ashley draw a sigh. "I wonder if Lady Clayborne has also come to welcome me back to Town."

Leonora cast him a curious look. "I believe she once disapproved of your friendship with my sister."

His expression revealed nothing. "If that was so, I do not recall. It was a long time ago."

"My dear," Lady Clayborne greeted her, "such a triumph! A veritable hurricane. It is a far greater success than I dared to hope."

As Sir Ashley got to his feet, Leonora said, "Christobel will be most gratified to hear you say so. She has put a good deal into the success of this evening." For a moment she hesitated before adding mischievously, "Aunt Eudoria, I believe you are acquainted with Sir Ashley Warrender."

Lady Clayborne's manner grew positively icy. "Indeed, but if I remember correctly, it is a good many years since we have had the pleasure of seeing you in Town, sir."

He inclined his head. "In the past few years there have been no greater pleasures than those at my country estate, ma'am."

The countess smiled frostily. "Your presence here now points to the fact you have decided there are greater diversions in Town."

It was not exactly a question, and he did not condescend to answer it. Instead he bowed stiffly to the two ladies. "I beg of you excuse me, my lady, Miss Hamilton. I am engaged to stand up with Lady Castlereagh."

Both ladies watched him go, Leonora feeling decidedly dissatisfied by their conversation, although she wasn't sure why. Then Lady Clayborne turned to her. "Lady Castlereagh, indeed. How toplofty he has become of late. Are we to be pleased by his reappearance in Town, I wonder?"

"Pray tell me why you have taken him in dislike, Aunt. He appears to have been made most welcome elsewhere."

"Oh, indeed. He has charm in abundance, I do not doubt, and I am more than grateful for his assistance to you, but he has the reputation of a fortune hunter. I would wish you to be warned."

"He now has a fortune of his own, Aunt," Leonora replied, feeling distinctly uncomfortable.

"So I am informed, but that makes no matter. It is, I confess, a most mysterious matter. His mother was Philomena Pendleton, daughter of the Earl of Kirby. She married an utter wastrel, which was typical of such a goosecap. I believe young Warrender favors his father in looks and in nature. Now, my main purpose in having this coze is to tell you I finally decided there is to be a masquerade held in your honor at Clayborne House."

"Thank you, Aunt. I am sure it will be a splendid diversion."

"There is no doubt about that. I shall put the arrangements in hand on the morrow. Now, tell me, Leonora, is there any young man whom you yet favor?"

Leonora was forced to laugh. "No, I regret to inform you there is not."

"It is difficult for me to keep note of who is favorite, since you are living with your sister."

"I am sorry about that, Aunt," Leonora replied, hiding a wry smile, "but be assured either Christobel or I will keep you informed."

Lady Clayborne looked satisfied, and her niece was relieved to see her next partner approaching. Lady Clayborne saw him, too, and she beamed with pleasure. "So it is to be my dear Freddie who is standing up with you for the country dance. You must allow him to present his own crowd of acquaintances to you. They are all supremely eligible, you know."

The thought of choosing a husband from the ranks of Freddie Littleborough's rackety cronies almost made her laugh, but she forebore to do so.

"Is Mama being her usual overbearing self?" the young man inquired as he led her into the set.

"I am afraid so," Leonora replied, her eyes alight with amusement.

"Don't let her bully you," he advised.

"It is exceedingly difficult to gainsay Aunt Eudoria."

Her son nodded grimly. "I do know that," he agreed and they both burst into peals of laughter.

They were still laughing merrily when Leonora caught sight of Sir Ashley again. It caused her something of a shock to see that his partner was none other than her own sister. Christobel was laughing at something he had said, and Leonora was surprised to note that he was more at ease than she had ever seen him before. At Hevening House he had been utterly restrained, somewhat warmer on reacquaintance here in London, but now, watching him with Christobel, she could not help but note the transformation.

Her gaze lingered on them until Freddie said, "Leonora?" and she gave him her attention once again.

When a short time later Leonora faced Sir Ashley in the set, his manner had resumed its more usual coolness, and the unease she had experienced at the sight of him with her sister increased now to pure resentment.

Chapter Six

𝒯he sidewalks of Bond Street were thronged with strollers, enjoying the displays in the many bow-fronted shop windows. Carriages of all sizes and styles dashed along the street, weaving their way between those which waited for their owners to return from the tempting emporiums that sold all manner of goods.

Living deep in the heart of the countryside, Leonora had learned to be satisfied with the goods Christobel brought with her when she visited Talworth, or had purchased small items from the peddlers who called from time to time. However, freed from those constraints, she now purchased all she needed with alacrity, delighting the merchants of the Strand, Oxford Street, and Bond Street.

Town life had unexpectedly become very pleasant, especially since each letter received from Talworth assured her of her mother's well-being as well as her delight at Leonora's success. Each day brought a shoal of new invitations to all the most prestigious diversions, and she could not help but be flattered by the attentions so many young gentlemen heaped upon her. Sir Philip's house-steward was nowadays almost fully employed, taking in calling cards and gifts from those who would set themselves up as suitors and vied for her favor.

To Leonora it was an entirely satisfactory situation, even

though she had no favorites among them. The Season had only just begun, so she did not consider that odd, except that so many debutantes were already declaring their interest. One or two were betrothed, but they were very highborn and the marriages were contracted often for purely dynastic reasons. Leonora could only be glad she was free to follow her heart, although she had no notion where that might lead.

The strangeness she had experienced at the beginning of her stay no longer teased her. Since arriving in London, she had made many acquaintances and most of them were now so involved with their own romantic affairs, they hardly ever alluded to Leonora's encounter with Captain Starlight, which could not fail to please her. However, despite being so well occupied, her mind often returned to that event, which seemed like a dream now, except that her memory of the highwayman remained crystal clear and often came to haunt her in her waking moments in the night. With Sir Ashley Warrender resident in Town there was a constant reminder of all she sought to forget, and she could not help wishing he had remained at Hevening.

Coming out of the mercer's emporium after purchasing further supplies of ribbons and lace, Leonora once again found herself approached by another debutante of her acquaintance, moreover one whom she found far more congenial than the obviously envious Lady Henrietta Drewe. Leonora still smarted at her aspersions about her abduction, and could not help but recall the girl's smug, self-satisfied expression as she partnered Sir Ashley Warrender afterward.

"Miss Hamilton," Rosalind Harries greeted her, "allow me to congratulate you on a superb diversion last evening. It was most enjoyable, and I am by no means alone in thinking so."

Leonora smiled with genuine pleasure as her maidservant hovered near the carriage. "Oh, I am gratified to hear you say so, Miss Harries. I am greatly looking forward to your come-out ball."

The girl dimpled prettily. "I am in a fidge about it, I own, lest it not be the success others have been."

"You need have no fear on that score. Your mama will make certain it is a brilliant success."

The other girl looked suddenly coy. "I made acquaintance

65

with Sir Ashley Warrender last night, and I am bound to confess, I envy you your encounter with him. How romantic it must have been to have been rescued from peril by such a fine gentleman."

Leonora forced a smile to her face, even though she hated the mention of it. "There was nothing romantic about it, I assure you."

"Mayhap not at that precise time, but it is all forgotten now, I daresay, and I could not help but note he was most attentive to you last night during supper."

"And to several others, too," Leonora hastened to point out.

"It would suit the tattle-baskets admirably if you and he were to make a match."

The girl eyed Leonora curiously, but she could only feel annoyed, for she was only too well aware of what the gossips were saying. She knew that the current *on dits* circulating about the town paired her with Sir Ashley, and she could only look forward to the day when they were proved wrong.

Once again Leonora smiled, but this time it was more sweetly. "But it most certainly would not suit me, Miss Harries. Pray excuse me now. I needs must return to my brother-in-law's house with no further delay. The shops are so inviting, I have stayed out far longer than I intended."

"How tempting it all is, I agree. Papa is forever lamenting the cost of my Season. He declares he is likely to be in dun territory before it is half over!"

"Hello there," a voice greeted them, and both young ladies looked around to see Freddie Littleborough coming toward them, swinging his silvertopped cane as he doffed his high-crowned beaver. Leonora noted that the points of his shirt collar were so high, he could scarcely move his head.

"What a pretty pair to encounter on such a gray morning," he greeted them, and Rosalind Harries flushed deep pink.

Noting their apparent interest in one another, Leonora left them conversing in a lively manner a few minutes later, when she returned, at last, to her carriage, which was standing nearby.

However, just as she was about to get inside, she heard a familiar voice cry, "Miss Hamilton. I say, Miss Hamilton! Hold hard there!"

Leonora immediately greeted Captain Symington with genuine warmth as he weaved his way between fast-moving carriages to join her at the other side of the street.

"How well blue velvet becomes you, Miss Hamilton, but on reflection there can be nothing which does not."

"Such flummery, sir," she responded, lowering her eyelashes. "You surely did not risk your life on the road just to compliment me on my bonnet."

"Can there be a more worthy reason?"

"How gallant you are, sir. Am I to assume you are shopping for gewgaws this morning?"

He laughed. "Gentlemen are wise enough to shop in much safer areas, away from the eyes of ladies. Jermyn Street is sufficiently far removed from here, I fancy."

"I did not think you would want ribbons or lace, sir."

He glanced across the street, where Gentleman Jackson's salon was situated. "I was partaking of a little instruction in pugilism. Unfortunately I have just been informed that my cousin has decided to use the gymnasium during his stay in Town, which I can only hope is a brief one. I deemed it prudent to leave before the sight of him cast me into the dismals. Now, having encountered you, Miss Hamilton, I am heartily glad that I did."

Leonora looked suddenly troubled. "I cannot help but think it a pity you and he, being kinsmen, are not on better terms than you are."

"You must not let it trouble your head, ma'am. Our mutual dislike is good-natured enough."

Hating herself for probing further, nevertheless she asked, "Is it merely his acquisition of Hevening that teases you about him, Captain Symington?"

The young man threw back his head and laughed. "Good grief, no!" he declared. "We have disliked each other heartily since childhood, but you must forgive me for saying so, ma'am, for I know you must regard him as a savior. It is understandably so. No one should be surprised if you favor him above all others."

Leonora was immediately uncomfortable and felt bound to reply, "I shall be forever in his debt, sir, but that does not mean I must consider him a saint."

"No man would claim to be that," he answered with a smile,

"at least none that I have encountered. However, there are certain ladies whom I would deem angels."

His dark, penetrating stare was almost as discomforting as his cousin's just then, and she said quickly, "Pray excuse me, Captain Symington. I really must delay no longer. My sister will be wondering where I am."

"It is indeed odd that she does not accompany you today. You are normally inseparable."

"Lady Langridge is all done up after last night and needs must rest awhile today."

"It is all to your credit that you, Miss Hamilton, retain your freshness after such a long and arduous night."

"I enjoyed myself thoroughly, and I could scarce sleep afterward."

"One would never know by looking at you."

"Captain Symington, I must not delay any longer in taking my leave of you, for you are like to turn my head with your flummery."

He smiled engagingly. "Allow me the honor of handing you into your carriage, ma'am."

As the carriage set off, making its slow way along Bond Street, Leonora drew a deep and profound sigh. She found the enmity between the cousins disturbing, feeling, as she did, an odd loyalty to Sir Ashley, which conflicted with her attraction toward the dashing army captain.

As she stared out of the window, deep in thought, she suddenly started when she found herself looking directly at one of the passersby. The woman momentarily stared back at Leonora, and after looking alarmed, she hurried on at a much faster pace than she had hitherto been walking.

After gasping with shock, Leonora called for the driver to stop. Before her maid could follow, she climbed down from the carriage and began to pursue the woman, inviting curious glances from other pedestrians who got in her way.

"Stop!" she called. "Stop there, I say!"

The woman did pause to look back and then she began to run. Leonora was greatly hindered by the number of people on the pavement. Somewhere at the back of her consciousness she saw one of her aunt's friends who said in shocked tones:

"Miss Hamilton, what are you about? This is most unseemly."

However great the disparagement and from whatever source it came, Leonora could not stop her pursuit, for the woman had now turned the corner. Leonora could not risk losing sight of her, even if it did mean inviting the disapproval of one of her aunt's toplofty cronies. As Leonora turned the corner, a figure loomed large in front of her, causing her to gasp in alarm. Try as she might, she could not avoid a collision, and she gasped again when she was held tight in a grip she could not escape.

As she struggled to free herself, a familiar voice asked, "Miss Hamilton, what in heaven's name is amiss?"

All at once she ceased to struggle as she looked up into the now familiar features of Sir Ashley Warrender, as inscrutable as ever. "Thank goodness!" she cried, scarcely able to catch her breath.

When he released her at last, she was thankful to step back a few paces. "The woman—Meggy! Captain Starlight's accomplice. I saw her!"

"When?" he snapped.

"On Bond Street just now! I was pursuing her when she ran down here. You must have seen her go past you."

"I have only just come out of my lodgings and saw no one until you came around the corner."

Leonora's eyes grew wide with shock and disbelief. "You must have seen her!"

"I assure you, I did not."

When Leonora looked around at last, it was to see that the street was all but deserted. Compared to Bond Street close by, it was a haven of solitude.

"She did run along here!" Leonora protested. "She must have gone into one of the houses. There is no other explanation. Sir Ashley, you must summon assistance and have each house thoroughly searched."

He laughed and it was a harsh sound. "Miss Hamilton, you must see the impossibility of doing so."

Once again she began to become anxious. "You must. Oh, I beg of you!"

"Do see reason, ma'am. There is no evidence of her being here."

"I saw her as plain as I am seeing you, sir! What other evidence do you require?"

"I do not doubt you saw someone you thought looked like the wretched creature, but do you truly believe a tobyman's doxy would stroll along Bond Street and not invite discovery?"

"Her mode of apparel was quite different today. When I saw her just now, she appeared almost fashionable and not at all as she had on that night."

When he began to look even more skeptical, she could have hit him. There were no doubts in her mind that the woman had been the creature who called herself Meggy, and she was still somewhere in the area close by.

"Miss Hamilton, I have never doubted that your experience was a most shocking one, and any possible reminder is bound to cause your sensibilities to be overset from time to time . . ."

"Oh, do not, I beg of you, patronize me. I know what I saw, and nothing is like to move me from that opinion."

Her eyes flashed blue fire. Not only was she growing more angry, but the more he doubted what she had seen, the more certain she became it was Meggy strolling along Bond Street. Despite her anger, Leonora could understand his doubts and that did nothing to soothe her wounded feelings.

Breathlessly she went on, "I would entreat you to consider that if the woman is in one of these houses nearby, the highwayman himself may also be with her. She was quite evidently his lightskirt, for I have never encountered such a low creature in all my life."

Sir Ashley's eyes narrowed. "Tell me, Miss Hamilton, if we were to discover him nearby, would you be able to identify him positively as the man who robbed your carriage and made off with you?"

Leonora bit her lip. "You already know that I did not see his face fully, but I certainly did see *her*!"

"On a dark night with only the one candle?"

"Oh, this is outside of enough," she protested.

"If we do discover the woman you saw a few minutes ago in one of these houses, she is likely to say your attic's to let, or some such thing. There would be no evidence, I regret to say. I doubt if

70

someone as cunning as Captain Starlight would keep the proceeds of his thieving ways about his person."

"This is useless," Leonora cried in exasperation. "I must take my leave of you, for I can see you believe me unhinged by the whole affair."

As she turned on her heel to go, he caught her by the arm. "You are not unhinged."

She stared at him for a long moment, unable to tear her gaze away, but his eyes were so full of passion, she couldn't bear to look any longer. She detached herself from his grip, feeling even more ill at ease than before.

When, in an effort to escape his discomforting company, she began to walk back toward Bond Street, he fell into step beside her. "Don't think I am unsympathetic, Miss Hamilton. I, more than anyone, wish to bring this felon to book, and anyone who consorts with him, but I fear the only way it can be done is if they are apprehended during or just after a holdup. You do see the difficulty, do you not?"

She turned to look at him, all at once her anger abating. "Yes, Sir Ashley, I do."

Her carriage was awaiting her at the side of the road, and he handed her into it. Immediately her maidservant began to exclaim her dismay and concern, but Leonora was not listening. Just as the carriage was about to set off, Sir Ashley said:

"Miss Hamilton, I beg of you to believe I want desperately to apprehend this villain before he brings grief to anyone else."

She didn't answer. She was still convinced he had not believed her, but she knew she was not mistaken, nor could she comprehend how he had not seen the woman who had been running as hard as she. Leonora sank back into the squabs and found tears of frustration squeezing from beneath her lids. A memory of the night she had been abducted came back to her just then.

"Do you think it is true?" Mrs. Torrington had asked.

"Does it matter?" her brother had replied.

Belatedly she wondered if, like several others in town, he did not believe it had happened at all. Leonora let out a loud groan of dismay that caused her maid to be alarmed anew.

For the first time Leonora wished she had stumbled into some

farmworker's cottage rather than the newly splendid mansion of
the proud and disdainful Sir Ashley Warrender!

Chapter Seven

*L*eonora continued to feel resentful about Sir Ashley's attitude. Nothing and no one could shake her belief that it was indeed
Meggy she had seen, and whenever she thought of that vile creature remaining free and at liberty so close at hand, the angrier she
became.

However, the prospect of attending the Haymarket Theater
cast it to the back of her mind for a short while, and she ceased to
seethe at one gentleman's cavalier attitude toward her when she
could take some solace in the extraordinary amount of attention
she was receiving from many others.

From the moment she arrived at the theater, she was surrounded by admirers, something to which she was now becoming
somewhat accustomed. This particular evening's performance of
Cardeno was popular with the haut ton because Robert Elliston
was acting onstage, and he had a reputation for being superb.

As the Langridge party made its way slowly to the box, it was
stopped at every step by acquaintances eager to claim a connection with the young lady who escaped the clutches of a highwayman. At last Leonora, her sister, and brother-in-law were
ensconced in their box with its view, not only of the stage, but
also of the rest of the theater. All three occupants were kept busy
acknowledging the smiles of their acquaintances who filled the
boxes all around. Young bucks sitting in the pit noisily claimed
the attention of those young ladies who had caught their fancy.
Some of them also called out to the Cyprians who occupied
boxes alongside those of the ton. There were few better show-
cases for their charms.

Leonora drew her spangled shawl around her and shivered

with pleasure. "This is quite the most exciting evening," she murmured.

"You have not had the pleasure of seeing Mrs. Siddons, as I did when I came out," Christobel informed her. "Oh, do look, dearest, there is Mr. Brummel. He always looks so disdainful. I do believe he would rather be gaming than theatergoing this evening."

"He comes only to cut people," Sir Philip declared as he put down his quizzing glass. "The man is utterly impossible."

"But so elegant," was his sister-in-law's rejoinder.

"Sartorially there is no one to compare," Sir Philip agreed, albeit grudgingly. "However, I don't believe that gives him leave to be so toplofty. He is not so highborn as those he would disdain."

"If it were not for Mr. Brummel, gentlemen would still be wearing paste buttons and powder in their hair," Leonora pointed out, realizing Sir Philip's dislike of Beau Brummel was probably because the dandy had disparaged some item of his apparel.

In his high neckcloth and stiff, pointed shirt collar, Sir Philip looked distinctly uncomfortable as he attempted to move his head. "I don't believe we ought to give him too much credit. He is able to bestow enough upon himself."

The two ladies laughed and then a moment later Christobel said, glancing across the auditorium, "Now, there is a gentleman of extreme elegance."

When Leonora followed her sister's gaze, she started, for entering one of the other boxes was none other than the object of her recent resentment, Sir Ashley Warrender. Naturally, Christobel was quite correct; he did look extremely elegant in his evening attire, although that was no more than was usual for him. He contrived to be fashionable and elegant while avoiding the more ludicrous extremes of the dandies.

To Leonora, Christobel looked a mite foolish as she fluttered her lace fan and smiled at him just as he caught sight of them. An indulgent smile tugged at the corners of his lips as he inclined his head toward Lady Langridge. Then he transferred his attention to Leonora, who was affecting not to notice his presence, but she did note he was a guest in the box belonging to the family of an extremely wealthy debutante, Lady Maria Tresco, daughter of the

Earl of Boscorran. Lady Boscorran looked a trifle flushed as did her daughter, but they both laughed and flirted with a more animated Sir Ashley Warrender than Leonora normally witnessed.

Christobel continued to smile across at him. "When Sir Ashley was last in Town," she said, addressing Leonora, who was directing her attention elsewhere, "I felt very strongly that he suffered keenly his lack of funds."

"He would," Sir Philip replied. "We all had sufficient for all our needs. Warrender was obliged to cry off so many diversions, simply for the lack of funds. His pockets were always to let in those days. Now I see he is so much in funds, I am positively envious of the fellow."

Christobel cast her husband a glance. "No wonder he is relishing his sojourn at present. He is bound to enjoy his popularity with those who would scarce acknowledge him a few years ago."

Sir Philip glanced across the auditorium. "It looks as though he will have ample revenge if he marries a great fortune." Christobel laughed and Leonora, who had been affecting not to listen, was wide-eyed at such revelations. "It would certainly come as a relief to some young bucks of my acquaintance," Sir Philip went on.

"Why is that, dearest?" his wife asked, swishing her fan to and fro, although it did not seem in the least warm to Leonora.

"Alby Norwood was as mad as a weaver the other day, he told me. During a nocturnal call on the Divine Clara, he discovered Warrender there before him. Alby reasoned that if Warrender marries in the near future that would curtail such visits—at least for a short while."

To her sister's surprise, Christobel laughed merrily at this news, and it was some small relief to her when the performance began at last, and she was able to give it her full attention, or indeed as much as she was able, for Sir Ashley's presence had somehow taken a slight edge off her pleasure in seeing *Cardeno*.

All too soon, however, the curtain came down, and after a brief discussion with Christobel, Leonora decided to leave the box and mingle with the crowds in the lobby rather than stay inside the box and receive their visits.

It was very crowded in the lobby, and Leonora was glad to be surrounded by her newfound friends. Most of them were more accustomed to the theater than Leonora, who had lived quietly in the country for so long, but she was glad of the opportunity to discuss the play, which diverted her mind. All the same she could not help but glance around nervously from time to time.

It was a great relief when she espied Freddie Littleborough, who came through the crowds to greet her. "You look as delightful as ever, my dear."

"Thank you, kind sir," she responded lightly. "You are the only young man in town I can address without inviting speculation."

His eyes twinkled. "I feel it incumbent upon me to warn you that Mama has chosen a likely match for you. She is determined the glory will be hers even if she is not bringing you out."

Leonora pulled a wry face. "Don't tell my sister. She will be mortified, but you may inform me of the name of the most fortunate of men."

"Duke Warnham."

"The Duke of . . . ?"

"No, chucklehead. Sir Marmaduke Warnham. He's a crony of mine. A match between you would certainly find favor in my eyes, and I vouchsafe he is a fine fellow."

"That is recommendation indeed, Freddie," she responded, not troubling to hide her amusement, "but I have had the pleasure of meeting the gentleman and even though my regard for him is marked, I feel both Aunt Eudoria's hopes and your own are bound to be dashed."

"So, you have thrown your cap over the windmill already?" he asked, his eyes alight with speculation.

"No!"

"I think you underestimate Mama," he warned.

"Freddie, *you* underestimate *me*."

Suddenly she started visibly when Captain Symington emerged from the crowds. For one moment she had thought him to be Sir Ashley Warrender.

"I was enjoying the play," he told her as Freddie took his leave of them, "but even such splendid theater is eclipsed by your presence, ma'am."

Leonora flushed slightly. "As always you are a tongue-pad, Captain Symington."

"Then every gentleman who admires you—and I know they

75

are legion—must stand accused of speaking moonshine. Surely you cannot be so cruel."

She laughed. He could always be depended upon to amuse her. "I do beg your pardon, sir. You can only be sincere, I am persuaded."

"None more so."

He smiled and the effect upon her was dazzling, causing her heart to flutter unevenly. In her confusion she fluttered her fan and murmured, "What a crush it is in here."

"You must allow me to fetch you some lemonade."

She was glad enough to let him go. His effect upon her was most unexpected as well as disconcerting. However, when his cousin suddenly appeared at her elbow, she wished she had not done so.

"Miss Hamilton, I do trust you have recovered after your fright on Bond Street."

Leonora eyed him coldly. He couldn't help but be aware of it. "Perfectly, I thank you, sir."

"Are you enjoying *Cardeno*?" he asked when it became obvious she had no intention of prolonging the conversation between them.

"Indeed. Mr. Elliston's performance, I am persuaded, cannot be bettered."

The ghost of a smile passed his lips. "I daresay you will find no one to gainsay you on that score. No doubt you will be looking forward to hearing the great Catalini sing at Covent Garden next Thursday."

Leonora had never felt less like conducting this kind of conversation, and certainly not with Sir Ashley Warrender. His manner was perfect and she could have hit him for his politeness. Suddenly she couldn't reply even though she was aware Christobel had spoken of them attending the gala.

"Considering you have been so long absent from Town, sir, you contrive to be seen in the most elevated company."

"It is always my aim to strive for the best in all spheres of my life." All at once he frowned. "If you will forgive my impertinence in saying so, Miss Hamilton, you look a trifle flushed. May I procure a glass of lemonade for you?"

Leonora snapped shut her fan. "No, I thank you, Sir Ashley.

76

Captain Symington has already done so. See, here he comes now."

Sir Ashley frowned again. "In that case I shall leave you in my cousin's more than capable company, ma'am."

Leonora smiled sweetly at last as he bowed stiffly. "Thank you, Sir Ashley, and do give Lady Maria my kindest regards."

Captain Symington handed her the glass and watched his cousin coldly as he made his way back to his party. "I see I am in time to rescue you from that arch toady."

Leonora laughed uncomfortably and replied as she sipped at her drink, "I fancy he does not toady to me."

"My cousin is famous for greasing the boots of heiresses. If he does not dangle after you, ma'am, he is as mad as you are fortunate. Indeed, I have to admire the fellow his presumption. In Lady Maria he has chosen a mighty fortune, which I own is typical. I have always followed my heart. That is why I am poor in financial terms but in no other."

He cast her a charming smile and she asked, "Tell me, Captain Symington, does your cousin dislike you as heartily as you do him?"

The young man laughed, not at all put out. "Very like, Miss Hamilton. Do not be misled by his outward charm. My cousin can be ruthless when the necessity arises." He took her empty glass and discarded it. "Regretfully, I am obliged to return to the pit and you to your brother-in-law's box, but I shall treasure this meeting as I have done all our others." He gazed deep into her eyes. "Mayhap we will meet again before too long a time."

When she took her seat once again, Leonora glanced across at the Boscorran box. Just at that moment Sir Ashley was laughing at something Lady Maria had said to him, and he appeared to be totally enchanted by her. It was plain, however huge a fortune possessed by the young lady, he was not averse to her company either.

Chapter Eight

From the very beginning, Lady Alleyn's rout was a great social success—especially as far as Leonora was concerned. She was left breathless by the sheer number of would-be suitors who flattered and fawned upon her. Dressed in a pale lilac satin gown with a low neckline and a flowing train, she was often complimented upon her appearance, something calculated to turn anyone's head. For some reason she found it comforting to have such adulation, even though it was something she would normally find amusing rather than flattering. She did note, with some satisfaction, that Lady Maria Tresco, despite her great fortune, was not as much in demand.

At the back of her mind Leonora still retained resentment toward Sir Ashley. Somehow she had placed him above the common horde of fortune hunters and chasers of lightskirts. Additionally she resented him finding her in such disarray in Conduit Street. On the first occasion she had been grateful for his help, but this time she experienced no such feelings, although if he had believed her story of seeing Meggy, it would have been worth any amount of discomfiture.

Ever since arriving at the Alleyn's Park Lane mansion, Leonora had been tensely awaiting his arrival, even though she could not be absolutely certain he had received an invitation. Reason told her that his aristocratic connections coupled with his newfound wealth would ensure that he obtained entry into most of the salons of the ton. There were also a number of debutantes who appeared anxious for his company. They, too, would ensure he received invitations to every diversion of any importance.

The circle of admirers that gathered around Leonora was some balm to her wounded pride, and her mind was being diverted from all her unwelcome thoughts when she caught sight of him at last. Being tall, he was easily seen even in so crowded a room. As always he was immaculately clad in evening dress. Leonora could find no fault with his appearance. As usual several ladies were eyeing him adoringly. Leonora had to admit, albeit grudgingly, that he was extremely handsome.

In a covert manner she watched as he conversed with first one lady and then another. She saw him smile and charm them with a few well-chosen words, leaving them to chatter excitedly and flutter their fans when he moved on. When he caught sight of Leonora, his smile faded somewhat, and she looked away quickly, angered that he had caught her observing him in so obvious a way. Her own fan became busily engaged cooling her flushed cheeks. How glad she was that the room was so warm.

A moment later she made a great effort to concentrate on conversing with the gentleman contriving to engage her attention. She was not entirely successful in doing so, smiling and murmuring a reply when called upon. Then, when she looked up again a minute or two later, Sir Ashley was standing at her side, which caused her to start, for he had made his way through the crush with surprising speed.

He bowed stiffly and exhibited none of the ready charm she had seen him extend toward others since his arrival. "Good evening, Miss Hamilton."

"Sir Ashley," she replied, bobbing a quick curtsy and averting her eyes from him.

One or two of the young men attending her withdrew as Sir Ashley informed her, "I have today received a communication from my sister, and she entreats me to convey her very good wishes to you."

Leonora kept her eyes downcast. His scrutiny of her was altogether too disturbing. "Pray reciprocate my warmest wishes to Mrs. Torrington when next you communicate with her."

"I will certainly do so. In the meantime may I engage you for one of the dances this evening, Miss Hamilton?"

"I'm afraid not," she answered, deriving some small satisfaction. "I am already engaged for every dance this evening."

He smiled faintly and looked not at all surprised. In fact, Leonora suspected he already knew and was asking only out of politeness, or even to vex her.

"That is a great blow to me, but I suspect I am not the only gentleman bound to nurse a disappointment this evening. In future, I shall be obliged to arrive as early as possible if I am to engage the most fetching females."

Leonora stole a glance at him, but she was unable to ascertain from his expression whether he was genuinely sorry or had asked her merely out of duty. During their encounter in the street she had gained the distinct impression he regarded her as a foolish, empty-headed chit. It was perfectly true she was engaged for every set, which was a blessing, she thought, for although she usually enjoyed dancing, with him as a partner it was clear she would not.

"You flatter me unduly, sir," she managed to answer at last.

"Indeed, I do not, ma'am. Your unavailability for dancing proves the point only too well."

She was just about to speak again when the fortunate young man who was to stand up with her for the cotillion arrived to claim her. Sir Ashley bowed briefly and withdrew. As the dance began, Leonora caught sight of him again, this time partnering Christobel, who was once more responding to whatever he was saying like a young girl, laughing and chattering excitedly. The sight of her sister with her one-time suitor filled Leonora with extreme disquiet. Indeed, it was beginning to seem that whatever Sir Ashley Warrender said or did caused her extreme discomfiture, and Leonora was at a loss to understand why. In the light of their initial meeting it seemed they should enjoy a great accord. She had the feeling it was also expected by all their acquaintances.

It came as some relief to her, after the cotillion came to an end, when she saw him leave the ballroom in the direction of one of the card rooms. Then she turned to her next partner, entering into the spirit of the country dance with her more usual gaiety.

The card room was a popular place for many of Lady Alleyn's guests, male and female alike. At some of the baize-covered tables large amounts of money were changing hands, and even some pieces of jewelry could be seen crossing the tables.

With his hands clasped behind his back, Sir Ashley Warrender wandered around the room, pausing now and again to watch some of the games taking place.

As one lady passed over her jeweled hair comb, she turned to him and said, "Sir Ashley, why not join us? I feel that you present a real challenge."

Ignoring her double entendre he nevertheless smiled with his customary charm. "The invitation is almost irresistible, my lady, but I must nevertheless decline the temptation—for now."

The lady laughed heartily as he moved on to one of the other tables where his cousin, Captain Symington, was engrossed in a game of faro. Sir Ashley noted with some surprise that his cousin appeared to be winning for once, and when one game was ended and a loser got to his feet, Captain Symington grinned at him.

"Look at this, Warrender. Some of the Kirby good fortune is mine at last, and not before time, I should say."

"If you possess any of the Kirby good sense, Symington, you will take your winnings and stand up from the table now."

"Unfortunately I have no other source of funds save these earned by my wits, Cousin. The duns require rather more than I have yet won, but the evening is still young and I have hopes that Dame Fortune will still be at my side when it ends." He took out a silver hunter and peered at it myopically. "At least I had a notion the evening was not yet well advanced." He looked up at his cousin again as he put away his watch. "Mayhap you'll sit down and game with me and my friends, and perchance I shall have the opportunity of winning some of that which should have been mine a long time ago."

Some fellow at the table let out a loud guffaw. Sir Ashley refused to be raised to anger by his cousin. He removed a jeweled snuffbox from his pocket, one which his cousin eyed jealously, took a pinch, and then returning it to his pocket, he sat down and placed a suede purse filled with coins on the table before him.

While the cards were being dealt, Captain Symington poured himself a glass of wine, and it was clear by his high color and slightly slurred speech, it was not his first of the evening. He was, however, triumphant when Sir Ashley lost the first game to him.

"It is clear that this is not the way you have made your fortune," Captain Symington sneered as he drained his glass prior to filling it once again.

"Only an utter fool would hope to do that" was his cousin's imperturbable reply.

"Why not reveal to us how a wise man may make his fortune? I do not doubt everyone is in a fidge to know."

Sir Ashley did not reply; he merely studied his cards. As the game progressed, he won several hands, causing Dermot Symington to grow more red in the face as he watched his winnings dwindle and his cousin's increase.

"I'm utterly dished up," complained a fellow player as he got to his feet. "Dancing will be my only indulgence for the rest of the evening."

Sir Ashley smiled faintly as he sat back in the chair. "Time, I think for us all to call a halt. The candles are beginning to burn low and there are a deal of fetching females in the ballroom. You, Symington, were never averse to the company of a fetching chit, I recall."

Anger flared in the young man's eyes. "You're merely afraid of losing what you have just gained."

Sir Ashley turned to his cousin. "There is no shame in taking one's winnings. If you had been of a similar mind, it could have been more to your advantage."

"What a prosy bore you are, Warrender. If I am not afraid of playing too deep, why should you?"

"Because I am not dished up, Symington, nor am I foxed."

"I am not foxed enough to know you never play unless you can be certain of winning."

Sir Ashley's face darkened. "Be plain, Symington. Do you accuse me? If you do, I warn you that I intend to take it amiss. You cannot impugn my honor with alacrity and hope to escape just retribution."

"You mistake me, Cousin," Captain Symington replied, laughing and placing one hand over his heart. "I could not call into question the gaming methods of such an upstanding fellow and rescuer of fair maidens."

"Miss Hamilton wishes the matter to be forgotten now."

"Oh, what fair maid would truly wish it?" Captain Symington scoffed. "How fortunate for you Captain Starlight infests the roads near Hevening, indeed, how *convenient*. He never used to in Uncle Horatio's time."

The other man jumped to his feet, his face dark with anger at last. A crowd began to gather around them, sensing an interesting confrontation was about to begin.

"Damn you, Symington! Out with it and be done, or hold your poisonous tongue before I thrust it down your throat."

Captain Symington chuckled as he got unsteadily to his feet and swallowed the last of his wine. "I never thought your sensibilities were so delicate, dear Cousin. Mayhap I have touched on a nerve. I am engaged to dance with the delightful Miss Hamilton, who, I declare publicly, has the prettiest ankles in town, for I have seen them."

One of his cronies tugged at his arm. "Come along, old fellow. You're too far in your cups to know what you are saying."

Sir Ashley's face grew even darker while his cousin was speaking. "This is out of all bounds. You slander a lady and I will not tolerate it."

"You mistake me, sir," Captain Symington replied, feigning surprise. "I praise her. I don't doubt you must harbor a fondness for the chit, but she most certainly doesn't like you, even though you have seen more of her ankles than has been the fortune to befall me."

Sir Ashley lashed out at him with his hand. "Enough! You are no gentleman, but that is no surprise to anyone. We shall meet over this, Symington. Name your seconds, the time, and the place."

Those enjoying the spectacle gasped in dismay as Captain Symington reeled from the slap. His smile disappeared at last as he steadied himself against a chair. "The time is now, at Lincoln's Inn Fields. By the time we arrive, it will be light enough."

"Let us contrive to resolve this matter amicably," someone said as those nearby began to chatter excitedly.

Sir Philip Langridge stepped forward as Sir Ashley stared implacably at his cousin. "You'll act for me, won't you, Langridge?" Captain Symington asked.

"Only if this cannot be resolved in a more sensible manner. You are both reasonable fellows, I fancy."

"Lincoln's Inn Fields," repeated Sir Ashley before he turned on his heel and strode out of the room.

* * *

Lady Dearden hurried into the ballroom, her entire body aquiver with suppressed excitement. She immediately espied several of her cronies and rushed up to them, chattering breathlessly before moving on to another group.

When Leonora came off the dance floor with Sir Marmaduke Warnham, she looked around for a sight of Captain Symington, whom she knew was to be her next partner and was bound to amuse her. He never failed to do so. Although she could not immediately see him, she soon became uncomfortably aware of the number of people who were talking between themselves in a most feverish manner and looking at her with even more interest than usual. It was evident she was the object of their excited conversation, but merely dancing with Sir Marmaduke Warnham could not possibly have caused it, unless, of course, Lady Clayborne had decided to spread the word that Sir Marmaduke and Leonora were about to make a match. However, Leonora was quite certain even her aunt would not be so foolish to do such a thing.

She was looking about her in perplexity when Christobel came hurrying up to her. "Oh, my dear, I have only just heard the news! I do not know what to make of it, I declare. Are we to be glad or devastated? I own, I am not sure what to think."

Leonora frowned. "Christobel, dearest, are you unhinged? What are you talking about? Indeed, what is everyone talking about? I assure you Sir Marmaduke is *not* about to come up to scratch."

Her sister's eyes opened wide. "Sir Marmaduke? Oh, no. I am talking about the duel."

"Duel?" Leonora repeated with an uneven laugh.

"La! I had not realized. You do not know."

"No, I do not. Will you be pleased to explain what you are talking about? What is all this about a duel, and why are you in such a taking?"

"Captain Symington and Sir Ashley Warrender! They are to fight a duel."

"I cannot conceive that this is so."

"Everyone is speaking of it, so it must be."

"Surely they have too much good sense for such tomfoolery, Christobel."

"I vow it is the truth. I have it from someone who witnessed the entire incident. Sir Ashley challenged his cousin in front of everyone in the card room only a short time ago. Lady Dearden witnessed it all. Apparently, when Captain Symington made mention of seeing your ankles the day you fell in the hall, Sir Ashley slapped him and called him out."

Leonora's hand flew to her mouth. "Dueling over me?" she gasped. "I cannot credit this. It is not to be borne."

"Don't get in such a taking, dear," her sister whispered while all those around them stared in interest. "You might be named as the cause, but it would take little for enmity to spill over between those two, and from all I have been told, Captain Symington was deep in his cups at the time."

"That makes the matter even worse. I cannot credit Sir Ashley being so foolish as to allow himself to be provoked by Captain Symington, especially if he is foxed and Sir Ashley is not."

"Men are always fools for their pride."

All at once Leonora looked at her sister with urgency. "Do you know when the duel is to take place?"

"Immediately, at Lincoln's Inn Fields as far as I am aware. Philip is acting for Captain Symington. I saw him leave only a short time ago with all the others."

"I must go there immediately and stop it."

"Stop it?" Christobel laughed. "My dear, you cannot. No man of pride and honor will retract, and as for you, you should be pleased. No man has ever fought a duel over my honor."

"I am out of all patience with you, Christobel. I cannot possibly subscribe to such foolish notions. You speak of me as if I had windmills in my head. I certainly will not have a death on my conscience, and I must confess, I am shocked at your attitude in this matter."

Without further ado, she hurried across the room, followed by her sister and scores of curious and, yes, envious glances. Protesting all the while, Christobel followed her sister into the carriage when it was brought around after what was to Leonora an agonizing wait. When it set off at last, she peered out of the window, urging the driver to go faster, but never before had she been forced to endure such an unending journey.

* * *

Several carriages were drawn up at the dueling site off the Strand, so Leonora's driver located it easily. As the carriage horses snickered softly, the gentlemen stood some distance away in a group. When Leonora arrived, they all looked up, but it was Sir Philip who came across just as she climbed down, so hurriedly she ignored the proferred hand of the footman.

"What are you doing here?" he asked, frowning as Christobel joined her sister. "We were expecting the surgeon, not a pair of females."

"I have come to put a halt to this lunacy, so you should have no need of a surgeon," Leonora replied.

"Christobel, you should have known better than to allow your sister to come here. This is none of her concern."

"You should know, dearest, a Hamilton can be headstrong when she so chooses. In all truth, I could not stop her."

He clucked his tongue with impatience as Leonora exclaimed, "None of my concern, indeed! They fight over me and I will not have it."

"You can do nothing to stop it, I fear. Believe me, Sir Aidan and I have tried our utmost. They are both stubborn and proud as the devil. Now, will you be pleased to go so we may be done with it and away to our beds as soon as may be?"

"Come, Leonora dear, let us be gone," Christobel urged. "You can now see, it is a useless task. Men are ever foolish, but we can do naught about it, I fear."

Leonora was hardly listening to her sister. She could see the seconds, Sir Aidan Dickinson and Major Foulkes for Sir Ashley, Sir Philip and Lord Kersdale for Captain Symington. In their midst the two protagonists were visible in their shirtsleeves, choosing their weapons. A clatter of carriage wheels and the pounding of hooves announced the arrival of the surgeon, who stepped out the moment the carriage came to a halt, clutching his black bag, the sight of which caused Leonora to wince.

As the seconds drew back and the duelists went to take up their places, Leonora rushed forward and stood foursquare between them. "I shall not move from this spot," she declared. "You will both be obliged to shoot me first if you are intent upon continuing this lunacy."

Captain Symington waved his pistol drunkenly in her direction. "Out of the way, Miss Hamilton. Let me kill the rapscallion with no further delay!"

When she looked at Sir Ashley, he was standing some distance away, his legs parted, his arms folded across his chest. He said nothing as she challenged him with her ferocious stare; he merely stared back at her, and she began to shiver beneath his scrutiny.

"You should be more prudent than your cousin," she told him.

"Symington has been angling for a confrontation with me for years. Let us be done with it once and for all."

Leonora stamped her foot in fury. "How dare you use my name in this tomfoolery!"

Sir Philip came up to her, saying gently, "You must believe me, Leonora, this has little to do with you."

He drew her gently out of the firing line and escorted her back to where his wife was standing. "Take her home, my dear. This is no place for ladies."

"No!" Leonora protested. "My name has been mentioned, so I bear the responsibility for what happens. If they intend to kill each other, they will be obliged to do it in front of me."

"This is most unusual," Sir Philip complained.

"My sister is a most uncommon female," Christobel told him, and he smiled faintly before going back to give the order for the duel to commence.

However, it was then that Sir Ashley spoke again. "Get the ladies out of here, Langridge."

"Haven't you got the liver to die in front of the ladies, eh?" taunted his cousin.

"Do let us be done with this," Sir Aidan complained. "I have already lost gaming time over this, and I do not wish to miss my engagement with the Divine Clara later today. If your shot goes awry, Ashe, I daresay you won't be in any hurry to enjoy her company."

Lord Kersdale laughed, and the men began to count their paces.

"They treat this as a game," Leonora said in an agonized tone.

"I daresay they will have placed wagers on the winner."

Leonora gasped at what she could only regard as foolishness and then closed her eyes and turned away. As soon as the pistols were discharged, she emitted a groan, but she had to look and face the worst.

Involuntarily her eyes went to Sir Ashley, and when she saw he appeared unhurt, Leonora was totally unprepared for the feeling of gladness she experienced. Seconds later, her feeling of relief evaporated as she looked to the other man. Captain Symington was still on his feet, much to her relief, but had dropped the pistol on the ground and was clutching his arm. His seconds seemed unconcerned with any injury that might have been sustained, merely paying and receiving monies won and lost in their wagers on the outcome. All four seconds were busy congratulating each other in the most vociferous manner.

After a moment or two Leonora realized there was a red stain on Captain Symington's shirtsleeve, and blood was oozing through his fingers as he clutched at the wound. When his seconds belatedly rushed him to his carriage, followed by the surgeon, Leonora cast Sir Ashley a furious look before hurrying away. She heard him call her name, but she didn't acknowledge it. She climbed into Captain Symington's carriage as he was eased back against the squabs. He looked deathly pale and the blood was now flowing freely from his wound.

When the surgeon tore at his shirt to reveal the dark, ugly wound, Leonora flinched but did not look away.

"Will he be all right?" she asked the surgeon, her voice a hushed whisper.

"He should be, if no infection sets in."

Captain Symington laid his head against her shoulder. "Unfair fight," he muttered. "Fired before the end of the count."

"Hush," she entreated. "Reserve your strength, my dear. Everything will be well."

Sir Philip gave him brandy from a hip flask, which Captain Symington swallowed eagerly, spilling half of it down his chin and shirt front. Just then, as the surgeon began to remove some ugly-looking instruments from his bag, Sir Ashley got into the carriage. He had replaced his coat and looked elegant enough to return to any diversion.

"How is he?" he asked.

His inquiry was of his cousin, but he was looking at Leonora, whose icy expression could not be misread. Before anyone could answer his question, she accused, "How could you, Sir Ashley?"

"It was a matter of honor," he explained, looking a trifle surprised. It was not for her to accuse him of cheating, but she was choked with emotion to think that he might. "Will he live?" he asked and looked so ironic it roused Leonora to even greater anger.

"No thanks to you," she retorted and Christobel, who joined them at that moment, touched her sister's shoulder.

"Come now, dear, we must go home. This is no place for you."

Without turning, Leonora replied, "I cannot leave now while Captain Symington is in such distress."

"It would seem that Miss Hamilton has taken my cousin's injury to heart," Sir Ashley explained.

"He was foxed," Leonora said, casting him a furious look. "You, Sir Ashley, were sober. I am as mad as a weaver about all this unnecessary suffering. As if poor Captain Symington had not endured enough pain and suffering in the Peninsula."

At the mention of his cousin's heroism, an inscrutable mask seemed to form over the other man's face, and he moved away as if stung.

"Don't leave me," Captain Symington murmured, and she turned her back deliberately on Sir Ashley and her sister, whom she was certain would champion him, to minister to the injured man.

A moment later the carriage door closed, and Leonora knew he had gone, taking with him her sister, which was an additional irritation. Foolishly she felt hot tears squeezing through her lashes, although she wasn't sure why. The surgeon passed her the brandy flask, and she administered some to the injured man. A moment later she braced herself as the surgeon prepared at last to remove the ball from Captain Symington's arm.

Chapter Nine

"Really, Leonora, over the past few days you have been as melancholy as a gib cat," her sister scolded. "You must make a true effort to come out of your ill humor. This is your come-out year, and you have already cried off several diversions that you cannot afford to do. Already one of your suitors has made an offer for another. It will not do, I say."

Leonora sat at the breakfast table, toying with a piece of toast that was no nearer to being eaten than it had been ten minutes earlier. "Had Viscount Trenton offered for me, I would have refused, so that is no odds to me."

"I daresay. It is of no real consequence, but you must, I beg of you, retake your place in Society."

"I cannot face it just now. Everyone knows about the duel and my part in it. The tattle-baskets speak of nothing else. If I was notorious over the Captain Starlight episode, now I am doubly so, and it is not to be borne."

Christobel laughed. "Dearest, it is wonderful! Every *on dit* in town for weeks has been about you. It could not be better, I assure you." When Leonora failed to be uplifted by this news, her sister went on, "No harm has been done. Captain Symington is recovering and Sir Ashley was unhurt." She frowned. "I have been wondering where he can be."

Leonora looked up at last. "What do you mean?"

"He appears to have left Town."

"Why does that concern you?"

Her sister looked surprised at the question. "Oh, I assure you it does not, but I am curious even though it was to be expected. He hasn't been seen since the duel took place."

"Good. I cannot bear to see him. If I never see him again, I will be well satisfied."

"My dear," Christobel said in awe, "I do believe you are in love at last. Yes, that is exactly the cause of your megrims. You have thrown your cap over the windmill at last!"

Leonora turned to look at her sister in dismay. "Faddle! If you persist in such nonsense, I shall be out of humor with you."

"You are already out of humor with everyone. I must have more hair than wit not to have suspected the cause of it though. You favored Captain Symington right from the moment you met."

"Captain Symington! This is outside of enough. Oh, Christobel, you are a goosecap. I find him amusing, I confess, and I was exceedingly concerned for his health after the duel, but I am not in love with him, I assure you."

"Dearest, you protest too much."

Leonora drew a deep sigh and was almost glad when Lady Clayborne was announced and then, almost immediately, ushered into the room.

When she sat down at the table, she looked uncharacteristically animated. "I confess I intended to call at the first possible moment to give you a set-down after you were seen acting the hoyden in Bond Street." Leonora did not trouble to explain the circumstances; it was enough that Sir Ashley Warrender considered her foolish. "But after recent events, I cannot in all conscience do so."

"That is a great relief to me," Leonora replied, scarcely hiding the irony of her words.

"Mayhap you can persuade my sister to go out, Aunt Eudoria," Christobel appealed to her. "She is being exceedingly foolish over this duel."

"My dear, of course you must go out. You must make the most of your moment of glory. You have had the most advantageous launch into Society of any girl I know. A duel, eh? It could not be more splendid." Leonora looked at her aunt in astonishment as she chuckled. "When I was a girl, there were three duels fought in my name. I was sorry when it appeared the practice was dying out, being unlawful, but now it seems it can still take place discreetly."

All at once Lady Clayborne looked at Christobel and affected her most disapproving expression. "My dear, I respected your wish to bring your sister out, but allowing her to remain indoors at home for almost a sen'night is outside of enough."

"I could not agree more, Aunt," Lady Langridge replied, drawing a deep sigh.

"You have been derelict in your duty toward her, and I can see I shall be obliged to intervene if Leonora is to effect a satisfactory match this Season."

"As you wish, Aunt," Leonora heard her say, much to her surprise.

"There, it is settled. You must attend as many diversions as you possibly can, and I intend to ensure that you do, Leonora."

"It is kind of you, Aunt," Leonora replied in soothing tones, "but it truly is not necessary. Mayhap I have been a trifle foolish over this, but . . ."

"I confess I had little regard for those scions of the Kirby family." Lady Clayborne went on, ignoring Leonora's protests, "But now I am bound to say they are finer gentlemen than I supposed." When Leonora looked away in disgust, her aunt continued, "You must begin to go out immediately, Leonora. There are so many diversions at present you surely do not wish to miss any of them."

"I'm persuaded everyone will look upon me oddly," she complained.

"They will look upon you only with envy, I assure you," Lady Clayborne told her. "I may also tell you that Captain Symington is not hiding away. He has been seen abroad on several occasions, enjoying the approbation of his peers. It seems in England the loser can often win, for I am informed Sir Ashley Warrender is not to be found anywhere near his usual haunts."

Leonora was surprised to hear about Captain Symington, and she somehow resented that he appeared not in the least chastened by the duel. At least Sir Ashley was displaying signs of contrition, but then he had cheated . . .

"She has already missed several important functions," Christobel interpolated in one of Lady Clayborne's rare pauses.

"Prinny is due to inspect his troops on Wimbledon Common today, and I have brought you vouchers for Almack's. I insist that you will attend on Wednesday evening. It is most important,

Leonora. Without an appearance at Almack's, you might as well go back to Talworth with no further delay."

"Would that I might," Leonora said with a profound sigh.

A frown formed on Lady Clayborne's brow. Then she looked first at Christobel and then back to Leonora. "Are you in love, child?"

Leonora gasped with exasperation. "Oh, I do wish everyone would stop asking me that!"

Lady Clayborne made a strange sound deep in her throat before getting to her feet. "Fetch your bonnet and pelisse, Leonora. You will go to Wimbledon in my carriage this morning. That is bound to forestall any worries you might have about appearing in public."

"Thank you, Aunt. It is very kind of you to trouble on my behalf, but I had it in mind to play with the children this morning."

"You have done nothing else save play with them all week," Christobel told her. "They will survive without you for a day."

"I really ought to pen a note to Mama. I have been remiss of late."

"I will not be gainsaid upon this," Lady Clayborne insisted, and Leonora did at last recognize her aunt's resolve. "You must go out, and immediately, so that your courage will not fail you for the future."

"It is not a matter of courage, Aunt. I merely don't wish to watch the Prince act the soldier like a child with his lead toys."

"Tush. You will enjoy the spectacle." Drawing a sigh, Leonora got to her feet as Lady Clayborne added, "It will give us an opportunity to have a coze, my dear. We can discuss plans for the masquerade to be held in your honor. I am determined it will be a brilliant diversion."

The ride to Wimbledon Common was a lengthy one, but Leonora was bound to admit to herself, she enjoyed the air after confining herself to brief turns about the garden for the past few days. She had known hiding away was foolish, aware she must emerge eventually, and the sooner she did so, the earlier she would overcome this strange embarrassment that assailed her.

Hearing that Sir Ashley Warrender was out of Town helped in some measure. Ever since hearing from Captain Symington's lips that his cousin had fired early, she knew she could not bear to see him. With luck he would not appear again this Season, but on realizing that, she felt oddly bereft. Being in his company was always more stimulating than with anyone else.

Wimbledon Common was, as expected, already crowded with people eager to witness the spectacle when they arrived. Lady Clayborne's driver had difficulty finding a space in which to park the carriage, but he did contrive eventually to squeeze it into a place between Lord Urden's curricle and Lady Fulton's barouche. Lady Clayborne had, for some time, been explaining all her intricate plans for the masquerade she was to hold at her mansion in Piccadilly, much of what she said going unheeded by her niece, who was often lost in her own thoughts. As soon as they arrived, Leonora glanced around fearfully, but saw only those who smiled and nodded in her direction in a friendly manner, much as they always did.

"You see," Lady Clayborne pointed out, "no one is looking at you askance."

"Yes, Aunt."

"You must own it would have been a pity to miss such splendid entertainment."

"Indeed, I do, Aunt."

"You will be pleased to see Freddie when he arrives. He was in a fidge to attend, although I suspect that was more in the hope of seeing Dorothea Harries's youngest girl."

For the first time Leonora looked at her with interest. "I had noted they were partial to one another. Do you consider . . . ?"

"Oh, I daresay, he will come up to scratch before long. Freddie has shown an inclination to become legshackled of late." Lady Clayborne chuckled and glanced at her niece. "You will be obliged to make haste yourself, my dear, lest Miss Harries becomes betrothed before you."

"She is most welcome, Aunt. The difference is Miss Harries has met a suitable match, whereas I have not—as yet."

"Freddie did make mention that Sir Marmaduke Warnham might also be here today," Lady Clayborne said airily.

"It looks as though *everyone* might well attend today," Leonora answered wryly.

"Prinny will not arrive until noon," Lady Clayborne was

94

saying, "but I note that Lady Hertford is already arrived." The two *grandes dames* nodded affably to one another as Lady Clayborne went on, "She has been good for the Prince, but I do feel for Princess Caroline, even though it is well known he never wished to marry her."

All the while she was speaking, Lady Clayborne nodded and waved her hand in several directions. In the midst of the nodding and waving she suddenly gasped. "Oh, dear. Brace yourself, Leonora. Captain Symington has arrived. He is certainly not hiding himself away."

Leonora, who had watched the troops assembling with great interest, started. When she followed the direction of her aunt's gaze, she saw that Captain Symington had arrived in what looked to be a brand-new high-perch phaeton, tooling the ribbons with his one good hand.

"My goodness," commented Lady Clayborne, raising her quizzing glass, "that is a very splendid conveyance. I wonder how he contrives to stump the blunt for those little extravagances? It is believed he is deep in dun territory."

"Both he and his cousin seem to be a trifle mysterious in that particular way." A moment later Leonora turned to her aunt. "You knew their family, did you not, Aunt Eudoria?"

"It was years ago, when I was a girl. Captain Symington's mother and Sir Ashley Warrender's were sisters, both of them acquaintances of mine. A pair of chuckleheads if ever there were. They came from a large family so they had small portions. Philomena became legshackled to Francis Warrender, younger son of Sir Delville Warrender. He soon disposed of the dowry and remained in dun territory for the rest of his life. Ernestine married Jonah Symington, who was both handsome and feckless, I am given to understand. Warrender has in some manner contrived to make his fortune, although no one appears to know how. No doubt, the Symingtons do not rejoice in the fact Sir Ashley has also inherited his uncle's baronetcy. In all truth, Leonora, I believe I did him an injustice all those years ago."

Leonora toyed with her mittens. "Christobel gives me to understand he was one of her suitors when she was a debutante."

Lady Clayborne laughed. "A persistent one, if I recall correctly, but it would not do. I could not, in all conscience, allow your sister to throw her cap over the windmill for a gentleman whose pockets were always to let. He had no prospects whatsoever. In retrospect, I have the comfort of knowing I was quite correct in doing so, for your sister is sublimely happy with Sir Philip. I only hope to see you so well settled."

Leonora felt her cheeks redden. Fortunately her aunt was too busy quizzing the crowds to notice her discomfiture whenever the subject of matrimony was mentioned.

Thousands of soldiers in brightly colored uniforms swarmed over the common while others ensured that the spectators did not come too close. Leonora could see Captain Symington strolling among the carriages and he appeared to be very much in demand, sporting a sling bandage to support his injured arm.

"Good morning, Lady Clayborne," he called as he approached. "Miss Hamilton, how pleasant to see you. I do trust that you are both well."

Lady Clayborne inclined an imperious head toward him as Leonora said, "I am happy to see you so well recovered."

The young man moved the injured arm in her direction. "It is of no consequence, I assure you." Recalling the agony of the removal of the ball, Leonora could only marvel at his fortitude. "There are those who believe it happened at Vittoria, and I will not gainsay them."

"Most, I am persuaded, believe you the loser in a duel."

He was not taken aback by her coolness of manner toward him. "The winner is, I understand, vanquished. He will be obliged to rusticate for the remainder of the Season, so I don't consider myself the loser, ma'am, far from it." He hesitated for a moment before going on, "I have a faint memory of your lending me succor in my time of need. Do assure me, ma'am, I was not dreaming."

She smiled faintly. "Be assured, sir, I should have done the same for Sir Ashley if he had been wounded in your stead."

"Then it is doubly fortunate that I *was* the loser. Your kindness was more than appreciated. Indeed, I shall treasure the memory."

"As you wish, Captain Symington, but I still regard it as foolhardy in the extreme. I should have thought you'd had enough of fighting in the Peninsula. You might have lost a limb or even your life. No gentleman can seek favor in my eyes by such cork-brained behavior."

All at once he looked uncharacteristically serious. "Miss Hamilton, I must seek to beg your pardon most heartily, even though it was not I who issued the challenge. I must take equal blame, but I would not for anything cause you anguish. My only excuse is that I was a trifle foxed and that coxcomb cousin of mine provoked me into such an ill humor, I scarce knew what I said or did."

Leonora could not help but be moved by such a heartfelt apology and replied, "If you were foolish, sir, you have suffered for it in full measure."

He smiled again then and looked more like his usual self. "Your solicitude is a balm to my pain, Miss Hamilton."

"And you, sir, are full of moonshine."

"You cannot conceive how relieved I am you do not take the episode amiss. Most ladies would wish only to champion the winner, however he had contrived to do so."

Ignoring his oblique reference to Sir Ashley's cheating, Leonora responded by saying, "I fear I must regard you both as a pair of chuckleheads."

He bowed and took his leave of the two ladies and as he strolled away to be greeted by two girls eager to question him about the duel, Lady Clayborne said, "There is no doubt he has much of the Symington charm."

"You sound disapproving of that, Aunt," Leonora replied, looking at her curiously.

"Not entirely, for this duel can do you nothing but good, but I would not wish you to look upon Captain Symington in a romantic light. He has no face but his own, and your portion is not large enough to support his extravagant ways."

"Contrary to what my sister believes, you may be assured, Aunt Eudoria, that I do not favor Captain Symington as a future husband."

"I am most relieved to hear you say so, for when you do marry, you must ensure it is to a man of position and wealth. His cousin is now far more suited in that respect."

Leonora drew in a sharp breath. "You never used to think so."

"You know full well why that was so. My objections no

97

longer exist, but I suspect that makes no odds, for he is not likely to reappear this Season, and you are bound to be settled long before it ends."

Leonora bit her lip, wondering if her aunt would still be as enthusiastic about Sir Ashley Warrender if she knew he had cheated during the duel.

When several of Lady Clayborne's cronies walked over to converse with her, Leonora was relieved. She climbed down when some of her own acquaintances approached, and she found to her relief it was not too much of an ordeal to speak with them. Although no one said as much, it caused Leonora no small amount of vexation to realize most of them believed she would marry one of the participants of the duel.

Eventually Leonora began to be glad she had come, even though there had been little choice when Lady Clayborne insisted. The day was a fine one, and the soldiers assembling on the Common were a splendid sight to behold. Sufficient to frighten Bonaparte, if he should see them. From time to time there were invasion scares, and such displays served to reassure the populace.

"His Royal Highness won't be arriving until noon," remarked one of Leonora's companions.

"My aunt likes to have a prominent view and that is why we arrived early," Leonora explained.

"Oh, indeed. She has sited her carriage close by Lady Hertford's, so that needs must be the best vantage point."

"There is Mama," pointed out another young lady, "conversing with Princess Lieven. I have it in mind she is attempting to procure vouchers for Almack's."

For the first time Leonora reflected upon how fortunate she was to be assured of the all-important right of entry to Almack's. An appearance at the assembly rooms was of the greatest importance to any debutante wishing for a successful Season.

She smiled suddenly when she saw Freddie Littleborough strolling toward her, accompanied by Rosalind Harries. Freddie was wise enough to choose a possible bride from the ranks of those approved by his formidable mother.

From the flushed appearance of the girl's cheeks, Leonora suspected that her cousin might indeed be in earnest about her.

Freddie was harmless enough, but Leonora certainly did not envy Miss Harries her future mother-in-law.

"You have become almost a stranger," Freddie greeted her.

"We looked to see you at Vauxhall Gardens last evening," Miss Harries explained.

"I was a trifle indisposed," Leonora replied, feeling foolish.

"Mayhap you caught a chill at Lincoln's Inn Fields," her cousin teased, causing Leonora's cheeks to grow pink.

"Tush, Freddie!" she responded. "I have heard enough on the subject to last the rest of this Season."

"My apologies," he answered with a laugh and then he asked, "How did Mama take the news?"

"Well, I am relieved to say."

"I have to tell you, Miss Hamilton," the other girl confided, "everyone is quite mad with envy. After Sir Ashley's rescue of you and now the duel, surely . . .?"

All at once Leonora gasped when she caught sight of Sir Ashley strolling toward her with Mrs. Torrington on his arm. Up until that moment they had not espied her, but it was only a matter of moments before they did. Although Leonora was always glad to see Anne Torrington, she had no wish to speak to her brother ever again. Indeed, like Lady Clayborne, she had convinced herself he would not be seen in Town again this Season. She had even persuaded herself that if she ever did encounter him again, she would by that time be married with an establishment of her own.

It was Miss Harries who caught sight of them next, and mischievously she tugged at Freddie's arm. "Should we not pay our respects to Lady Clayborne, my lord?"

For a moment the young man looked both surprised and unwilling, and then he too caught sight of the other couple approaching. "Oh, indeed, we must, and with no further delay, I fancy." He doffed his high-crowned beaver, "Leonora, dear, Miss Trencham, Lady Clara, good day to you all."

"There looks to be a match there," Lady Clara observed, watching them go.

"They are very well suited, I fancy," Leonora replied.

"Do you have vouchers for Almack's?" Miss Trencham inquired of her a moment later.

Reluctantly Leonora returned her attention to her friend. "Yes, yes, indeed. My aunt is an acquaintance of several of the patronesses."

The girl's eyes grew cold, and Leonora immediately wished she had not spoken, even if it was no more than the truth. "How incredibly fortunate you are."

Aware that Sir Ashley and his sister were coming ever closer to her little group, Leonora laughed uncomfortably. All at once her companions became aware of his presence, and they began to smile and nudge each other. Leonora was mortified. It was not to be borne.

When Anne Torrington clapped eyes on Leonora, her expression revealed her delight in seeing her again, while her brother displayed only his customary inscrutability. Leonora doubted if he would be pleased to encounter her, not after their last meeting. He must suspect she knew he had cheated, something for which she felt she could never forgive him.

"Miss Hamilton," Anne Torrington greeted her. "How good it is to see you again."

"And I you," Leonora responded with genuine warmth as her erstwhile companions wandered away, still chuckling and whispering between themselves.

When Leonora forced herself to look in Sir Ashley's direction at last, he doffed his beaver and nodded coldly to her. "Miss Hamilton."

She was glad enough to return her attention to Mrs. Torrington, who said, "We did hope to see you here today."

"When did you arrive in Town?" Leonora asked.

"Late yesterday."

"Seeing you in Town is quite a surprise to me, although, I confess, a most pleasant one, ma'am."

Anne Torrington looked abashed. "I will not deny I have always been reluctant to come up to Town, but Ashe contrived to persuade me on this occasion, and how glad I am that he did, Miss Hamilton. Everyone I have so far encountered has been so welcoming. A veritable avalanche of invitations arrived this morning, and it will be all I can do to choose which of them to accept. Recall, I am not accustomed to such a hectic life. It is many years since I was last here."

It suddenly occurred to Leonora that, for some reason, Anne Torrington was nervous, causing her to prattle on in such an uncharacteristic manner. Recalling her own uncertain feeling when she arrived in London from the country, she could readily sympathize.

"I will ensure you receive invitations to the diversions held in my honor," Leonora hastened to assure her.

"That is so kind of you. At least I know your kindness is genuine, and not because my brother has made a cake of himself."

Leonora had been wondering if Mrs. Torrington knew of the duel, and her own expression hardened at the mention of it. "I trust you do not hold me responsible, Mrs. Torrington, for I was as cross as two sticks when I heard of it."

"I blame Dermot Symington, but Ashe must have had windmills in his head to have called him out. You may be certain, Miss Hamilton, I have let my brother know in no uncertain terms of my opinion of his foolishness. You cannot be held in the least responsible."

"Now, now, my dear," Sir Ashley chided, not at all put out by the scolding, "Miss Hamilton has already made her feelings plain on that score."

"Such bravado," Anne Torrington protested. "You could have been killed!"

Sir Ashley smiled deprecatingly. "Not by Dermot Symington in his cups, I assure you. To suggest it is an insult."

"That is the least of it," Anne Torrington went on irritably. "Even now I am in fear of the law."

"I don't believe I am like to be thrown in jail," her brother teased, "but if by a mere chance I am, there will be a veritable crush of those who would wish to visit me."

He was looking at Leonora, but it was his sister who said, "Tush. You may jest, but I find the entire matter utterly disagreeable."

"There appears to be no end to the set-downs I am bound to endure, first from Miss Hamilton, and now from you, Anne."

He looked at her in a teasing manner that she evidently could not resist. Her face relaxed, and a moment later she looked past

101

Leonora and said, "Why, I do believe that is my old friend, Lady Jane Meering, over there."

"Lady Jane Furnow," her brother corrected.

Then Anne Torrington transferred her attention to Leonora again. "Do excuse me while I have words with her. We were once such very good friends, and it is an unconscionable time since we last met. Miss Hamilton, I do hope you will call upon me one day when we can indulge in a coze over a dish of tea."

"I would be delighted, Mrs. Torrington. You may be certain that I will."

The woman smiled with genuine pleasure before she hurried away, leaving Leonora distinctly uncomfortable in Sir Ashley's company.

"Mrs. Torrington appears to be in fine spirits," she said a moment later, in an effort to ease the void between them.

"She is in general, I feel, although as you may have noticed, she is a trifle apprehensive. It is some years since she last came to London, so I deemed it time for her to make a visit. Life has been somewhat mundane for her since Tom Torrington died."

"I can understand that being so, but I also know full well that Mrs. Torrington enjoys rusticating above all else."

"That is true of both of us, but all females enjoy the occasional delights of Town and my sister, I fancy, is no exception. She will find a stay tolerably amusing."

During their brief exchange both Leonora and Sir Ashley had focused their attention on the lady under discussion as she renewed an acquaintanceship, but when he at last transferred his attention to her, she murmured, "Would you be good enough to excuse me, Sir Ashley? I must rejoin my aunt. I see the lines are formed, and His Royal Highness will soon be arriving."

As she turned away, he fell into step beside her. "Allow me to escort you back, Miss Hamilton, seeing my cousin is not, as usual, here to do so."

Ignoring his sarcasm, she said, "We truly did not look to see you in London again for the remainder of this Season."

"Staying away was very tempting. Indeed, I was strongly advised to do so. It was certainly prudent to be absent for a few days until all the fuss and botheration had died down. In my experience other sensations soon become more prominent in people's minds. In any event, it appears my cousin has not felt the necessity to leave Town, and I am not the man to turn tail and run from a challenge."

Leonora paused to look up at him. "A challenge, Sir Ashley?"

His eyes met hers unwaveringly, a most disconcerting experience. "I felt it necessary to return to face up to the possibility of being thrown into Newgate."

"I am persuaded a sojourn in Newgate is not the most comfortable of experiences."

He drew a deep sigh. "As a magistrate I did visit that wretched place just after my arrival in Town, and I confess to you, Miss Hamilton, I did not much fancy staying longer than a half hour, but our gallant fighting men in the Peninsula experience far worse from all I am told, and those who travel in the depths of our merchantmen are similarly discomforted."

For a moment Leonora looked at him consideringly before answering, "I truly believe you are enjoying this gamble with the forces of law and order, Sir Ashley."

His answering smile was a genuine one and no less charming than his cousin's. "All challenges are enjoyable, Miss Hamilton, and I have faced many, I assure you. The more difficult it is, the more satisfying the success."

Leonora was forced to look away quickly as the waiting crowd began to cheer very loudly, signaling the arrival of the Prince of Wales. Some of the lower members of the populace booed, since the Prince was not popular among them, but as the crowd consisted mainly of members of the haut monde, the cheers drowned out most of the dissention.

When they arrived back at Lady Clayborne's carriage, Leonora's aunt cried, "La! Sir Ashley, I am bound to confess my surprise at seeing you here today. You and Captain Symington have been made bold by your meeting."

"Miss Hamilton is not welcoming of our presence, I regret to say, ma'am." he replied, glancing at Leonora's mutinous face.

"My niece is still a green girl, sir."

"I am bound to agree with her on the foolishness of the escapade, my lady."

"Captain Symington is not of a like mind, which is odd as he is the injured party."

"When my cousin is fully recovered, I shall trounce him again, this time at Gentleman Jackson's gymnasium, and no one can possibly think it amiss."

Leonora let out a gasp of exasperation as her aunt, to her astonishment, laughed. "I like your style, sir. Indeed, I do. Why do you not join us to see the review?"

"Alas, I cannot on this occasion take up your very kind invitation, much as I would wish to. My sister is waiting for me, and I must attend her with no further delay."

"You refer, of course, to Mrs. Torrington, do you not?"

"I do, indeed, my lady. She is only just come to Town."

"I shall make a point of calling upon her, sir, in the near future, you may be sure."

"She is just now feeling a trifle strange, having not visited for several years, so I am persuaded she will be honored by your condescension, my lady."

Lady Clayborne nodded imperiously and said, "Come along, Leonora. We must not miss the start of the review, which is imminent now."

Sir Ashley offered his hand to help Leonora into the carriage and as he did so, she noticed that there was a large piece of court plaster on his hand.

"You have been wounded, sir," she remarked.

"It is nothing, I assure you. The shot merely grazed me. Mine met a far more accurate mark."

Leonora gasped. "Do you mean to say that this happened at the duel?"

"Yes. I assure you, I rarely indulge in dangerous activities and never the twice in the course of a sen'night."

His irony was completely lost on her as he handed her into her aunt's carriage. Captain Symington had indicated that his cousin had cheated by firing before the full count, but he could not possibly have done so if he, too, was shot.

"Oh, do look, Leonora!" Lady Clayborne was saying. "How stout Prinny looks in his dress uniform."

Obediently Leonora did look, but what she saw certainly did not register in her mind. Even as the soldiers began to fire their guns and the noise was deafening, all Leonora could think of was that Sir Ashley Warrender was not a cheat after all, and the knowledge caused her no small amount of pleasure.

Chapter Ten

"*I* am so glad to see you have come out of your megrims," Christobel declared a few days later as they made their way to a breakfast at the home of Lord and Lady Dunwith. "Even if it was Aunt Eudoria who achieved it."

"I own I was being foolish," her sister replied, gazing eagerly out of the window.

"I did tell you no harm would come of that duel as far as the gentlemen involved were concerned. Philip informed me that Sir Ashley and Captain Symington were actually conversing quite convivially the other evening at White's."

For some reason that morsel of news did not entirely delight Leonora, who had been indulging in a good deal of contemplation of late, and in truth, she found her thoughts to be of an alarming nature.

"Philip declares that Sir Marmaduke Warnham and Major I'Anson are about to come up to scratch." Leonora looked at her in alarm as Christobel went on, "Well, do not, I beg of you, appear surprised, my dear. There are a dozen young men madly in love with you. There will be even more offers before long, and whether you wish to do so or not, you will be obliged to decide upon the one you prefer."

"Why? The Season is only weeks old."

"My dear," Christobel retorted, a touch of irritation in her voice, "these matters are decided very early. Only those with minute portions and hag features are obliged to wait. You do not match either of those descriptions."

"I couldn't possibly accept either of those gentlemen, worthy as they are. The truth is, I don't care a fig for either of them."

"Very well," Christobel said with a sigh of resignation. "I just pray you do not harbor a fondness for Captain Symington, as has long been my suspicion, for he simply will not do."

"You are beginning to sound just like Aunt Eudoria."

"She and I are united in wanting a brilliant match for you. Most of your suitors are suitable."

"If you truly believe that, mayhap you and she should decide between you, who I must accept."

"Tush! You will decide for yourself."

"Did you?" Leonora couldn't help but retort, glancing at her sister intently.

This was the very first time they had ever been truly out of patience with each other.

"What a crack-brained question. Of course I did."

"Looking back, do you have no regrets about your choice?"

Christobel Langridge looked shocked. "Do Philip and I seem to be at odds with one another?"

"No . . ."

"Then what are you about asking such a thing? I am well settled as anyone can see, with a full nursery to boot. Your marriage is the matter in question." When Leonora looked away, her sister said in exasperation, "You were always headstrong, and I don't doubt you will continue to be so in this matter, but do not, I beg of you, run off with one of the footmen as Belinda Conningsby did only a few weeks ago."

"You may rest assured that I will not; I have scarce exchanged a word with any of the footmen in your service since my arrival in Mount Street. In any event, do you regard me as such a goosecap?"

Lady Langridge smiled at last and as the carriage approached its destination and slowed down, she patted Leonora's hand. "No, indeed, I do not, but love often makes fools of all of us, I fear."

Leonora was tempted to ask if love had made a fool of her, but thought better of it, biting back the words that were on the tip of her tongue. Certainly Christobel had never appeared happier or lovelier than she did now. She looked no older than a debutante herself despite having four young children. The girl Sir Ashley Warrender had courted relentlessly could not have looked so different to the one who often danced with him now.

It came as a relief when the steps were let down, and they alighted outside Dunwith House to join the crowds thronging into the mansion. Once inside, Leonora found herself constantly importuned by various young gentlemen, something that she normally found diverting, but on this occasion she discovered herself glancing around from time to time to scrutinize the new arrivals. It was not until she saw Sir Ashley arrive with Mrs. Torrington that Leonora recognized it was he whom she was seeking, and the realization was a profound one.

Almost immediately he caught her eye and smiled, causing her to experience an immediate glow of warmth, which assailed her entire being. While her attention was being constantly diverted by importunate young men, and young ladies anxious to be considered one of her acquaintances, Leonora eagerly awaited the moment he reached her side. However, when she looked eagerly to see him approaching, she was disappointed that only Mrs. Torrington squeezed through the throng to reach her.

"What a crush!" she exclaimed with a laugh. "It is so good to see a familiar face."

Swallowing her disappointment, Leonora responded, "Do you not know anyone except me?"

"I do keep encountering old acquaintances at every turn, and I confess it is most pleasant to renew friendships. Only yesterday while I was purchasing a few gewgaws, I met Sir Hilary Tuckwell, an old acquaintance from my debutante days. Are you acquainted with him?"

"I believe my brother-in-law is an acquaintance of his. A most agreeable gentleman, I own."

Anne Torrington's cheeks were unusually pink. "I was surprised to learn he was widowed at the same time as I. Only fancy that!"

Leonora smiled faintly. It was beginning to appear that Sir Ashley might have brought his sister to London in the hope she would find a husband. It should not have surprised her, for it appeared he was a man who never made a move without there being a very good reason behind it.

Mrs. Torrington was staring past Leonora, who followed the direction of her gaze. "Is that not Lady Maria Tresco in the purple satin?" she asked a moment later.

"It is, indeed," Leonora replied as she looked upon the young woman who was happily conversing with those around her.

Sourly Leonora wondered why she was in such high spirits, for she was normally a trifle dour.

"So there is another of my acquaintance present today," Anne Torrington said. "Only the other day, Ashe took her riding in his curricle. I am so pleased he is enjoying this stay in Town, for he was so disappointed last time he . . ." Anne Torrington suddenly looked shamefaced as she cast Leonora an uncertain smile and then, in an unnaturally cheerful manner, exclaimed, "I do believe that must be Millicent Copley over there. How stout she has grown since I last saw her. I fear what they all must think of me, Miss Hamilton, for I notice most of my one-time acquaintances have grown prodigiously old."

Leonora could not help but laugh. "Older, perchance, Mrs. Torrington, but certainly not old. You need have no fear, for no one could possibly find your appearance wanting."

Anne Torrington dimpled at the compliment. She certainly looked far younger than she had when Leonora first encountered her in Dorset, despite her apparent unease over being in London. She noted, too, that the woman now wore far more modish gowns and because of that, once again Leonora experienced a feeling of warmth toward Sir Ashley.

"You really are the sweetest child," Mrs. Torrington responded.

"It was sincerely meant, I assure you, ma'am."

"I have always believed that Ashe had been given everyone's share of the family's good looks. At Hevening he was just my brother, but here in Town, I am quite taken aback at the number of females who seek his company at every turn. He has always resisted any temptation to marry in order to devote his energies to the estate, but I do suspect that will not always be so, despite past hurts . . . Ah, Sir Hilary," she said quickly, her cheeks growing pink again as the gentleman approached them. "Allow me to present Miss Hamilton whom I am pleased to regard as a good friend of mine."

For a few minutes the three of them conversed pleasantly, although Leonora's mind still pondered on what Anne Torrington had said. Had he hinted to his sister that he would in the near

108

future be making an offer for Lady Maria Tresco? she wondered. If that was what he intended and he was accepted, and she didn't doubt that he would be, it would be sweet revenge on all those who once snubbed him so roundly.

When a few minutes later one of Leonora's acquaintances approached to convey a new snippet of gossip, she was glad enough to leave Mrs. Torrington with a possible suitor. As the girl chattered on inanely, Leonora glanced around the room once more, but there was no sign of Sir Ashley, who was normally easily seen no matter how crowded the place. However, a few moments later, she did espy Christobel slipping out through the French windows onto the balcony beyond.

Frowning slightly, Leonora could scarce concentrate on what was being said to her and answered in monosyllables while all the time casting curious and worried glances toward the windows. As soon as she could take her leave of her acquaintance, Leonora began to make her way toward the area herself, although it was a painfully slow progression, for she was accosted at every step by those eager to engage her in conversation.

By the time she reached the French windows, Christobel had just stepped back inside. When she saw Leonora, she started with what looked suspiciously like guilt.

"Leonora, dear, you gave me quite a shock standing there. What are you doing?"

"More to the point, Christobel, what are you about?"

Christobel pulled her paisley shawl closer about her shoulders. "It is so warm in this room. I felt I should swoon if I did not take some air with no delay. You know how impossible it is to have a window opened at these functions. Everyone is possessed of a dire fear of chills."

"You are always remonstrating with me the perils of cold air." Christobel had the grace to look shamefaced, and her sister went on, "Mayhap we should leave if you feel unwell."

"No! No!" Christobel laughed. "There is no need for such drastic action. I am perfectly recovered now."

As if anxious to terminate the conversation, she moved away quickly. Leonora hesitated where she stood for a few moments until her sister was swallowed up by the crowd. Suddenly Leonora caught sight of her own reflection in the pier glass and noted her flushed cheeks. Feeling somewhat guilty, she slipped out onto the balcony to take in a few breaths of cool air in the hope her thoughts might take on some semblance of reason.

From that vantage point she could see into the garden, where several couples strolled, laughing and conversing between themselves. From the many *on dits* that came her way, she knew many ladies and gentlemen were enjoying illicit affairs and at such gatherings as this often took the opportunity of planning liaisons while walking in the garden, ostensibly for all to see. However, all gardens had a hidden arbor or summerhouse where privacy could be had.

It was chilly on the balcony in contrast to the heat inside. Compared to the babble of noise inside, it was a haven of peace with only the occasional shout of laughter or bird cry to intrude on her solitude. Leonora pulled her shawl more tightly about her shoulders and was about to go back inside when she changed her mind and went down the steps into the garden instead. She felt foolish, but was aware her sister was not one for a turn around the garden and never had been. Leonora had been the one glad to stay in the country with their invalid mother. Stuffy drawing rooms had never troubled Christobel before.

One couple ran past her, laughing, and she wandered hesitantly into the garden. Others nodded and smiled as they strolled past. Just as she approached the Broad Walk, she drew back in shock when she saw Sir Ashley Warrender striding purposefully toward her. The sight of him out there caused her spirits to sink, for she imagined he was the reason for her sister's uncharacteristic venture into the garden.

For some time she had half suspected the reawakening of their regard for each other, and this was proof enough of Christobel's infidelity. She was only one of many who took on a *chèr ami* after dutifully marrying and producing an heir. Christobel had married rank and fortune, as befitted her station, but she evidently could not deny her heart when her old love returned to London. Leonora would be the first to agree that Sir Philip, fine man that he was, was also a trifle dull for someone as ebullient as her sister.

Despite her suspicions, Leonora was unprepared for her own feeling of devastation to be proved correct. At Hevening she had

110

considered Sir Ashley Warrender to be above other men, even if she had not liked him overmuch. Now her feelings had taken on a decidedly different turn, but she had to acknowledge, he was probably as capable of shabby behavior as any other gentleman. What she had not suspected was how miserable the knowledge would make her. All at once she wished she had not given in to her curiosity and remained in an ignorance that was, if not blissful, certainly more comfortable.

"Miss Hamilton," he called as she made to turn away.

Leonora drew a deep sigh, for she had hoped he had not seen her. It would do her sensibilities no good at all to be considered a spy. When she pretended she had not heard, he called her again, more loudly.

This time she stopped and turned toward him, and the sight of him looking so debonair, caused her eyes to mist. Two sisters in love with one man, she thought. How ironic that was. How the tattle-baskets would love to know that *on dit*.

"It appears everyone is in need of air today," he remarked as he approached, "but you must have a care not to contract a chill," he added when he was closer.

Just at that moment Lord and Lady Castlereagh strolled past, nodding affably, and when they had gone, Leonora retorted, "My sister has not, so I doubt if someone with as stout a constitution as I will succumb."

He fell into step beside her when she began to walk, in her confusion, away from the house instead of toward it.

"I did encounter Lady Langridge only a few minutes ago," he told her. "She, too, was finding the atmosphere inside a trifle . . . heavy for her comfort."

Leonora was surprised he had admitted seeing Christobel and wondered if he would have if she hadn't mentioned it first. "It is not like her to do so," she replied, eyeing him covertly.

He appeared unperturbed. "Nor you, I fancy, but it is even more crowded than usual in there. For those of us who live mostly in the country, we need space and air around us."

She looked at him in some surprise before admitting, "Yes, I suppose it is so." She glanced behind her at the retreating foreign minister and his wife. "How good it is to see Lord Castlereagh here today. Mayhap the war is going in our favor if he can take time off from his duties."

"I believe the latest news from the Peninsula is heartening."

They had come to a charming walled garden that was sheltered. Leonora turned to make her way back to the house, but he barred the way.

"It is still stuffy indoors, so why not let us stay here awhile?" he suggested.

Leonora was more than a little hesitant. While one part of her perversely wanted to be in his company, another told her she would be foolish to remain.

"I really should be getting back," she told him. "I am persuaded Lady Maria is in a fidge to converse with you."

He smiled, and she felt her will melt. "She will wait," he said softly, and Leonora knew she didn't have the will to argue.

"Well, I agree it is exceedingly pleasant out here . . ."

"Do you realize, Miss Hamilton, this is the first opportunity I have had to converse with you alone since we were at Hevening? Do you recall our conversation in the summerhouse?"

"Yes," she answered, and her voice was no more than a whisper.

It seemed so long ago. She could scarce recognize herself as the same person.

"You are so much in demand, it is not like we shall have many opportunities in the future," he went on.

His eyes held hers in a captive gaze, and almost against her will she sat down on a rustic bench, where he joined her, sitting altogether too close for her comfort. His arm was lying along the back of the seat, very close to her shoulders, and involuntarily she drew the shawl closer about her as if it might afford her some protection from him.

"What a pretty garden this is," she murmured, feeling self-conscious.

She was desperately afraid he might guess her feelings, transparent as she regarded them to be, and that would never do. Christobel could wear her heart on her sleeve, but Leonora was determined no one would ever know how she felt about this most enigmatic of men.

"It was a trifle ordinary before you entered," he told her, and

112

she didn't know how to respond to his flattery. She knew he was a practiced exponent of the art. Fortunately he went on quickly. "I have wanted an opportunity like this since returning to Town. I believe I owe you an apology, Miss Hamilton."

She looked at him in surprise. "I am not aware of any misdeed, sir."

"I have it in mind you do not forgive me for wounding Captain Symington."

She drew in a sharp breath. "It appears you were both injured, and I assure you, my concern would have been aroused for anyone in a similar situation. There is no reason for you to believe . . ." she began to protest but he put one finger to her lips to silence her.

"Why then do I feel you bear me a degree of resentment?"

"You are mistaken, sir," she answered coldly.

"Since my arrival in Town, I have looked for some degree of warmth in your manner toward me, but it has been sadly absent. You display cordiality to others, so I must ask myself what I have done to offend you."

Leonora's eyes became downcast, for she could not deny it. "You may be certain, I did not intend to appear cold, Sir Ashley."

"My pride and arrogance are mayhap too closely related if I demand your friendship."

"No, no," she protested, shaking her head, "that is not so. I owe you a great debt."

"You owe me nothing. I want no duty-bound accord between us."

"I am at a loss to know what you want."

"Are you?" he asked, and there was a surprising bitterness in his voice. When she raised her eyes to look at him at last, he went on, "Mayhap your feelings toward me are more similar to mine than I could dare to suppose."

All at once she was unable to hold his penetrating gaze for fear that he would see the truth in her eyes. "Your feelings for me, sir . . . ?"

He stroked her cheek gently with the back of his hand, and she was aware of the red mark where the ball had grazed it. All at once she was assailed by an urge to press it to her lips and beg his forgiveness for misjudging him so.

113

"Dearest Leonora, with all the adulation heaped upon you of late, you still have not guessed how much I adore you."

"Ashley," she murmured, her heart filling with love and joy where there had been misery only a short time before.

Captain Symington had been wrong about him cheating during the duel so, reason told her, it was entirely possible she could be in error about his relationship with Christobel. Just at that moment she didn't care about anything that occurred outside the walled garden. If he adored her because she reminded him of Christobel or even if he was in love with both of them, it did not matter.

He cupped her face between his hands and drew her closer to him and when their lips met for the first time, Leonora knew it was something she had wanted since first meeting him. It was her very first kiss, but she responded to his ardor with every fiber of her being, until nothing or no one else existed beyond the boundary of their arms.

Chapter Eleven

On the following morning Leonora was up early. In truth, she had hardly slept. Throughout the night her mind had returned to that magic interlude in Lord and Lady Dunwith's walled garden. She relived every word and each embrace that had been exchanged between them. Only when it was absolutely necessary for them to return to the house did they do so, remaining close for the rest of their stay.

No one suspected, and Leonora hugged close to her the knowledge of what had occurred between them. She had thought the encounter with Captain Starlight had changed her life. Now she knew nothing could have changed her life to the extent of that one brief assignation.

On waking she knew at last what it was to be in love, and the feeling was too good to waste in sleep. Fortunately Christobel was still abed when Leonora put on her feathered blue bonnet and velvet pelisse and set out, accompanied by her maid, to walk to Conduit Street. She carried with her an engraved invitation to Lady Clayborne's masquerade in the event Mrs. Torrington had not received one, having come so lately to town.

A shiny new high-perch phaeton was standing at the curb outside Sir Ashley's lodgings. Resplendent in yellow paint, Leonora eyed it admiringly. Just as she was doing so, he came out of the house wearing a many-caped driving coat and shiny Hessian boots.

When he saw Leonora, his face broke into a smile of welcome, and her heart filled with gladness as he ran down the steps toward her.

"My dear," he said as he raised both her hands to his lips, never taking his eyes from her face. "How delightful you look—as always."

Recalling their heated kisses the day before, she was all at once abashed, feeling her cheeks grow pink.

"Your tongue is as smooth as Captain Symington's," she told him in an attempt to hide her own embarrassment.

He stepped back, feigning outrage. "What a dire insult. If you were a man, I would call you out for that affront."

Leonora laughed and then told him, "I beg you not to be downcast, but I am come to call upon Mrs. Torrington. I have an invitation for her."

He let her hands go at last. "Oh fie! I thought you might have called upon me." She smiled at his teasing as he went on, "Anne is gone out. We rustics do not lie abed. Your call is opportune, however. Mayhap you would do me the honor of riding with me in my new carriage. There is no other I would as lief have up beside me."

"This is yours?" she gasped.

"It is, indeed."

"I was only just now admiring it. How splendid it is."

He turned to her maid, who was hovering nearby. "I shall return your mistress home." Then he took Leonora's hand and helped her onto the box. As he climbed up after her, he said, "You have the honor of being the first female to travel in it."

"First?" Leonora responded with mock outrage. "I trust, sir, I shall be the only one."

"My dear, when the females in this town clap eyes upon it, the street will be filled with those waiting their turn."

She laughed as he took the ribbons and started up the team of magnificent horses. A moment later he went on, "I am beginning to enjoy London as I never did when my pockets were to let."

"So I had noticed. I had heard you were a trifle wild in your youth."

"Are not all young men? My excesses, I regret to say, were restricted by a severe lack of funds."

"That is something that evidently does not affect you now."

He glanced at her, smiling wickedly. "Sadly I haven't the partiality for wild living that I had then."

"I confess, I too have enjoyed my sojourn, but in all honesty, I am bound to say I would not like to live here more than in the country."

"Then it is likely you will not have to do so. I have an excellent land steward, but I, too, prefer rusticating. I believe we are of one accord in that matter."

She cast him a loving glance. "In many others, too, I fancy. I have taken an unconscionable time in realizing it."

He turned to smile at her, and their eyes met for a long moment before he returned his attention to the road. They quickly arrived in Grosvenor Square, where he drew up in front of one of the splendid new houses that had been built there in recent years. Leonora cast the building, with its three storeys and Greek columns, a curious look.

Sir Ashley climbed down and then came around to help her alight from the carriage. For a long moment they stood by the curb gazing at each other, and Leonora's heart was beating so fast, she wondered if he could hear it. A moment later he stepped away and indicated that they should enter the house.

She hesitated, and he said in a soft voice, "Trust me, Leonora."

Just at that moment she had never trusted anyone more, and she followed him into the large hall with its marble floor and classical columns. A double staircase soared up to the first floor, and as yet, empty niches marched up the walls just awaiting statuary.

Sir Ashley removed his coat and threw it over the newel post, followed by his high-crowned beaver, something that made Leonora laugh.

"Brummel would be outraged by your treatment of your clothing," she pointed out, still feeling a little uneasy at being alone with him in what appeared to be an empty house.

"I don't give a fig what Brummel thinks of anything," he admitted, coming back toward her. "It is your opinion that matters to me above all else."

A noise somewhere behind them made her start, and her eyes opened wide when she saw Anne Torrington come toward her. The woman's surprise was equal to Leonora's.

"Miss Hamilton! I expected Ashe to join me here, but what a double pleasure it is to see you."

"Miss Hamilton called to see you this morning, Anne," her brother explained, "so I brought her here."

"I'm so glad that you did. Why don't you show her around the house, Ashe? I am persuaded Miss Hamilton will find it interesting."

"That is an excellent suggestion."

Anne Torrington smiled again. "Do go along with Ashe, Miss Hamilton. I have not yet explored all the domestic offices, but I will join you both presently."

When she hurried away, Sir Ashley ushered Leonora toward the long, curving staircase. As she went toward it, Leonora smiled warmly.

"Your sister is the dearest person."

He smiled, too. "Yes, I know it. I am the most fortunate of men."

As they walked up the stairs, Leonora said, "I am exceedingly curious about this house. Who is the owner?"

"All will be clear presently," he told her, maddeningly. "Just follow me around for now."

Leonora felt she would be willing to follow him anywhere. Being in his company, wherever that might be, was delight enough, and she questioned him no more.

He ushered her through the various salons and apartments, all of them beautifully proportioned, just waiting for curtains and furnishings. Leonora could easily envisage it in its complete state.

117

Ornamental plasterwork lavishly decorated every ceiling, each of which was supported by marble pillars.

When they reached the part of the house that was eminently suitable for a nursery suite, Leonora felt embarrassed, but then they moved on until at last they returned to the main drawing room with its view over an, as yet, uninspiring garden.

At a loss as to what to say, Leonora stared out at the garden, imagining how it would look after gardeners had set to work on it. After standing there for a minute or two, she heard him coming across the room toward her, and before she could turn to face him, he had enfolded her in his arms, pressing his lips to the side of her neck. Leonora shivered with delight and allowed herself to wallow in his embrace. She had thought of little else since the previous day, but the reality was so much better than the memory.

"Do you like the house?" he asked, his lips close to her ear.

"Oh, yes, indeed," she sighed. "It is a most beautiful house."

"I'm so pleased that you like it."

"How can I not?"

"Shall I purchase it?" When she gasped, he went on, "Will you furnish it in your own exquisite taste and live here with me as my wife?"

Leonora turned at last to face him, her eyes brimming with tears. "Oh, yes, yes, I will."

"Then the house will be ours."

When she went back into his arms, she whispered, "I love you so much. I never thought I could be so happy."

"I loved you from the moment I set eyes upon you," he whispered against her hair.

"How I wish I had known. You appeared to favor others."

"Ah, but that was only to salve my pride when you were so cold toward me."

"I do know you were once fond of my sister."

Her heart was beating fast as she spoke, and she stayed in his arms, not daring to see his face.

"Was I? I daresay I was for a short while, but I was a callow youth then. Perchance what I found congenial in her for a very short while, I have come to love in you. Be certain that I do love you, Leonora."

Satisfied at last, she asked, "Shall you call upon Sir Philip?"

He held her away so he could look at her. "I have a far better idea. After Lady Clayborne's masquerade I shall be obliged to go to Hevening on a matter of business."

Her face crumpled at this unwelcome news. "I shall miss you so."

"Have no fear, I shall be away for the least possible time, but while I am in the area, I will take the opportunity of calling upon Sir Hector to ask his permission to marry you."

"I must own that is a splendid notion. He will be so glad to see you. He holds you in such high esteem."

"So it is likely he will not reject my offer?"

Leonora's face creased into a smile. "He would not dare. His daughter's happiness depends upon it." Slyly she added, "Even Lady Clayborne looks upon you favorably now."

He laughed. "Which proves what a difference is made by a fortune and a title."

"It makes no difference to me," she vowed. "I would have loved you had you been a pauper."

"I know," he whispered, "and if you were a serving wench, I should love you in equal measure."

"It is going to be so difficult for me to keep my own counsel when all I wish to do is proclaim to everyone in sight we are betrothed."

"It would not be right until I have contrived to speak to your father."

"I know, and it will not be for long even if it does seem like forever before you return to Town."

"Before I go, we are engaged to attend the masquerade. It will be odd if we do not recognize one another in our disguises."

"That is impossible for me. I would know you anywhere."

"Just to be certain no importunate fellow is mistaken for me, I may as well tell you I shall be the one in the black and silver domino."

"And mine is blue and gold. Our love will be concealed behind our masks and dominoes."

"Like the masquerade, that situation will not last for long. I am anxious to proclaim to the world what a fortunate fellow I am."

All at once she became serious. "I never believed this degree of contentment was possible, and I owe it to you."

119

"Our happiness is dependent on each other, that much is certain now."

He kissed her again, and they remained clasped in one another's arms for some considerable time until Mrs. Torrington's footsteps could be heard on the stairs. When she entered the drawing room, Leonora and her brother were standing some yards apart, demurely discussing the respective advantages of Mr. Hepplewhite's furniture over that of Mr. Sheraton's.

"I cannot conceive why you insist upon calling around at Conduit Street, for I am persuaded Mrs. Torrington must have received an invitation to the masquerade from Aunt Eudoria," Christobel declared as she and Leonora returned from the shops the following day. "After all, it is patently obvious Aunt Eudoria regards that family favorably now."

"I cannot be certain of that, even though not to invite the savior of one's niece might be regarded as *mauvais* ton."

Christobel laughed. Leonora was glad to see her sister's ill humor had gone and hoped that it would not return when she learned she was to marry Sir Ashley. Leonora believed she knew her sister well enough to think that she would hide her own disappointment and be glad for her. After all, Christobel had a husband of her own.

Although Leonora had noted her sister's mood, Christobel did not seem to notice that her manner was brimming over with happiness. It was for the best, Leonora decided, seeing she was obliged to hug the knowledge to her for a few more days. Soon Christobel and the entire haut monde would know that she, Leonora Hamilton, was betrothed to Sir Ashley Warrender. Repeating that fact to herself caused Leonora to shiver with delight.

"In any event," Leonora went on, smiling to herself, "I feel it my duty to call upon her. I haven't yet done so."

"I am aware you have cause to be grateful to her, but I am bound to confess, she is scarce the kind of sister I would have imagined Ashley Warrender to have. I have always found her a trifle dull, and he is such a Corinthian these days. He always did have a good deal of style, even when he was out of funds."

"She was very kind to me when I was at Hevening."

Christobel smiled. "For that she has earned my eternal gratitude, but I fear if you are still determined to call upon her, you will be obliged to do it without my assistance. I am all done up, and if I am to attend Aunt Eudoria's masquerade this evening, I shall have to rest in the meantime."

The carriage took them back to the Langridges' house, and then Leonora continued on to Conduit Street. Secretly she was glad Christobel was not up to accompanying her to call upon Anne Torrington. There was always a chance of seeing Ashley while she was there, and that would be an additional pleasure before the masquerade. Tomorrow he would be on his way to Dorset to speak with her father. They could be married very soon after his return to Town, and the thought of that caused her to hug herself with delight.

Alighting from the carriage outside Ashley's lodgings, she was disappointed not to see his phaeton at the curb, but she had already known it was doubtful he would be at home at that time of the day. She hurried up the steps and was admitted by a servant and shown into a small parlor, which was quite different to any of the apartments in the new house she would share with him in Grosvenor Square.

A few minutes later Anne Torrington joined her, looking somewhat flustered, her lace cap slightly askew. However, she greeted Leonora as warmly as ever.

"Miss Hamilton, my dear, how very kind of you to call. I'd been hoping you would. It is always a genuine pleasure to see you."

"And I you, you may be sure, ma'am," Leonora responded warmly.

Mrs. Torrington made a wry face. "I have had a sufficiency of callers since my arrival, but all of them appear to have daughters just come out! Needless to say, I did not tell them my brother is almost certainly a confirmed bachelor like his uncles, Desmond and Horatio. Even though he has appeared, of late, to be dangling after Lady Maria Tresco, I have long since despaired of his ever marrying."

Leonora was tempted to laugh out loud and tell her future sister-in-law that it was not so, but once again she did resist the temptation. It would not be right even to hint at it while Ashley was away.

"Will you take tea with me, Miss Hamilton?"

"I would not wish you to go to any trouble, ma'am. I only called to bring you an invitation to Lady Clayborne's masquerade. I had it with me yesterday, only I forgot to hand it to you in all the excitement of viewing the house."

"Ah yes, it is kind of you to trouble yourself on my behalf," the woman replied, looking suddenly troubled, "but Lady Clayborne did send one with one of her servants. It is exceedingly condescending of her, I own. When you arrived just now, I was expecting delivery of my domino."

She rang for tea and until it arrived they chattered on various subjects. Then, when the servant arrived with the kettle, Mrs. Torrington busied herself preparing the tea, which she then poured into delicate Rockingham cups.

"The house in Grosvenor Square is a very fine one," Leonora observed as she accepted the cup.

To her surprise Anne Torrington started and began to appear uneasy again. "Oh yes, yes indeed it is. Ashe has decided to buy it, you know."

"He seemed certain he wished to do so yesterday, but are you not pleased, Mrs. Torrington?"

The woman appeared to force a smile to her face. "You may be sure that I am, even though I considered he should think on the matter a little longer." Leonora remained unconvinced of the woman's sincerity as she invited, "Do have a biscuit, Miss Hamilton."

She took one and bit into it thoughtfully, all the while observing the woman. She was not wrong. Anne Torrington was ill at ease, much as she had been at the military review just after her arrival in Town. The danger of her brother being arrested for dueling was almost certainly over now, so it could not be that that was causing her so much anguish.

"Are your children both well?" Leonora ventured.

"Oh yes, indeed, although I miss them sorely as you might imagine," she replied, her manner warming a little.

After a moment Leonora once again ventured to say, "I do beg your pardon if I am incorrect, ma'am, but I fear you are a

122

trifle out of humor today. Mayhap I have come at an inconvenient time."

"No, no," Anne Torrington hastened to assure her. "It is always a pleasure to see you, as I am sure you know." After a moment's pause she went on, "It *is* a splendid house, is it not? When we remove there, I daresay I shall send for the children and have them by me." She paused to draw a profound sigh. "The phaeton is such a fine carriage, is it not? A few years ago I would not have believed it possible for my brother to own either that or the house."

"All credit is due to Sir Ashley," Leonora told her, still feeling puzzled. "One hears so often of fortunes being lost, not so often of them being made."

"Just so," Anne Torrington replied, looking even more miserable.

At this point in the conversation Leonora frowned. "Mrs. Torrington, what is troubling your head? I am bound to confess, it is most unlike you to be out of humor, and I would like to feel, as a good friend . . ."

"Ashe has been such a good brother to me since my husband died, Miss Hamilton, none better."

Leonora felt a flush of warmth flow through her veins. "I do not doubt it for one moment. He is a very fine gentleman."

"We have wanted for nothing, the children and I. Roger and Thomas are down for Eton . . . I could not possibly have managed without . . ."

"You do not need to sing Sir Ashley's praises to me, Mrs. Torrington. I am very well aware of his worth."

The woman could not meet Leonora's steady gaze. "Of course, you, too, have reason to be grateful to him, and I know you have a fondness for him, and that is why I am tormented so."

For the first time Leonora could see tears in the woman's eyes, and she began to be truly alarmed. She moved to join her on the sofa. "Mrs. Torrington, whatever is amiss? I cannot leave with you in such torment."

Anne Torrington wrung her hands together. "You look upon my brother with fondness, so perchance it is just I share my concern with you."

123

"Yes, you must tell me," Leonora urged, stifling her own sudden unease.

"You must vow to me not to breathe a word of what I say to another living soul."

"You know I will not."

"Swear it."

Leonora hesitated before affirming, "I will take your confidence to the grave, ma'am."

Anne Torrington shook her head. "I believe I am being a foolish woman, fit for Bedlam to worry so. It is disloyal at the very least."

"Is it concern for Sir Ashley which teases you so?" Leonora asked gently.

"Yes." The word was wrung out of her.

"I am persuaded you are very fond of your brother."

"Oh, yes, I love him dearly."

"Then you will be obliged to face him with your concern."

"I cannot!" Mrs. Torrington declared, looking horrified.

"Then do tell me what is troubling you so."

The woman looked away. "At the heart of the matter is the mystery of how he has made his fortune. So many have alluded to it since I am come to Town."

Leonora relaxed a little and smiled reassuringly even though Mrs. Torrington stared blindly ahead of her. "Gentlemen do not discuss their business dealings with ladies."

"He will not discuss it with anyone. Oh, he appears to answer the questions put to him, but in essence he says *nothing*. He always was as close as oak when it suited him."

"Mrs. Torrington, I regret to say I am at a loss as to what is plaguing you so."

"You must have heard that a very few years ago, we were as poor as church mice, struggling for survival as a family. Inheriting Uncle Horatio's estate was no help, for it was virtually bankrupt. Ashe even came to London in his desperation in search of a wealthy bride, but those he was partial to would have none of it—quite understandably—so after that, he set out to make his own fortune."

"And . . . ?" All at once Leonora experienced a great sense of foreboding.

Anne Torrington swallowed hard before speaking again. "That night, the night you were found near the house . . ." Leonora started slightly. "Ashe had only just arrived home when you were found. His horse was wet through from being ridden hard—a dark horse. He went straight out with Jemma after he had returned and that was when he found you."

Leonora laughed in bewilderment. "Mrs. Torrington, just what are you trying to say?"

"Captain Starlight," she answered with some difficulty. "Each time he has struck somewhere in the area, Ashe has been out of the house. I had never given it a thought until the night you arrived. Moreover, since he came to London, Captain Starlight hasn't held up any coaches at all. Not one. It is wicked of me, Miss Hamilton, but all the while Ashe has been here in London, I have been praying Captain Starlight would hold up the stage so I should know it is not my brother who commits these dreadful crimes."

Leonora sank back into the cushions of the sofa, her mind reeling. "My goodness," she said after a moment, "you cannot possibly imagine . . ." When Mrs. Torrington made no reply, Leonora sat up straight again. "No! It was not your brother who abducted me, ma'am."

"How can you say with such certainty? You did not by your own account see his face."

"That is so, but I do know it was not Sir Ashley. There is no question of it, I assure you. You must believe me, ma'am."

After what seemed to be an agonizing few moments, the woman's face relaxed at last. "Thank you, Miss Hamilton. That is precisely the reassurance I have been seeking."

"Whatever put the notion into your mind?"

"A number of things. The repair of our fortune, his being out of the house whenever Captain Starlight struck, and the fact he always engaged in hazardous pursuits as a boy. It is all a non-sense; I now acknowledge that. I am bitterly ashamed of myself for even mentioning it."

"It is as well you did, for now your mind is put at rest."

"I am a goosecap, am I not?" Anne Torrington asked, smiling faintly. "A highwayman, indeed. My dearest Ashe could not possibly be that creature. I do believe, I was becoming unhinged to

125

think so. Will you ever forgive me for plaguing you in such an unnecessary manner?"

Although she was now as much disturbed as Mrs. Torrington had been, Leonora smiled reassuringly. "You need not ask it of me. We will never again refer to this conversation, and I beg of you to cast all thoughts of it from your mind, as I am determined to do.

"Now, do tell me about your domino. Mine is blue and gold . . ."

When Leonora left the house some time later, Anne Torrington was more like her natural self. However, Leonora's mind was still troubled by what she had been told. It seemed inconceivable that Anne should ever connect her brother with such infamy, but then no one else was closer or knew him so well. Leonora could not admit to knowing him at all, even though she loved him so much.

Learning every facet of each other's character was a pleasure to come, and it was one she looked forward to with relish. Even so, what Anne had said went around and around in her mind as the carriage set off. She laid her head back against the squabs and closed her eyes, which was a mistake, for immediately her mind conjured up a picture of Captain Starlight, something she had hoped was put behind her forever.

It did seem, however, that the specter was never far away from her after all. The highwayman, as she recalled him, was of a similar build to her beloved Ashley, and by his sister's testimony, he had been out for hours that evening.

That in itself was not incriminating, but all at once her eyes opened wide with shock when she suddenly recalled the day she had seen Meggy in Bond Street. The woman had disappeared almost outside Ashley's lodgings! He must have seen her, and yet he had categorically denied seeing anyone.

In an effort to contain such alarmist thoughts, Leonora put one hand to her head. This was far worse than the abduction itself, for her fear was even greater. Beads of perspiration broke out on her brow.

Once again her mind returned to the day she had seen Meggy, recalling as best she could everything about it. Suddenly she sat up straight, crying out in anguish before sinking back again, looking bleak.

"On a dark night with only the one candle?" he had scoffed, referring to her ability to have recognized the woman.

How could he have known there was only the one candle in the cottage unless he had been there himself? she asked herself. It was not something she had told him, for it was of no consequence at all.

When the carriage jerked to a halt outside her brother-in-law's house, the footman immediately came to let down the steps and open the door. He affected not to notice the tears streaming down Leonora's face. When she climbed down at last, she hurried into the house and up the stairs to be alone with her utter desolation.

Chapter Twelve

"If you insist upon being so Friday-faced, Leonora, it is as well you are to wear a mask for most of the evening."

Christobel Langridge cast a disapproving look at her sister as they rode to Lady Clayborne's masquerade. During those moments when she could penetrate her own misery, Leonora had been tempted to find an excuse to miss the event, but short of expiring, she knew it was not possible to do so. Philosophically she appreciated it was necessary for her to speak with Ashley before he left for Dorset to seek her father's approval for their marriage. Bleakly she acknowledged that tonight might well be her last exchange with him, and she desperately sought the necessary courage required to tell him they could not, after all, be married.

"I have the headache," Leonora replied at last, fighting back her tears.

The number she had shed since realizing Sir Ashley Warrender was Captain Starlight was sufficient to fill the lake at Hevening.

127

Christobel sighed. "I should not be surprised to hear you say so, for I must own, the past few weeks have been particularly hectic. I do not suppose it will do your social standing any harm if you were to cry off a few diversions."

"I will be glad to do so," Leonora replied, showing signs of relief.

"In the meantime do contrive to enjoy this evening's diversion."

"I will try," her sister lied.

"Aunt Eudoria will have contrived to make it superb, you need not doubt. One thing I must own about her and that is her total commitment when she decides to put on a diversion. On one occasion she wore a gorgon mask to a previous masquerade. She had no notion why everyone found it so amusing!"

Leonora laughed brokenly as their conveyance arrived in Piccadilly, which was choked with carriages going in the same direction. It seemed an age before it was their turn to be let down, and the strain on Leonora was beginning to tell. Her despair was so much deeper after that brief glimpse of happiness in his arms.

The Langridge children had an automaton in their nursery, to amuse them. As the masquerade got under way, Leonora felt like that automaton, going through the motions, speaking to the other guests and even joining in the lighthearted search to discover who was behind each domino and mask. It was in a sense ironic, for she could hide her misery behind the golden mask, through which should have shone her triumph that evening.

"So this is my golden angel," a voice said close to her ear, causing her to start.

When she whirled around, fearfully, she realized the voice and the face behind the mask were those of Captain Symington. No longer did he and Ashley seem so alike. Leonora just wished she had paid more attention to Captain Symington when he had accused Ashley of being treacherous. Both cousins it seemed could lie easily when it suited their purpose.

"I have it in mind," he teased, "that there is a beauty hidden from me."

Leonora was in no mood for a flirtation, especially with one of Ashley's kinsmen. Tragically for her, it had turned out that they were both rogues, the only difference being that Dermot Symington made no pretence about it.

"Mysterious lady, will you dance with me?" he persisted.

As dancing precluded the necessity of conversing, Leonora was glad to acquiesce. She noted that the evening had got off to an excellent start and everyone appeared to be enjoying themselves, all except for Leonora herself. Misery pervaded every part of her being, but a small voice told her it was fortunate she had discovered Ashley's secret before their betrothal was formally announced. Worse still, she might not have made the discovery until after they were married, and that thought did not bear contemplating.

When Captain Symington escorted her to the edge of the floor and seemed disposed to linger, Leonora eagerly accepted an invitation to stand up for the next set. When it had finished, she made her customary review of the guests and was shocked to see Ashley standing by the dance floor, even though she had been constantly seeking out his presence.

Seeing him dramatically enveloped in a black domino, which now could only painfully remind her of his guise as Captain Starlight, she fought back the tears which were once again threatening to overwhelm her. Not for the first time that evening was she glad of the mask, which hid her misery from the world.

Just as she gazed across at him, he turned to her, and she could see that his mask was one that only covered the lower part of his face. Ironically it was this that confirmed finally what she already suspected. He was Captain Starlight. The question of his newly acquired fortune was no longer a mystery to her.

Faced with the indisputable fact of his treachery, the room whirled around her. Her legs became weak and she staggered slightly, reaching out for something on which to steady herself.

All at once she found herself being helped to a chair by Sir Marmaduke Warnham, to judge by his voice, and a vinaigrette was being held up to her face. Someone loosened the strings of her mask and gently removed it, so she no longer had that behind which to hide her heartbreak. She attempted to free herself from the overwhelming concern of others, but someone said:

"Hold still, Miss Hamilton, and you will be recovered in a moment."

Leonora looked up to see a mass of masked faces surrounding her. She was just about to laugh out loud at the sight of them when Ashley pushed his way through the crowd.

"What is it that afflicts her?" he asked in a worried tone.

"The heat, no doubt," someone replied, and she felt cool air as someone swished a fan in her face.

"Stand back a little. She needs air," another ventured.

"Poor child. It has all been too much for her."

"Allow me," Ashley suggested, and she felt the loving strength of his arms around her, raising her to her feet. "I'm going to take you out of here," he said, and the concern in his manner would have been sufficient to break her heart had it not been shattered already.

Just then, however, she was glad enough to allow him to support her, and she leaned on him as he led her from the ballroom, watched by a score of curious eyes. As she enjoyed their closeness for the last time, Leonora recalled her ride on Captain Starlight's horse, how she had tried to have no contact with him, but failed and felt the strength in him then. Such duplicity must be remembered whenever his voice and his manner attempted to make her oblivious to it.

With great gentleness he led her down into the hall, where it was both cool and quiet, and eased her onto a sofa. He removed his mask, but to Leonora it was as if he still wore one. His expression was tense and he regarded her with concern.

"Do you feel better now?" he asked.

"Yes, I thank you," she answered, averting her eyes from his worried gaze.

"You must have a heed for your health, my love. All the hurry-scurry of the last few weeks must have been too much for you." When she made no answer but merely fanned her rosy cheeks, he went on, sitting beside her, "First thing on the morrow I leave for Dorset, and I must insist that you rest while I am gone."

She turned to him then, snapping shut her fan. "Sir Ashley, when you are there you must not on any account approach my father on the matter we discussed yesterday."

He looked shocked, which did not surprise her. It certainly wounded her as much as it did him. When his eyes opened wide, she was forced to look away. Whatever he was and whatever he had done, she still did not wish to cause him pain.

"Why, Leonora? Do you now prefer that I speak to Sir Philip and ask his approval?"

"I want you to speak to no one. The fact is, I do not now wish to marry you."

Before he could exclaim his surprise, Christobel came hurrying down the stairs, having dispensed with her own mask and domino.

"Leonora, dearest, I have only just been told of your indisposition. Whatever is amiss? Are you ill?" When she saw the tears trembling on her sister's lashes, she cried, "La! You are overset. I should have heeded the signs this afternoon. Never mind. We shall go home immediately, and you must be put to bed with a brick and a posset." She looked at Ashley. "I do thank you for your assistance, sir. Will you be kind enough to remain with my sister while I send for our carriage?"

Unaware of Sir Ashley Warrender's grim expression, Christobel rushed off to instruct the lackeys. The moment she had gone, he turned to Leonora once again, saying in an urgent tone:

"Did I hear you correctly?"

"Yes." Her voice was a barely discernible whisper.

"I cannot believe you mean this, Leonora. Do I have Lady Clayborne to thank for this change of heart?"

"My aunt knows nothing of my . . . of our . . ."

"Love," he supplied in a clipped tone. "Then I beg of you to tell me what has occurred to change your mind. Is there another?"

"No!"

"You must forgive my perplexity, Leonora, but only yesterday you were as happy as I at the prospect of our being wed."

"I do mean what I say, sir. Be assured, I do not want to marry you."

"Would you like more time to consider?" he asked, his voice growing soft again.

"There would be no point, I fear. My mind is quite made up, and I would not for anything have you remain hopeful of a further change of mind. I shall not marry you and there's an end to it."

"Leonora!" he said in a low urgent voice. "What has happened to change your mind? You must tell me. I beg of you. I insist upon it."

"It makes no odds. Can you not see that?" she whispered. "It is over."

"In heaven's name . . . !"

As Christobel came back with a footman who carried Leonora's cloak, she jumped to her feet and hurried toward them. Hugging the cloak about her, she hurried toward the door as the Langridges' coach rumbled to a halt outside. Sir Ashley had jumped to his feet and followed her partway across the hall. At the door Leonora paused and turned to look at him through her tears.

Her last impression was of a man in as much torment as herself, and she supposed even rogues could fall in love. It might have been possible for her to disregard his secret life, so great was her need for him, if it were not for the nagging fear that one day he would be caught—and hanged. That was one aspect of his life of which she wanted no part.

The dream was a vivid one. Leonora was dressed in her wedding finery with orange blossoms in her hair. As she waited for her love, Captain Starlight, in his dark frieze coat and battered beaver, came to claim her. He came closer and closer, and Leonora knew she could not escape him. She would be in his power forever, and there was nothing anyone could do to prevent it happening. In her dream she was both afraid and happy, and only when he was about to take her into his arms did she awake with a start.

Even though she immediately knew she was safe, she still shuddered and sank back into the lace-edged pillows to stare up at the tapestry tester above her head. Today should have been the happiest day of her life, the beginning of something so wonderful she could not have begun to imagine it before.

Instead she was about to begin a life of wondering what might have been if Sir Ashley Warrender had been the man he appeared to be to the world. Now she would never marry, for if she was not to be his bride, she would accept no one else, rather than play out a sham for the rest of her life.

Eventually she supposed she would return to Talworth House

to be with Mama and to take up good works in the village, rather like poor Miss Denton. The spinster was rumored to have suffered unrequited love in her long-ago youth and since then had devoted herself to visiting the sick and the needy of the parish.

Tears of self-pity pricked at her eyes again when she saw the kind of future she had to look forward to, reflecting that she would never again experience the sweet kisses or the glorious passion that had flared between her and Sir Ashley Warrender. Her throat felt choked when she recalled that he would be by now well on his way to Hevening never to know why she had rejected him. For the first time she wondered how she could face Mrs. Torrington with any degree of equanimity, and if it would be at all possible in the future to see her without the risk of also encountering her brother.

It was, of course, possible that Mrs. Torrington would also return to the country and that would solve the problem. She might even marry Sir Hilary Tuckwell and have a separate establishment from her brother.

She might well do neither of those things, though, Leonora recognized. Even though Anne Torrington would prefer to return to Hevening, with Sir Ashley purchasing a house in Grosvenor Square, he would require a hostess—at least until he found a bride. Leonora bitterly reflected he would easily find a bride now. His newfound wealth, his charm, his fine appearance, would ensure it. Only his poverty had prevented it before. Leonora could think of a half dozen debutantes who would eagerly accept an offer of marriage from him, and their fathers would be no less pleased.

If only, she thought to herself, if only we had not encountered Captain Starlight that cursed day. But they had, and it had affected her life even more profoundly than anyone could have suspected.

Suddenly the door to her bedchamber flew open, and Christobel came rushing in, breathless and waving a letter in front of her. Leonora sat up in the bed, scarcely heeding her sister's agitation. No news could be worse than what she had learned about Ashley. Even if Bonaparte had invaded, Leonora could not care about it.

"Leonora, I know I intended to allow you to rest today, but you must get up immediately."

"Why? It is raining outside and my head aches."

"Oh, fie to your megrims. This note has just arrived from Papa. Mama is taken ill, and we needs must go to Talworth without delay!"

All thoughts of her own unhappiness immediately left Leonora's mind. "Oh, no," she gasped. "How bad is it?"

"I don't know! Papa says we must go with no delay, so it needs must be serious indeed."

"Let me see that letter." Leonora scrambled over the bedcovers to snatch the missive from her sister's trembling hands. "It really is outside of enough. If Papa has sent for us, she must have had notice to quit, Christobel!"

Christobel put one hand to her head. "Oh, I beg of you do not say so. This could not come at a worse time. Philip tells me Lord Kelsdon is coming to make an offer for you."

Leonora swung her legs over the edge of the bed. "Oh fie to Lord Kelsdon. He's a toadeater and I dislike him intensely. You cannot have thought I would wish to become legshackled to *him*."

Christobel sighed and shook her head before she turned and hurried toward the door. "And here I was actually anticipating your Season with pleasure. What a chucklehead I must be to think I would see you soon settled."

As she paused by the door, Leonora was already raiding the press for a gown suitable for traveling. "I shall send your maid to pack a cloak bag, and in the meantime I had better order our traveling carriage to be brought around from the mews. I do hope we will reach Talworth in time. I shall never forgive myself if we are too late."

Chapter Thirteen

"*I* fear I will be obliged to give your papa a set-down over this to-do," declared Lady Hamilton, who was sitting up in her bed and looking not in the least in danger of dying. "There was no cause for him to send for you in the middle of Leonora's Season. It really is outside of enough."

Her two daughters were seated at either side of the bed, and it was Leonora who replied, "Papa considered it necessary, and no one could be more delighted than Christobel and I that our journey was entirely uncalled for. In any event, Doctor Belston has ordered you to rest. There has been some cause for concern, so you need not seek to gammon us, Mama."

Lady Hamilton sighed. "My dears, I do nothing else save rest. I just regret having brought you from London in the middle of your Season. The journey alone is sufficient to overset the most sturdy constitution."

As Leonora recalled a previous, disastrous journey, Christobel glanced at her worriedly. "Leonora was in need of a respite, Mama. She's all done up, and it is my fault entirely. I fear I have accepted too many invitations on her behalf in my enthusiasm to give her a brilliant Season."

"I'm persuaded you meant it for the best, Christobel, but I did have it in mind that Leonora looked pale."

"You must not concern yourself with me, Mama. All I need to do is cry off a few engagements, that is all."

"Your letters to me have been most informative, so I do know how many engagements you have attended. The one thing you have failed to do is give any intimation of a likely young man. I refuse to believe there are none who favor *you*, my dear."

"There are a score, Mama," Christobel answered. "Leonora has just failed to grow attached to any of them. It might be

135

difficult for you to conceive it is so, but I do assure you of the veracity of what I say. Leonora has allied herself to one young man, and he is quite unsuitable. To give my sister her due, she is fully aware of it."

"What of Sir Marmaduke Warnham?" the girls' mother asked.

"What do you know of Sir Marmaduke, Mama?" Leonora asked in astonishment.

"Your aunt, Lady Clayborne, wrote to inform me that he was most suitable, and in earnest."

"Mama, I believe I am the better judge of who is suitable," Leonora replied, looking wry. Then, with a purposeful air, she closed the book of poetry she had been reading to her mother and said, "I believe it is time for you to rest, Mama. Christobel and I will come back later and read to you again if you wish it."

Lady Hamilton smiled as her younger daughter stood up to adjust the pillows. "I must own that it is good to have my girls back home, even if it is only a short respite."

As they made to leave, Christobel said, "Next time we come to Talworth, Philip and I will bring the children."

"That is a time to which I look forward with great relish, although invariably the children exhaust me. I daresay I shall not recognize Cyrus. He will have grown so big."

When Leonora closed the bedroom door behind her, Christobel said, drawing a profound sigh, "It is such a relief to see her so much recovered."

"Indeed, it is," Leonora agreed in heartfelt tones. "I never dared to hope she would be so well. I had steeled myself to face the worst when we left London."

Christobel looked at her sister and smiled. "Papa is busy with his land steward and Edmund with his lessons, so shall we take a turn in the conservatory? It is always pleasant in there."

"That would be most enjoyable."

Since arriving back at Talworth, Leonora had had little time to brood about Ashley. Being removed from London and all the places where she was likely to encounter him was also a great balm. What she dreaded now was returning to see him at every function she attended. Even worse would be those who expected her to choose a husband from her many suitors. She wanted

136

Ashley and no one else, not even the most illustrious title and greatest fortune in the land.

"Now we know for certain Mama is not given notice to quit," Christobel said as they entered the conservatory with its views of the garden, "we needs must make arrangements to return to Town. We have been absent for long enough."

"I have been giving some consideration to that matter myself," Leonora replied in a careful tone. "Mayhap I had best stay awhile longer, to help nurse Mama."

Her sister looked shocked at the suggestion. "Leonora, this is the middle of your Season. You cannot rusticate *now*! Mama is well looked after here, you need not doubt."

"I would not be easy in my mind if I were so far away while she is still recuperating."

Christobel let out a gasp of exasperation and sat down on a seat near an orange tree. She took out her sewing before asking, "Do you recall when I went up to London for my own Season?"

Leonora was glad enough of a safe topic of conversation, and she smiled at the recollection. "Indeed, I do. I missed you sorely."

"And I you, but I wrote to you regularly, giving you all the news of my activities."

"I was, I confess, a trifle envious of you," Leonora answered with a laugh.

"It was the first time we had ever been apart. You were the very first person I told about my feelings for Philip before Mama or Papa, or even Aunt Eudoria."

"Yes, I recall very well. It was devilishly difficult to keep my own counsel on the matter. Fortunately Philip did come up to scratch, and I could tell whom I pleased that my sister was to marry Sir Philip Langridge."

They both smiled fondly at the recollection of all the excitement that ensued, and then Christobel said, "Leonora, we were so very close then. What has happened in the time since?"

Leonora started and then laughed uncomfortably, knowing what her sister said was the truth, but she could not possibly confide in Christobel, of all people, about Ashley Warrender.

"We are still close, dearest," she murmured a moment later.

"It is not as it was. You must know it. There are times when I feel we are almost strangers."

Leonora looked down at her hands, which were clasped demurely in her lap. "Christobel, the truth is we are no longer children. You are married with children of your own. It is plain we have changed, even if it is only in a small way. I am still, and always will be, exceedingly fond of you."

"When you came to Town this Season, I had hoped you would regard me as a confidante in the same way I looked upon you."

"If there was anything to confide, be certain it would be with you," Leonora assured her, feeling a mite uncomfortable.

"Then why have I, for this past sen'night, sensed you are in some measure of torment?" When Leonora opened her mouth to protest, her sister still went on, "I do understand some of the conflicts you must be experiencing. When you first suffered the megrims, I considered you must be in love, and Captain Symington appeared to be the obvious candidate. He is so handsome and charming, and was always at your side even though he is unsuitable. I was persuaded it must be him, but since we came down to Talworth, I have had time to reflect, and I have come to the conclusion that I have been a goosecap to think you so foolish. It is Sir Ashley Warrender who has won your heart, and you encouraged Captain Symington only—I cannot conceive why—to keep Sir Ashley at a distance. Am I not correct, dearest?"

When Leonora did not answer, her sister went on, "I cannot conceive of a reason for your vexation of spirit if it is so. When I recall his concern for you at the masquerade, and his attentiveness on other occasions, it is patently obvious to me that just a little encouragement from you is all that is required to bring him up to scratch."

"I have no intention of encouraging him, Christobel. Indeed, I have refused his offer."

Once again her sister let out a gasp of exasperation. "I do not understand your attitude, Leonora. He is eminently suitable and if you harbor a fondness . . ."

At this point Leonora turned to look at her. "Christobel, you favored him once, did you not?"

"I believe I have mentioned that fact."

"Do you still have a fondness for his company?" Christobel looked outraged, and her sister went on, not troubling to hide her bitterness, "You did wish for intimacy, so by all means let us confide in each other now you have expressed a wish to do so."

Christobel smiled faintly and touched her hand. "Indeed, and no, I do not still harbor a fondness for him beyond what is normal, although I confess to being delighted to see his good fortune. I also find him charming company. That has not changed. He never made an offer for me, but if he had there was no real contest between him and my dear Philip. We are far better suited than Ashe Warrender and I ever were, and I had the good sense to know it at the time."

"So it was not just his lack of fortune and the pressure from Aunt Eudoria which parted you?"

"I assure you it was not."

However, Leonora was not so easily assured. "When we attended the Dunwiths' soirée, you went into the garden . . ."

"Ah yes, I do recall," Christobel answered, returning her attention to her sewing. "The heat was so great, I could bear it no longer."

"A little while later I, too, decided to take the air and discovered Sir Ashley was also in the garden . . ."

Again Christobel put down her sewing in exasperation. "Oh really, Leonora, this is outside of enough. You cannot think that I had an assignation with him." When Leonora merely returned a steely gaze, Christobel went on, exhibiting extreme patience. "I am a married woman with four children in the nursery. How could you possibly think it of me?"

"Lady Falkham has six children and still contrives to pursue a liaison with Sir Montague Speers!"

"I own it is not like me to take the air, but I did feel faint, and I feared I might once again be increasing. However, I am glad to report it is not so. I did encounter Sir Ashley when I was strolling in the garden, and because I have always enjoyed his company, I did contrive to engage him in light conversation. However, he was not as sociable as I had always found him to be, so I returned to the house, and he set off down the Broad Walk, where I believe he was bound when I first encountered him. At the time I considered him to be a little unnerved, and I did wonder if he was on his way to a liaison, but in retrospect, I suppose that is as fanciful as your crack-brained notion about me."

It did afford Leonora some measure of relief to hear her sister's explanation, and she no longer doubted it, but sadly it was now of no consequence. Leonora had been quite willing to accept his relationship with Christobel, providing it was now over. Since coming to Town and listening to the *on dits*, she had come to learn few men were paragons of virtue. What she could not accept was his role as a lawbreaker and the possible consequences.

Christobel continued to look concerned for her sister. "Dearest, I do pray this notion you had was not the reason for your ill humor of late."

Leonora cast her sister a faint smile. "I assure you, it is not."

"Then . . . I have it in mind there is no reason why you should not encourage Sir Ashley to pay court to you."

Leonora drew a deep sigh. "I confess to you that I do harbor a definite fondness for the man. You, of all people, should understand why." Christobel nodded sagely. "But it will not do. I cannot elaborate on my reasons. Sufficient to say, they are sound. He and I can have no possible future together."

Her sister looked alarmed, but before she could question Leonora further on the matter, Sir Hector came hurrying into the conservatory, and he was evidently in a great state of excitement.

"Ah, so there you are, ladies! I have been scouring the house and grounds for you both for an age. Such a to-do. I scarce know whether I am on my head or my heels."

Both young women got to their feet. "Mama," Leonora said as his excitement communicated itself to her. "She is not . . . ?"

"What? Oh, no, no," he hastened to assure her. "Your mama is sleeping soundly."

"Then what has occurred to put you in such a taking, Papa?" Christobel asked, looking amused.

"I have just been apprised of the most remarkable piece of news. Jack Carter has only just ridden over from Wolvercome to tell me of it. I have left him in the study partaking of a glass of Madeira so I can communicate it to you with no further delay."

"What is this news, Papa?" Leonora asked, casting a perplexed glance at her sister.

Sir Hector's eyes glowed. "Captain Starlight." Leonora started at the mention of the name. "He has been apprehended at last!"

140

Leonora felt her head reel, and she reached out for the support of a nearby chair. "Where? How?" she begged.

"Oh, how splendid!" Christobel declared, echoing her father's delight.

"Are they absolutely certain that they have apprehended the right man?" Leonora asked rather breathlessly.

"It appears there is little doubt of it. I am not certain of the details, but Mr. Carter informs me he was apprehended last night in the process of robbing the stage. He has been clapped in the jail at Wolvercome, but he is not to remain there for long; the military have been summoned to escort the villain to London. The trial is to be held there, which will no doubt be followed by execution at Newgate. I must rejoin Mr. Carter, but I had it in mind, you, Leonora my dear, would wish to hear the splendid news as soon as was possible."

As he turned away, Leonora belatedly called after him, "Papa, is there any news of his real identity?"

"Mr. Carter has no notion. All will be told in due course, I daresay. The trial will be a most interesting one. It is a pity it will be held in London, for that is one trial I should enjoy attending. When I think of that fiend I shudder, especially when I contemplate what might have happened to you, my love."

"He would not have harmed me, Papa," she told him with certainty.

"I was not so sure," Sir Hector replied.

When he had gone, Christobel said, looking as triumphant as their father, "Why do you look so Friday-faced? You should rejoice in this moment. Justice will be done at last, and you will know of his execution. Mayhap you will wish to attend."

When Leonora shuddered expressively, Christobel said in a more muted tone, "I fancy all this will do is revive the horror for you. Come now, I suspect your sensibilities have been overset, however good the news may be, and I suggest we retire to our rooms to rest awhile before dinner. The past few days have been exceedingly tiring, I find."

When Christobel hurried away to her room, she left Leonora still feeling stunned. His apprehension had always been a real possibility, but so soon after discovering that Captain Starlight was Sir Ashley Warrender was such a shock.

141

How could she bear to know he was to be executed along with common criminals? she asked herself and shuddered again. Not Ashley. Not the man whom she had declared to love forever.

As she wandered back toward her room, she knew with certainty she could not stand by and allow it to happen. Whatever he had done, she still loved him deeply.

When her thirteen-year-old brother came down the corridor toward her, Leonora didn't even acknowledge him, so deep were her thoughts.

"Let us have a game of cricket before dinner?" he asked.

"Not now, dearest," she murmured.

The boy looked vexed. "You never used to be so Friday-faced before you left for London," he accused.

"Edmund, I need your help," she blurted out.

The boy's manner brightened. "Oh, surely, Lee. What do you want me to do?"

"Do you think you could find me a pair of your breeches, a hat, and a riding coat?" she asked.

Edmund laughed. "What do you want them for?"

"Does it matter?" she asked, unable to hide her impatience. "You said you would help."

The boy looked suddenly cunning. "Is it a lark?"

"Yes." Leonora forced her own laughter. "You're so quick-witted, Edmund. You guessed immediately."

"What kind of a lark?"

"I cannot tell you until it is over. It needs must be a surprise."

"Are we to do it together?"

"No."

His face twisted into a look of disgust. "Lee, you have become quite disagreeable of late."

"Don't set your face against me now," she pleaded.

The boy looked stubborn. "You've become as close as oak of late."

"Will you do it?"

For a moment he didn't reply, but then he said to her great relief, "Oh, very well."

"Then be quick about it. There is no time to lose."

He still looked reluctant, adding, "Only if you vow to tell me all about it when it is over."

"I will. Go along now, Edmund. Hurry!"

She watched him run back along the corridor before she turned to go in the direction of her father's gun room.

Chapter Fourteen

The chestnut mare galloped across fields and jumped over hedgerows, urged on by her rider's cries and the flailing of her riding crop.

Dressed in her brother's breeches, her hair concealed beneath a battered old hat, and her shapely curves disguised by a frieze coat that Edmund had undoubtedly snatched from the servants' quarters, Leonora had not paused to contemplate any of the dangers that might arise out of her pose. Desperation made her oblivious to it and drove her on.

Riding astride the horse, she kept to the fields, for she did not wish to be seen in the vicinity, not that anyone could have recognized her in her disguise. Fortunately the jail was situated on the edge of the town, and she could easily approach it unseen.

Time was the real enemy. She was all too well aware she must free Ashley before the military arrived to take him to London, and also before his true identity became known. Only then would he have a chance of freedom.

Leonora slowed the mare down as they approached Wolvercome, and as soon as the jail came into sight, she found a thicket of trees in which to tether her horse. Although it was an agony to do so, she hid in the thicket for a short while so she could observe the jail. When no movement could be discerned during that time, she began to move stealthily closer to the jail.

It was a small building. Crime, Captain Starlight apart, was not a great problem in the area, and the turnkey was paid by the parish for very little work. The jailing of the notorious Captain

Starlight would be the summit of his career. He would sup free ale at the inn on the strength of it for many a long year.

The jail, she knew, possessed but one cell, always sufficient for the occasional drunkard or beggar to be confined. There was also a small room for the jailer, so he could keep guard over any prisoner.

Moving stealthily along the wall, Leonora slowly straightened up to peer through the window. Silas Hughes, the turnkey, was sitting at his table, a bottle and two glasses before him. Leonora could only hope he had been celebrating his good fortune for some time. It would certainly make her task easier if he had.

Suddenly she froze on hearing a noise not far away. Trembling, she looked around but could see no one. After a moment she allowed herself to breathe again, but it was a few minutes before she felt steady enough to go on.

Taking one last glance around her, she reached for the pistol she had tucked into her waistband and drew it out at the ready. Her hand was trembling, and she made a conscious effort to still it. However, her concern for the man she loved made less of her own fear, and she thrust open the door with a boldness she did not feel and stepped inside brandishing the pistol in front of her.

Silas Hughes jumped to his feet. "Hell and damnation!" he cried, stepping back.

Bolder now, in the face of the man's fear, Leonora moved farther inside, keeping the hat low over her face. "The keys, jailer." When he reached for them, she ordered, "Open the cell door and be quick about it, or I'll let you have it right in the breadbasket."

He fumbled with the keys for a few moments, never taking his eyes off the pistol, which she had cocked at the ready. Leonora moved forward a little farther, but kept well out of his reach, hoping he would not sense her fear. From the look of him, he was so frightened himself, he could not possibly be aware of it in others.

It seemed to be a long time that he fumbled with the keys until he found the correct one, which he put into the lock. When the door swung open, it revealed a dark void within.

"Now, tell him to come out," she ordered.

"Out yer come!" bellowed the turnkey.

When no one came out, Leonora moved forward to peer

inside, and just as she did so, she felt a hand in her back, pushing her hard. Crying out in alarm, she fell headlong into the cell, the pistol slipping from her hand as the door was slammed shut behind her.

Leonora whirled around in alarm to the sound of much laughter outside. "Just as well I answered a call of nature, Silas," chortled the new arrival.

"Now we've got the two of 'em," Silas Hughes boasted.

"Let me out!" Leonora called, panic rising in her fast as she looked around the miserable cell.

Only a small grille near the ceiling allowed in a little light. It was also extremely cold and damp in there. Leonora shuddered at the sight of a spider scuttling into a corner, and a scraping sound in another part of the cell told her that rats probably lived in there, too. She had contrived to escape from Captain Starlight's cottage, but Leonora knew there would be no such escape from this place.

Silas Hughes peered through the grille in the door. "You were too late, lad. 'is lordship's gone an hour ago. Gone to meet Jack Ketch." He laughed nastily again before adding, "There'll be the two of you on the gibbet afore long. What a sight that'll be."

Gone! Leonora sank down on the rickety wooden bench, which was the only piece of furniture in the cell. It was all for nothing after all, she thought in despair. It was all she could do to choke back hysterical laughter. She was too late! How the tattle-boxes would love this when the news became known in London. It would cause a sensation in town, but this time Aunt Eudoria and Christobel would not be so pleased by her notoriety.

Even in the midst of her desolation her thoughts were of the man she loved. She wondered if she would be able to see him when they took her to Newgate. It would be something if she had an opportunity to explain why she had cried off their betrothal, and at least they would die together. The thought somehow gave her no comfort, and she buried her face in her hands and began to weep.

Sometime later—she had no notion of how long—Leonora heard the outer door close, and she grew even more afraid, for they would surely transport her to Newgate without delay so she could stand trial alongside Ashley. No doubt he would defend

145

her, but so great was the outrage against tobymen it would be to no avail. When Leonora thought about it, she really did not mind, for she no longer wanted to live in a world without him. Discovery as a woman would not save her. Women went to the gibbet as often as gentlemen. She only regretted the pain that her family were bound to feel.

Through her fear and worry she could hear voices conversing with apparent urgency in the outer room, and she wondered what shackles would feel like against her skin. Such a short time ago Ashley had kissed her, praising the softness of her skin, and her hair, which would soon be matted and filthy. The recollection of the tenderness between them made her eyes mist with tears.

A few moments later the cell door creaked open, and she started. Light flooded into the murky depths of the cell from a lantern held aloft by Silas Hughes.

"Stand up, lad," he ordered, and Leonora did so.

She blinked, blinded momentarily by the light.

The man who had accompanied him seemed to fill the doorway. "Leave him with me awhile," he told the turnkey, taking the lantern and hooking it on the wall.

Again Leonora blinked, but she could see no better than before. The voice of the newcomer was so familiar, but she knew it was only her imagination playing cruel tricks upon her.

"If the lad's facy with you, sir, you leave 'im to me," Silas Hughes said in an ominous manner. "I'll curry 'is 'ide for 'im."

He closed the door behind him as the newcomer said, "So you're Captain Starlight's accomplice. You don't look at all fearsome to me, but we shall see."

He put one booted foot on the bench, and with her eyes downcast Leonora could see only the riding crop he was slapping against the shiny leather.

"Take off your hat, boy," he ordered.

Leonora did so, allowing her hair to fall to her shoulders. The man gasped. "Leonora! What the devil!"

Her head snapped up at last, hardly daring to believe her eyes, which were now accustomed to the light. "Ashley? Is it really you?"

Her joy was so great she flung herself into his arms, which closed about her, holding her near. He could not have been

146

unaware that she was trembling from cold, fear, and now utter delight.

"I feel that this must be a dream, Leonora. Why are you here and dressed as a boy?"

"I thought it was you they'd arrested," she told him, her words tumbling out almost incoherently. "I was so afraid you'd be executed if you were taken to London, so I resolved to try to get you out, only they locked me in here instead. I must have windmills in my head to think it of you."

He held her away, looking into her tearstained face. Then he led her to the bench and they both sat down. He kept his arms around her all the while, and she reveled in his closeness as never before. One fact kept repeating itself in her mind; he was not Captain Starlight! He was not going to the gibbet!

He put one hand to her brow. "There appears to be no fever."

"Only madness, but it is gone now."

"Then mayhap you can explain the reason for all this nonsense?"

"Are you all right, sir?" called the turnkey.

"Perfectly," Sir Ashley replied, before returning his attention to Leonora once again.

"It is of no account now. You are not after all Captain Starlight. That is all that matters to me."

A great sigh escaped his lips. "So that is it. You thought I was Captain Starlight."

"Forgive me, dearest," she begged, fearing his anger when she saw his lips form into a grim line. "I am the most foolish of females. How could I have thought it of *you*?"

"Pray do not beg my forgiveness, Leonora. I must first of all get you out of here. Only then may we talk and resolve these matters."

"They think I am the tobyman's accomplice," she said, choking back a high-pitched laugh. "They'll never let me out."

"The turnkey has no authority. Fortunately I do."

He picked up her hat and pushed it onto her head, clumsily tucking her hair into it. "Keep your face averted and allow me to speak for both of us," he told her. "Do you understand?"

Leonora nodded, and he drew her to her feet calling, "Jailer, open up!"

When he did so, Sir Ashley pulled Leonora outside the cell. "This is no tobyman," he informed Silas Hughes. "This lad is the son of a good family who foolishly came here as the result of a wager with some of his cronies."

He pushed Leonora roughly toward the door as the turnkey cried, "Well, I never!"

Sir Ashley tipped him a substantial vail. "Take this for your trouble, Hughes. You were not to know this isn't Captain Starlight's confederate. You exhibited extreme bravery when you apprehended the lad, and it has been noted, I assure you."

The turnkey looked foolishly pleased with the praise while all the time Leonora kept her face averted.

"Lor' thank yer kindly, sir. What yer gonna do with the lad?"

"I shall take him home, and his father can administer the thrashing he undoubtedly deserves for this escapade. It was good work, though, Hughes. I shall make certain it is made known in the county."

All the while Sir Ashley was edging Leonora closer toward the door. As they reached it, Silas Hughes bowed low. "Thank yer, sir. Thank yer kindly."

Once they were outside the jail, Leonora longed to give Sir Ashley a hug, but he asked in a low voice, "Where is your horse?"

"In the thicket."

He untied his own, and together they went to find her mount. As soon as she was mounted, they both rode hard until they reached Talworth House. Only then did they give in to the tension within them both and clung onto each other in sheer relief.

Leonora quickly discarded the coat and hat and then left him in the drawing room with a decanter of brandy while she sped away to make herself more presentable.

When she saw her reflection in the cheval glass, she was horrified by her appearance, and as quickly as she could contrive, she washed away all the awful grime of the jail. When that was done, she changed into a becoming gown and dressed her hair as was befitting a lady. Sometime later she started down the stairs again, only to encounter Edmund, who appeared to have been waiting to waylay her.

"So you're back," he greeted her. "Was it a great lark?"

"Wonderful, and I vow I shall tell you all about it on the morrow, dearest."

As she made to move past him, he asked, "Why can't you tell me about it now?"

Leonora smiled sweetly despite her desperate impatience to be back in the company of the man she loved. "Because I have a visitor in the drawing room, and it would not be polite to leave him there."

The boy made a wry face. "A *gentleman* visitor, no doubt."

Leonora could not help but smile. "Yes, indeed, Edmund, you are quite correct. I have a gentleman visitor and a very special one, I must own."

Her brother did not appear impressed. "Why, oh why do one's sisters have to become females with windmills in their heads as soon as *gentlemen* come to call?"

Nothing could dismay Leonora now, and she chuckled, replying, "One day, dearest, you will know the answer to that question."

When she went into the drawing room, her heart grew full again at the sight of Sir Ashley. He stood up to greet her, and then came to take her hands, which he raised to his lips.

"Now you are more like my dear Leonora," he told her, "but be certain, I shall never love you more than I did when I discovered the risks you were willing to endure for my sake. You took an immense risk, and even now I shudder to think of it."

"It is of no matter now. You are not Captain Starlight on your way to Newgate, and neither am I, which should be a relief to us both."

"Is that which caused you to cry off our betrothal, Leonora?"

The painful reminder made her eyes cloud as she nodded. "Do forgive me, I beg of you. How I ever imagined you . . ."

"Leonora," he said abruptly, "we must talk about this."

"Can we not just put it behind us now?"

"Presently I hope we can do that, but there are certain matters that must be aired between us. Then, if you still wish it, we can begin again."

Leonora looked perplexed. "*If* I wish it . . . Ashley, you are alarming me."

He gave her no comfort but led her to the sofa by the fire.

When she sat down, he remained standing, resting one arm on the mantel and staring into the flames.

"What I am about to tell you must never be repeated to another living soul. I want you to understand that." When she made no reply, he went on, "Will you vow to me you will not speak of it once it has been discussed between us now?"

Leonora was even more perplexed and more than a little concerned. Of late when anyone wished to speak with her in a confidential manner, it boded ill.

"Of course, if you wish it."

"It is not merely a wish; it is an absolute necessity." He drew a sigh before going on. "Some months ago it became known that two agents of Bonaparte's regime were traveling to England to bring much needed funds to a network of spies in this country." Leonora frowned. "Lord Castlereagh entrusted me with the task of stopping the money reaching its destination."

"You!" she exclaimed, still somewhat puzzled by what he had so far told her. "Why, Ashley? Why you?"

"There are different ways to serve one's country."

"I still cannot credit what you are telling me."

He kept his back to her, and she missed his closeness just then, needing his reassurance. "Our information was scant, so we knew little of the matter, save the fact there would be a man and a woman traveling together from the coast to London. It was charged to me to stop them at all costs and confiscate the monies."

Leonora's hand went to her lips. "I see it now," she whispered in awe. "It *was* you. You thought Papa and I were French spies!" He didn't answer, and she went on, "It was their money you were searching for in our carriage and among my clothes."

"It was a rather large amount. Disguising myself as Captain Starlight seemed a good way to stop the traffic when a likely carriage came along. We stopped several before yours came along. You and Sir Hector were the only male and female traveling together."

"How could you have thought it of *us*?" Leonora demanded, suddenly angry.

"I cannot blame you your outrage, Leonora, but recall they

150

would not travel carrying Boney's tricolor. It was evident to us they would appear to be ordinary travelers."

"You could not have thought that I . . ."

"Once you were at the cottage, I suspected I had made a mistake, but I had no option but to carry on and hope I was correct, after all. If I was harsh with you, it was only because I believed myself dealing with ruthless people who allowed nothing and no one to stand in their way.

"When my colleague returned to tell me the agents had been apprehended elsewhere, it was too late to make amends to you. We left the door unlocked so you could make your escape when we had gone."

For a moment there was a silence while Leonora digested what he had told her, and then she gave a strangled laugh. "How ironic I was found in *your* carriage drive."

He turned then to face her at last. "Mayhap it was not so surprising as the cottage was also on my estate. I was glad you were found there. It gave me an opportunity to make some small reparation for all the hardship and fear you were obliged to endure. I had never disliked myself so much in all my life."

"Did Mrs. Torrington know?"

"She knew nothing of the matter. As I said, it was important for as few people to know as was possible."

"So it *was* Meggy I saw in Bond Street. You did hide her from me."

"Yes," he answered heavily. "You should despise me for the wrong I did you."

"I can see you were in an impossible situation."

"Your generosity does not ease my conscience, I fear."

He looked at her appealingly as she asked, "And who is the real Captain Starlight?" Suddenly an awful thought struck her. "Oh, Ashley, it wasn't . . . it isn't . . . your cousin?"

To her surprise he laughed. "No, indeed it is not."

"What a relief," she murmured, feeling foolish. "I fear, I am seeing highwaymen everywhere."

"My cousin has not, I assure you, the wit. I would also like to point out that robbing coaches and carriages cannot possibly maintain the kind of lifestyle we have both come to enjoy.

151

Symington merely sends the duns to me. He knows full well I will not allow him to bring ill repute upon our family."

Leonora felt both foolish and angry. "My goodness, how very shocking that is, and he is a war hero."

Again Sir Ashley laughed. "While we are speaking between ourselves, let me assure you he is no such thing. He was cashiered for selling supplies to the enemy." All at once his smile faded. "Well, my dear, it seems it is I who has to beg *your* forgiveness. It may have been an error, but your fear must have been real enough. You may be certain I have not forgiven myself for putting you through that ordeal."

"Oh, you need not beg my pardon for doing your patriotic duty. I can only commend you for that. It is I who have been a goosecap ever to think you a rogue."

He came to sit by her at last, once more taking her hands in his and raising them to his lips. "Your generosity is remarkable, my love."

"It is my love for you that makes it so." A moment later she asked, "Who is the real Captain Starlight? Do you know?"

"A man called Ralph Stanley." When she frowned, he added, by way of explanation, "He has a small holding at the other side of Wolvercome."

She smiled suddenly. "While we are speaking between ourselves there must be no more secrets between us, so tell me how you made your fortune."

"With difficulty, Miss Hamilton, not roguery, I assure you," he teased.

"If you are considered a rogue, it is entirely your own fault, for you have always been as close as oak about it."

"Has it not made me a more intriguing fellow?" She laughed and he went on, "When I failed to find a wealthy wife some years ago—for which I am now most heartily thankful—I went to India and returned with sufficient funds to begin to put my estate to rights. At that time Tom Torrington was alive, and I had only myself to consider. I had been told there were fortunes to be made in the East, and it seemed a worthwhile risk rather than remain a basket-scrambler for the rest of my life. When I returned, I continued to use some of the contacts I made in India and became involved in several lucrative business matters. I still do from time to time."

He fingered the material of her gown. "The company in which I have a substantial interest brought this material into England."

"Had I known, I would have bought several more lengths," she told him, "but I am sorely disappointed in the prosaic manner by which you have made your fortune."

"If you prefer, you may recall I was Captain Starlight for a day. My true business, however, is far more lucrative than riding the high toby, but a trifle less romantic."

As she laughed, he drew her into his arms and kissed her, and she gloried in a love that she had thought would never be hers.

After a while he held her away from him again. "Am I to take it your objections to our marriage no longer exist?"

Her face radiated her happiness. "I am only thankful you still want to marry me."

"I would never want anyone else," he vowed.

"Then let us be married while we are here in the country. I see no reason for us to return to London just now."

"I shall send for Anne on the morrow. She will not wish to miss our wedding."

Leonora smiled her agreement and vowed never to reveal that Anne had also believed him to be Captain Starlight. That was the one truth which would never be spoken between them.

When the door opened a moment later, Christobel stood there looking astonished. "Sir Ashley!" He got to his feet and bowed. "Edmund told me Leonora was entertaining a gentleman, but I never imagined . . . Does this mean your differences are now resolved?"

Sir Ashley glanced at Leonora before answering, "You may take that to be so, ma'am."

Christobel smiled with sheer pleasure. "How splendid. I could not be more pleased." Leonora got to her feet to be embraced by her sister. Then Christobel looked at Sir Ashley. "I presume you will wish to speak with Papa."

"As soon as it is convenient for him."

"I shall go immediately and inform him, sir," Christobel promised as she backed toward the door. When she reached it, she hesitated before saying thoughtfully, "However, I feel it only fair to warn you, I might be an unconscionable time locating him. I do hope you will not mind the wait."

As the door closed behind her, the lovers burst out laughing. When Sir Ashley turned to Leonora, he said, "I have always harbored a great liking for your sister and never more than now."

Leonora went into his arms once again, rejoicing in her good fortune. If her feeling of happiness at that moment was a harbinger of good things to come, the future was going to be quite, quite wonderful.

Love Finds a Way

Chapter One

If there was one thing the Countess of Fossborough enjoyed more than playing host to fellow members of the beau monde, it was relaying a particularly juicy morsel of gossip to her cronies.

It was to this end that her elegant barouche drew up in front of the Honorable Mrs. Vere Radleigh's house in Cavendish Square, and her ladyship stepped out the moment the lackey let down the carriage steps. Lady Fossborough could hardly suppress her eagerness as a liveried footman led the way up to Mrs. Radleigh's drawing room. Her impatience could best be seen by the way the ostrich feathers on her modish bonnet quivered constantly even when she was still.

At last she was ushered into Mrs. Radleigh's sanctum where it pleased Lady Fossborough to see that her friend was entirely alone.

"Why, my dear Mirabel, what a pleasant surprise this is," Mrs. Radleigh greeted her breathless friend.

She had been reading the latest edition of *The Ladies' Magazine*, which she had discarded the moment the countess entered the room, sensing that she was about to be privy to a morsel of information of monumental proportions.

"I am able to stay only a few minutes in all conscience, but I knew I could not go about my business until I had apprised my dearest friend of the most remarkable news that has only just been related to me."

Lady Fossborough seated herself on a sofa facing her friend and systematically stripped off her calf-skin gloves while Mrs. Radleigh smiled knowingly.

"How good you are to think of me, Mirabel. Do tell of this latest *on dit* that has brought you here in so precipitate a manner. I am persuaded you must have pressing business elsewhere."

"As I have told you, I have only just heard and could scarce believe my ears! I immediately thought, 'I'll warrant Vere does not know of this. Or mayhap she does and has not apprised *me* of the fact.' After all, you have been on exceeding close terms with him for a long time. . . ."

Mrs. Radleigh, a noted beauty, looked amused. "Mirabel! Just what are you prattling on about?"

Lady Fossborough was taken aback. "You do not know?"

"I do not know if I do or not, for I am quite dizzy to hear you prattle on so."

"Crandon," Lady Fossborough replied. "Brett Crandon has come up to scratch. I was never more shocked in my life, and I dare say I am not wrong in supposing you will be similarly afflicted."

Having at last related the remarkable piece of news the countess sank back to assess the effect her words had had upon her friend, and she was rewarded by a look of incredulity that came upon Mrs. Radleigh's face.

"Brett Crandon is to become riveted? Are you quite certain?"

"I could not be more so, for I have heard it from the lips of the chit's proud mama only this morning in Wigmore Street. She could scarce concentrate on choosing a length of chintz at Clark and Debenham. I can report that for one who normally sings small she was quite naturally in high snuff. Which lady with a marriageable daughter would not be? What a catch! After all these years he has finally succumbed to being shut in the parson's pound!"

Mrs. Radleigh sat forward slightly, having regained a little of her composure. "I am bound to confess, my dear Mirabel, I am quite stupefied to hear this news. I had Crandon down as a confirmed bachelor. Indeed, he always declared to me he was!" After making the admission her face suddenly became pink.

Lady Fossborough said, "There is no doubt for several years past he has been pursued by chits just out and their ambitious mothers. I confess I favored him myself when Dilys made her debut, for a short while only. Dilys found him excessively condescending and considered his humor somewhat mystifying."

"Oh, indeed," Mrs. Radleigh agreed ironically.

"In all honesty, Vere, it is as well he displayed no interest, for

Dilys is sublimely happy with dear Matlock, to whom she is better suited. It must be a trifle difficult to keep pace with such a nonpareil as Crandon." She paused to cast her friend a curious look. "I recall he was quite friendly with you at one time."

Mrs. Radleigh's cheeks took on a deeper hue. "Oh, indeed. I found him an amiable companion until I grew weary of his company."

Lady Fossborough laughed and looked unconvinced. "I had never considered Crandon as *amiable*. However, I'm persuaded you must have the greater knowledge than I of his nature. It is a great relief to me that the news has not given you an attack of the vapors. Sally Bayliss, whom I have just left, was obliged to call her abigail to administer hartshorn. I dare say she will have to burn feathers, too."

"I am made of much sterner stuff than Sally Bayliss, I assure you, Mirabel. In any event it is nothing to me now if Crandon becomes legshackled. You did not make mention of the chit to whom he has become allied," she said a moment later, a note of coolness creeping into her voice.

Lady Fossborough smiled with grim satisfaction. "Did I not? How very forgetful of me. It is Jeanne Montescue's daughter."

The other lady gasped. "La! I cannot credit that."

"I can assure you it was Jeanne Montescue who was crying roast meat all over Clark and Debenham this morning."

"I had always assumed if Brett Crandon ever fixed his interest, the chit would be a first-rater. There were times when I believed he was waiting until Princess Charlotte was of marriageable age. In my opinion no less would do for him."

Her friend laughed merrily at the observation. "Mayhap Her Royal Highness has turned out to be a little more plump and plain than pleases his lordship."

Mrs. Radleigh sighed. "Yes, I daresay she would have to be fetching as well as being well endowed."

"You must own the Montescues are quite respectable, and the chit has a fair portion."

"Fair? I daresay it is, but it is not in the least overwhelming, nor is her beauty. How odd it is, for I should not have considered a nonpareil such as Crandon to be at all suited to a drab like Allegra Montescue."

"But it is not Allegra he has offered for," Lady Fossborough informed her in clipped tones, savoring the news she was about to administer. "It is, in fact, Laura Montescue. Lord Crandon is betrothed to marry Laura Montescue."

Mrs. Radleigh's laughter rang round the elegant drawing room. "Oh, now you are gammoning me!"

"No, I vow to you, Vere, I do not. It is indeed the younger Montescue girl he has offered for."

"But she is only just out. A green girl fresh from the schoolroom."

"Indeed."

"I recall she was being ardently pursued by Julia Marsham's cub, *and* from all I observed of the matter the chit was head over ears in love with him."

"Becoming Marchioness of Crandon cannot compare to being plain Mrs. Marsham, however well connected he might be."

"Tush. Crandon will eat such a green girl for supper."

"Confess, he is devilishly attractive," Lady Fossborough teased, "so you cannot blame an untutored child being over-whelmed by his undoubted charm."

"Oh, indeed," her friend agreed, sighing profoundly, "but what can have possessed Jeanne Montescue to allow her younger daughter to become betrothed while the older is still unwed? I have always thought well of Mrs. Montescue, but now I declare she must be positively idiotish."

"Do you really think so? Only consider carefully, Vere. If you had two unmarried daughters, would you refuse an offer from the Marquess of Crandon for one of them simply because the older is not yet settled? I think not, my dear."

Mrs. Radleigh nodded her head sagely as she drummed her fingers on the brocaded arm of her seat. "How amazing it is. I had no notion he was paying court to her."

"Nor I, and if I did not know of it, Vere, you may be certain it was not at all apparent. Of course, Lord Crandon has always been a creature of sudden caprices. Don't you agree?"

"Men of passion always are." She frowned suddenly. "I still cannot conceive of a prime blade like Crandon legshackled to anyone, let alone one of the unremarkable Montescue girls."

"In my opinion they are tolerably handsome."

"But not true beauties, either of them."

"Laura Montescue is the handsomer of the two, but Allegra has more spirit."

"Undoubtedly, but others have greater beauty and larger portions, I fancy."

"Neither can compare with you in your youth, Vere," Lady Fossborough added slyly. "You were considered a great beauty."

The other woman bridled. Her much-lauded eyes, of violet hue, grew wide and her ample bosom heaved. "My dear Mirabel, only the other evening Lord Belton declared I was the most handsome female in all London!"

Lady Fossborough's eyebrows rose a fraction. "Who could possibly quarrel with the opinion of one who is such an arbiter of female beauty? Are you and he on the closest of terms?"

Mrs. Radleigh smiled. "You may take it to be so."

"It is a great relief to me to learn that you will not be bereft of Lord Crandon's company in the future."

"You must not fear for any lady of his acquaintance, for I doubt if impending matrimony will curtail Crandon's immense appetite for female companionship. If Crandon is ever brought to heel by a female, I doubt if that green girl is the one to do it."

"Now, now, Vere, we may be as surprised by his fidelity as by his betrothal."

"Do not depend upon it," was Mrs. Radleigh's dark reply.

Lady Fossborough gathered up her gloves. "If anyone has been rash enough to wager upon where his lordship might fix his interest, I fear they must have lost their purses. Well, I must depart. I intend to call upon dear Isabella Kaydale, for I'll warrant she does not know this news as yet."

Mrs. Radleigh smiled sweetly. "You really must hurry, my dear, for I dare say the announcement will appear in the *Morning Post* on the morrow, and then everyone will know."

As she pulled on her gloves Lady Fossborough ignored her friend's sarcasm and replied, "I do not suppose I will really believe it until then. No, not even then. I will not believe it until I see them together. The Montescues are holding a rout in their honor."

"It is Allegra Montescue I truly pity. Last Season everyone was quite persuaded Dudley Rymington would offer for her, and then he married Petrina Pelham instead. That was most perplexing."

"Mayhap it is understandable," Lady Fossborough contradicted. "Miss Allegra Montescue is something of a hoyden, and no gentleman wants a wife who is better at tooling the ribbons than he!"

Mrs. Radleigh nodded. "Wagers were lost at White's on that occasion, and as you have said, Mirabel, it is certain the gamesters will not benefit from this particular alliance. Crandon will be pleased about that; he rejoices in confounding people."

"Did he confound *you*, Vere?" her friend asked sweetly and was rewarded by a dark look.

"I cannot help but think how galling it must be to witness one's younger sister's betrothal before one's own," Mrs. Radleigh went on as if the question had never been asked.

"Happily it did not happen to me."

"Nor I," Mrs. Radleigh said with feeling. "I had so many suitors it was exceeding difficult to know which of them to choose."

The countess smiled. "I recall it very well indeed, Vere. You chose the wealthiest, did you not?"

Satisfied to have surprised her friend with such astounding news, the countess sallied forth to inform another of her cronies. Remaining in her drawing room, Mrs. Radleigh was left to reflect on the brief attachment she had enjoyed with the young Marquess of Crandon several years earlier. Drawing another deep sigh, she turned moments later to take up her magazine once more and help herself from a dish of comfits at her side.

The Marquess of Crandon, whose name was often on the lips of ladies of the ton, was aware that he was about to cause more gossip than ever before. As he paced back and forth in front of the fire in a drawing room in his house in Piccadilly, he displayed none of the fashionable boredom that came so easily to him in company.

Enclosed behind high brick walls and gates of exquisitely wrought iron bearing the lion rampant escutcheon of the Carlyon family, Crandon House was simply one of the most lavish in the capital. The splendid drawing room was decorated in the Chinese style with carpets brought from the Orient, lacquered cabinets designed by Mr. Chippendale, Coromandel screens and brocaded chairs and sofas. The Chinese drawing room was only one of the many exquisite rooms in the house. The ballroom possessed several of the largest Venetian chandeliers in the country. When lit they utilized several hundred candles that reflected dazzlingly off the walls which were paneled with mirrors.

The Marquess of Crandon had grown wealthy over the centuries by a mixture of astute trading in both the East and West Indies, and by clever marriages to considerable heiresses. Now that the Napoleonic Wars made trading difficult, the Crandon wealth was in no jeopardy, for those clever marriages had endowed the present marquess with land in several English counties.

The present holder of the marquessate, Brett Frederick Denholme Carlyon, was considered by his peers to be a consummate whipster, a tulip of fashion, and a Pink of the Fancy. To the females of his acquaintance Lord Crandon was quite simply one of the most handsome and charming Corinthians of the ton.

The fact that he had reached almost the age of thirty and remained a bachelor had proved a challenge to a great number of females, but his manner of evading their advances was invariably gentle and charming, and few had reason to dislike him afterward. In a similar fashion, after he had enjoyed a discreet relationship with various married ladies of the ton, all were left with fond memories of him rather than resentment.

However, the news, about to break, that he was to marry Miss Laura Montescue would shatter the hopes of many and infuriate more than a few. Ever since he had entered Society on the completion of his education, Lord Crandon had been eagerly sought by Society hostesses to adorn their diversions. His elegant figure was to be seen at all fashionable assemblies and frequently at Carlton House where his opinion on matters of taste was eagerly sought by the Prince Regent himself.

Lord Crandon was also held to possess a keen wit and was a superb raconteur, whereas his sartorial elegance was invariably admired by male and female alike, compared often to that of Beau Brummel himself, although the marquess would be the first to deny any similarity in their mode of apparel.

Today, as the fashionable world was about to receive the astounding news that he had come up to scratch at last, he was dressed in a buff-colored coat that was a credit to the art of the great tailor, Stultz, and his neckcloth was tied in an immaculate bow that defied criticism. His pale buckskin breeches were entirely wrinkle-free and showed a fine leg, and his knee-high Hessian boots were polished to a mirrorlike sheen with not a blemish to mar them. As he paced the length of the fireplace the tassels on the boots swung to and fro, indicating a state of agitation Lord Crandon rarely displayed in public.

Seated on a brocade sofa close to the fire was a young lady clad in a white muslin gown, its plainness broken only by the wide pink satin sash that encircled her tiny waist. A head of dark corkscrew curls framed a pale heart-shaped face, and her navy-blue eyes, fringed by long, dark lashes, bore a striking similarity to those of the marquess.

"I am bound to confess to you, Brett," she told him, "I was never more surprised in my life than when you informed me with no prior warning that you were about to become betrothed."

The marquess stopped pacing at last and looked at her. "It should not surprise you that a man of my age wishes to engage in matrimony, Lucrezia. There are those who say it is long past the time for me to settle down, and I am inclined to agree."

The young lady smiled fondly at her brother. "Oh, do not think for one moment, dearest, I am not happy for you, for I assure you I am, but I am quite overset by the suddenness of it all."

The marquess's face relaxed a little. "In all truth, my dear, so am I."

She laughed, and he went to sit at her side. "Why did you not warn me?" she asked, a note of reproach in her voice.

He looked a little shamefaced. "In all truth, Lucrezia, there was no time. I do want you and Miss Montescue to like one another."

"Oh, Brett, if she makes you happy I cannot help but love her!"

"You and she will be the greatest of friends."

Lucrezia Carlyon gazed at her brother adoringly. "You must be very much in love to have offered for her with no prior warning to your closest relative."

"There were some very good reasons for my doing so," he answered, looking troubled again.

"Oh?"

He looked uncharacteristically sheepish. "I was foxed at the time I offered for her."

Lady Lucrezia laughed as she replied, "Fudge, Brett! I have never seen you in the least bosky even after you have cracked open several bottles. I'm persuaded you are gammoning me."

"No, I assure you I am not, although I forbid you to repeat it to any of those prattle-boxes who are eager for every morsel of gossip."

"I still believe you're shamming."

His smile faded somewhat. "It is of no matter. Mayhap a few bottles are all I required to make me sensible of the attractions of matrimony."

"My head is quite in a whirl," she confessed, and he smiled wryly.

"So is mine. I was as drunk as a wheelbarrow and still suffer the consequences. However, Miss Montescue is quite, quite delightful, I assure you. She is no hag-ridden harpy."

"As if you would offer for anyone other than a beauty," his sister scoffed, "but," she added, looking more troubled, "I do hope you haven't been too precipitate."

"Don't you think it time I became legshackled?"

"Indeed I do, but . . ."

"Miss Montescue will make the perfect wife. She is quite handsome, you'll agree, and she has a considerable portion to her name. Good land in Shropshire that will be a great asset to me."

"How romantic you are," she scoffed.

The marquess was looking extremely serious. "For someone in my situation there are greater considerations than romance."

"I cannot conceive of anything of more import than love and romance."

He smiled faintly. "I am the last of the male line, Lucrezia. It is time I provided an heir to the title."

"I am becoming out of patience with you, Brett! You talk of Miss Montescue as if she were one of your brood mares at stud. I am beginning to pity her most heartily."

"If you do you are quite alone, my dear. I'll wager everyone else will be envying her greatly."

"Oh, your overweening vanity!" Lady Lucrezia cried, laughing anew.

"And recall," he went on quickly, "you are to make your debut next Season. As my wife, Miss Montescue will be able to supervise your come-out. It will be rather convenient, I fancy."

The girl looked skeptical. "I scarce think a girl not much older than I am, just out of the schoolroom, will be of much value in that capacity. In all probability she will be in an interesting condition by then."

Her brother got up rather abruptly and began to prowl the room again. "I am persuaded you do my future wife an injustice."

"I do not mean to, I promise you, Brett. I only wish to assure you there is no need for you to marry on my account."

He looked surprised. "I have no intention of doing so. I am not so unselfish."

Lady Lucrezia cast him a wry look. "What does Mrs. Radleigh think on the matter, I wonder?"

The marquess looked irritated. "I see little of Mrs. Radleigh of late. She became a trifle tiresome, like most females."

"You are outside of enough!" his sister responded, refusing to become annoyed. All at once she dimpled, "I am going to be quite envious of your bride, I warn you."

"You will have no cause," he responded, still seeming to be irritable.

"You must understand, Brett, I have never been obliged to share you with another female before."

"Selfish baggage," he responded, the indulgent tone returning to his voice. "You will be wed yourself within a twelvemonth with no thought for me, I daresay, when you throw your cap over the windmill for some young cub." Then he added, "Lucrezia, you have been dear to me since the day you were born, and you will always have a special place in my life even when you are, yourself, married."

She shivered slightly. "How exciting it will be, living in London with you while your wedding is being planned, and then having a Season of my own immediately afterward."

"One thing is not in doubt—there will be many young bucks eager to make your acquaintance even before your come-out."

"If the formidable Lord Crandon doesn't frighten them all away," she replied, making a wry face.

"You may be sure I will do that only if they are considered to be unsuitable."

"Mayhap there will be occasions when we are like to disagree upon that score," she pointed out, looking amused.

He smiled. "We shall see. I do not believe it will happen, for I have the utmost confidence in your good sense, my dear."

"In any event there is little point in discussing the matter at length, for it is all in the future, Brett."

"Not as far away as you would believe. A few months—no more—and you will make your debut."

"By then you will have acquired a wife," she said gleefully, "and for now I only wish to know about *your* future. Tell me everything about Miss Montescue, Brett. I would not for anything wish to be considered ignorant when we eventually meet."

He sat down beside her once again. "What can I tell you? She is handsome, but I believe I have already told you that, and well connected. Her mother came to England as an emigrée from France when she was a young girl. Unlike many others, however, her family were able to bring with them substantial wealth. Mr. Samuel Montescue is connected to the Earl of Brixton. What else do you wish to know?"

"Everything! What of the rest of the family. Surely Miss Montescue has brothers and sisters."

The marquess paused to consider for a moment before replying, "There is an elder brother, Mr. Barnaby Montescue. He fancies himself as a bang-up blade and a top-sawyer."

Lady Lucrezia laughed delightedly. "No one could reach your heights, I fancy, Brett."

"I would not dream of telling him so, but he has the makings of a Corinthian."

"I don't doubt I would like him. Are there any other brothers or sisters? I feel it is fair to warn you I do so hope for a large family."

Her brother frowned slightly before answering, "Miss Montescue has an older sister, Miss Allegra Montescue."

"No doubt as she is older she is married and has an establishment of her own."

167

The marquess hesitated for a moment before answering, "Not as yet."

Lady Lucrezia gasped. "She is not wed? Is she hag-ridden?"

The marquess stared down at his perfectly manicured nails. "By no means. I believe you will find her as handsome as her sister."

"But if her younger sister is to be married before her that is quite dreadful, Brett."

"You must not concern yourself on the matter, Lucrezia. The older Miss Montescue is not without her admirers. It is always possible she will, after all, marry first."

"I am bound to confess, Brett, if I were in her place I believe I would feel quite humiliated."

"Yes," he said heavily, "I daresay there is a possibility of her feeling that way, but if she is, she is bearing it well, I assure you. You must bear in mind I could not hold back, for it is always possible she will never marry, so how could I possibly wait? Her parents could scarce refuse me in order to salve their other daughter's pride."

"No, I suppose not, for you are not the most patient of men. I daresay once you decided to come up to scratch you were most *im*patient, but I am bound to declare I am full of sympathy for the poor creature."

The marquess took her small hands in his and raised them to his lips. "You have a kind heart, my dearest Lucrezia. It is to be hoped that no gentleman will take advantage of it."

Her eyes were full of amusement. "It would be just if anyone did, for *you* have taken sufficient advantage of ladies' hearts during the past few years."

He laughed. "You have not lacked gossip while you rusticated, my dear."

"If only some of the *on dits* I have heard are true you have been a considerable rake, Brett. Do you intend to reform once you are wed?"

"How can you doubt it?"

His own eyes sparkled, and she cast him a disbelieving look as the door opened to a soft knock and Miss Chapstone, Lady Lucrezia's governess, came in.

She curtseyed before saying, "Pardon the instrusion, my lord, but it is time for her ladyship's dancing lesson."

As Lady Lucrezia got to her feet, the marquess said, "We must not keep the caper-merchant waiting, but when you have finished your lesson we can go riding in the park if you wish."

"If . . . ! In your new racing curricle, Brett?"

He looked amused. "Naturally."

"I will look forward to it with relish, you may be sure."

When she had left the room his indulgent smile faded, to be replaced by a frown as he began to stare sightlessly into the leaping flames of the fire once again, his hand clenched into a tight fist on the mantel.

Chapter Two

*M*iss Allegra Montescue smiled until her face hurt.

The ballroom of her home in Mount Street was crowded with the most elevated members of the beau monde, which was only to be expected after her sister had made the match of the Season, and even the most prominent members of Society wished to be included in the celebration. After all, the future Marchioness of Crandon was bound to be a leading hostess of the ton after her wedding, and there were few who would wish to be snubbed by her once she attained that lofty situation, even though as Laura Montescue she had scarce caused anyone to take undue note of her in her first Season.

Beneath the chandeliers hundreds of guests milled around the happy couple. Fabulous jewels, draped around necks and wrists and adorning the ears of the ladies, glittered in the light of hundreds of candles. A great wave of chattering and laughter swelled through the house, and Allegra continued to smile, nodding affably to those who greeted her.

Usually she was able to dance until dawn with no ill effect

whatsoever, but on this evening her feet in their satin slippers ached abominably, and she longed to sit down in a quiet corner. However she knew full well that on this particular occasion she could do no such thing. Not that any observer would guess her discomfort, for her smile was ever present as she acknowledged the greetings of her friends and acquaintances.

Now and again Allegra glanced across the room to where her sister, younger by a year, stood proudly at the side of her husband-to-be. Laura, a diminutive figure, especially when dwarfed by the tall marquess, whose height enabled him to be seen even when fully surrounded by others, looked lovely in pink satin, a simple necklace of pearls circling her throat. Laura was evidently enjoying her moment of splendor and no one—certainly not Allegra—could blame her for it.

In appearance there was a marked likeness between the two sisters. Both possessed glossy chestnut hair worn in the very fashionable corkscrew curls framing an oval face, a slightly retroussé nose, and large emerald-green eyes. Allegra was an inch or two taller than Laura, and her figure was more rounded, but it was their personalities that showed the greatest difference.

Laura was considered to be far more biddable even though she did possess a streak of willfulness in her character, whereas the older Montescue girl displayed a certain hoydenish quality, which often brought frowns to the faces of her elders. She was fond of racing her brother's high-perch phaeton, a practice admired in gentlemen but considered *mauvais* ton when indulged in by young ladies of breeding.

It was generally acknowledged by the beau monde that the Montescue girls were tolerably handsome, sufficiently well connected, and possessed of fair portions. However, it still came as a great surprise to most members of the ton when it was announced that Laura Montescue was to marry the very eligible Nonesuch, the Marquess of Crandon.

It came as no less of a shock to the Montescue family, for it was generally expected that Allegra would be the first to marry. Moreover, Lord Crandon had not shown a marked predilection for Laura until the very day he had offered marriage. Up until that moment Mr. Montescue had expected to receive an offer of marriage from Geoffrey Marsham, and very satisfactory that would have been, too.

Very naturally, the news had been greeted with great delight by the girl's family, except for Laura's sister, who might have been expected to display a certain amount of jealousy of her sister's good fortune, but did not. She was merely concerned for Laura's future happiness, feeling that her sister had simply taken on more than she could possibly manage.

"The evening appears to be going splendidly," Mrs. Montescue said to her older daughter as the last of the guests were greeted.

"Undoubtedly, Mama," Allegra agreed.

She could not recall when the house had been as full before. Dressed in a plain white muslin gown, cut low at the neck and adorned by a green sash that matched exactly the color of her eyes, Allegra Montescue just then looked even younger than her sister.

Jeanne Montescue put one hand on Allegra's arm, and when she spoke there was only the slightest trace of a French accent in her voice. "I am so happy this evening. Laura looks so beautiful—just as she ought—but how I wish we were also celebrating *your* betrothal, my dear. You also deserve to be as well settled as your sister."

Once again Allegra glanced across at the marquess and her expression became uncharacteristically hard. "In all truth, Mama, I'd as lief remain a spinster than marry someone like Lord Crandon."

Mrs. Montescue looked greatly troubled by her daughter's declaration, knowing that such passion was not usual in one so even tempered. "Oh, I do wish you would like your future brother-in-law."

"Surely it is sufficient that he and Laura are in accord."

"You sound as if you doubt it is possible. I cannot help but wonder if we were correct in allowing this betrothal to go ahead, for I believed your sister enamored of Mr. Marsham, but she insists it is Lord Crandon who holds her affection now."

"I'll wager that his lordship can be persuasive when he so chooses," Allegra answered, and she could not help the note of bitterness that crept into her voice. It was a failure she immediately vowed not to repeat.

"It is apparent to me that you are still of the opinion that it was Lord Crandon who influenced Sir Dudley to offer for Miss Pelham instead of you."

"Yes, Mama, I am, but I must one day thank his lordship for his trouble, for it is now evident to me that Sir Dudley and I were not in the least suited, and he and Miss Pelham are."

"That at least is a blessing, but why should Lord Crandon do such a thing?"

"I have no notion," Allegra answered truthfully. "Mayhap he sensed my dislike of him and did not wish me to marry his friend."

"Oh, surely he would not be so cruel or selfish."

Just at that moment the man in question, perhaps sensing he was the object of their attention, glanced across the room and caught Allegra's eye. For a moment he stared at her, and then he smiled, inclining his head slightly. Allegra responded in a similar manner before returning her attention to her mother once again.

"We know so little of him, Mama, but I suspect he could be cruel and unforgiving to those who cross him. Now he is to be my brother-in-law, and I can do nought about it, not that I would wish to as long as Laura is happy, and it appears that she is."

For a moment or two Mrs. Montescue continued to look troubled and then her still-beautiful face broke into a smile. "Here is Barnaby. How splendid he looks in his new evening coat. He admires Lord Crandon so much, you know."

Allegra's face also broke into a smile of genuine pleasure as she too espied her brother approaching. Barnaby Montescue possessed his fair share of the family's good looks. He presented a tall, elegant figure, even if the points of his shirt collar were a little too extreme and his neckcloth was tied into a bow that was rather more elaborate than good taste decreed. His dark blue evening coat looked well on him, and the gold buttons shone with a military brilliance enhanced by the candlelight.

"I am so very proud of all my children," Mrs. Montescue confided as he joined them.

"Mama, no one who did not know us could possibly guess you had a grown-up brood," he responded, much to his mother's delight. "And you, Allegra, must be the most divine creature in the room save for Laura, who naturally sparkles with incandescence this evening."

Mrs. Montescue laughed, saying, "I had no notion you were such a tongue-pad," before she drifted away to enjoy the envy and congratulations of her friends.

"What moonshine!" his sister gasped. "How I pity the poor creatures you fill with flummery."

"There are more than a score of them, and I assure you they do not complain."

"I do not doubt it, but perchance now Laura is to be wed you will emulate his lordship, who has for many years enjoyed a similarly rakish reputation, and settle for one of those poor females whom you have given good reason to hope."

Barnaby Montescue threw back his head of chestnut curls, arranged à la Brutus, and laughed. "Oh no, Ally, I could never aspire to Crandon's heights. He is a true Corinthian and bang up to the mark. I shall relish having such a nonpareil as a brother-in-law, I assure you. Have you, by any chance, seen his gift to our sister on this auspicious occasion?"

Allegra became wide-eyed. "No, but I imagine it will be something quite splendid. Jewelry, perchance?"

"Lady." His sister merely looked perplexed. "The most splendid roan mare you have ever clapped eyes upon was brought round to the stables this afternoon."

"A mare?" Allegra asked laughingly. "Doesn't his lordship know that Laura dislikes riding above everything else? The poor creature is like to grow old and stiff in her stall."

"Evidently Lord Crandon does not know of our sister's aversion to riding. Mayhap she will now learn to love the saddle."

Allegra subjected him to a disbelieving look. "I should not depend upon it, Barnaby. Nothing has prevailed upon her so far."

"I am told the power of love is very great indeed," he joked and then, in the face of his sister's frozen expression, he went on quickly, "Piers Westcott tells me that Crandon paid fifteen hundred guineas at Tattersall's for her."

"That is a huge sum!" Allegra gasped.

"The bidding was lively, but in any event Crandon can

173

easily afford it. You must go to the stables and see her at the first opportunity."

"I will, but it is a great pity that Laura will never appreciate such a splendid gift."

"The mare will need regular exercise, so I daresay it will be for us to keep her in shape." He glanced around, drawing in a deep breath of excitement. "This is quite splendid, Ally. Having Crandon as a brother-in-law—even a future one—can do nothing but good for this family."

"Do you really think so?" she responded without enthusiasm.

"Oh, come now, even you must know own he's an out-and-outer."

They both glanced across the room to where the happy couple was surrounded by a crowd, eager to become ingratiated with the future Marchioness of Crandon. Involuntarily Allegra shivered.

A moment later Allegra's attention was diverted when her brother exclaimed, "Good grief! Who is that exquisite creature talking to Laura?"

"Lady Lucrezia Carlyon," she answered without hesitation. "She's Crandon's sister. She is just come up from Crandon Park and will make her debut next Season."

"I had no notion he possessed a sister."

"That is not so surprising as it appears she is only just out of the schoolroom, which cannot be said of his lordship, I fear."

"What a beauty." Barnaby looked at his sister again. "Laura will be scarce over her wedding trip when the chit comes out. Our poor sister is going to have her card filled from the outset."

Allegra smiled sadly. "Position brings its responsibilities, as Laura will discover before too long."

He chuckled. "I'll warrant she has not considered that aspect of the parson's mousetrap. Come along, Ally, let us join them. I'm in a fidge to make acquaintance of this precious bit of muslin."

His sister smiled wryly. "Later, Barnaby, but you go along and make Lady Lucrezia's acquaintance. I can see you are in a fidge to do so. I feel bound to warn you, you will not be alone."

He grinned endearingly. "She is bound to find that *I* have the greater address. Crandon and Laura are, naturally, leading the first set, but will you stand up with me?"

"It will be a pleasure to stand up with a Dasher."

He hurried away watched by Allegra who smiled wryly, although she sincerely hoped her brother would not attempt to practice his seductive charm on the sister of the Marquess of Crandon. Future brother-in-law or not, Barnaby was likely to find himself at the end of the muzzle of the marquess's duelling pistol if he trifled with Lady Lucrezia Carlyon.

After a moment she made her way to where she had espied a rather forlorn-looking young man, scowling in a corner, drinking deeply of champagne. Out of the corner of her eye, Allegra had noted he had partaken of several glasses, but as she approached him his expression lightened a little.

"Miss Montescue, I am bound to tell you you look utterly charming this evening."

"Thank you, Mr. Marsham, but it is no use mincing words with you of all people. Your eyes are only for Laura, and I fear this is not the most enjoyable of evenings for you."

The young man drew a deep sigh, and Allegra pitied him with all her heart. He was a pleasant-looking young man without being in the least remarkable, and certainly not possessing any of the forceful presence of Lord Crandon. However, she liked him and believed his unprepossessing manner far more suited to Laura's nature than that of the man she had decided to marry. Laura was fond of having her own way, but Allegra could not envisage the marquess allowing her such license, while Geoffrey Marsham was so adoring he would very likely let her have her head.

"I cannot believe this evening is taking place at all," he admitted. "It is almost as if I am dreaming. Up until the very day Crandon offered for her and was immediately accepted I was so certain Laura favored me. I was never more shocked in my life."

Allegra put a comforting hand on his arm. "All you can do now, Mr. Marsham, is put the matter out of your mind."

"Do you think it possible?" he asked, and the bitterness was very evident in his voice.

"You have no choice in the matter, I fear. Your future must now lie in another direction."

His eyes, filled with misery, met hers. "I shall never meet another who means as much to me as your sister, Miss Montescue. There, I have laid bare my feelings to you."

"I do truly pity you, sir."

"I'm persuaded you have suffered a similar disappointment not too long ago."

She smiled faintly. "I don't believe I ever felt as deeply for Sir Dudley as you do for Laura."

His eyes glittered darkly as he put aside his glass, looking past Allegra. "I do not believe I shall remain here much longer, Miss Montescue. Your sister approaches, and I have no mind to wish her happy."

As Allegra turned on her heel the young man made his escape. Laura Montescue watched him go, looking astonished.

"Where has Geoffrey gone?" she asked the moment she reached her sister. "I hoped to have words with him."

"I fear you are obliged to wait, for he couldn't stay any longer. You should understand his feelings, Laura. He really is as melancholy as a gib cat."

The young woman looked not in the least regretful. "He may act the mooncalf, but he will recover his spirits soon enough. Have no fear for him." Then she looked at Allegra. "Isn't this the most heavenly rout you have ever attended?"

"It is a veritable squeeze. I am ... so very happy for you, dearest," Allegra forced herself to say.

"I didn't think it possible to be so happy. All I need now to make life absolutely perfect is for you to become as well attached as I. Crandon is the most wonderful man in the universe!"

"Not so long ago you were declaring Mr. Marsham to be that, Laura," Allegra could not help but point out gently.

Laura Montescue became rather flushed. "That was before I came to know his lordship. There is no comparison, I assure you. I do want you to become better acquainted with him, Ally, so you might like him a little more. Oh, I am fully aware you are less than enthusiastic to have him as a brother-in-law, but I know when you are better acquainted you cannot fail to like him."

"I'm persuaded you are right," her sister replied, exhibiting no enthusiasm.

"He always speaks so highly of *you*." When her sister failed to respond Laura went on, exhibiting slight irritability, "Oh, you cannot possibly still attach blame to him because Sir Dudley cried off."

"That is of no account to me now. Sir Dudley is legshackled to the former Miss Pelham, and I can only be glad for them."

The younger Montescue girl looked doubtful at such a spirited declaration before she said, "There is always Sir Angus Beane. He has been so attentive toward you of late. I am almost certain he is in earnest."

Allegra could not help but laugh. "Sir Angus Beane! La! What a funster you are, Laura. Is everyone so despairing of me they would pair me with that man-milliner?"

Laura flushed slightly. "If you wish to be married, Ally, you will be obliged to learn not to be so particular."

"You were!"

The girl's cheeks grew even more pink. "I find Sir Angus perfectly charming, if you wish to know my opinion."

"Your opinion is, as always, welcome, dearest, although in this instance it does not, unfortunately, tally with mine."

The younger girl looked suddenly coy. "We are destined not to agree upon the subject of gentlemen."

"It is fortunate we are not obliged to do so."

"Why exactly do you not favor Sir Angus? He is perfectly presentable I find."

"He is too old."

"He is not so much older than my own dear Crandon."

Allegra almost winced at the reference to the marquess and then she replied, "Recall that Sir Angus is a widower, Laura."

"That can only be reckoned to be a misfortune, Ally. You cannot blame him for seeking connubial bliss."

"Having married and squandered one fortune he is now dangling after another," Allegra answered wryly. "I trust my family wants better for me than that."

"I think you mistake him. I truly do. He always displays a true fondness for you. You could settle for worse, I assure you."

Her sister nodded, thinking of Lord Crandon. Then she asked, "Where is Papa? I haven's seen him in an age."

Laura made a wry face. "I believe he has gone off in one of his humdudgeons."

"It is only what I feared."

"At first he feared that the heat and crowds would bring on an attack of the ill humors, but then someone unthinkingly opened a

177

window close by his chair, and now he believes he is in the first throes of a chill, so Mama administered some of his drops and he is resting in the library."

"I declared this evening would be too much for his constitution."

"One could positively guarantee it," Laura added, exhibiting no sympathy for their stricken parent. "They're about to announce the first dance, Ally," Laura said a moment later in great excitement. "Come along! Crandon and I are leading the set and you are to partner Barnaby if he can tear himself away from Lady Lucrezia. I own she is quite delightful, but I feel our brother to be moonstruck."

"That is nothing out of the ordinary," Allegra replied laughingly.

"I declare I shall remember this evening for as long as I live!"

With rather less enthusiasm Allegra followed when her sister led the way. As she took her place in the set next to Laura and Lord Crandon, Sir Angus Beane, standing at the edge of the dance floor, raised his quizzing glass to scrutinize her the better.

"The betrothed couple make a handsome pair, don't you think, ma'am?" he asked of the lady standing at his side.

Mrs. Vere Radleigh agreed but with rather less enthusiasm than most. "Oh indeed. They do look well together. However, in my opinion it is more important to deal well together."

Sir Angus looked amused. "Do you believe they will not?"

Mrs. Radleigh considered a moment before replying, "It will be interesting to observe the course of their marriage. If you wish to know my opinion of the matter, it is a very unlikely match."

"Your close acquaintanceship with his lordship no doubt gives you the knowledge to proclaim it, ma'am."

The woman glanced at Sir Angus. "Oh yes, I know Crandon very well indeed." She hesitated before adding, "It is rumored that the older Miss Montescue will very soon follow her sister down the road to matrimony."

The dandy smiled stiffly. "A lady as fetching as Miss Allegra Montescue cannot possibly remain unmarried for much longer."

"It is common knowledge that the Montescue girls are very well endowed, although Crandon can scarce be considered a fortune hunter. He is as rich as Croesus. However, I'll warrant there are others who are not as far up in the stirrup."

Sir Angus remained unimpressed by the lady's innuendos. "Crandon gambles deep; his horses do occasionally fail to win their races."

"Your aspersions are a nonsense, sir. If Crandon happened to be in dun territory, which I assure you he is not, he would choose to wed a greater fortune than that possessed by Laura Montescue."

Sir Angus dropped his quizzing glass and turned to smile at Mrs. Radleigh once again. "Mayhap he is simply in love with the chit."

His statement caused Mrs. Radleigh to laugh uproariously. "Oh no, Sir Angus, I do not believe that is the answer either."

"Alliances between two people are often a puzzle to others, ma'am. It was just so when I wed my own dear wife, but we enjoyed a great accord until her unfortunate demise."

Mrs. Radleigh cast him a disbelieving look and then he asked, "Shall we join the set, ma'am?"

"I would be delighted, sir," she responded, allowing him to lead her out into the midst of the colorful throng on the dance floor.

Chapter Three

As the evening progressed Allegra watched worriedly as her brother was to be seen more and more in the company of Lady Lucrezia Carlyon. Barnaby, like so many bucks of the ton, enjoyed flirting with pretty girls, most of whom had just come out into Society and were receptive to the attentions of a handsome young beau.

Allegra was fully aware that he had broken several hearts with his flirting and was usually seen in Hyde Park at the fashionable hour every day riding in his high-perch phaeton with one or another adoring young female at his side. As the heir to a considerable fortune he found mothers were usually glad enough to allow him to escort their daughters, but Allegra was very much afraid he could not play fast and loose with the Marquess of Crandon's sister and be allowed to escape the consequences.

Most ladies of the ton, both young and old, vied for a flattering word from the most elegant Corinthian in town, the Marquess of Crandon, so it seemed odd to her family that Allegra disliked him so heartily. She could not quite recall when she had first taken him in dislike. It was most likely, she thought, during the previous social Season, her first, when the dashing Sir Dudley Rymington courted her in earnest.

From the outset Allegra had found herself attracted to this member of the Four-in-Hand Club—like Lord Crandon—which consisted of only the finest horsemen in London. Whenever any of them were seen abroad in their specially built carriages, phaetons, curricles, gigs or cabriolets, drawn by the finest horses in the land, heads naturally turned to watch and to admire.

Immediately after she made her debut, Allegra was in great demand, but almost at once she found herself attracted to Sir Dudley. It was generally believed he would before long make an offer of marriage, so it came as a great shock when he became affianced to Miss Pelham instead. Lord Crandon, who was known to be a crony of Sir Dudley, and Allegra seemed to start out with a mutual antipathy toward one another, although she could think of no real reason why it should have been so. It was because of this unspoken dislike on both their parts that when Sir Dudley, with no apparent reason, cried off, Allegra suspected the marquess to be behind the matter. In fact she was certain of it, for no other reason was forthcoming. Needless to say, afterward her antipathy toward Lord Crandon became something much more deep-rooted, so that when the marquess made his surprise offer of marriage for Laura, Allegra was shocked for more than one reason.

The sight of Barnaby approaching in the company of the very pretty Lady Lucrezia Carlyon did nothing to calm her unease. One alliance in the Crandon family was more than enough, although she was convinced it was not possible for her brother to be in earnest on such short acquaintance. She had seen him entranced on many previous occasions, and Lady Lucrezia was not even out of the schoolroom as yet.

"Ally, I want you to make the acquaintance of Lady Lucrezia. She is in a great fidge to meet *you*."

Again Allegra smiled. This time it was more genuine, for she had no intention of blaming this schoolroom chit for her brother's shortcomings.

"Lady Lucrezia, you cannot help but be aware you have come to Town at a very auspicious time."

"Indeed I have, Miss Montescue, and I could not be more delighted; otherwise I should have been obliged to rusticate at Crandon Park for another six months at least."

"So the betrothal has served a very great purpose," Allegra replied wryly, liking the girl's ingenuity immediately.

"I was never more surprised when Crandon announced himself to me."

"As were we all," Barnaby interposed.

Lady Lucrezia looked at him in surprise. "So it was not apparent to you either that Crandon was in earnest."

"It was as much a surprise to all of us," the young man assured her. "I am bound to commend your brother's good sense, however."

"I had quite decided Crandon would remain a bachelor to the end of his days. He has never been in earnest before. There are only the two of us left, and I was resigned to having no nephews or nieces. Happily that is not likely any longer."

"Do you enjoy your stay?" Allegra asked politely.

"I have been here such a short time, but naturally it is exceeding blissful to me. When Crandon marries Miss Montescue I shall feel as if I have gained two sisters and," she glanced shyly at Barnaby, "another brother."

"Good grief!" the young man exclaimed. "That is not at all what I hope for! At least not as far as I am concerned!"

The girl blushed to the roots of her hair. Allegra had expected the only sister of Lord Crandon to be at least as toplofty as he, but she was delighted to discover Lady Lucrezia entirely unspoiled. Whatever her attitude toward the marquess, Allegra felt she could like his sister, which was something of a relief.

"I am obliged to beg your pardon," Barnaby told them, looking truly regretful, "but I am engaged to stand up with Lady Dorothy Memlock and must leave you for the moment."

"Barnaby, only a sen'night ago you were crying roast meat because Lady Dorothy condescended to ride with you in the Park," Allegra chided him.

The young man appeared a little discomforted by the disclosure as he took his leave.

Lady Lucrezia watched him go before saying, "Mr. Montescue is utterly charming."

For once his sister could wholeheartedly agree. "Indeed he is, and I would like to take the liberty of saying he appears to be charmed by you, my lady."

Again the girl blushed and said as she glanced around with bright eyes, "I do believe I am as happy as your sister tonight."

"No one could be," Laura replied, coming up to them at that moment. "I have never experienced so many people wishing to toady to me. I am accustomed to bucks toadying but not toplofty matrons."

Allegra could not help but laugh. "I am afraid you must grow accustomed to toad-eaters now you are betrothed to the Marquess of Crandon."

"I daresay I shall contrive to do so," she replied airily. "Crandon has bought me the most fetching mare, so it appears I must also learn to like riding."

"Don't say you do not," Lady Lucrezia gasped, "for my brother is a keen rider."

"I know," Laura responded, looking wry. "His lordship may well be disappointed in me."

Her future sister-in-law laughed merrily. "That is not possible, Miss Montescue."

A moment later a young buck claimed the blushing Lucrezia for the cotillion, and the girl excused herself shyly.

"We will, mayhap, have a further coze on another occasion," she ventured.

"I'm persuaded there will be many more opportunities in the time to come," Allegra assured her.

When she was out of earshot Laura sighed. "She is something of a prattle-box, is she not?"

"Her excitement makes her garrulous, but I find her utterly delightful. Don't you?"

"Oh, indeed."

Allegra eyed her sister wryly. "Barnaby is also in agreement with me on that score."

Laura looked at her sister askance. "Is not every chit delightful for a short time to our brother?"

"I am bound to say he appears to be more than usually impressed on this occasion."

"I have no notion what she has been saying to you and Barnaby—exclaiming her delight at everyone and anything I don't doubt—but to me Lady Lucrezia has been prattling on about her coming Season. She is looking forward to discarding her governess when *I* launch her into Society. Crandon failed to make mention that I would be responsible for his sister when he offered for me."

"Would that have made any difference to you if he had?"

"No, but it is quite a responsibility, and I'd as lief not be obliged to bear it. Oh, Ally, I shall have enough to do just being Lady Crandon next Season."

"You will contrive, dearest," Allegra assured her.

Once again Laura sighed. "I daresay, only it all seems a bit much all at once. I'm persuaded when the time comes I shall enjoy being Lady Crandon and acting toplofty to one and all!"

Allegra could not help but laugh despite her prejudice, for she was unable to imagine her sister in such a role. Just then the marquess himself emerged from the crowd, and Allegra's smile faded just as Laura's appeared.

He somehow contrived to be looking at Allegra as he addressed his bride-to-be. "Time for us to stand up together again, my dear. It wouldn't do if it is said we have already parted brass rags."

Laura chuckled. "No one who has seen us together this evening could possibly think so."

The marquess continued to look at Allegra as he put his arm loosely around Laura's waist. "Miss Montescue, you are now the only female member of the family with whom I have not yet danced this evening. I cannot possibly allow that situation to continue."

183

Allegra immediately averted her eyes, for his searching look was most uncomfortable. "You must not let it tease you, my lord. You are naturally much in demand and no one, much less I, will take it amiss if you do not stand up with me this evening."

"The demand does not always come from those one prefers," he replied, exhibiting his customary irony.

"That is one penalty of popularity," Allegra responded.

"Well, if we do not stand up together, Miss Montescue, I assure you *I* shall take it amiss. Will you be kind enough to stand up with me for the next country-dance?"

She nodded, knowing it was a necessary evil she must endure for the sake of family harmony. "If you wish it."

"I do. Come along, Laura. The sets are being made up for this dance."

Laura, however, exhibited no eagerness to be gone. She cast her sister a thoughtful glance before saying, "As a gentleman of some consequence, my lord, I do wish you would prevail upon my sister to encourage Sir Angus Beane's suit."

Allegra looked up in alarm as he replied, casting her a sardonic look, "As I am not yet a member of your family, it would be impertinent of me to do so, Laura. In any event, from all I have observed, Miss Montescue is quite capable of deciding whom to encourage for herself. She has displayed that capability readily in the past."

As he led his bride-to-be away Allegra let out a long breath. She had little time, however, to reflect upon their exchange as someone said:

"They do look exceeding happy, Miss Montescue."

When she looked around it was to see Sir Angus Beane standing nearby. "Yes, they are in high snuff," she admitted, although it did not become her to be so false.

In her opinion they were not in the least suited, but were she to voice that opinion to anyone other than a member of her immediate family she would be considered to be suffering envy.

Up until now she had always been regarded as rather too plain-spoken, and it did not suit her to be obliged to hide her true feelings about the marquess and his relationship to her sister, although she sadly acknowledged it would have to continue for

184

some considerable time to come, perhaps for the rest of their lives. The thought depressed her even more.

"I have heard it said that *we* also make a handsome pair," Sir Angus persisted.

Allegra smiled sweetly. "Your hearing is evidently far more acute than mine, sir."

Not in the least put out he asked, "You would do me a great honor if you would condescend to stand up with me for the cotillion, ma'am."

She inclined her head in agreement and as he led her toward the dancers he said, "It has been most frustrating for me to try and approach you this evening, Miss Montescue. You have been so much in demand by one and all."

"It is not every day that one's sister becomes affianced to the scion of such a noble family."

"I am fully aware he is regarded as a great catch."

"No one is in any doubt about that, sir," she answered, unable to keep the ironic tone out of her voice.

"Quite so," he responded. "It is to be hoped, Miss Montescue, that your sister's betrothal does not cause you any feeling of irritation."

"Indeed it does not!" Allegra retorted, casting him an outraged look. "Why do you think it should be so?"

"Knowing you to be possessed of such a generous spirit, ma'am, I doubted it myself, only there are those present this evening who do not know you so well as I and believe you would resent not only your sister's undoubted good fortune, but the very fact she is to be settled in her own establishment ahead of you."

Allegra was able to successfully contain her irritation, although she was only too well aware that there were many present who pitied her with all their hearts and regarded the betrothal as a humiliation for her. Many of them were not slow in saying so in no uncertain terms. That was why she knew she must be vigilant and show her pleasure unendingly so that the tattle-baskets would be confounded. They were not to know that all her concern was for Laura's future happiness and not her own.

"It is inevitable people should think in such a manner," she answered carefully, "but as you say, sir, they do not know me well, otherwise they would appreciate I only wish my sister happy."

"That is no surprise to me, and, of course, it is assumed—no, known—you will yourself be settled before long. Such a course can only confound those who spread unkindnesses with such ease."

His words only caused her to smile wanly. Fortunately, the music was striking up, precluding any further conversation with Sir Angus, for Allegra was only too well aware that one encouraging word from her would send him rushing to seek out her father for permission to marry. What she feared most was his insistence upon doing so with no such encouragement forthcoming. Sometimes she felt like the tightrope walker she had seen recently at Astley's Amphitheatre. One false step and she would topple to the ground.

As the dance began she caught sight of Lord Crandon who, up until that moment, had with Laura been in amiable conversation with Mrs. Radleigh, a woman known to have enjoyed for a time a close relationship with the marquess. Although the affair was believed to be over some time ago Allegra had a sudden vision of her sister's marriage in which Lord Crandon would enjoy the company of a demi-rep, while Laura who, from the outset of her Season, had been pursued by adoring beaux, would eventually console herself with a number of *chers amis*. The thought depressed Allegra even more as the dance began, although she was fully aware that many a successful alliance proceeded in a similar manner.

When Allegra faced the marquess across the set at one point during the cotillion, he smiled faintly at her, and she inclined her head slightly, unable to prevent herself from admiring his appearance, if not his harsh nature. Not for the first time did she wonder what had prompted him to offer for Laura with such suddenness. Even though her sister had attracted the attention of countless young men during her one brief Season, it seemed odd to think that someone as proud and as experienced as the Marquess of Crandon was suddenly so impetuous as to fall in love with such a green girl. Personally Allegra doubted if he was capable of falling in love with anyone, but that was one observation she determined to keep to herself.

When the dance ended Sir Angus persisted to remain at her side, but almost immediately the marquess came to claim her for the promised country-dance, and Allegra was obliged to tense herself to face the ordeal.

"You have the devil's own luck, Crandon," Sir Angus declared. "The most fetching females in the room are your future kin."

The marquess's eyes sparkled with some emotion she could not recognize as he replied with aplomb, "You are mistaken to put it down to luck, Beane. It is by design." He then addressed Allegra whose cheeks had grown somewhat pink. "Miss Montescue, our set I believe."

As he led her back toward the dance floor she did not know what to say to him. That was one of the things that confounded her about him; as convivial as she was with everyone else of her acquaintance, conversation with Lord Crandon was always extremely difficult. She sometimes wondered if that was because there often seemed to be an unspoken meaning behind much of what he said to her.

"My sister appears radiant this evening," she ventured.

"You can rest assured I shall endeavor to make certain she will remain as happy as she is this evening in the time to come, ma'am."

Allegra could not help but laugh, albeit harshly. "You will have me to contend with if she is not."

His dark eyes opened wide with mock horror, and she noticed for the first time that they were not brown as she had supposed but a most unusual shade of the darkest blue.

"That is a threat, is it not?"

"Only if you see it as one."

"You may be certain it has instilled in me the utmost terror, Miss Montescue."

Allegra smiled wryly while nodding to a nearby acquaintance. "I do not believe for one moment that anything or anyone terrifies you, my lord."

"Then you cannot be held to know me so well."

She leveled a look at him. "No, I do not suppose I do. Does anyone?"

He paused to consider for a moment or two. "I believe my future wife may come to do so."

She put her head on one side to consider him the better. It was difficult to discern when he was serious or jocular. "I cannot say whether that is a good thing or not," she answered at last.

To her surprise he laughed, and she smiled uncertainly as those around them glanced curiously in their direction, no doubt certain that they were enjoying each other's company hugely. It suddenly occurred to her that he might be amusing himself at her expense and the now familiar anger toward him began to kindle in her breast. Having him as a brother-in-law was going to be well nigh unbearable.

Chapter Four

The mare moved like the wind. Allegra reveled in the feel of the animal's power and strength beneath her. What a fool Laura was not to appreciate such a sublime gift, she thought, as she galloped through Hyde Park. Suddenly, though, Allegra recalled that Lady had been a gift from the marquess to her sister and all at once she felt bereft.

Not long ago she too had experienced love—or what she had thought to be love. After the first pangs of disappointment had faded away Allegra had put Sir Dudley's defection to the back of her mind, insisting she had not been left to wear the willow, but just then, enjoying the gallop on this superb animal, she had felt the lack of love in her own life most acutely.

She slowed her gallop, mainly to allow her groom the opportunity to catch up with her. When he did so she continued her ride, but this time at a more sedate canter. The mare, however, seemed anxious to be given her head and as an accomplished horsewoman herself, Allegra could not resist the temptation.

Hyde Park at that time of the morning was fairly empty of

riders. It was not until the fashionable hour of five o'clock that the beau monde arrived in their elegant carriages or on superb horses to see and be seen by others. This, however, was as Allegra liked it to be, so she could leave the carriage paths and gallop across open fields, though that did mean the occasional scattering of a dairy herd.

So great was her enjoyment of the ride, allowing Lady to show her paces, she scarcely noticed another rider rapidly bearing down upon her across the turf. Only when she became aware of pursuit did she pull in Lady's reins and gently slow her pace once again.

When she glanced behind it was to see the marquess riding a gray stallion of magnificent proportions. Moments later he came abreast of her and reined in his own mount, and Allegra prepared herself for an encounter with the one man she would have chosen not to see.

"Good morning, Miss Montescue!" he greeted her heartily. "I did not believe any female capable of being abroad at such an hour. You cannot have gone to your bed until dawn. Your stamina is to be admired."

"I fancy there are few enough gentlemen who are able to totter out of bed at this hour after an evening's revelry, so I declare your stamina equal to mine."

His eyes sparkled with amusement. "I have not been to bed," he confessed. "It would be too great a pity to miss a ride on such a brisk morning for the sake of a few hours between the sheets. You are evidently of the same mind." It was then he gave the mare his attention. "It is good to see Lady's needs are not being neglected."

Allegra closed her eyes in sudden anguish as she sat back in the saddle. "Oh, my goodness. I do beg your pardon, my lord. It has only just occurred to me you must have thought it was Laura who was riding Lady."

His answer was to roar with laughter, which caused her to look at him askance. "Indeed I did not! There are few enough females who have as good a seat as yours, Miss Montescue. I knew exactly who was riding Lady the moment I clapped eyes upon her."

189

Her relief was tempered by puzzlement. "You do not mind that I ride your gift to my sister?"

"Mind!" He continued to look amused. "I could not be more delighted to see the mare so well suited. I confess now it was crackbrained of me to buy Lady as a gift for Laura."

"You may be certain she is exceeding grateful," Allegra hastened to tell him.

He looked wry. "I daresay she is, but no one can deny that Lady suits you far better than she. Laura will not gainsay me if I present Lady to you. . . ."

"Lord Crandon!"

Her eyes had opened wide with shock, but he raised one gloved hand to silence her protests. "Have no fear, Miss Montescue, she will be delighted to be relieved of the responsibility of exercising her as you well know. I will buy Laura something she will appreciate far better than a piece of prime blood."

"Even so, I couldn't possibly accept something of such great value," she gasped. "Truly I could not."

"I am afraid I must insist upon it, and when you become better acquainted with me you will appreciate I do like to have my own way."

Her eyes met his for a long moment, and it was as if a silent battle of wills was ensuing until he looked past her, and his face became set into a forbidding countenance.

"It appears we have met at an inopportune time, Miss Montescue."

When she looked around in some puzzlement she saw Sir Angus Beane approaching on his hack, which was exasperating to her. The marquess raised his high-crowned beaver hat and rode on. Allegra watched him go, feeling bemused. She was tempted to call him back, but could think of no reason why she should.

When Sir Angus greeted her from a distance, she reluctantly turned her attention to him, but she did feel unaccountably annoyed by the instrusion.

"Why, my dear Miss Montescue, what a pleasant surprise."

" 'Tis amazing how crowded the Park is becoming at such an early hour," she snapped.

He was evidently nonplussed, for he glanced into the distance at the marquess who was riding toward the park gates. "I do trust I have not interrupted anything of importance."

At this point her irritation increased considerably. "I resent your inference, Sir Angus!"

"Oh, I do beg your pardon most heartily, ma'am. I recall now how much you dislike Lord Crandon."

"I neither like nor dislike him, you may be sure," she replied, gripping Lady's reins as tightly as she was holding on to her own patience.

"Now I have had time to ponder upon the matter it seems to me my arrival must have furnished you with considerable relief."

"Do not presume that to be so," she snapped.

"You are very loyal to your family's needs, ma'am. I do admire that in you. Mayhap you would honor me with your company while we ride."

"I had, in fact, completed my ride and was about to return home, sir."

"Then I will have the pleasure of escorting you as far as Montescue House. I assure you no one you don't like will be allowed to accost you while you are in my company, ma'am!"

Without agreeing to allow him to accompany her Allegra turned her mount and rode off at a spanking pace.

"What a rum prancer you're riding," he remarked, displaying no difficulty in keeping up with her. "I recall that Crandon outbid everyone else for this daisy kicker at Tattersall's." When she made no answer he went on, "I do suspect Crandon left so abruptly because he believed *we* had an assignation. He looked mighty miffed about it, too." He laughed softly, as if he liked the notion.

This raised Allegra's irritation anew. "I cannot conceive of him being so unchivalrous as to think me capable of such a thing, but even if he were to be nonsensical and consider it, I declare it is nothing to Lord Crandon if I do have an assignation with any gentleman."

"I admire your spirit, ma'am, but you may well find you are sadly mistaken," Sir Angus refuted as they rode through the park gates.

"I do beg your pardon," she responded, looking up at him in some alarm.

"Crandon is so full of his own consequence it is very like he

191

considers himself the head of your household now, with responsibility for you and your family. It is very like him to take such a toplofty notion into his head."

"If he does harbor such nonsensical notions, Sir Angus, I assure you he is bound for a bitter disappointment. Papa may not be of the most robust constitution, but he is most definitely the head of our household and is like to remain as such for the far foreseeable future."

"How glad I am to hear you say so, ma'am. You are indeed a woman of spirit, and I cannot tell you how much I admire that in a female. It is reassuring to hear that there is one person who is resistant to Crandon's toplofty ways."

"Your worry on my behalf is mistaken, sir."

"Fortunately, once you are yourself wed you will no longer be obliged to be accountable to him."

They had reached Montescue House and a lackey came forward to help her dismount. As the groom led Lady away, Allegra returned her attention to Sir Angus.

"You may be certain, sir, I am not accountable to Lord Crandon now or in the future. Good day to you, Sir Angus."

He bowed in the saddle. "Good day, Miss Montescue. I look forward to seeing you again in the very near future."

When she strode into the hall she felt far from relaxed after her ride and blamed Lord Crandon rather than Sir Angus for that, although she'd have preferred not to have encountered either of them. In the future, she decided, she would ride in St. James's Park even though it was much smaller, with little scope for a true gallop, but at least there she might be able to preserve her solitude.

After she had changed out of her riding habit and into a striped poplin gown, she went to her father's study, where she found him ensconced in a high-backed chair close by the fire with his gouty foot propped on a low stool. A screen had been drawn across the window embrasure to ensure no draughts reached him, and he wore over his frogged dressing gown a paisley shawl with a tasseled cap on his head.

"Papa?" she enquired timidly as she entered the darkened room with a degree of hesitancy should she find him asleep.

"Allegra, my dear," he responded, his voice barely audible.

"Do come in and sit beside me for a while. It always does me good to see you, and make no mistake I am badly in need of someone to divert me."

She came further into the room as he put aside the book he had been reading. "Poor Papa. Do you feel very queer?"

"I am, I thank you, a little better. Dr. Pomfret called in this morning and prescribed a new physic for me, which I believe will be beneficial. Of course the rout did not improve matters. The excessive heat and all those crowds are never healthful, and then some jobbernoll opened a window. It could have made an end of me."

Allegra sat down close by him on a stool. "It was a splendid evening, Papa. I'm persuaded Mama must have told you all about it. Laura was a triumph, and I can only be sorry you missed the most of it."

He laughed feebly, waving one bony hand in the air. "I'm persuaded I was not much missed."

"I for one missed you."

He patted her hand gratefully. "Crandon and Laura were the center of attention and quite rightly so."

"We were all very proud of her," Allegra confirmed.

"It was a proud occasion, I am bound to own." He frowned. "Where is the chit? I scarce see the child of late."

Allegra smiled faintly. "I believe she and Mama are drawing up lists for the wedding and trousseau. It appears to be an onerous task."

Mr. Montescue laid his graying head against the chair back. "Such a hurry-scurry. It is exceeding wearing on the nerves, and that does not take in the expense of it all. This wedding will make an end of me. Just you see if it doesn't."

"Fudge, Papa! Don't you wish to see your daughter wed to the Marquess of Crandon in style?"

"I liked that young Marsham. He seemed to me to be a modest fellow, not that I don't favor Crandon. No father could deny the advantages of such a match for his daughter. It's just that Marsham seemed to suit Laura's style. I daresay I am just a foolish old man to say so."

"No, Papa," Allegra answered heavily. "I thought so, too, but it

193

is Laura's choice that matters, and Mama is crying roast meat all over town!"

"That comes expensive."

"We can afford it, can't we?"

"That is not the point." He looked exasperated. "What's the use of railing? Females always have windmills in their heads when it comes to matrimonials. Who am I to complain? Who will listen to an old man given notice to quit? It is Barnaby we should ensure is safely riveted before he games away the very roof over our head."

"Papa," she said with infinite patience, "I am quite certain Barnaby does not game deep."

"Females don't enter gaming halls, so how can you say with such certainty? In any event it is time he became legshackled. He needs an heir. There is every chance he might come into a title. Brixton's in the Peninsula. If he goes to Peg Trantum the title comes to me, and everyone knows I am not long for this world."

Allegra laughed softly. "Oh, Papa, you mustn't be blue-deviled over Brixton. You will live for a long time yet, and as for your relative he is also like to survive. We are now winning in the Peninsula. Wellington is holding the lines at Torres Vedras, and Beresford has defeated Albuera. We must be thankful that the French are in retreat at last and not be in the mopes."

"No one hopes that those successes are sustained and repeated more than I do, but one can never be certain about anything."

"We must remain hopeful, Papa," she insisted, adopting a bright tone of voice that was always difficult to sustain in her father's company.

"You have all the optimism of youth, which is just as it should be, but life is always exceeding unpredictable, my girl."

At this pronouncement Allegra could not help but laugh. "Indeed! Who would have thought Laura would become betrothed before I am."

"Or that the poor King would take leave of his senses, leaving his crackbrained son to become Regent? That is one reason I have reservations about Laura. Crandon is one of Prinny's Carlton House Set and there isn't a more rackety bunch in the Kingdom."

"Lord Crandon is not in the least like Prinny." Allegra surprised herself by speaking up for the marquess. "You must not

194

concern yourself over Laura—or Barnaby. They're both as right as a trivet."

"What of you? Must I concern myself over you?"

"Certainly not!"

"Do you have a beau? I'll warrant you do not, my girl."

"Only if you include Sir Angus Beane," she answered with a smile.

Mr. Montescue clucked his tongue. "I trust you do not favor *his* suit. He always was a scapegrace as well as a basket-scrambler. He ran off with Walter Grimond's chit and saw an end to her. I trust he doesn't come to me for permission to address you, 'cause I shan't give it."

"I am very glad to hear you say so, Papa, for he and I are not at all suited."

"I recall I once saw you and Crandon dancing together at Almack's. *Entre nous,* I am bound to confess at the time I considered you to be handsome together.

A look of horror came over Allegra's face and she hastened to say, "Now, don't you think you should rest for a while, Papa?"

"Ah yes, I believe I shall. I am weary. Is it true Lord Byron is about to have a poem published?"

"So I am told. Publication is said to be imminent and everyone is in a mighty fidge to read it. Hatchard's is bound to sell out on the day of publication."

"Then it is as well I sent Randall to order a copy this morning. It is strange to me to think of that rapscallion as a poet. It must be because of his lame foot."

Allegra looked puzzled. "I truly cannot perceive a connection between his talent for writing poetry and his lame foot, Papa."

Mr. Montescue made a sound of annoyance. "Is it not obvious to you? He cannot dance and therefore he must direct his energies elsewhere."

His logic made Allegra laugh once again. "From all the *on dits* I have heard of late, it is very evident his energies have been directed elsewhere."

Mr. Montescue chuckled. "Once his poem has been published, he will be even more in favor with the females of the ton."

Allegra got up from the stool and placed a kiss on her father's brow. "I shall go immediately and ask Cook to prepare you a posset, Papa, and then you will be able to rest."

He patted her hand once again. "You are a good girl, Allegra. I am very proud of you. It is you who deserves the elevated marriage far more than your sister."

"You are very wrong, Papa. I truly believe I will be more content in some country parsonage than a grand house."

He chuckled again. "We shall see. Yes, we shall see."

It was with some feeling of relief that Allegra hurried out of the room, closing the door gently behind her. For a moment she sank back against it, drawing a deep sigh.

Her father had been a semi-invalid almost as long as she could recall. During her childhood she occasionally reflected how odd it was that a woman as beautiful and vital as her mother should have settled for someone like Samuel Montescue.

Naturally, Jeanne Montescue had occasionally been prevailed upon to tell the story of her escape from the Terror in France, and Allegra supposed her mother must have been very afraid and alone during those first few years in England. In any event she had always displayed the greatest patience and care toward her husband, and unlike other women in a similar situation she had never encouraged eager gentlemen to become her court of assistants, despite many attempts from those who wished to become her lover.

When Allegra entered the drawing room, no one else was present, and she sat down at the pianoforte, glad of the solitude that had been difficult to find since Laura's betrothal. As she picked out a desultory tune she allowed herself to reflect upon her meeting that morning with the marquess. Up until that moment she had fought to keep it to the back of her mind, but now her cheeks flamed at the thought he could consider her foolish enough to make an assignation with Sir Angus Beane. It was evident he held her in a very low esteem and she wondered why, although that had not prevented him offering marriage to her sister. It was possible she had not given him true credit for being in love with Laura. Why else would he wish to marry her? she wondered. There was no doubt in anyone's mind he could very easily make a much more advantageous marriage elsewhere.

However, the realization that this could be a love match after all did not cheer her, which Allegra found odd.

Her reflections were rudely interrupted when the door flew open and Laura rushed in, her curls flying, her cheeks ruddy, and her eyes wide.

"Oh, Ally, I am so glad to find you here! I cannot find Mama anywhere in the house, and I simply had to speak to someone!"

Allegra immediately jumped up from the stool in alarm. "What is amiss, Laura? Why are you in such a taking? Calm yourself, dearest, and tell me all about it."

The girl took a deep breath and then thrust a flat box toward her sister. "Look! Just look. I cannot speak! I am as dizzy as a goose!"

Casting her a curious and rather worried glance Allegra took the box and opened it, gasping as she saw the contents. Nestling on a pad of black velvet was the most magnificent collar of emeralds and diamonds Allegra had ever clapped eyes upon.

"How splendid this is," she murmured, her own eyes growing wide. "No wonder you are speechless. I am at a total loss for words myself."

"They arrived only ten minutes ago—by messenger. They're from Crandon, needless to say, but do read the message. You will be quite agog when you do, I assure you."

Her sister exhibited extreme reluctance to invade Laura's privacy. "Should I? I'm persuaded the message was for you."

Laura was now much calmer, but her eyes remained filled with excitement. "Please do. In any event it concerns you, too."

Slowly Allegra unfolded the parchment headed by the marquess's coat of arms. Unaccountably her own heart was beating faster. *Your sister looks better on Lady,* she saw written in a strong even hand. *These will look better on you.*

As Allegra put down the note, Laura squealed with delight. "Can you believe such generosity? I confess I find it devilishly difficult. Have you ever seen anything so beautiful as this?"

Allegra was immediately put in mind of Lady, but she shook her head. For once words deserted her.

"Do say something, Ally," her sister urged, laughing all the while.

"You must excuse my staying mumchance, dearest," Allegra

heard herself say. "I am almost overcome." A moment later she asked, "Are those jewels part of the Crandon collection?"

"I don't believe they can be, for the messenger was from Garrard. I don't suppose I shall be allowed to wear any of the Crandon jewels until after I am married." She bit her lip. "Oh, heavens, Ally, I am so afraid."

Her sister looked at her in alarm. "Of Lord Crandon?"

"Of being his wife. He has such large establishments, here and at Crandon Park, not to mention bringing out Lady Lucrezia. Me!"

"You will contrive," Allegra told her in a dull voice. "His lordship must believe you possessing all the qualities he looks for in a wife."

"If only you too were settled, you could help me. You were always so much more accomplished in domestic matters than I. How can I possibly learn to be the kind of wife Crandon expects of me when most of my time will have to be devoted to supervising routs and balls for Lady Lucrezia's Season? I will be totally overset, I assure you."

"Lord Crandon will understand you're a greenhorn."

"Oh, I do hope you are correct, Ally. He is quite particular you know."

"He loves you, Laura," Allegra told her through strangely stiff lips.

The younger girl smiled. "Yes, yes he does," and her uncertainty seemed to disappear. "You must now own he is quite, quite splendid."

"He is generous to a fault, I grant you."

"I cannot conceive why he sent me the mare in the first place."

"Mayhap he believed it would please you. Everyone knows her to be a prime blood."

"Tush! Everyone knows ever since my fall I do not go riding unless it is unavoidable. You are the horsewoman in the family. He should have sent it to you in the first place. In the face of your disapproval of him it would have been a fine sweetener."

Allegra walked over to the window and glanced out into the street below. "He couldn't do that," she answered, biting her lower lip thoughtfully.

When she turned around again it was to see her sister removing

198

the collar from its box. She glanced gleefully at Allegra. "Help me fasten it, do. I cannot wait to show it to Mama!"

"Why don't you show it to Papa when he wakes up?" Allegra asked as she came to do her sister's bidding. "He will be so pleased to see you. You don't bear him company often enough."

Immediately her sister looked crestfallen. "Oh, must I? Papa invariably depresses my spirits so. He's always riding grub when I'm with him. There is nothing I can do that pleases him, whereas you are so good and patient with him. I . . . well, I am bound to admit I find him difficult."

"You must always make allowances for his megrims. He's not always up to the knocker, Laura."

"Faddle! He's as fit as a flea, and we all know it."

Allegra smiled faintly. "Unfortunately, dearest, he does not. He truly believes he has been given notice to quit, and nothing will persuade him otherwise."

"That is only because everyone encourages him in his humdudgeon. No doubt he *will* curl his heels up—in about sixty years' time. In all honesty, Ally, I am out of all patience with him."

"Dr. Pomfret doesn't think him in a humdudgeon."

"That quack! Papa's vapors and ill humors have no doubt made him a rich man." She paused in her tirade to admire the collar in a mirror before turning to look at Allegra. "I know full well why you have taken Crandon in dislike, but do tell me exactly what it is you dislike so much about Sir Angus Beane?"

For a moment Allegra was taken aback by her sister's question, and then she walked across to the harp in the corner. "If I am pressed to tell you, I dare say it is the color of his eyelashes."

For a moment or two Laura did not respond and then she burst out laughing. "Now you are roasting me!"

Allegra began to look amused, too. "No. I vow it is the truth. He has sandy-colored hair and his eyelashes appear to be non-existent. I don't like that."

Laura clapped her hands together. "I know exactly what you mean now! Crandon has the most heavenly dark eyelashes. Have you noticed them? Of course you have not, but I assure you it is so."

"Laura, at Lady Kaydale's assembly we have been asked to play a duet," Allegra reminded her, anxious to steer the conversation away from both the marquess and Sir Angus Beane. "Do you recall?"

"Yes, but in all the hurry-scurry of late it has scarce been in the forefront of my mind."

"That is very understandable, but we do need to practice a little so that our playing is of one accord."

"I feel too excited to concentrate on such mundane matters, but I will try. At least once I am Lady Crandon I shall not be called up to play music in public. That can be safely left to the new debutantes just come out."

As Laura went to take her place at the pianoforte and her sister to the harp, she caught sight of her reflection in the pier glass and paused to finger the collar of emeralds and diamonds that sparkled wickedly at her throat, but looked a trifle incongruous against the material of her muslin day dress.

"They are a mite too grand to wear while practicing music," she murmured.

"Why don't you take them off," her sister suggested.

The girl chuckled. "No, indeed I will not. I shall continue to wear them at every opportunity, or at least until I have something of equal splendor to take their place!"

As she began to tighten the harp strings Allegra drew an almost imperceptible sigh, and if anyone had asked her why, she would have been hard put to say why she felt quite so low-spirited.

Chapter Five

"Three dozen pairs of silk stockings," Mrs. Montescue read off the list as the carriage jerked to a standstill outside the mercer's emporium in Pall Mall.

She looked across the carriage to where her two daughters were sitting and asked, "Do you really think three dozen pairs of silk stockings will suffice?"

"Mama," Laura protested, "if they do not I assure you when I am the Marchioness of Crandon my husband will allow me sufficient pin money to purchase more."

Mrs. Montescue looked outraged. "I do not doubt for one moment the veracity of that, but do you really think I would allow you to go to your husband without sufficient stockings in your trousseau? Credit me with greater sensibility, Laura. No one is going to say your father is a nip-cheese."

"As if Crandon would be so high in the instep." Laura turned to Allegra and said wryly, "You will be obliged to endure this, Ally, when you become betrothed, and I dare say I will go through it all again when Lady Lucrezia is settled. Let us hope that is sooner rather than later, unless she is obliging enough to elope!"

"If you consider it easy to see a daughter married in the proper manner I assure you it is not," Mrs. Montescue told them, and then, glancing out of the carriage window, "Come along now, girls. We have much to do today and no time to waste in useless tattle."

She climbed down, followed by her daughters who both looked fetching in the latest style as decreed by illustrations in *La Belle Assemblée*. Laura wore blue velvet and Allegra burnt-orange watered silk, each with matching bonnets, generously feathered and beribboned.

As Mrs. Montescue swept into the emporium, Laura put one hand on her sister's arm to hold her back. "I have been meaning to have words with you all morning, but have had no opportunity, especially as you insist upon rising early to exercise your mare." She hesitated a moment before saying, "Minnie Carver confided in me last night—and I don't doubt her veracity—that Sir Dudley and Lady Rymington are back in Town."

Allegra started slightly but recovered sufficiently a moment later to retort, "Oh? What is that to me?"

The young girl looked disappointed at her sister's reaction to the news. "I had it in mind you would wish to be informed so as to be prepared for their appearance in polite circles."

"Thank you for the consideration, dearest, but I can assure you no preparation is necessary, for I assumed they would return as soon as their wedding trip was over, so it is no surprise to me that they are returned to Town. It is, in fact, inevitable."

"How will you behave toward him when you do meet?" Laura asked breathlessly.

"With the usual propriety," Allegra answered in some surprise. "You surely did not think I would indulge in an attack of the vapors the moment I clapped eyes on him, or take to my daybed. I am not so foolish."

"Well, I admire your pluck, for I shall not relish meeting Mr. Marsham in the future. He was quite persuaded I would marry him and is said to be desolate."

"That is not so surprising," Allegra pointed out. "Everyone thought so, too. You need harbor no fears for me, however. I only wish Sir Dudley and his bride happy. He and I would not have suited after all."

"That is a considerable relief to me, you may be sure. For some while I was persuaded you appeared to believe yourself in love with him."

Allegra smiled faintly. "The next time I throw my cap over the windmill, be very sure I intend to do it with more care."

"I hope that does not mean you intend to treat every gentleman who wishes to pay court to you with disdain, just because one cried off," Laura ventured, displaying uncharacteristic perspicacity.

"I think we should join Mama before she becomes as mad as a weaver over our absence," Allegra suggested, guiding her sister toward the door and effectively ending their conversation.

They had only just completed their lengthy purchases when Lady Lucrezia Carlyon came into the emporium, accompanied by a lady clad in darkest bombazine whom the young lady introduced as her governess, Miss Elvira Chapstone.

"How happy I am to see you," the girl enthused. "I had it in mind to call upon you as soon as I was able."

"We are scarce at home nowadays," Laura told her, laughing gaily. "Mama is intent upon buying up the entire stock of every emporium we patronize."

Allegra gave the girl an encouraging smile. "We would

always be happy to see you whenever you are able to call, you may be sure."

"How kind of you to say so, Miss Montescue. No wonder my brother is constantly singing the praises of you all!"

"We are about to visit the milliner," Mrs. Montescue informed the girl. "Mayhap you would like to join us." She glanced at Miss Chapstone as Laura shot a vexed look at her sister who affected not to notice it.

Allegra's heart swelled with gratitude toward her kindhearted mother who must also have realized how lonely London would be for Lady Lucrezia with only the sour-faced Miss Chapstone for company and a brother hell-bent on his own pleasures.

"If you would care to leave her ladyship with us, ma'am," Mrs. Montescue told the governess, "we will return her to Crandon House when we are finished with our shopping."

"Oh yes, Chappie," Lady Lucrezia enthused, turning to the woman, "do allow me to stay with Mrs. Montescue and her daughters. After all, we are almost related."

"Lady Lucrezia can partake of tea with us at Mount Street and then she will be returned home in our carriage," Allegra added, and the girl's eyes gleamed as if offered a great prize.

"Very well, my lady," Miss Chapstone agreed unsmilingly at last. "I shall inform his lordship of your whereabouts should he wish to know where you are."

All four ladies watched the governess's departure in silence, and then excitedly Lady Lucrezia turned to the others. "Chappie is the dearest thing, but she will insist upon continuing to treat me as if I were still in the nursery. La! By this time next year I might be preparing for a marriage of my own!"

"If you are not, my lady," Mrs. Montescue replied, looking wry, "something will be gravely wrong."

"Of course," Lady Lucrezia went on, still appearing ebullient, "the problem is I was such a sickly babe and had to be coddled. Crandon was always very exacting with the servants when it came to my care and comfort, and poor Chappie is afraid of him." Lady Lucrezia laughed gaily. "Afraid of Brett! La! As if he is in the least alarming, but naturally as his only sister and so much younger to boot I daresay he is the slightest bit protective of me still."

As they left the emporium, bowed out by the owner, Lady Lucrezia chattered happily to Mrs. Montescue while Allegra and Laura followed behind. They were held to be a particularly handsome group by those who observed them leaving.

"I have the oddest feeling Lady Lucrezia is going to be as a shadow to me," Laura complained to her sister, her voice a low whisper.

"Shame on you, Laura, for your uncharitable thoughts," Allegra chided. "Can you not see how lonely she is?"

"Do not seek to persuade me that Lady Lucrezia is in need of anyone's pity. No one is more privileged than she."

Allegra shook her head sadly. "Only think, dearest, Lady Lucrezia has been living at Crandon Park with Miss Chapstone for company, seeing her brother only occasionally. Now she is come to London she must see us as the family she never had, so it really is incumbent upon us to look kindly on her plight, for we have always had each other for company and that, I'm persuaded, is a great blessing."

"It is evident to me you and Lady Lucrezia are becoming as thick as inkle weavers," Laura replied.

"One cannot help but like her. She is so lively and unaffected. In fact, it is difficult for me to believe she can be Lord Crandon's sis . . ."

Laura cast her a sharp look. "You still hold him in dislike, don't you?" When her sister did not answer Laura went on, "I'd have thought his gift to you of that splendid mare would have changed your mind about my husband-to-be."

At the reminder Allegra felt her cheeks growing hot. "I am indebted to him, you may be sure, but it is evident the gift was only made because he wished to please *you*."

"I do not doubt that for one moment," Laura replied haughtily as they went to join their mother and Lady Lucrezia who were climbing into the carriage.

Not far away, in Bond Street, the Marquess of Crandon parked his curricle at the side of the street, which was particularly crowded with elegant carriages, so his skill at maneuvering was observed and very much admired by all who witnessed it.

When he jumped down from the curricle his lordship handed

204

the ribbons to his tiger and paused for a few moments to exchange words with the fellow. The marquess, who was wearing a Belcher handkerchief, knotted loosely around his throat in honor of the great fighter, was just about to go into Gentleman Jackson's gymnasium, when he espied an acquaintance striding purposefully toward him.

The marquess hesitated only a moment before greeting him heartily. "Rymington! So you're back in Town at last! I am bound to own it is good to see you in merry grig for an April gentleman."

Sir Dudley Rymington's manner, however, displayed no such pleasure in seeing a friend. "Crandon, you scoundrel!" he growled. "I've a mind to call you out."

It was evident that the marquess was both taken aback by the attack as well as slightly amused. "What the devil has caused you to fly out at me in this way?"

"How dare you ask?"

"Come now, tell me what has caused your choler, my friend?"

"Friend? How dare you claim me as a friend? You are no friend of mine but a rapscallion, and you will meet me or I will acquaint everyone with your perfidy."

The marquess's half smile faded and a steely look came into his eye. "Hold hard there, Rymington! Guard carefully what you say or you might have cause to regret your rashness."

"Will you or will you not meet me, Crandon?" Sir Dudley insisted, to the great interest of several lackeys bored at being left in charge of their masters' carriages. This was precisely the kind of diversion they had been seeking.

"You would not wish to make your bride a widow so soon after the nuptials, I fancy."

"That is assuming you will be the victor, and I beg you not to depend upon *that*!"

Once again the marquess's face relaxed into a smile. "Come, Rymington, let us crack open a bottle of wine together and discuss your grievance in a more civilized manner than you propose. Whatever annoyance you harbor toward me cannot possibly warrant this degree of incivility."

A second later Sir Dudley had whipped his kidskin gloves across the marquess's face. Up until that moment the exchange

205

had been proceeding in relative privacy, but when it happened all eyes turned upon the two gentlemen. Grooms and lackeys as well as pedestrians just passing by paused, for no one was ever in any doubt when a challenge to a duel was issued even if it was against the law to indulge in such chivalry. Duels still often took place and even government ministers had been known to flout the law when honor was deemed to be at stake.

The marquess's face twisted with fury. His eyes grew darker as he hissed. "Hell and damnation, Rymington! Don't be such a clunch! This can only end in disaster for us both, and you know that full well."

Sir Dudley threw his head back in triumph. "Does the great nonpareil refuse to settle a matter of honor?"

"If I do agree to meet you you'll discover you've pulled a boner, my friend."

"*If?* The Nonesuch shows the white feather? Is that how it is to be?"

The marquess glanced around and then took Sir Dudley's arm, saying softly, "I have a far better solution to whatever hurt you believe yourself a victim, one which will not run foul of the law."

"So now the mighty Crandon is wriggling out of his obligations," Sir Dudley smirked.

"Do not provoke me too far, Rymington," the marquess warned.

Sir Dudley's eyes flashed with fire. "That is precisely what I am trying to do."

"This nonsense is the outside of enough. What say you we take this matter into Jackson's and fight it out under his rules? Would that satisfy you?"

Some of Sir Dudley's anger faded then. When he glanced around at the keen interest all about them he became suddenly self-conscious.

"Very well, we shall settle this matter in a bruising match, but I give you fair warning, Crandon, be prepared for me to trim your coat!"

When Barnaby Montescue entered his house it was to see his sister Allegra laughingly skipping down the stairs with Lady Lucrezia Carlyon at her side.

206

He had been in the process of handing his hat and riding whip to the house steward, but then he just stood and stared, a slow smile spreading across his face.

"What a vision of loveliness to greet a fellow's return home," he declared.

The young lady blushed, and Allegra laughed. "Lady Lucrezia, I don't believe my brother is addressing me in this instance!"

"I have enjoyed the most splendid day in the company of your sisters," the girl told him when she recovered her composure.

"You may be sure I envy them your delightful company with all my heart," he responded.

Allegra shot him a warning look. "I feel obliged to warn you that my brother, charming as he may be, is a habitual tongue-pad."

"I could not be more sincere," the young man protested, and Allegra had the profound feeling he was, for once, speaking the truth.

The young lady looked all at once coy, throwing her head back so that her curls bounced enticingly. "You may be assured my brother has counseled me on such matters, Mr. Montescue. He has warned me of those who would seek to fill me with moonshine and grease my boots."

Barnaby looked outraged. "I sincerely trust you do not look upon me as a toad-eater, my lady."

She smiled engagingly. "Indeed I do not, sir. I am persuaded you can be nothing but sincere." When Allegra chuckled, Lady Lucrezia went on, "My brother has become allied to the most delightful family in all London. I can only admire his choice."

"We are similarly delighted at our sister's good fortune," the young man responded.

"I believe the carriage has arrived to take you home, my lady," Allegra informed her as it could be heard rattling to a halt outside the door.

"It has been the most delightful day," Lady Lucrezia repeated. "I cannot recall ever enjoying myself more."

"It is only the first of many such occasions, I hope," Allegra told her in all honesty. "You are always welcome at Montescue House whenever it pleases you to call upon us."

"Hear, hear," Barnaby echoed, "but it is surely too early for

207

you to return to Crandon House unless you have a prior engagement."

Lady Lucrezia looked a little dismayed. "No, I do not, but my brother . . ."

"I have it on very good authority, ma'am, that his lordship is otherwise engaged." Allegra cast him a curious look, but he continued to address the younger girl. "Mayhap you would come riding with me in the Park, and afterward I will return you to Crandon House."

The girl almost skipped with delight. "I have longed to ride in your high-perch phaeton, Mr. Montescue. It looks to be a most splendid carriage."

"Then let us not delay a moment longer." He nodded to his sister. "Allegra."

Lady Lucrezia glanced at her, too, and Allegra said, "Enjoy your ride," but her mind was troubled.

Someone as young and unworldly as Lady Lucrezia was vulnerable to first love, and Barnaby was a handsome young man, accustomed to making ladies' hearts beat the faster with a flattering turn of phrase. Allegra knew she would hate for Lady Lucrezia to have her feelings bruised.

There was, however, little time for her to dwell upon such discomforting thoughts, for before she had a chance to leave the hall Sir Angus Beane arrived, sweeping off his high-crowned beaver hat as he entered the house. Allegra eyed him with no pleasure. His buff riding coat had far too many capes for true elegance and the buttons, as big as saucers, looked ridiculous when compared to the more refined style of Corinthians like Lord Crandon.

"Miss Montescue," Sir Angus greeted her smilingly. "How fortunate to find you so close at hand. I called in the hope you would be free to ride with me this afternoon."

As he looked at her hopefully she was tempted to refuse, but then she answered, "Thank you, Sir Angus, I will fetch my hat and pelisse if you will but wait a moment."

"For you, ma'am, I will exhibit the utmost patience, just as I have been obliged to do for the past several months."

Allegra was somewhat discomforted by that declaration, and as she hurried toward the stairs he went on, "I happened to see Mr. Montescue driving away with Lady Lucrezia Carlyon just now. He is no doubt aware, as I am, that Crandon is not like to see them."

Allegra paused by the stairs. "I doubt if Barnaby is much troubled whether Lord Crandon sees him or not."

"Indeed, it is all in the family, is it not? No doubt Mr. Montescue informed you of the reason why his lordship is otherwise engaged."

"We had weightier matters to discuss."

"Then allow me to be the first to apprise you of the fact that your brother and I, among others, have benefited handsomely today from wagers placed on the outcome of a mill between Crandon and Sir Dudley Rymington. I know you to be acquainted with the both of them."

His words had the desired effect on Allegra, who gasped. "I cannot credit that, sir."

"I promise I am not shamming."

"I did not wish to insinuate that you were." After a moment's hesitation she asked, "Who was the victor?"

"Need you enquire? It was Crandon who dealt poor Rymington a rather ferocious facer. However, you need not concern yourself for Sir Dudley, Miss Montescue. Apart from a few bruises he has not suffered as greatly as he might have done."

At this she stiffened and asked coldly, "What precisely do you mean by that, sir?"

"I meant nothing untoward, I assure you, ma'am."

"Was the mill instigated for gaming purposes?" she asked, rather hesitantly.

"From all I observed and was told, Rymington flew out at Crandon, and they decided to settle in that manner. No one is quite certain what caused the kickup between them, but Finney Dodswell's tiger witnessed Sir Dudley challenge Crandon to a duel, and it was his lordship who persuaded him to fight at Jackson's instead."

"I cannot credit this, Sir Angus, so you must forgive my surprise. Sir Dudley and Lord Crandon always seemed to be the closest of friends. Surely Sir Dudley has only just returned to town with his bride. What can have occurred to make them resort to fisticuffs?"

Sir Angus took a pinch of snuff before answering, "Gentlemen

209

often fight over the merest trifle, Miss Montescue. Those two are keeping as close as oak as to their reasons, but I can only cry roast meat, for Mr. Montescue and I wagered upon Crandon to win. I do not like the fellow in the least, but it was evident to me Rymington stood little chance of acquitting himself as well as Crandon, who is known to be a Pink of the Fancy." As her thoughts milled around in her head Sir Angus went on, laughing disparagingly, "Brummel arrived as soon as he heard of the wagers and promptly put his purse on Rymington. For all his affectations as an arbiter of fashion, he is a deucedly bad gamester."

As Allegra made her still-thoughtful way upstairs she met her sister. Laura glanced down into the hall, a slow smile coming to her face.

"Are you actually demeaning yourself by going riding with Sir Angus this afternoon?"

Irritably Allegra replied, "I see no harm in it, and I do need some fresh air."

"And a rest from prattle-boxes I don't doubt."

"It might surprise you to learn that I do enjoy Lady Lucrezia's company, Laura. I cannot conceive why you do not."

"Oh, you may be sure I find her tolerable, merely a trifle wearing on the nerves after a short while."

"I am surprised to hear you say anyone is wearing on the nerves if Lord Crandon is not."

"It seems to me that Sir Dudley's defection has unhinged your reason. I have it in mind you cannot like any gentleman now."

"Oh, why do we quarrel over trifles?" Allegra asked with a sigh.

"I agree it is foolish. It doesn't matter a whit whom we dislike as long as we continue to like each other." As Allegra nodded her sister said, "I observe I shall be the only one of us to remain unescorted this afternoon. It is quite provoking to think I am betrothed and yet my husband-to-be has not called to take me riding."

"He must be otherwise engaged," Allegra suggested, after hesitating for a moment.

There was time enough for Laura to hear the story of Lord Crandon's bruising match from others, she thought, and there would be many only too eager to recount the tale at the earliest opportunity. Hearing it certainly troubled Allegra, although she could not for anything think why, and she was still frowning when she came back down the stairs some few minutes later.

Chapter Six

*T*he assembled crowd at Lady Kaydale's Park Lane mansion applauded enthusiastically when the Montescue sisters finished their duet for harp and pianoforte and curtseyed prettily.

For Allegra it had been quite an ordeal, for all the time they played she was fully aware that Lord Crandon had been standing at the back of the room watching them with unwavering attention. His scrutiny of them—or more probably that of his bride-to-be—did not dismay Laura one jot, and she had played with all her usual sureness.

For the first time Allegra envied her sister for being so sure of herself. Allegra supposed that Laura had no reason to be any other than sure of herself; she had caught the most eligible bachelor in the beau monde and as a consequence was much sought after by all her acquaintances.

However, Allegra's brief envy vanished quickly. It was impossible to sustain it when she knew full well life as Lord Crandon's wife would not be easy. He was such a difficult man to know, and she was certain her sister had not made a start in doing so. Moreover, it must be near impossible to please him. Philosophically, Allegra decided that if her sister was not much concerned then she should not worry herself on that score either.

"Miss Montescue, I am bound to own you acquitted yourself brilliantly in the duet."

When she looked up from her thoughts it was to see Sir Dudley Rymington standing in front of her. His face wore a diffident smile, and her heart leaped slightly, but not for the more obvious reason. He no longer had the power to affect her emotions, but this was the very first time she had set eyes on him since his marriage, and others would be observing the meeting with keen interest.

The first thing she noticed about him, apart from the anxious look in his eyes, was the shiny bruise on his cheek and the piece of court plaster adorning one brow. The sight of his injuries caused her lips to quirk, although she disliked herself heartily for being so well amused by his hurt, slight as it appeared to be. Had the two gentlemen fought a duel, as it was reported Sir Dudley had wished, it was likely he would have emerged in a far worse condition than this. The Marquess of Crandon was a noted shot.

"You are very kind to say so, sir," she answered in as cool a manner as she could contrive.

As she spoke she suddenly realized how foolish she had been ever to consider herself in love with this man. Just then she experienced a great feeling of liberation. While she had been constantly denying her disappointment when he gave her the go-by, now she knew it to be a truth.

"I would want you to be aware that my very high regard for you will never wane, Miss Montescue."

Allegra stiffened with outrage. "Again it is kind of you to say so." Then she asked with a deliberate casualness, "How does Lady . . . Rymington? I have not as yet clapped eyes upon her."

At the mention of his wife's name the young man appeared more discomforted, but Allegra did not pity him. "I am glad to say she is in rude health, I thank you."

"I must look to see her tonight and address her myself as soon as may be."

"Lady Rymington is not present this evening, I regret to inform you. She had . . . the headache and was obliged to remain at home. It is a great disappointment for her, having only just returned to Town."

"And to you, I do not doubt."

"Indeed."

Allegra smiled faintly. "No doubt we shall have many other opportunities to enjoy a coze."

"Miss Montescue . . ." he began, and she leveled him a cold, appraising look.

"I must beg your pardon, sir, but I can linger not a moment longer, for I observe my brother signaling to me."

That was not strictly true, but something told Allegra that Sir Dudley was on the brink of an indiscretion, and she pushed her way through the crowds until she saw Barnaby, who looked well pleased with himself having just stood up with one of the Season's great beauties. Nothing was more certain to bring a smile to his face.

"Barnaby, I have been in a fidge to speak with you since yesterday. Have you a moment?"

"You are sporting your bracket-faced look, Ally. I do hope you do not wish to give me a setdown on some score, for I am in high snuff this evening and in no mind for a scolding."

Her face relaxed into a smile, for she had been unaware of looking severe. "I just wish to speak to you of Lady Lucrezia Carlyon."

"Ah!"

"I do trust you are not filling that child's head with a bag of moonshine, Barnaby."

"Child? She is scarce younger than you and Laura. Very soon she will be of marriageable age, and there will be many tongue-pads filling her head with flummery."

"When that time arrives—and not before!—Crandon will be looking for a dynastic match for his only sister, even if you do declare you are in earnest, which I take leave to doubt of you!"

"But I am in earnest, Ally," he declared to her astonishment. "You can take it I am, for the first time, madly in love, and I fully intend to offer for her the moment she comes out."

"Barnaby, I could not be more pleased for you, and she is the dearest person I know, but Crandon might take issue with you over your intentions. Your expectations might be considered excellent, but I do not doubt his lordship will be looking to the peerage for a match for his sister."

"Oh, faddle, Ally. You credit him with being too toplofty. You always do. He is not the devil incarnate, you know."

Allegra smiled wryly. "I have never maintained he is as bad as *that*."

"Do you believe he is hard-hearted enough to maneuver her into a loveless match, all for position? I think not, in all truth.

213

From all I have observed he is exceeding fond of his sister and will abide by her choice as long as he isn't an out-and-out muckworm."

"I do hope you do not underestimate his lordship, dearest," Allegra answered doubtfully. "No one wants for your happiness more than I, you may be sure."

Barnaby looked impatient. "You speak as if we were beneath him, but you must recall he is to marry our sister, so he must regard us sufficiently up to snuff."

"Oh, I do not forget," she said wistfully before returning her attention to him. "Let me assure you, Barnaby, if Lady Lucrezia is to become my sister-in-law at some time in the future I could not be more pleased, but are you certain she returns your feelings?"

"Not as yet. I would not expect her to declare herself so soon, especially as she is not yet come out, but I am persuaded she will look upon me favorably when the time comes. I believe I have an advantage in the family connection and will exploit it, you may be certain. I am determined not to have the worst end of the staff."

"As long as you are certain in your feelings," she warned. "Up until now you have not been known for your constancy."

"I am a reformed character from now on, I assure you."

"What of Mrs. Armitage?" she chided.

"I am done with Cyprians," he said in a whisper.

Allegra allowed herself a smile. "Good. Much as I would hate for Lady Lucrezia to be left wearing the willow for you, Barnaby, I would be most anxious for you not to provoke his lordship into any rash action. I know you are aware of his contretemps with Sir Dudley Rymington."

Barnaby chuckled merrily. "Our future brother-in-law acquitted himself splendidly. I only wish you could have seen him, Ally. You could not help but be proud of the connection."

"Do you know why they fought?" she asked, frowning slightly.

"I regret I do not, although I shall not complain, for it was advantageous to me and several others of my acquaintance. We are all much plumper in the pocket. No one can know what their quarrel was about because both participants are staying mum—

chance as to the reason. Good Lord!" he suddenly exclaimed as the orchestra struck up for the first dance, a gavotte. "Just look at our sister!"

Mystified, Allegra followed the direction of his gaze and was amazed to see her sister partnering her erstwhile suitor, Mr. Marsham.

"That is very civilized I am bound to own," she said a moment later. "I dare say Mr. Marsham is over the dismals."

"If Lucrezia became riveted to another I don't suppose I should *ever* recover."

Allegra was both shocked and surprised by the intensity of her brother's declaration, for even now she did not entirely believe he was in earnest, but she supposed if a rake like Lord Crandon could settle down, it was entirely possible for her brother to do so also.

When she gave Barnaby her attention again he took out his snuff box, which he proudly showed to her. "Crandon must consider me handsome, Ally, for only this afternoon he sent me some of his snuff made specially for him at Berry's."

"An honor indeed," she agreed, eyeing the brown concoction with some interest.

"Why don't you try some," he invited, and she laughed, although she was touched by the honor he wished to bestow upon her.

"No, I thank you. Ladies usually do not, and it is not a habit in which I would wish to indulge."

"Lady Borrowdale enjoys a very superior blend, I'll have you know."

"She also swears like a fishwife and rides on a man's saddle! I doubt you would favor such behavior in me."

They were still laughing together when Sir Angus came to claim her for the next set.

"Another winner of the mill," Barnaby greeted him.

"You must prevail upon your future brother-in-law to fight more often. That should not prove difficult, I fancy, for he finds it easy to be quarrelsome."

"In this instance," Barnaby reminded him, "it was Rymington who picked the quarrel."

The young man bowed and went to claim his next partner. Sir

Angus watched him go for a few moments before returning his attention to Allegra. "When you witness your sister's felicity and indeed that of your brother—if I am not being indiscreet in that observation—I am persuaded you would mayhap wish to be in a similar situation," he told her as they took their places in the set.

"I daresay it is every female's wish to be settled, Sir Angus," she answered firmly.

He looked so satisfied she realized too late he had mistaken her meaning entirely. "Perchance you would not be averse to my calling upon your father in the not too distant future, Miss Montescue."

He watched her carefully as she protested, "Oh no, I beg you do not, sir, for Papa is not in plump currant at present and tends to ride grub with all those who trouble his head. You would not find favor in his eyes at this moment, I assure you. Naturally, it is all we can do to cope with the arrangements for Laura's wedding at present."

"It is certain your family would only delight in making similar arrangements for you."

Allegra was almost panic-stricken as she replied, "I could not possibly think of imposing it upon them at this time. Nothing must detract from Laura's triumph."

"Your consideration of everyone's sensibilities is admirable," he countered. "As I have already been at pains to point out to you, I am a patient fellow, although I only think it fair to say there are many who look upon us as a pair."

"Do they?" she asked in some surprise. "How strange you should say so, for I was not aware of it."

"Such modesty," he told her admiringly to her utter chagrin as the dance began.

While Allegra automatically executed the dance steps her mind worked frantically to think of a suitable manner in which to dispose of her unwanted suitor once and for all. At the same time Laura Montescue was making her purposeful way through the crowds toward the man to whom she was betrothed.

Eventually, after rebuffing several young men who wished to stand up with her, Laura was able to join the marquess, who was just then engaged in conversation with a few of his acquaintances. Although she looked anxious she affected a smile and for a few moments joined in the amiable conversation. However, as soon as she was able to draw her future husband to one side she did so, affecting an air of urgency.

"Have I told you you look ravishing tonight, my dear?" he asked.

Her cheeks immediately became tinged with pink. "I thank you, my lord. It has already been remarked upon by many, but the declaration has all the more value coming from you, naturally."

"You honor me indeed. Why have I gained the distinct impression that you wish to address me on a matter of some import, Laura? You appear to be in something of a pucker."

Again she flushed. "Is it any wonder I am in a fidge? When I was dancing with Mr. Marsham a short time ago he informed me that you and Sir Dudley Rymington fought yesterday. Fought! I could scarce believe my ears, although I do not doubt his honesty for one moment."

"Oh *that*," his lordship answered, taking out his jeweled snuffbox and enjoying a leisurely pinch before returning the box to his pocket. "It was a bruising match, no more, so I have no notion why news of it has put you in this taking, my dear. It was not, after all, a duel."

"From what I have been told, it was as much as a duel."

"Fustian! It was of no import whatsoever."

"I am not so unsophisticated I do not know gentlemen enjoy mills, but I do wish I had heard of it from your own lips. It is quite mortifying to be told of one's affianced husband's actions by a stranger."

The marquess looked amused. "I take leave to doubt that Mr. Marsham is a complete stranger to you, Laura, but do accept my heartiest apologies for the omission. You are quite correct, of course; I should have made mention of it to you straight away and spared you this horrid shock to your sensibilities."

The young girl looked mollified, but she did eye him suspiciously for a moment or two for signs of sarcasm. Not having detected any she then asked in a careless fashion, "What . . . did you quarrel over?"

He subjected her to one of his enigmatic smiles, which invariably infuriated her sister. "That, my dear, is a matter between Sir Dudley and myself."

Laura stamped her foot in vexation. "You are being exceeding provoking, my lord."

"I daresay I am, but if we are shortly to be wed, I believe it is time you began calling me Brett."

Her cheeks grew even more pink, and she began to fan them furiously. "I take leave to warn you, you shall not mollify me in that manner."

"Very well," he agreed good-naturedly, "I shall not."

A moment later she cast him a sideways glance while still retaining her air of grievance.

"Do you still insist upon remaining mumchance on why you fought with Sir Dudley, even to me?"

"I believe I must."

"Why?"

"Because you really would not wish to know the reason, I assure you." While Laura continued to look mutinous he added softly, "Come now, my dear, what business gentlemen have between themselves is not for the ears of ladies. After all, you would not wish me to quiz you when you exchange *on dits* with your cronies over a dish of scandal broth."

"That is not precisely the same. You are being horridly cruel to me, Crandon. Indeed you are."

He smiled faintly as he slipped one finger between the emerald collar and her throat. "There are few who would agree with that score, my dear."

As Laura made a strangled sound in her throat, Lady Lucrezia came bounding up to them, a vision in pale yellow sarsenet. "Is this not famous? I have stood up with Mr. Montescue twice and the evening is scarce yet begun!"

Laura eyed her coldly. "If I were you, Lady Lucrezia, I should exhibit the utmost caution with regard to my brother and his excess of flummery. He is known to be a callous breaker of hearts."

The girl's look of abject pleasure was replaced by one of dismay as Laura cast the marquess a cool look and walked away, her head held high.

"I cannot credit Mr. Montescue with such callousness," the girl said, "but she is his sister and knows him the better, I daresay."

"Do not heed anything Laura says this evening, Lucrezia," her

218

brother warned her. "I fear she is suffering a fit of the megrims and is like to ride grub for the rest of the evening."

"I cannot conceive why she should be cast in the dismals. It is such a lovely evening. Mayhap it is you who has put her out of humor, Brett."

He laughed then. "Yes, I daresay there is a grain of truth in that accusation."

"Shame on you for using her so ill."

"You mustn't concern yourself with Miss Montescue, Lucrezia. She will soon enough regain her spirits. The place is crowded with those who would seek to fill her head with flummery, and nothing is more conducive to her pleasure than that."

"I pity poor Miss Montescue, for I fear she has not found favor in your eyes this evening."

"Oh no, quite the reverse is true!" he protested, laughing again.

His sister eyed him with patent disbelief. "Miss Laura still has my sympathy, although I am bound to confess I cannot like her quite as well as Miss Allegra. However, I am truly delighted you are to marry her, otherwise I should still be rusticating at Crandon Park with only Miss Chapstone for company!"

He smiled down at her. "I am gratified to hear you say so, for it means that at least *you* are pleased."

Lady Lucrezia looked somewhat perplexed. "Does that mean you are not? Oh, do not say you are about to cry off this marriage, Brett. I would not wish to be on the outs with the Montescues now they are so welcoming of me in their home."

He traced his finger idly across her cheek. "You mustn't allow me to gammon you."

She smiled shyly. "You are so much more sophisticated than I, Brett."

"That can only be a good thing," he told her.

"But you are better acquainted with Mr. Montescue than I. Is he as his sister says? I don't wish to make a cake of myself, but I do confess to liking him exceeding well."

Once again he subjected her to his fond gaze. "Like most young gentlemen, Montescue can claim his fair share of maidenly conquests, but as it is far too soon for you to set your cap at any one young man," her cheeks grew pink, "I believe it is best to make as many acquaintances as possible before your come-out."

219

"But what of Mr. Montescue, Brett?" she asked breathlessly.

The marquess drew a small sigh. "There is no reason why young Montescue should not be numbered among them. One cannot blame the cub for trying to compound his family's good fortune."

"How can you be so condescending toward your future family?" she asked in some surprise. "You do not talk like a man who has lost his heart."

He continued to look down upon her, an enigmatic smile playing around the corners of his lips. "You could not be more wrong, my dear."

His sister smiled happily then. "I am so glad to hear you say so, Brett. Your lack of matrimonial ambition did concern me for a very long time."

"Had I known that it teased you so greatly I should have considered myself on the catch much earlier," he said, causing her to blush once again.

"There is much you could teach anyone about flummery. Now will you stand up with me for the next set? Mr. Griggs, my dancing master, believes I need much more practice before I make my debut, and it won't matter in the least if I step upon *your* toes."

"I am much indebted to you for the warning!" he answered laughingly, taking her hand in his and leading her into the set.

Although she was partnering Mr. Marsham for that particular dance, Allegra found herself on several occasions facing the marquess, and she could not help but think that he looked very splendid in his dark blue evening coat and satin breeches. In fact she was quick to tell herself, as soon as the thought crossed her mind, that he and Laura made a handsome couple.

When the dance was over Allegra breathlessly said to Mr. Marsham, "I was so glad to see you standing up with my sister earlier this evening, sir. I am persuaded she would wish to remain on good terms with you."

"You may rest assured I shall always be at Miss Montescue's service, ma'am. She can never be anything but dear to me."

"I am gratified to find you over your disappointment."

"Alas, I cannot confess to that, ma'am. I shall in fact never be reconciled to her marriage to any other man. Indeed, I have decided to continue to live in hope of her changing her mind until she leaves the church a marchioness. I do not intend to lose this particular struggle without a very determined fight."

Allegra cast him a startled look. "Mr. Marsham, I am bound to confess you are alarming me in no small degree."

He smiled and so confident was his manner she was alarmed anew. "You must not let the situation tease you. I do have cause for considerable hope, for I am by no means certain your sister is indifferent to me."

"Has she given you cause to hope?" Allegra asked in some further alarm.

"Miss Montescue always behaves with the utmost propriety, as I am sure you are aware." Allegra allowed herself a small sigh of relief. "However, it is true one cannot blame any female for being flattered by the attentions of such a Corinthian as the Marquess of Crandon, but I am far from persuaded the matter is ended with their betrothal."

"I beg you not to live in too much hope, lest the eventual disappointment is the greater, sir."

He was, however, not listening to her. He glanced past her, saying with a clear note of satisfaction in his voice, "Here comes one gentleman who is most definitely aware of his error of judgment. What fools we are for love, Miss Montescue."

Before she had any opportunity to reply to his bitter retort he had moved away and his place at her side was taken by Sir Dudley Rymington. In view of what Mr. Marsham had told her, Allegra felt greatly discomforted.

"Supper is about to be announced, Miss Montescue," he told her. "Would you do me the honor of allowing me to escort you this evening?"

Before she had any opportunity to think of an excuse to refuse him Sir Angus Beane came rushing up to them, saying, "I am afraid not, Rymington. Miss Montescue is already engaged to accompany me into supper."

For once she was actually glad to see Sir Angus. On this particular occasion he was definitely the lesser of the two problems. Casting her admirer a regretful look she walked away with Sir Angus, who as usual flattered her endlessly. Allegra allowed him to chatter on, scarcely hearing what he was saying, for her mind was full of what Mr. Marsham had said and also Sir Dudley's unwelcome attentions.

Supper was set out in the conservatory. An enormous table almost groaning beneath the tempting morsels of every type of food imaginable filled the length of it, and the guests eagerly surged forward to fill their plates.

Sir Angus chattered on inconsequentially as they ate, and it occurred to Allegra that he was confident of one day becoming her husband. For her own part, she doubted if she would ever be so desperate for marriage to accept him. She wanted so much more. Aware that her mind could well be full of the many novels she borrowed from the circulating library, she knew she wanted to be thrilled when she was held in strong arms and welcome the feel of her loved one's lips upon hers. If such a man did not come her way, Allegra knew she would be far happier as a spinster, however much others pitied her that unenviable state.

When she glimpsed in the crowds Laura, Lord Crandon, Barnaby, and Lady Lucrezia conversing convivially together in a corner, she could not repress a feeling of dismay at their happiness in one another's company. Her only admirers were a newly married man and a fortune-hunting widower.

When the music started up again it appeared that Sir Angus was determined to remain at her side for the rest of the evening and so indicate to everyone they were a couple. Allegra, however, had alternative plans.

When they arrived back at the ballroom she said, looking a mite sheepish, "I do believe I have left my fan in the conservatory."

"You must allow me to fetch it for you," he immediately offered.

"I couldn't possibly allow you to do so," she responded and hurried away before he could argue the point.

The conservatory was now empty save for the servants clearing away what was left of the splendid array of food. Her fan was exactly where she had left it on a chair, and she retrieved it gratefully, feeling more than a little reluctant to return to the melée, knowing that Sir Angus and Sir Dudley awaited her there.

She could only hope that in the time to come Lady Rymington would not often suffer the headache and be more at her husband's side. Recalling the timid girl, much given to the vapors, who had made her debut at the same time as she, Allegra somehow took leave to doubt it.

When she turned on her heel, knowing she could not linger in the conservatory for much longer, she started with alarm to see the marquess standing in the doorway. She suspected he had been there for some few minutes, observing her unseen. She hesitated, expecting him to stand to one side to allow her to pass, but he did not, instead coming further into the room toward her, and there was a purposeful air in his manner that did not reassure her one bit.

"How oddly peaceful it is in here now," he remarked, pleasantly, "unlike the babel of confusion only ten minutes ago."

Allegra smiled faintly. "I do confess to finding the peace quite wonderful."

She had never failed to feel uncomfortable in his company, and it was never more evident than now. Despite the presence of the Kaydale servants who were hurrying to clear away so that they could retire, Allegra and the marquess were effectively alone, and that had never happened before. Moreover, the situation was not a welcome one now.

"Are you seeking Laura?" she asked, clearing her throat nervously under his dark scrutiny, which had never been more disconcerting in its intensity.

"No. I have in fact left your sister safely in the company of Mr. Geoffrey Marsham."

Allegra's eyes narrowed slightly. "Do you not mind?"

He appeared surprised at her question. "Why should I mind? I have nothing to fear from Geoffrey Marsham, Miss Montescue. There is no doubt now that it is me she will marry."

"Poor Mr. Marsham," she could not help but murmur as she averted her eyes from his.

It was not until he spoke again that she realized he had heard what she had said. "Do not worry your head on his account. Geoffrey Marsham will be endowed with true happiness in due course."

"You cannot possibly know that," she responded.

"Rely upon it," was his soft answer. He came further toward

her. "When he is at last settled, his happiness will be all the sweeter for the pain he suffers beforehand."

He sounded so insufferably sure of himself Allegra was suddenly angry. "You will be obliged to excuse me, my lord. . . ." she said, making a determined effort to go past him at last.

He barred the way, looking down into her eyes, a stance so disturbing that she immediately backed away.

"Are you so anxious to return to your admirers?"

She looked at him levelly, drawing a deep breath. "No, I am merely in a fidge to escape your company, my lord."

He appeared not at all put out by her admission. "I won't detain you a moment longer than is necessary, you may be sure."

"I regret to inform you, my lord, you shall not detain me at all," she responded.

"Sit down, Miss Montescue," he ordered, causing her to start. "I wish to have words with you and now seems as excellent an opportunity as any we are like to have."

"There is nothing you can have to say to me which will be of the slightest interest, I fear."

The marquess placed a gilded chair before her, eyeing her levelly. "Sit down, Miss Montescue."

To her amazement and chagrin Allegra found herself seated in the chair. He brought over another and sat facing her.

"There has been between us a certain reserve, the reason for which I am unaware. However, it is certain that before long you and I will find ourselves related. There is even an outside chance that my sister will settle for your brother. . . ."

"He is only the first gentleman to pay court to her," she pointed out quickly.

"I am sufficient of a romantic, Miss Montescue, to know first love is often the last, and the couple display disturbing signs of being smitten."

Allegra was more than a little taken aback by this statement from the renowned rake, Lord Crandon. Surely Laura could not be the first to claim his heart, she thought. Indeed, she had been quite certain all along he could not possibly be in love with her sister, or any other creature, so great was his arrogance and consequence.

"What concerns me more is *our* relationship," he went on.

224

"Ours?" she asked in astonishment, her lips twisting into a travesty of a smile.

"Yes, ours, Miss Montescue," he answered coldly. "In the time to come we are bound to find ourselves in each other's company, more than would otherwise be normal." Allegra looked away in distress when she acknowledged the truth of that statement. "I know how fond you are of both Laura and Barnaby, and, I suspect, of my sister."

"That is certainly true, but . . ."

"Is it not evident to you, my dear, we must, for the sake of our loved ones, find some manner of accord in our behavior toward one another?"

As he spoke Allegra stared down at her folded fan, toying with it idly. When she made no reply he went on, "It cannot be so difficult for you to make the effort."

She looked up at last then, smiling slightly. "I regret you feel it necessary to speak to me in this manner, for I can assure you, my lord, I do not find your company in the least uncongenial."

He smiled and she knew, as she had intended him to do, that it was not the truth. However, he sat back in the chair that was patently too small for him and appeared at ease.

"I cannot conceive why you are so concerned," she went on, displaying resentment. "After all, once you and Laura are wed you will not be obliged to visit my house as often, so it is like we shall not be in each other's company as much as we find ourselves of late."

"One day in the not too distant future I don't doubt you will be settled with an establishment and family of your own. So will Lucrezia and Barnaby, whether together or with others. It would be pleasant for you and your family to join us at Crandon Park, which is a huge pile. It is a house made for the use of families." He looked all at once wistful. "In fact, I am bound to confess to you it is a very long time since children played on the lawns of Crandon Park."

As his words died away into silence Allegra scarcely knew what to say to him and then realized she was not called upon to comment when he got to his feet.

"I am glad we have had the opportunity of holding this conversation, ma'am. No doubt you will agree with me over much I

225

have said." He towered over her for a long moment before he added, holding out his hand to her, "Let us return to the others before we are missed."

Rather reluctantly Allegra gave him her hand as she got to her feet, withdrawing it almost immediately. As they walked together back to the ballroom her mind was in a turmoil, envisaging the unlikely possibility of staying at Crandon Park in the future, watching his and Laura's children growing up in those idyllic surroundings. The thought of being with Barnaby and Lady Lucrezia afforded her rather more pleasure, for although Allegra could acknowledge there was a great deal of common sense in what the marquess had said, she could not for one moment envisage being able to tolerate his company the better in the future however more conducive it would be to family harmony.

What is more, she was disquieted by noting that, as Laura had stated, he did indeed possess the most wonderful long, dark eyelashes she had ever seen in a man.

Chapter Seven

*L*ady Lucrezia soon became a regular caller at Montescue House. Allegra was always glad to see her, mainly for her own sake, but also because Laura had become less of an amiable companion of late. Allegra felt that the betrothal had put a barrier between them. It was not because Laura had become too full of her own consequence. Rather the opposite was true; she seemed to be in a less ebullient mood than at the time of her engagement.

Allegra felt she could, in a way, understand her sister's loss of high spirits. Now that all the furor and excitement of the engagement period had died down, she was left with her mother fussing endlessly over lists, and a father constantly predicting imminent financial ruin.

By comparison, Lady Lucrezia Carlyon was invariably good-natured and eager to join in whatever pursuits were undertaken by the two sisters. Today Allegra and Lady Lucrezia pored over fashion magazines while Laura embroidered delicate flowers upon handkerchiefs for her trousseau. For once she was quite content to do so.

"Have you decided on the design of your wedding gown?" Lady Lucrezia asked Laura, glancing up from the magazine.

"Not as yet."

"There is a most fetching one here," Allegra pointed out. "It would suit you admirably, but naturally there is still ample time for you to decide."

"Mrs. Dunn, the mantua maker, is awaiting the latest fashion plates from Paris," Laura told them, looking all at once wistful. "She has undertaken to bring them round here directly when they arrive and then a decision can be arrived at."

"I shall not wish to rival you," Lady Lucrezia confided, "but I have in mind the prettiest gown to wear on that day." She looked at Allegra then. "I do beg your pardon if I am being presumptuous, Miss Allegra, but is there a chance of your being married before too long?"

Allegra looked momentarily startled before she laughed, a mite harshly. "Goodness me, no!"

"Oh, I thought Sir Angus Beane . . ."

Laura chuckled over her sewing as her sister replied. "Do not even think of Sir Angus as a suitor, dearest. The very notion is the outside of enough."

"This is a great pity, I fancy," the young lady said, casting Laura an uncertain look.

"Because this is my second Season?"

All at once Lady Lucrezia looked shamefaced. "Oh, I would not for anything wish to infer . . ."

Allegra laughed again, but this time it was more lighthearted. "You need not suffer any embarrassment on my account, my dear. My situation may concern others, but I assure you it does not confound me."

"I only made mention of the matter because my brother told me you had your admirers."

"And so she does," Laura agreed, chuckling into her sewing.

Just then Allegra's manner grew decidedly colder. "I can

assure you both I'd as lief remain a spinster for the rest of my life than marry a man I did not hold in the greatest affection."

"Bravo!" Allegra's cheeks grew bright red when she saw Lord Crandon standing in the doorway, still wearing his caped riding coat. "Truly a modern woman, which is most admirable."

Lady Lucrezia immediately got to her feet, looking delighted to see him. "Brett, how good of you to come. I'm persuaded Miss Laura was not expecting you, and so the surprise must be all the sweeter."

As Laura put away her sewing she displayed none of the pleasure Allegra might have expected her to show at the arrival of her future husband.

"I hoped you, Laura dear, would do me the honor of riding in the Park this afternoon," he told her.

"I regret I cannot, my lord," she replied, getting to her feet. "Mr. Marsham has already bespoken the honor, and as you had not I could think of no good reason to refuse his entreaty."

The marquess did not look as disappointed by the blow to his hopes as might have been expected. He merely said, "While I cannot hold you in blame it is a great pity, Laura, for I had quite made my mind up to ride in the Park this afternoon. Mayhap on the morrow?"

Laura's face relaxed into a smile. She looked almost coquettish. "As you wish, dearest. I am much relieved you do not take the news amiss. After all, you cannot in all conscience expect me to sit at home with hands folded in the event you might happen to call."

Allegra looked at them anxiously as did Lady Lucrezia, for both awaited his explosion of anger that did not come. "How right you are, Laura," he agreed, displaying an equanimity none of them thought he possessed.

Laura herself seemed a little surprised as well as relieved. As she reached the door she said, looking now a little mischievous, "As you have come equipped for a drive why don't you take my sister in my stead?"

Because she didn't wait for a reply she didn't hear the marquess say, "What a splendid notion! Miss Montescue, do not say you too are engaged this afternoon."

In desperation Allegra looked appealingly at Lady Lucrezia,

who told her in a pert manner, "You need not concern yourself on my account, either of you. Barn . . . Mr. Montescue is calling for me shortly."

"You must take pity upon me, Miss Montescue," the marquess told her. "The two ladies closest to me are obliged to cry off, and you will make a delightful companion, I fancy." While Allegra desperately racked her brain for an excuse he went on slyly, "After our conversation the other evening I had it in mind you might wish to indulge my wishes in this matter."

Allegra could not help but cast him a wry look as she answered, "Very well, my lord, if you insist upon it."

"I do."

In fact, as she put on her chipstraw bonnet and fastened the ribbons, she marveled at her own compliance with his wishes once again. It seemed amazing to recall that while Laura habitually flouted his wishes she, Allegra, had begun to obey him.

When she went down into the hall Laura was just being handed into Mr. Marsham's gig while the marquess watched. Mr. Marsham eyed Laura's future husband warily, saying, "I will take the utmost care with her."

"I have every confidence in you, Marsham," was his lordship's inscrutable reply.

As they drove away Laura waved cheekily to the marquess who raised his hand in an answering salute.

Mr. Marsham continued to look uneasy. "It is a great relief to me that Crandon does not take amiss my riding with you."

"I can assure you he does not. I cannot conceive why you should consider him an ogre. He is most amiable as well as being sophisticated."

"So I have discovered," the young man replied, looking more at ease now.

"I have informed him he cannot in all conscience expect me to await his convenience. If I did I would be doomed to stay at home most days of the week, which would be insufferable to me. It was evident he was much surprised when I informed him I was already engaged to go riding with you, but I am bound to say he hid his disappointment tolerably well."

Mr. Marsham then drew his eyes from the road to cast her a perplexed look. "But, Miss Montescue, I was most astonished to find him at your house, for I chanced upon Lord Crandon in White's earlier today and made mention of our appointment then. He intimated on that occasion he had no objection whatsoever."

Laura looked aghast. She glanced back to see her husband-to-be handing Allegra up onto the box of his racing curricle. She started to say something but then fell silent, pushing her hands into her muff as she faced forward once again.

Just as the marquess climbed onto the box next to Allegra and took up the ribbons, Barnaby Montescue drew up outside Montescue House in his high-perch phaeton. He jumped down, proclaiming, "This is quite like a family outing, Crandon."

"I cannot conceive why you should think so," the marquess replied with marked coolness. "None of us is as yet related." The young man's ready smile faded a little and then the marquess went on, "My sister is inside and I am sure I am not mistaken in declaring she is awaiting your arrival in quite a fidge."

Giving them a cheery wave, Barnaby then went into the house and the marquess flicked his whip over the backs of his team, which set off at a lively pace.

"You are being exceeding generous allowing Barnaby to see so much of your sister before her come-out," she said rather hesitantly as they set off.

He cast her an inscrutable look. "Do you think I should disapprove of Barnaby? After all I am going to marry his sister."

Allegra laughed, albeit uncomfortably. "No, indeed not, only she is not yet out and obviously destined for a very elevated marriage."

"That is a distinct possibility," he admitted, "but for now they believe themselves in love."

"It is a great relief to me to learn you are taking so generous a view of the matter," a statement that caused his lips to quirk into a smile.

"Can I believe you consider me rather less of an ogre than before, Miss Montescue?" When she bridled noticeably he went on quickly, "Credit me with a little good sense, my dear. Were I to forbid them to meet so often I daresay they would consider themselves ill-used and contrive to do so in secret, which is not desired. Love always finds a way." He drew his eyes from the

230

road to look at her momentarily. "It invariably does, don't you think?"

Allegra drew a profound sigh. "It will not for poor Mr. Marsham, I fancy."

He glanced at her again. "Or perchance for Sir Angus Beane?"

Allegra once again felt the familiar discomfiture. "I cannot speak for Mr. Marsham, whom I have always considered to be in earnest, but I am persuaded whatever else he feels, Sir Angus Beane is not in love."

"Oh, Miss Montescue, you do yourself a grave injustice. Your modest fortune is not the most admirable quality you possess."

His declaration caused her cheeks to grow rosy. They had reached the gates of Hyde Park and she could see Mr. Marsham's gig ahead of them. In an effort to change the subject of their conversation she told him, "You may be glad to know that Lady is thriving."

"Just as I knew she would in your ownership."

"You couldn't have known it when you bought her," she contradicted and then, when he made no reply, she went on quickly, "I don't believe I have properly expressed my gratitude to you."

"Your pleasure is gratitude enough, Miss Montescue."

Once again Allegra felt herself flushing and went on quickly, "Our stables are becoming exceeding well stocked of late, my lord. Only the other day Barnaby bought a fine piece of prime blood at Tattersall's."

"I know. I was there when he made the purchase."

"Mayhap that is the answer to his skill in choosing such an excellent goer."

"I can assure you, ma'am, your brother made the purchase with no help from me. You might be surprised to know he beat the bargain entirely on his own and he has a good eye for cattle."

Her heart swelled with pride at her brother's prowess and with gratitude for the marquess's magnanimity. It was quite evident to her he was determined to be on the best of terms with his future relatives, and she could only admire the desire in him.

"His skill cannot possibly equal yours," she responded. "Your judgment when it comes to horseflesh is well known and there can be no finer mare in all England than Lady."

When he looked at her she could not mistake the mockery in

his glance, and she was puzzled by it until he said, "So you will own, Miss Montescue, that I am not wrong in everything I do."

Allegra gasped. "I have never asserted that you are!"

"My mistake, ma'am, for which I heartily beg your pardon."

She cast him a suspicious look, for humility was not a quality she acknowledged in him, but she was bound to admit his generosity, his indulgence of both her brother and sister as well as Lady Lucrezia, which had come as a welcome surprise to her.

When she espied Sir Angus Beane hacking toward them she braced herself for a sarcastic comment from that gentleman, and she was not disappointed.

"How famous! I have only just bade farewell to Miss Laura and Mr. Marsham, and now I chance upon Miss Allegra with you. None of you will ever find life dull."

"That depends upon with whom we are obliged to associate," the marquess responded with a quick flash of wit that caused Allegra's lips to twitch, especially when she glimpsed the annoyance on Sir Angus's face.

She gained some satisfaction from the realization the two gentlemen heartily disliked each other, although she could not understand why she should be so pleased to know of it.

Without giving Sir Angus any further opportunity to make acid comment, the marquess flicked his whip over his team and they moved on, only to be overtaken by Barnaby's phaeton going at some speed. To continue in such a fashion he was obliged to leave the path and all the other carriages in his way and plunge into the field beyond.

As they passed the curricle the young couple waved. Allegra caught a fleeting glance of Lady Lucrezia, whose cheeks glowed pink and eyes were bright and wide. The ribbons on her bonnet were flying wildly as she desperately and laughingly attempted to hold on to it.

"Dash it all!" the marquess exclaimed, looking suddenly alarmed. "The cub's showing off. I hope he has a mind to Lucrezia's safety."

Although Allegra fully understood and sympathized with his alarm, she said in a soothing tone, "You mustn't worry, my lord. Barnaby is a fine whipster, and he would take no chances with Lady Lucrezia, I am sure."

The marquess's face relaxed into a faint smile. "You must forgive me my concern, Miss Montescue. Lucrezia is very dear to me, and being protective toward her has become something of a habit."

"Naturally. One would expect nothing else."

"We are closer than most owing to there being only the two of us. My responsibilities have often been that of a mother and father rather than brother."

"Lady Lucrezia would do any parent great credit," she told him.

"It is kind of you to say so, ma'am. You must understand our parents lost several children at birth between Lucrezia and I. When she was born it was our mother who died."

Allegra looked dismayed. "How dreadful for you that must have been."

"She was sorely missed," he admitted sadly. "I was old enough to know what had happened and was prepared to hate the creature responsible for my loss. However, I was not prepared to find her so entrancing."

His recollection moved Allegra profoundly. "On that score I am bound to agree with you most heartily, my lord. I have become exceeding fond of her myself."

"And she of you," he assured her, casting a glance in her direction once again. "I don't suppose I am revealing any secret in telling you that, Miss Montescue." She smiled with pleasure. "And I am bound to express my gratitude to you on her behalf for the friendship you have offered. She knows so few people in Town as yet. You have made her feel very welcome."

Once again Allegra felt her cheeks growing pink. "You have no need to thank me, my lord. It is a pleasure, I assure you. I hope we will always remain close in the future."

A whisky driven by Sir Dudley Rymington drew abreast of them. His bride was at his side on this occasion, and she carried a parasol to shade her pale cheeks from a very weak sun.

Sir Dudley nodded coolly to the marquess. The bruise on his cheek had become yellow and the cut over his eye was now free of court plaster, but he still bore the signs of his disastrous fight with Lord Crandon.

Allegra forced herself to cast the newlyweds a warm smile

despite her feeling of discomfort. "Welcome back to Town, Lady Rymington."

"Thank you, Miss Montescue," the other lady replied.

"I do hope you are feeling recovered now. Sir Dudley informed me the other evening when we met at Lady Kaydale's assembly that you were a trifle off the hinges."

"I am fully recovered, I thank you," she replied, casting her husband a cold look, "but because of my indisposition I have not arranged any social functions of my own, or attended anyone else's."

"You may be certain everyone will be delighted to see you."

Lady Rymington smiled slightly. "I am much surprised to see you two together in this manner, for I was given to understand it was Miss *Laura* Montescue who was betrothed to marry Lord Crandon."

"Your information is correct," the marquess replied, giving her an urbane smile, "but the sisters are so close I do not dare neglect Miss Allegra for fear of Miss Laura's wrath. Good day."

As they rode on Allegra's laughter rang out merrily. "Poor Lady Rymington. I fear she will contrive to find the matter most perplexing."

"It is intended that she should. Does seeing them together trouble you?"

"No, it does not!" she protested. "I only wish everyone would stop believing I am wearing the willow for that man."

"I am much relieved to hear you say you do not. You and he would not have suited, you know."

Allegra gasped at his presumption. "How dare you say so?"

"As a soon-to-be relative I believe I have the right to be plain-spoken with you. I recall that you take pride in doing so."

Her eyes narrowed with fury. "I beg of you do not believe because you are to marry my sister you are entitled to be free with me, my lord, for I assure you it is not so!"

"I would not dare!" he said, appearing aghast, but Allegra distrusted his stance. There seemed to be a twinkle of mockery in his eyes.

A moment later she admitted, "I have myself concluded Sir Dudley is well suited in his choice of bride, but that does not give you leave to say so."

"I am utterly shamed, Miss Montescue," he said, and never was his irony more marked. In the face of it Allegra could not sustain her irritation. "I had it in mind you were a lady who spoke plainly and would wish me to converse in a similar manner. I apologize if I am in error," he continued.

She did not reply. She really did not know how to, for she was surprised to discover how stimulating she had found his company despite all their disagreements. The realization was most disconcerting to her.

A moment later he handed her the ribbons and when she looked at him questioningly there was a light of amusement in his eyes as he said, "Laura tells me you are as fine a whipster as any gentleman, Miss Montescue."

Recognizing a challenge when it was issued, Allegra took his riding whip and sent the team charging for the park gates, watched admiringly by several riders and pedestrians nearby.

Although she was mindful of the advice that no gentleman wished to marry a female who rode better than he, it hardly mattered in this instance, for this gentleman was her sister's husband-to-be.

Chapter Eight

"*I* was never more shocked than to see you racing Crandon's curricle through Hyde Park!" Laura declared the very next morning over breakfast. "I dare not imagine what Mama will say when she comes to hear of it, let alone Papa, who will no doubt suffer one of his spasms!"

"Humbug!" Allegra replied, biting into a slice of toast and signaling the lackey to pour more coffee. "Crandon handed me the ribbons, but I was not racing." She smiled at the recollection. "Well, at least not very much."

"Crandon is so proud of his curricle. I am astonished to learn he allowed a female—any female—to drive it."

As Laura peered at her sister over her cup Allegra said, "In any event, if we are speaking of yesterday afternoon, more to the point is why you accepted Mr. Marsham's invitation after treating him so shabbily. What were you thinking about?"

Laura shrugged. "He asked me. What was I to do?"

"You could have refused. Now he is like to believe you held out hope to him where I fancy none exists. It would have been far kinder to have refused."

"Fudge! Your notion of kindness is not mine, I assure you. Just because I am to marry one gentleman does not mean I should snub all others. In any event, Crandon can be shockingly negligent."

"You never used to be so missish, Laura."

"Becoming betrothed to Crandon has proved to me my own worth. You may be certain Crandon will not cast off his friends just because he is to become riveted to me!" She smiled suddenly. "How could I refuse Mr. Marsham, Ally? He is always so glad of my company. In all truth, I had no notion he cared so much. Now I feel I have sufficiently ruined his life without refusing an innocent invitation to ride in his gig."

"He will recover given time and the opportunity to do so," Allegra pointed out, but noted that her sister did not look reassured on that score.

"If I can bestow upon him the tiniest morsel of happiness it is incumbent upon me to do so."

Allegra cast her a disbelieving look. "What faddle! You are simply casting him the crusts from your bread."

Laura took one last sip of her coffee before she got to her feet. "Crusts are very welcome to a starving man," she said cheekily, adding in a sly manner, "I notice Sir Angus Beane has sent you violets this morning. How good and clever of him to ascertain they are your favorite flowers."

"Did you tell him they were my favorites?"

"I may have let the fact be known," the girl replied in an artless manner, which only fueled her sister's annoyance.

"Laura! I am out of all patience with you."

236

"Do not accuse me of being missish when you indulge in these artless manners."

Laura hurried out of the breakfast room and as she did so passed her mother on the way in. Mrs. Montescue had one hand clasped to her head as she complained, "Your papa is not at all well today. I have been obliged to call in Dr. Pomfret."

"Oh, dear," Allegra murmured.

"I am persuaded he will soon be recovered," Laura said as she left the room.

"When Dr. Pomfret has left I shall go up and read to him," Allegra promised. "Papa received a copy of Lord Byron's new poem yesterday, and I dare say he will enjoy hearing me read it to him."

"He does so enjoy your company," Mrs. Montescue told her as she sat down at the table. "The pity is Laura is always too busy to spend time with her father."

"She has a deal to do before the wedding, Mama."

"I cannot help but wish at all times that you shared her good fortune."

"I am quite content with my present situation, Mama."

Jeanne Montescue searched her daughter's face carefully. "Are you truly, dearest?"

"Yes, truly, Mama," Allegra answered with a smile. "Laura is not to be envied her choice of husband, whatever everyone else chooses to believe."

The housemaid returned with fresh coffee which Mrs. Montescue indicated should be left on the table.

When the servant had left the room Allegra said, "You seem more than usually concerned this morning, Mama. Papa's condition is not worse than usual, is it?"

Mrs. Montescue smiled faintly. "Oh no. You must not put yourself into a pucker. I imagine he believes he has contracted another chill. Nought will convince him otherwise, I fear."

The news caused Allegra to relax somewhat, but she saw no sign of corresponding relief in her mother. "Then there is something else that troubles your head this morning."

"It seems so foolish even to think on it."

"On what, Mama?" Allegra insisted. "What can have put you so out of countenance?"

"You will consider me a chucklehead."

"No, I will not. If it is at all possible I would wish to help you solve any puzzle that teases you."

Mrs. Montescue swallowed noisily. "It's Laura."

"Laura! Nothing on earth ails Laura just now. She is in high snuff, you may be sure."

"That is not precisely my concern, which, I am bound to own, is a most foolish one, for any mother would be crying roast meat to have her daughter marry Lord Crandon."

Allegra frowned. "But am I to take it you do not cry roast meat any longer?"

"That is why I consider myself such a gudgeon."

At this point Allegra smiled. "Tush, Mama. You are possessed of more good sense than any other female I know." Mrs. Montescue smiled faintly at her daughter's praise. "What has prompted such a fidge, Mama?

"Has Laura made mention to you of any doubts in her mind? For if she has I am given to believe it is quite natural in a prospective bride," she said a moment later when her mother did not reply.

"The doubts are all mine, my dear," Mrs. Montescue admitted at last. "Your sister, as far as I am aware, is still as right as a trivet."

"Then you must not concern yourself."

"Try as I might, I just cannot envisage your sister as Lady Crandon. The more I think on it, the more I come to believe she will be putting herself in the wrong box when she marries the marquess."

"Mama, you trouble your head unnecessarily. Laura is quite content when she envisages her future, despite the occasional panic when she thinks of herself in such a toplofty situation."

"Is she truly content, Ally? Lord Crandon is such a nonpareil. He will expect much of her with no quarter given, I fancy."

"Laura is sensible of her own consequence, Mama, but you have prepared her well. Indeed, you have prepared both of us. As for Lord Crandon, you must not concern yourself on his account, for I have noted since their betrothal he has been most indulgent of Laura. Whatever she does or says seems to fill him with lelight. He sees nothing wrong in anything she is wont to do, which I am bound to own I consider remarkable in him."

Mrs. Montescue smiled with relief at last. "You do relieve me, dearest, and I am more than grateful to you. In all honesty, I have found Lord Crandon far more indulgent than I had envisaged at the outset. Mrs. Radleigh proclaimed him a veritable ogre when their friendship ended, but I should have known better than to believe her Banbury tales. You are quite correct, my dear, I am queer in the head even to think on it."

When she got to her feet she added, "I must go up to your papa with no further delay for I have left him long enough. He is bound to grow querulous."

"Tell him I will be along presently."

Her mother smiled. "I will. I can always rely upon you, if not the others, to raise your father's spirits. Barnaby is gone out already. He is scarce home at all nowadays."

"Young men lead such hurry-scurry lives, Mama," Allegra told her with a laugh.

Mrs. Montescue now looked a good deal happier than she had only a few minutes earlier. "The box on his phaeton is high enough to serve a suspicious husband. I declare one can see directly into first-floor windows."

Allegra laughed, but the moment her mother had left the room Allegra's expression became serious once again. She poured another cup of coffee for herself and stared thoughtfully over the rim.

After reading to her father for some time and then seeing him settled for a morning nap, Allegra found herself somewhat at a loss. Laura's company was not always convivial nowadays, and in any event, Allegra had seen her leave the house on an errand that she did not announce to anyone else. Laura's betrothal to Lord Crandon had seemed to change her in an almost indiscernible way, which Allegra supposed was quite natural. Soon Laura would be taking up a very lofty position in Society and sadly Allegra was bound to acknowledge that her sister's marriage was likely to widen the chasm between them.

Mrs. Montescue was engaged in domestic matters that had become somewhat more onerous since Laura's betrothal. Allegra did her best to alleviate some of the burden, but Jeanne Montescue took pride in running her own household, and she did it with great efficiency.

After wondering listlessly for a short while what she should do next, Allegra dusted her cheeks with rouge, added pomatum to her lips, and donned a bonnet and pelisse before going out accompanied by one of the footmen. It was only a short walk to Piccadilly, and as it was a time when gentlemen were usually not at home, she had no compunction about approaching Crandon House in search of the uplifting company of Lady Lucrezia Carlyon.

As Allegra recalled her brother speaking earlier of a mill between a fighter called the Boilerman and another who gloried in the name of Grub Jenkins, she fully expected that Lord Crandon would also be attending with many other bucks of the ton who enjoyed such meetings and was herself in no danger of encountering him.

Crandon House was a much larger establishment than her own home. When she stepped into the hall with its soaring twin staircases and atrium adorned by countless paintings and marble statuary, she was very much impressed by what she saw.

After announcing herself to the house steward, she was informed that her ladyship was out. Disappointed, Allegra turned to go home, but she did pause to look around at the magnificence her sister was about to enter. To Allegra it was rather awe inspiring, and although she would not have made mention of the fact to their mother, she also found it difficult to envisage Laura in so elevated a position. Much would be expected of Laura as Lady Crandon, but Allegra did not doubt that Laura would contrive very well indeed and become an exemplary wife of the marquess.

She cast a regretful smile at the house steward and was just about to leave when she froze, catching sight of the marquess himself coming down the stairs. For one moment she considered making a dash for the door, but then he caught sight of her, too, and paused on the landing, evidently as surprised to see her as she was to see him. Then, without uttering a word, he continued slowly down the stairs while she waited in the hall, wretched and embarrassed.

He was dressed for riding in a buff-colored coat, his Hessians gleaming, the tassels swinging as he came slowly down the stairs.

"Miss Montescue, what can have moved you to honor me with this call?" he asked, smiling urbanely when he reached the bottom of the stairs.

The assumption she had come to see him annoyed her, but she contrived to contain her feelings to answer politely. "I called in the hope of seeing Lady Lucrezia, but I discover she is not at home."

"Ah yes, Lucrezia. I am given to understand Miss Chapstone has taken her off on some kind of improving expedition this afternoon. She will regret having missed your call."

Allegra kept her eyes averted, finding his scrutiny of her uncomfortable. She could not credit he would truly believe she had come to see him. He could not possibly be so arrogant, but she was not sure.

"It is no matter, my lord."

He smiled faintly as he replied, "There really is no need for you to rush away now you are here."

She found herself smiling foolishly. "You are evidently on your way out, and I would not wish for anything to detain you."

"You do not detain me, Miss Montescue. Mayhap you would like a brief look at your sister's future home."

She froze on the spot. "I believe I shall wait until Laura is ensconced here."

"I'm persuaded she will be delighted to learn you intend to become a frequent visitor." He paused for a moment before he added, "Allow me, at least, to show you one thing of which I am most proud."

At last Allegra allowed herself to look at him. "From the little I have observed you have a great deal here of which you can be proud."

A fleeting smile crossed his face. "You are too generous in your praise, ma'am. Come."

He began to lead the way up the stairs, and when she hesitated to follow, he paused to look at her questioningly. After that brief hesitation Allegra surprised herself by following him up the stairs, indicating to her footman that he should remain in the hall.

Halfway up the stairs she hesitated as they passed a painting of

241

a particularly fetching female. Noting her interest the marquess paused and said, "John Partridge painted that portrait of my mother just after I was born."

"It is evident she was very lovely," Allegra said truthfully.

"Yes," he answered, drawing a sigh, "that is undoubtedly so, but it is said he flattered her more than is usual by a painter because he fell in love with her during the commission."

Startled, Allegra heard herself asking, "Was it unrequited love, my lord?"

He looked grim and for a moment she wondered if she had made a grave mistake in voicing the question, until he replied with no rancor apparent in his demeanor, "As far as I am aware." Then he nodded in the direction of a portrait of a gentleman in a peruke wig. "That painting, by Thomas Gainsborough, is of my father, the seventh marquess."

Recognizing a similarly arrogant look upon the painted face, the dark, mocking eyes and severe set of the lips, Allegra could not help but retort, "I note the resemblance."

They had reached the first floor landing where she noted a bronze bust set upon a marble tochère. Again the features were strongly reproduced and she commented, laughing suddenly, "This bronze is of you, my lord."

"How strange you should think so. It is in fact my grandfather. He was something of a rake."

"That is most remarkable," she told him, making no attempt to hide her amusement.

He, too, looked amused. "I am not shamming. He possessed a notorious reputation."

"Do you believe such a characteristic can be inherited from our ancestors?" she asked wryly.

He appeared to consider for a moment or two before he replied, looking as amused as she now, "I daresay it is entirely possible."

When she realized she was beginning to enjoy herself in his company she said abruptly, "What is it you wished to show me?"

"It is over here," he answered, turning away from her rather suddenly.

He had brought her to another painting, and when she looked

242

at it she gasped with pleasure. "It's a Canaletto," she breathed. "How lovely it is. How fortunate you are to possess it."

Her words evidently pleased him as he acknowledged, "You are more knowledgeable than most young ladies."

"Our governess was most punctilious in ensuring we enjoyed a rounded education," she replied, feeling satisfied at having surprised him. Then she returned her attention to the painting. "When I look at this I can almost imagine myself in Venice. It makes it very real to me."

"When Boney is defeated you will be able to go there and see what it is like for yourself. My father enjoyed a Grand Tour in his youth; I missed mine owing to hostilities in the area, but I am confident very soon we will be free to journey wherever we wish once more."

She cast him an uncertain look for a moment or two. "I really should be returning home now. I am honored you have invited me to see the Canaletto. We have nothing so splendid at Montescue House."

He laughed then. "I cannot entirely agree with you on that score." When she realized he was referring to Laura she was forced to look away quickly. A moment later he hastened to say, "I beg of you don't go so soon. You would not, I fancy, had Lucrezia been at home." She made some sound of protest but he went on quickly, "Take a glass of ratafia with me in the library before you go on your way and then, if you consider yourself late, I shall be honored to drive you back to Mount Street."

Before she had a chance to refuse more insistently and make her escape he had opened a nearby door. All at once, finding him so mellow, even willing to drink ratafia, which was regarded as not at all the thing among fashionable gentlemen, Allegra was reluctant to cause any friction between them. However, it was with considerable reluctance that she preceded him into what she discovered to be a lofty and exceptionally well stocked library.

Once again she found herself looking around with interest, but this time at the shelves full to the ceiling with books, while the marquess went to a side table near his desk to pour wine into two glasses.

"When Laura comes to live here she will have no cause to visit the circulating library," Allegra remarked.

"Do not be so sure. I have none of Mrs. Radcliffe's gothic romances, or indeed Byron's epic poem, although it appears I shall be obliged to purchase a copy of *Childe Harold's Pilgrimage* if his fame continues apace."

Allegra laughed and went to take the glass he offered, studiously avoiding that most disconcerting scrutiny to which he invariably subjected her. She went to sit in a leather-seated chair that faced a large mahogany desk which he perched on the edge of. All at once she felt self-conscious and stared down at the glass. What am I doing here at Crandon House with this man I dislike so heartily? she asked herself. Only just at that moment she found she could not dislike him half so much. It would be easy, she thought, to forget the wrong he had done her. It might even be possible, she considered, to forgive it.

A moment later she asked, "Has the Canaletto been in your family for a very long time, my lord?"

"I have only just acquired it." When she looked at him in surprise he smiled and went on, "That is why I am so pleased. You are one of the first to view it, in fact. My agents have been scouring the country for just such a work."

"You are very discerning."

"So I am told," he answered, suddenly looking grim. Then after he had taken a mouthful of wine he went on, "But it will remain here for only a short time."

"Are you removing it to Crandon Park?" she asked, exhibiting some surprise.

If he had bought it hoping to impress Laura he would be in for a disappointment, she thought, for a painting would excite her sister no more than Lady had.

"No. It was bought as a gift for the Regent, to adorn the newly renovated walls of Carlton House."

"How very generous of you, my lord," Allegra gasped, her eyes wide.

He went to refill his glass before coming back to the desk and sitting on the edge of it again. "I don't blame you your surprise, Miss Montescue, but you should understand Prinny is an old friend of mine."

"He has recently alienated so many of his acquaintances, including Mr. Brummel, I am told."

"I know he has courted a good deal of unpopularity of late, but he *is* our future king, and as he is always in dun territory, there are some of us who deemed it appropriate to supply him with works of art for what will undoubtedly become a palace when it is entirely finished. Whatever else are his faults I assure you he has exquisite taste."

"So I am given to understand," she answered, sipping at her ratafia wondering why she felt so uncomfortable and content, both at the same time.

"When the restoration of Carlton House is complete," he told her, "you will no doubt see it for yourself."

Allegra laughed uncomfortably. "I don't doubt that as your wife Laura will often be invited to His Royal Highness's diversions, but I cannot envisage ever having an opportunity to go there myself."

"You cannot possibly know that," he responded.

She was aware he was looking at her again, although she kept her eyes averted. His leg was swinging gently by the edge of the desk and all at once there was a silence broken only by the ticking of a clock somewhere nearby. Suddenly there seemed to be an almost tangible element in the air, but although it was something Allegra could not recognize, it alarmed her just the same.

A moment later the great double doors to the library burst open and Lady Lucrezia came rushing in, still wearing her bonnet and pelisse.

"Miss Montescue! How splendid you have called! When Whittaker told me I could not have been more delighted, although disappointed I was not actually at home when you first arrived."

Immediately Allegra experienced a great feeling of relief and got to her feet, putting her half-finished glass of ratafia down on the desk. As she did so she glanced hesitantly at the marquess who also stood up, but his attention was all for his sister now.

"Good grief, Lucrezia!" he exclaimed, looking amused, "You look in high snuff."

"It has been, I am bound to confess, the most sublime afternoon. And now with your permission, Brett, I wish to take Miss Montescue to show her some of my most recent purchases and solicit her esteemed opinion on them."

245

He appeared philosophical when he glanced at Allegra. "By all means, ladies. It is my misfortune that Miss Montescue came to see you and not me."

As Allegra sketched a curtsey she felt awkward. "I am obliged to you for your hospitality, my lord," she murmured.

"It has been my pleasure," was his perfunctory reply.

Lady Lucrezia slipped her arm around Allegra's waist and began to lead her out of the library. "Chappie and I visited the British Museum to view the Egyptian relics this afternoon, and then we went to Lord Elgin's house to see the frescoes he brought back from Greece. Have you seen them? I am bound to confess myself quite amazed. . . ."

When they reached the door Allegra paused to glance back to see that the marquess was now standing by the side table pouring another glass of wine. He did not look up, and after a moment she followed Lady Lucrezia out of the room, closing the door behind her.

Chapter Nine

*B*y the late afternoon St. George's Field was crowded with a great miscellany of aristocratic carriages, all of them lined up so they could obtain the best view of Mr. Sadler's balloon, which was due to ascend in celebration of the Prince of Wales becoming Regent at last.

Allegra and Laura accompanied their mother in a splendid barouche. Once it was in place Laura eagerly scanned the other carriages for sight of friends, frequently calling out when she espied one.

"There are so many people here today," she remarked.

"While the war with Boney continues," Allegra pointed out, "there is little to celebrate, so any occasion is like to bring out a crowd."

"Do you truly regard Prinny's elevation to Regent a reason for celebration?" Mrs. Montescue asked, making her daughters laugh.

"There are many who would dispute it," Laura acknowledged.

"I have it in mind I should have stayed with your papa today," Mrs. Montescue said a moment later, looking suddenly unhappy.

"Humbug!" Laura replied. "He will be perfectly safe at home with his faithful Randall in attendance."

"Laura is correct, Mama," Allegra pointed out. "Papa is in safe hands, and you are bound to enjoy the spectacle we are about to see. Prinny himself is due to arrive shortly."

"No one wishes to see *him* even if the balloon ascent is in his honor," Laura pointed out, waving frantically to one of her acquaintances.

"You do look a trifle pale," Allegra told her mother, glancing at her worriedly. "You are in need of this diversion."

Mrs. Montescue smiled. "You are correct, I fancy, and much wiser than I. I am, I fear, turning into a goosecap."

"A most delightful one," her elder daughter responded laughingly.

"Ally, do look at Minnie Carver's bonnet," Laura cried. "Is it not the ugliest one you have ever clapped eyes upon?"

"I don't consider it to be so ugly," Allegra replied.

"It is hideous and her hair is as straight as a pound of candles. She is totally unable to curl it properly, you know. And why, oh why, does Isobel Chetham always wear gowns that are a season out of mode? She is such a dowd despite all her airs of modishness. She has never appeared in high feather yet."

"Mayhap we are fortunate in having the advice of a mama who still retains all the modishness of a Frenchwoman."

Their mother laughed disparagingly. "It is a very long time since I deemed myself a Frenchwoman. I was not much older than Lady Lucrezia when I arrived here. I have been in England longer than I ever was in France, you know."

"When Boney is finally defeated you will be able to go back to Paris, Mama," Allegra told her, injecting a tone of brightness into her voice.

"Everything will have changed greatly, so I am not so sure I would want to do so."

"I would!" Laura argued. "I should like to walk along the banks of the Seine and in the Tuileries."

"I believe I should like that, too," Allegra agreed.

"I shall prevail upon Crandon to take me as soon as we are able," Laura mused. "He will not be able to refuse me. How romantic it will be."

Mrs. Montescue glanced worriedly at her elder daughter before she said quickly, "Your Papa was greatly cheered by your visit this morning, dearest."

"When I read to him I was most impressed by Lord Byron's poem, Mama. It is certain to be a great success."

"It is already," her mother replied. "Everyone is talking about it, and Barnaby has instructed his barber to arrange his hair in a similar style to his lordship. All the young bucks are like to do so within a sen'night."

"You must read it, Laura," Allegra told her. "I found it exceeding moving, as did Papa."

"Faddle! You know full well I cannot abide poetry. And who could conceive of Lord Byron, of all people, writing in a sensitive manner? I had always considered him exceeding uncivil."

"I confess to be in a fidge to read whatever he writes next," Allegra admitted. "I shall tell him so the very next time I encounter him."

Laura cast her sister a mischievous look. "He is very handsome if one is able to disregard the limp, and I have heard tell he is a danger to females. Naturally, he will never be a Corinthian like Crandon, but you might find him interesting, Allegra, sharing a pleasure in blue-stocking pursuits."

Allegra took no exception to her sister's words and she laughed good-naturedly. "You must stop matchmaking for me, Laura. First Sir Angus and now Lord Byron. Where will it end?"

"With your wedding 'tis to be hoped. Oh, why does it take so long to inflate one balloon?"

"It is very large," her mother pointed out. "Look, here comes Barnaby! How fine he looks. What a pleasure it is to see him."

"Good day to you, ladies!" he called as he approached the carriage, his curly locks now arranged in a careless disarray favored by the lauded poet. "Three ravishing females in the one conveyance. I declare it is all too much for a fellow."

"Such flummery," his mother replied, looking nevertheless pleased.

"This is not an event which would normally find favor with you, Barnaby," Allegra told him, and he immediately looked abashed.

"In all truth I did not come to see Prinny parade his *chère amie*, but I have it on very good authority that Crandon will be accompanying his sister here this afternoon."

All three ladies subjected him to an amused look and he went on, "No doubt that is why you are here, Laura."

His younger sister appeared taken aback for a moment before she answered, "Yes, indeed. Naturally I am in a fidge to see them."

"Mayhap you would wish to take a stroll with me while the balloon is being prepared, ladies."

"Yes indeed," Allegra enthused, allowing him to hand her down. "It is a rare occasion when we are able to enjoy a coze together, Barnaby."

Surprisingly Laura demurred. "I think one of us should remain in the carriage with Mama."

Mrs. Montescue immediately protested, but Laura would not be moved. As they walked away from the barouche Allegra found herself feeling guilty, for she was not sorry to be away from her sister's company. Of late she had found Laura difficult to understand, and she was often saddened by the certainty that Laura's marriage would cause a greater rift between them.

However the marquess envisaged their future life, Allegra was quite certain she would not wish to visit them often, which was odd as she now felt less bitter toward him than at the beginning of his betrothal.

"I hear you were seen racing Crandon's curricle in the Park the other day," Barnaby said when they were out of earshot of those in the barouche.

"If you hadn't been so intent upon impressing Lady Lucrezia with your own prowess, you would have seen for yourself it was nothing of the sort," she retorted. "I do hope no one will make much of it."

"No, indeed. I know how proficient you are tooling the ribbons. It was, after all, you who taught me! I was only surprised you condescended to be in Crandon's curricle after declaring loud and often how disagreeable a fellow you considered him to be."

The reminder caused Allegra some considerable discomfort as she replied in a careful tone, "Lord Crandon and I will never be fond of one another, Barnaby, but I am bound to confess I no longer find him quite so horrid as I once did. In any event, for Laura's sake I must make some effort to accommodate him."

"If you were a fellow you would appreciate his qualities the better."

"Why is that?" she asked, with genuine interest.

"Need you ask! He is such a nonpareil. One can only learn from being in his company. That is why I consider myself so fortunate in Laura's choice of husband."

Very soon after Allegra and her brother had strolled away from the barouche, deep in conversation, Sir Angus Beane approached the carriage.

"A very good afternoon to you, ladies," he greeted them, sweeping off his high-crowned beaver hat and smiling at mother and daughter charmingly.

As Mrs. Montescue inclined her head toward him in acknowledgment of the greeting, Laura said, "No doubt you had hoped to find Allegra with us."

"I am always delighted to see any of the Montescue ladies, ma'am. However, I am bound to confess it is not often one finds Miss Allegra missing from your party."

Laura grinned knowingly. "You need harbor no fear, Sir Angus. My sister is not far away today. You will be relieved to learn that she is strolling with our brother. You are certain to encounter her before long."

"In the meantime I would be greatly honored if you two ladies would accompany me for a brief stroll."

Mrs. Montescue declined politely but added, "If you wish to go, Laura, by all means do so, dearest, for I shall be perfectly comfortable here. I have a splendid vantage point."

"You are most generous, ma'am," Sir Angus told her before he handed Laura down from the carriage. "How charming your

250

mother is," he said as they moved away. "You are a much-blessed family."

"We think so," the girl agreed. "I'm so glad the weather has remained clement for the balloon ascent. Prinny should be arriving soon, and no doubt Lady Hertford will accompany him. I believe they have become exceeding close of late. He doesn't give a fig for popular opinion, does he?"

"I fear not, but I am told her ladyship has had an improving effect upon His Royal Highness." Laura paused to cast him a curious glance and he added, "It is said they read a chapter of the Bible together every day."

She laughed merrily as she glanced at him. "Sir Angus, I am persuaded you are roasting me. I don't believe that humbug for one moment."

"I own it is devilishly difficult to credit, ma'am, but I do have it on very good authority." He glanced at her before venturing, "Plans for your wedding must be very well advanced now."

"Yes, they are," Laura replied, laughing mirthlessly. "We scarce have time to devote to anything that is not connected to the wedding, but it is all quite exciting I am bound to confess."

"I don't doubt it is a most pleasant time for you. However, your happiness is bound to be tempered with a small degree of concern for the future of your sister."

She gave him a curious look. "Allegra? What is she to do with my wedding, pray?"

"To be plain, Miss Montescue, I welcome this opportunity to seek your counsel on a matter of the utmost import to me, and, I believe, ultimately, to your sister."

"Yes?" she said breathlessly.

As they walked Sir Angus kept pace with her, swinging his ebony stick as he did so. "I don't believe you can possibly doubt my devotion to your sister, ma'am."

"It is my opinion you have been most attentive."

"My regard I feel has been evident for some time. However, you may also be aware of some reserve in Miss Montescue's manner toward me, and she refuses to give me any hope for the future."

"There are times, Sir Angus, when I truly do not understand my sister. She can be a trifle unfeeling, I fear."

251

He smiled faintly as he nodded to a passing acquaintance. A young buck called to Laura from the box of his whisky, but she affected not to hear him.

"I believe Miss Montescue has had good cause for the dismals of late, so you should not castigate her, ma'am."

"I daresay," Laura answered grudgingly.

"But you do know her as well as anyone," he persisted, "and what you could condescend to tell me, if you will—for I am certain sisters enjoy a close degree of intimacy in their conversations—is, do I have reason to hope, in your esteemed opinion?"

The young woman paused to draw a faint sigh as she turned to face him. "My sister has always been one to hold her cards close to her chest, sir, which I regard as a great failing in a female. Myself, I am always open. My feelings are evident for all to discern, which I believe is more usual in a female."

"Quite so."

"However, I am bound to say your feelings in the face of my sister's coolness toward you do you much credit."

He smiled faintly again. "I am indebted to you for saying so, ma'am, but I am not so certain my regard for her will be, in the fullness of time, to my ultimate advantage."

"You must not lose hope, sir."

"It is particularly vexing to me as I have enjoyed connubial bliss, and I am in a fidge to enter into the blessed state once again."

They continued to walk as they conversed. After a moment's thought Laura said, "If you are truly in earnest, Sir Angus . . ."

"Do not doubt it for one moment, ma'am!"

"I can confide in you that Allegra has not totally taken you in dislike, for her objections, as confessed to me, have a hollow sound to them. You may well be obliged to become more insistent. Oh, I do not for one moment believe she is entirely indifferent to you. I'm persuaded no female could retain a cold heart toward a gentleman who evidently cares so deeply. I could not. In my opinion, you have treated her with far too much patience."

"Miss Montescue, I am greatly relieved to hear what you have had to say, and even more indebted to you for your encouragement."

"I have thought upon the matter a great deal of late, you may

252

be sure, and it has occurred to me that my sister's reluctance to encourage you—or indeed any other gentleman who displays a partiality—is due to her unfortunate experience when she set her cap at Sir Dudley Rymington."

"The fellow always appeared to be a ninnyhammer to me. He must be queer in the attic if he preferred Miss Pelham to your sister." He frowned suddenly. "Mayhap there is some connection between Sir Dudley's attachment to your sister and his bout of fisticuffs with Lord Crandon."

As he cast Laura a speculative look her cheeks became pink. "I doubt that, sir."

"Naturally, but unlike you, ma'am, I am not in any position to know their reason, whereas you surely do."

"You may be certain Crandon has not confided it in me," she told him, her manner outraged.

"I would have thought a couple about to be riveted would enjoy a greater degree of intimacy." When she made no reply, he went on, "There are those who are making wagers on the reason for their mill. . . ."

"Oh, how insufferable these gamesters are."

"Indeed," he agreed. "I would have no part in such wagers, you may be sure, so the reason for their fight is of no import I fancy."

Slightly mollified, Laura replied, "That is precisely my opinion of the matter, Sir Angus."

Her face broke into a smile of pleasure a moment later at the sight of Geoffrey Marsham approaching them in the company of a number of his friends.

One of Sir Angus Beane's eyebrows rose a fraction before he said, "I believe I am able to leave you with all good conscience, Miss Montescue. Mr. Marsham will, no doubt, escort you back to your mother's side. Once again, I do thank you most heartily for your good counsel."

Laura turned to him and smiled almost absently, "Oh, it was a pleasure conversing with you, sir. After all, we may yet become connected by marriage."

"You may rely upon it, ma'am," were his parting words.

Laura forgot her conversation with Sir Angus almost immediately when she joined Mr. Marsham and his friends, who were in great spirits and making a good deal of noise with their raucous

253

laughter. Their company, Laura decided, cheered her greatly, being rather less decorous than that of her husband-to-be.

Meanwhile, in another part of the field, Allegra remained in the company of her brother, and whenever they were not engaging in an animated conversation with friends and acquaintances they came upon, she was obliged to listen to Barnaby singing Lady Lucrezia's praises.

At length she was bound to say, laughingly, "Barnaby, you do not have to elaborate on Lady Lucrezia's qualities to me. I am fully aware of them, I assure you."

He looked immediately abashed. "You must consider me a lobcock, but I do beg you to understand that this is the very first time I have felt quite like this."

"It is natural, I own."

She frowned suddenly at the realization that Laura never wished to proclaim Lord Crandon's virtues to anyone who might listen.

"Now, if only you were settled," he said, becoming serious at last. "I would be in high snuff."

"I thought you were!" she responded wryly, and then more seriously, "Oh, Barnaby, I am becoming out of patience with those who seek to see me married. I am perfectly content to wait until the time is right."

He subjected her to an unusually searching look. "Do you truly not mind our sister being married before you?"

"Indeed not. If it is what she wishes, then I can only be truly happy for her."

The young man looked considerably relieved before he said, "I'll warrant Geoffrey Marsham is not. The hoyden insists upon encouraging him even now, and that I fear does not bode well for his equilibrium."

"Today we need not concern ourselves with poor Mr. Marsham, for I left Laura quite content in the barouche with Mama." Suddenly Allegra frowned. "You do not think this sudden re-attachment to Mr. Marsham indicates that she regrets accepting Lord Crandon, do you? Only the other morning Mama confided in me she felt Laura is not suited to becoming married to someone as toplofty as his lordship."

Barnaby threw back his head of tawny curls and laughed

heartily. "What a notion! You're a goosecap even to consider it. Our sister will revel in being Lady Crandon. Can you not see her weighted down with the Crandon jewels, being insufferably condescending to one and all?"

His words made Allegra laugh, too, albeit uneasily. She had no notion from where her unease originated, for she was bound to agree with Barnaby on the matter. Laura had always engaged in haughty mannerisms when it best suited her to do so.

It wasn't possible to discuss the matter further, for they caught sight of Lady Lucrezia coming in their direction at that moment. When she reached them she was breathless with excitement and her eyes were shining.

"How fortunate to catch sight of you so soon after our arrival!" she declared. "Just as I climbed down from the curricle I saw you both walking in our direction."

"Where is Lord Crandon?" Barnaby asked. "Surely he hasn't abandoned you among this rackety crowd."

"Indeed he did not. When he saw you so close by he went immediately to seek out Miss Laura, and I came over to join you. He knew I would be in very good company with my dearest friends."

The crowd erupted into noisy cheers mixed with some jeering. Barnaby said, "That is no doubt the Prince arrived at last. Let us go closer to see him."

"I believe I had best return to Mama," Allegra announced diplomatically, even though Lady Lucrezia looked a trifle crestfallen. "We shall no doubt meet again later."

Allegra wandered away, casting her brother and his love an indulgent look. They appeared so happy in one another's company she could not help but feel wistful as well as pleased for them.

When she declared herself willing to wait for an equitable match, she had meant it sincerely, but all at once she did wonder from where he might come. At the beginning of her first Season there had been any number of young bucks eager to pay court to her, but after her swift attachment to Sir Dudley Rymington, many lost interest, finding themselves more willing sweethearts. Now, like Sir Dudley, they were almost all married, and she had no fancy for any of those who were left.

The familiar cry of the gingerbread seller broke into her disturbed thoughts. "Tiddity-dols, tiddity-dols," he cried as he moved through the crowds, and Allegra dipped into her reticule for a penny to buy a piece.

Most of her acquaintances were now returning to their carriages to witness the balloon's ascent, which was imminent, judging by the excitement evident all around her. She could see that the balloon itself was now almost fully inflated, but she made no haste to return to the carriage, despite having declared her intention of doing so.

After speaking with Lady Lucrezia it was evident the marquess would be there with Mama and Laura, and even though Allegra felt she was now on better terms with him than ever before, the continuation of that situation was dependent upon not being in his company too often, and she still experienced a great feeling of discomfort whenever she was obliged to be in close proximity to him.

The Prince Regent was still making his stately way around the field accompanied by an equerry and his current favorite, Lady Hertford. Although his presence was the reason for this gesture of celebration, he received a mixed greeting, for he was not well liked. Many regretted that the old King was now sufficiently incapacitated by illness to necessitate his rackety son being declared Regent. It was also considered that he treated his wife, Princess Caroline, shockingly, so it was not all cheering for the portly Prince, but there was sufficient of the ton present to make it a tolerable triumph.

"Miss Montescue, I have been seeking you out for an age."

Allegra was so surprised to be confronted by Sir Angus at that moment the gingerbread slipped from her fingers.

"Have no fear for that, my dear, for I shall buy you more," he declared. "As much as you wish."

"It is of no account, sir, for I have eaten sufficient."

When she looked around for an acquaintance who might join them she saw to her dismay that she was some considerable distance from her mother's carriage. So profound were her thoughts, she had walked away from and not back in the direction of the barouche as intended. In fact, it was in this part of the field that the less affluent members of the crowd had gathered.

"I must return to my party," she told him.

"Mrs. Montescue, I may tell you, is quite content. At least that is what she declared to me a short while ago when we conversed, but if you are intent upon joining her, do allow me to accompany you. There are some unruly elements abroad on such occasions."

There was no doubting the truth of that statement, so she did not demur for once. In any event, it was evident he intended to remain at her side however much she protested, and she bowed to the inevitability. She could not for one moment understand why Laura considered him a fitting partner or believed she harbored a secret fondness for him. He did possess, though, if not fortune, an old title, and Allegra suspected that even her mother would not be unreceptive to the notion of having him as a son-in-law. Not for the first time the very notion made her shudder.

"Miss Montescue, I fear you are being very cruel to me," he told her as she walked along in silence. "You give me absolutely no hope for the future."

Still not looking at him she replied, "I regret I cannot, sir."

"I have it in mind you are fearsome of upstaging your sister's nuptials. Mayhap Crandon has even warned you against such a move."

Allegra could not help but laugh at the suggestion, although it was all at once evident to her that he believed it might be so.

"You must surely own, sir, that it would be unfeeling of me to spoil her triumph which is looked to be a considerable one," she agreed at last.

He put one hand on her arm and when she looked up at him, there was an expression in his eyes that she had never noted before, and it disturbed her greatly.

"But what of me, Miss Montescue? Of my feelings? Do I not deserve some consideration? I am in earnest, as you know full well, and I am out of all patience."

"I truly regret that, sir," she answered with a sigh, averting her eyes from his at last, "but I do not wish to marry you, and there's an end to the matter."

Suddenly he smiled, which was disconcerting after her declaration. "You display the greatest unselfishness, but I cannot believe you would not enjoy astonishing everyone with your own marriage."

Allegra's eyes narrowed with surprise as Sir Angus looked at her in triumph and then went on to explain, "If we were to leave here now we can be well on our way to Gretna Green before anyone knows we are gone. Think of the surprise we will occasion in our families and acquaintances."

If he had not looked so utterly serious Allegra would have laughed out loud at his suggestion. As it was she replied in as demure a manner as she could contrive, "No, I thank you. It is not the manner in which I envisage taking a husband, and even if it were, I must reiterate you are not that man, Sir Angus."

"I am persuaded you have not, as yet, thought on the advantages of such a marriage."

Allegra fought hard to contain her exasperation, although she was beginning to wonder if he might be a lunatic. "There are few enough advantages to a marriage between us, I fancy."

"You would have the advantage of being able to attend your sister's wedding as Lady Beane. If that alone does not attract you, do you doubt my ardor, Miss Montescue?"

"No," she admitted with a sigh. "Oh, do forgive me, but a marriage without love, for that is what it would be on my part, cannot be advantageous to either of us. Can you not see that?"

"I can only be aware of the reason for your coldness toward me, but be sure you will soon forget your previous disappointment in my arms, ma'am." He caught hold of her wrist and began to pull her along. "Come, my carriage is waiting nearby. We must waste no more time if we are to reach the border and be back within the sen'night."

"Sir Angus!" she protested, partly outraged and partly afraid. "Have you not heard a word I have spoken? I shall not marry you in any circumstances, and I demand that you unhand me this instant! This is outside of enough."

Sir Angus Beane appeared to be unmoved by her pleas. "Young ladies invariably insist upon being missish, but I see past the protestations to someone willing and eager to be a woman."

At this point in her futile struggle, witnessed by several amused bystanders, she became truly afraid. He was very strong, and only then did she recall he had contracted his first marriage at Gretna in the face of the disapproval of his bride's family.

"Sir Angus, I must protest!"

Allegra continued to struggle, hampering their progress but unfortunately not arresting it. She considered appealing to those nearby for assistance, but feared they were more like to help Sir Angus.

"Sir Angus!"

The voice boomed out and his grip slackened on her wrist but not sufficiently to enable her to disengage herself until an ebony cane crashed down on his arm. With a cry of pain he let her go at last.

The marquess, who had wielded his cane to such effect, looked furious as he confronted Sir Angus. "How dare you treat my future sister-in-law in so cavalier a manner?"

The other man looked almost afraid as he pulled at his coat and made a valiant attempt to smile. "Crandon, what foolishness is this? There is no need to get on your high ropes. Miss Montescue and I were merely funning."

"You have a humor not shared by others, Beane," the marquess replied in clipped tones. "Having traveled all this way I doubt if you will wish to miss the balloon going up, so I will escort Miss Montescue back to her carriage myself."

Still looking somewhat discomposed, Sir Angus tipped his hat and strode away from them, and only at that moment did Allegra allow herself a sigh of relief. When the marquess transferred his attention to her she knew her eyes were still wide with fear and her face pale beneath the brim of her poke bonnet.

"Did he hurt you?" he asked abruptly, and she felt he was angry with her, too.

She shook her head even though her wrist still bore the imprint of Sir Angus's fingers. What is more, she felt the marquess noted it, too. Abruptly he raised her hand, examined it carefully and then, to her astonishment, pressed it to his lips briefly before he allowed it to drop.

"Why was he holding on to you in that manner?" he asked.

"He . . . was taking me to a better vantage point to see the balloon going up."

The look he cast her was a plainly disbelieving one. "I give you fair warning, if I ever catch him setting as much as one finger on your person again, I shall thrash him unmercifully."

Allegra was still reeling somewhat from what had happened,

259

and she heard herself saying, "As you did with Sir Dudley Rymington?"

"In just such a way."

"What reason did you have then?"

"One day I will tell you."

"You may be sure I do not wish to know," she retorted breathlessly, her eyes flashing with green fire.

"If that is, in fact, true, you are the only female in Town who does not."

"You may be certain of it."

"Come, your mother is concerned for your absence," he said a moment later and began to walk away.

After hesitating for a moment or two Allegra had no option but to follow, whereupon he said, "You really must be more discerning in the future in your choice of companion."

Glad as she was for his timely intervention, Allegra gasped. "I resent the implication that you know best who I should choose as an acquaintance, my lord."

"If you find Sir Angus Beane amiable, then I must heartily beg your pardon."

"That is not the point! It does not augur well for the future, when you are married to my sister, if you insist upon approving *my* acquaintances! Constant interfering in my life will be most unwelcome, I assure you!"

A nerve at the corner of his mouth tightened, and Allegra was certain his chin jutted more than was usual. "Very well, Miss Montescue," he replied as the crowd roared nearby, "in the future when I see you with Sir Angus Beane and your face registers the utmost distaste, I shall simply assume you are enjoying his funning."

He strode on ahead swinging his cane. All at once Allegra's eyes filled with tears of despair. He had reverted to his hateful self again after she had almost decided he was tolerable. The disappointment she experienced on that score felt like a physical pain.

Allegra was forced to strive to compose herself when she saw Barnaby and Lady Lucrezia bounding toward them. They were totally unaware of any friction between her and the marquess as they all chattered excitedly between themselves about the balloonist who was now gliding gently away into the distance.

Chapter Ten

*W*hile Allegra had always felt uncomfortable in Lord Crandon's company, she now also dreaded all future encounters with Sir Angus Beane. However, immediately after their encounter in St. George's Field he appeared to have absented himself from fashionable circles, much to Allegra's relief. On this one occasion the marquess's incivility had been of some value to her. She hoped that from now on Sir Angus would be sensible of her disinterest in him and leave her alone.

Allegra had always enjoyed all the diversions available in the Season, but since that day she became rather wary in the event Sir Angus attended. She felt she would not know how to behave in his company and especially feared Lord Crandon's temper if he saw Sir Angus anywhere near to her.

When an invitation was received to an assembly at the home of Lord and Lady Broxbourne, Allegra was able to relax a little, for Lord Broxbourne was a relative of Lord Crandon and as such was unlikely to invite Sir Angus Beane, and as Lady Broxbourne insisted upon filling her house to capacity with guests at all her diversions, it was possible Allegra might evade the marquess, too.

By the time the Montescue party arrived the house was already crowded. The sound of music reached them before their carriage turned into Hanover Square.

As they alighted from the carriage Laura turned to her sister and said, "I do hope you will find the evening diverting, dearest, for it seems to me you have suffered a definite vexation of spirit of late."

Allegra was not pleased to learn her unhappiness had been noticed, especially by Laura who was lately concerned only with matters particular to herself.

"I believe it is just a touch of tiredness that affects me of late," she explained.

The girl looked suddenly coy. "Or mayhap the absence from Town of Sir Angus Beane?"

Allegra gasped with vexation at such a mistaken observation.

"Come along you two," their brother urged. "Let us not miss one moment of the assembly."

Before Allegra could think of a suitably cutting reply, Laura said to Barnaby, who was following with their mother, "Oh, how anxious you are to be with your Lady Lucrezia."

"Do not tease your brother," Mrs. Montescue admonished as the young man's cheeks grew rather ruddy. "In any event, are you not in a similar fidge to be with Lord Crandon?"

"Naturally," Laura replied, though she exhibited no real enthusiasm at the mention of her beloved's name, "but I would not be so unfashionable as to show my impatience."

"Then it is my opinion you cannot truly be in love," Barnaby responded, putting an arm around each of his sisters and hurrying them into the house.

"What a squeeze!" Mrs. Montescue declared as they entered the main salon, which was fairly seething with exotically plumed ladies and elegantly clad gentlemen.

Clad in pink sprigged muslin Allegra was at first fearful, but then she relaxed in the company of several of her acquaintances who made diverting conversation. Lady Lucrezia, she noted, was accompanied by Miss Chapstone, who remained seated in the corner with some of the other chaperons. The sight of Miss Chapstone gave Allegra hope that Lord Crandon had, for some reason, been obliged to cry off.

When Lady Lucrezia succeeded in pushing her way through the crowds, she looked so radiantly happy Allegra actually envied her. "I am so excited, Miss Montescue!" she confided. "Your brother was kind enough to send me a copy of *Childe Harold's Pilgrimage*—as if flowers, marchpane, and comfits were not enough! Now, imagine, I have actually spoken to the poet himself." She nodded in the direction of a crowd that had gathered at the far side of the room. "Is that not truly amazing?"

Allegra could not help but smile as she found Lady Lucrezia's enthusiasm pleasant as well as infectious. "Lord Byron is socially prominent. You are like to encounter him often."

"Unfortunately Lady Caroline Lamb, for some reason I cannot comprehend, seems unwilling to allow anyone too close to him, but I was able to tell him how much I enjoyed reading his poem even though I am not quite sure of what it is about."

As they engaged in a lively discussion of the merits of the new literary sensation, Barnaby came to claim Lady Lucrezia for the next dance. Allegra was still smiling as she watched them go, and it was just then that she caught sight of the marquess who was in conversation with her sister.

He appeared to be listening intently to what Laura was saying, and they seemed very much of one accord. Involuntarily Allegra recalled how he had kissed her hand, something she was unable to put out of her mind however hard she tried. It was a gesture she considered entirely out of character.

"I am out of all patience with my sister," Laura was confiding in a low whisper to her husband-to-be.

"Are you and she on the outs with one another?" he asked, displaying no real interest. "What can she have done to have vexed you so?"

"It is not as you might think, but I cannot help be downish over her attitude toward likely suitors."

"Ah!"

"I am afraid she will be obliged to remain a spinster. This is her second Season, you know."

"If Miss Montescue does not mind the prospect of being an old tabby why should you?"

"Is it not evident why I am so concerned? At the moment she makes a good companion to our mother and nurses Papa devotedly whenever she is called upon to do so, but one day it will be incumbent upon us to care for her." She sighed. "Unmarried females are always a botheration, I find."

"I have always regarded your sister as the least troublesome of females, Laura, and I am persuaded she will continue to be so. Don't get yourself into a pelter over this."

Laura was staring thoughtfully ahead, scarcely heeding his words. "I dare say she will go to Barnaby sometimes and even Lady Lucrezia, if she marries another, for they have become as

263

thick as inkle weavers of late, so it is like the burden will not be entirely ours."

The marquess smiled slightly. "You are so unselfish, my dear."

She flushed with pleasure, unaware of his sarcasm. "You may be certain Allegra is very dear to me and her welfare is of the utmost import, but I am sensible that my duties as a wife are paramount and as *your* wife they will be onerous indeed."

"Quite so," he agreed good-naturedly, smiling ironically.

When she caught sight of Geoffrey Marsham across the room her cheeks grew more pink.

The marquess noted Laura's smile and said, "You mustn't trouble your head over your sister, my dear. It is possible that her future will be more brilliant than anyone yet envisages for her."

"In all truth I cannot conceive of that."

"I am rarely wrong, Laura. It is very like your sister will become more elevated than you. You would not mind that, would you, dear?"

She cast him a curious look before saying, "I had no notion that Mr. Marsham would be here this evening. I was not aware that he was acquainted with either Lord or Lady Broxbourne."

"Nor am I, but he must be," the marquess told her, and then, "Do allow me to fetch you some champagne, Laura. Your glass has been empty for some minutes."

"No, no," she hastened to say. "My cheeks are sufficiently flushed. I thank you, but I am obliged to beg your pardon for a while, for I have espied a very old acquaintance across the room and would have a few words with her."

"By all means do," he told her, but then put one hand on her arm as she made to go, drawing her back toward him. "After all, very soon now you and I will have all the time in the world to enjoy one another's company to the exclusion of everyone else."

Laura's eyes opened wide with alarm as she looked up into his smiling ones before she drew away and hurried across the room leaving the marquess looking sardonic as he watched her go.

Despite her current lack of suitors Allegra did not find herself short of dancing partners. She was known to be surefooted and an amiable partner to boot, so she remained in demand whenever the music struck up. On occasions throughout the evening she encountered other members of her family during the dancing, including her mother, who looked more carefree than she had appeared for some time.

"This may be quite a squeeze, but I am enjoying myself hugely," Mrs. Montescue confided before being whisked away to dance a quadrille.

As Allegra smiled at her mother's retreating figure Lady Broxbourne bore down on her, saying, "My dear Miss Montescue, I have only just now been saying to Mirabel Fossborough that Crandon's alliance with your sister has made him far more amiable than I can ever recall."

Allegra smiled sweetly, enquiring, "Do you really think so, my lady, for in all truth I had not noticed it."

Lady Broxbourne looked a trifle taken aback, and Allegra was glad to be claimed by her next partner and led away to join the set rather than discuss the finer points of Lord Crandon's good nature with his devoted relative.

When a waltz was announced a little later in the evening it caused a good deal of excitement among the guests, for it had only recently been declared respectable by the lofty matrons of the ton, enabling debutantes to participate without causing widespread disapprobation to be heaped on their heads.

Allegra could not help but smile as she watched the laughing, blushing ladies being led onto the dance floor for the only dance that required a gentleman actually to hold his partner in his arms.

The first time Allegra recalled waltzing had been with Sir Dudley Rymington prior to the announcement of his betrothal to Petrina Pelham. The waltz was not often performed, for even now there was still a belief among some members of Society that the dance was in some way immoral. Allegra had always thoroughly enjoyed it, but she was glad to see that Barnaby and Lady Lucrezia were watching from the edge of the dance floor. It would not have been proper for a girl not yet out to participate in this particular dance.

"Miss Montescue, our dance, I think."

She gasped when she turned to see Lord Crandon towering over her. After their last encounter she had certainly not looked to stand up with him for any of the dances. The thought of dancing the waltz with him was truly shocking to her.

"I do not recall you engaging me, my lord."

He looked amused. "From what I observe you are not engaged for this dance."

"What makes you so certain?" she challenged.

He looked even more amused which irritated her. "Why, Miss Montescue, any gentleman so engaged would have already claimed you."

Allegra drew a deep sigh before informing him in an even voice that did not entirely hide her irritation, "I do not wish to dance the waltz. I do not like it."

"That is not my understanding after observing you on various occasions, and ever since Lady Jersey waltzed at Almack's no debutante need worry about the consequences of what was once considered to be an indiscretion."

"I do not concern myself with Lady Jersey," she retorted, "or, indeed, for the opinion of anyone else."

"Then it is evidently me whom you find unacceptable as a partner."

Allegra smiled tightly, avoiding meeting those irony-filled eyes. "If you insist upon thinking so I shall be unable to persuade you otherwise, I am sure."

"Did we not, the other evening, agree upon an accord, ma'am?" he asked in a soft voice that did not in any way disguise the cold note that had entered his manner.

Once again Allegra smiled. "It did not, I believe, include waltzing, my lord."

She would have brushed past him, only he stood foursquare in her path. "I think it only fair to inform you, ma'am, that I regard your attitude as dismissive."

At last Allegra looked directly at him. "It was intended that you should."

"I see," he breathed, and she shivered slightly, sensing in him a dangerous anger, but something drove her on.

"Just because you are to marry my sister does not mean I should cease to dislike you. It is regrettable, I own, and a fault in my character I dare say, but it is also a fact I am unable to change however hard I may try. Now, be pleased to allow me past."

"No, by jove, I will not!" When her eyes opened wide in alarm he added, "At least I will not until you explain the reason for this unwarranted attack, which I do not believe I have either earned or deserve."

She now drew a sigh of resignation, realizing it would be as well for them to air their grievances once and for all. Those around them were so intent upon either participating in the waltz or watching those who did that little attention was being given to Allegra and the marquess, who appeared to be enjoying just an animated conversation.

"Yes, I daresay you are perplexed," she answered at last. "Your confounded arrogance would have me like you even for the wrong you have done me."

"Miss Montescue! I must protest!"

"To be plain, my lord, I can neither forgive nor forget that you, in some manner, induced Sir Dudley Rymington to offer for Miss Pelham rather than me."

"Good grief!" he exclaimed, looking truly amazed. "I should have thought you would wish to display your appreciation rather than your anger."

Allegra's face plainly registered her shock, for this was not the response she would have expected. "You do not deny it?"

"No, indeed, I do not."

She looked away in distress and tears came unbidden to her eyes although why she should be so shocked at his admission she could not quite understand. Perhaps she had hoped she was mistaken in believing him guilty after all.

"Oh, you are abominable!" she whispered, clenching her hands into fists at her side. "My sister is to be pitied heartily in her choice of husband."

"Would you truly want one so easily swayed in his resolve?"

"You and Sir Dudley are both the most despicable gentlemen I have ever encountered," she declared. "I cannot conceive why you should wish to behave in so horrid a manner."

His expression gave nothing of his feelings away as he answered, "It is held to be my nature, is it not?"

His answer maddened her beyond belief, for she was certain he was mocking her. Before she lost her temper entirely, Allegra did brush past him and this time he made no effort to prevent her going. Her cheeks were red with fury as she pressed her way through the crowds in an effort to escape his odious presence, which would only be a temporary respite at best. She was fated to meet him at every turn. She was so angry and upset she didn't even notice that a couple of her friends attempted to attract her attention.

The insolence of the man, she fumed, to admit his complicity in spoiling her chance of marriage, to revel so blatantly in his wickedness. It was beyond her belief, and Allegra could not recall ever being so angry before in her life. He was far more evil than she had imagined in her bleakest moments, and she despaired of her sister's future.

On her way out of the ballroom she glanced back to see him leading Mrs. Radleigh into the whirling throng of dancers, and then she hurried out in the hope that a little fresh air would calm her heaving breast and cool her flaming cheeks. If fortune was for once kind to her, she might be able to enjoy her solitude until the end of the evening, which had suddenly become an ordeal to be endured rather than a carefree diversion.

Almost blindly she stumbled along until she found a quiet spot where the music was just a distant sound. Allegra sank back against a marble pillar, taking quick gulps of cool air into her lungs. The future did not bode well if she was forced to be in the marquess's company at every turn, and there was no doubt, as he was soon to be her brother-in-law, it would be necessary, if only occasionally. How could she possibly bear it? she asked herself.

When she closed her eyes she could see his mocking look as plainly as if he were still standing in front of her. She disliked him with good reason, but she could not for anything understand why he should hate her so. He was madly in love with Laura and appeared to like Barnaby well enough to allow him to pay court to his sister. Allegra could not help but wonder what was lacking in her that had incurred so strong a dislike in him.

Her wretched thoughts were interrupted at last by the sound of a soft chuckle nearby, which caused her to blink back her unshed tears, adjust her paisley shawl, and check her curls for disarray with a quick touch of her hand.

In a determined manner she straightened her back and raised her head in the event she was seen, aware that she had inadvertently stumbled upon an assignation.

As they were half-hidden in an alcove, it was only when she

moved away that she noticed who the couple happened to be. Clasped tightly in each other's arms and kissing with a passion that took Allegra aback were Barnaby and Lady Lucrezia.

Allegra felt she must have uttered some small noise borne of her shock, but the couple remained unaware of anyone nearby. For a few moments she was shocked at the impropriety of what they were about, and then Allegra felt nothing but relief that it was she and not Lady Lucrezia's brother who had seen them.

When it became apparent they were too lost in their ardor to notice anyone, she walked back toward the ballroom, her mind full of agitation, although it was for quite a different reason than before. She was just about to go back into the ballroom when she caught sight of the marquess standing near the entrance in conversation with Mrs. Radleigh and several other people of his acquaintance, so she immediately drew back before he could see her and walked a little way in the other direction, her mind in a turmoil.

As she wandered aimlessly she resolved to give her brother a severe trimming at the earliest opportunity. She would acquaint him in no small measure with the dangers of trifling with the Marquess of Crandon's only, beloved sister. Feeling satisfied that this was the correct course to take in the matter, Allegra decided to try to return to the ballroom once more, but as she turned on her heel she experienced a feeling of intense mortification at the sight of Laura in the company of Mr. Marsham ahead of her.

They were not, like the other couple, kissing, but Laura certainly had the look of a woman who had recently been kissed very thoroughly. Mr. Marsham had his arm about her waist while she rested her head contentedly upon his shoulder, and he was whispering to her in a manner that could only be described as intimate.

With Barnaby and Lady Lucrezia, Allegra had not cared if they saw her, but on this occasion she did not wish to be seen and to be obliged to confront her sister. It was best if she pretended she did not know Laura was being untrue to her future husband, and, accordingly, she moved quickly away.

Several people were coming out of the ballroom as Allegra once again attempted to return, and they appeared to be rather the worse for drink. In their stumbling haste they almost swept her off her feet and she reeled back, only to find herself being steadied by the last person in the world she wished to encounter, the marquess.

"You look a trifle flushed, Miss Montescue," he told her as he gazed down at her. "I fear I have put you out of countenance. Allow me to take you outside for a few moments."

In normal circumstances she would have been quick to absent herself from his company, but she was more concerned for the well-being of the two young couples, and when he began to lead her back toward the hall a ripple of lunatic laughter bubbled up in her throat. She contrived to suppress it, but her voice was a trifle hoarse when she managed to protest, "No! No, not out there. I'd as lief go onto the terrace, if it is all the same to you, my lord. It is a trifle hot in here and I do feel unsteady. You'd oblige me by offering me your arm."

One dark eyebrow quirked upward in surprise as he replied, crooking his arm obligingly, "My pleasure, ma'am."

While he escorted her toward the French window Allegra glanced worriedly behind her. There was no sign of either young couple who were, no doubt, still enjoying each other's company.

When they reached the terrace, they interrupted yet another couple who had sought solitude in which to tryst. When Allegra and the marquess came out of the ballroom the other two returned, looking both amused and embarrassed.

Although she was glad to have averted a catastrophe of gigantic proportions, Allegra was immediately discomforted to find herself alone with him and so turned away to take in deep gulps of cool air that were more welcome than she had envisaged. A moment later when she realized he was watching her she wondered what she should say now.

"Shall I fetch Mrs. Montescue out to attend you?" he asked, looking at her with some concern.

She managed to shake her head. "I am perfectly recovered now, I thank you. I merely felt the heat momentarily. You may return to the ballroom if you wish."

"I do not wish. I have no intention of leaving you here, but you must have felt the heat sorely indeed to solicit the help of one who is so abominable to you."

At the sight of the mocking gleam she detected in his look the all-too-familiar anger welled up inside her, and she made to brush past him and return to the other guests. He put two hands on her shoulders to stay her, staring down into her eyes.

"No, you shan't escape me so easily, you little vixen."

"Lord Crandon, I demand you let me go! Have you not yet injured me sufficiently?"

"I doubt if your injury can begin to compare with mine. After being roundly set down by you on so many occasions of late, Miss Montescue, I demand recompense and I declare I shall have it!"

All at once Allegra felt afraid and her heart was beating noisily within her breast. He had a well-earned reputation for ruthlessness. She had seen for herself the result of his fight with Sir Dudley, heard him threaten Sir Angus, who had taken him seriously enough to absent himself from town, and she feared desperately for her sister and brother should they be discovered and incur his wrath. It had even been rumored he had once shot a man in a duel. What revenge for perceived insults would he inflict upon her, she wondered?

"You would not dare!" she challenged.

"Dare?" he echoed with a harsh laugh. "Of course I dare. Who is there to stop me doing exactly what I wish? Not even your razor-edged tongue, young lady."

She made one last vain attempt to free herself from his grip before his mouth came down upon hers. His fingers chafed her shoulders through the thin muslin of her gown, but the harsh touch of his lips on hers aroused in her a feeling other than outrage. It was not until they were interrupted by another couple seeking solitude that she was able to tear herself away from his grip, which had ceased to be odious the moment his lips had touched hers.

When she reached the window she paused to glance back, to find him glowering darkly after her, and then she rushed back into the ballroom to escape a situation she could not begin to understand. Escaping the maelstrom of her own feelings was not going to be quite so simple.

Chapter Eleven

"*M*ama, I do wish you would not fuss so," Allegra complained. "There is very little wrong with me."

Allegra was sitting up in her four-poster bed, propped up on lace-edged pillows. At frequent intervals her mother insisted upon putting her hand to Allegra's brow.

"Dr. Pomfret declares you have a mild fever, dearest, and insists that you remain in bed until it abates. How unfortunate it was he had called to see your papa this morning."

"Dr. Pomfret calls upon Papa *every* morning." Suddenly Allegra looked up at her mother in alarm. "Papa does not know I am indisposed, does he?"

Mrs. Montescue's eyes rolled upward. "It would be more than I dare do to tell him. Normally you have such a strong constitution, but I must own our social life of late is sufficient to make an end of the most sturdy morale. Now, dearest, you must stay here and rest as much as you are able."

Gladly Allegra laid her head back on the pillow, drawing an imperceptible sigh. Of course, this could prove to be a most welcome respite. As long as she remained indisposed, she would not be obliged to be in Lord Crandon's odious company.

The very thought of him caused her cheeks to flame. She had been loath to think it, but there was no doubt now that he and Laura thoroughly deserved one another.

"There is no mistake," Mrs. Montescue was saying, "you do have a fever. You are being very brave about it, but you must have a care for your health. I shall go and ask Cook to prepare some beef tea."

After tapping lightly at the door, Laura put her head around the crack. "So you are awake. May I come in?"

In truth, Allegra was not at all anxious to see her sister, but nevertheless answered, "Please do."

When she came further into the room Allegra was amazed to note how carefree she appeared. Allegra could not imagine how it was possible. It appeared her sister was about to marry one man while still harboring a fondness for another. It was not so remarkable a situation, except that Laura seemed determined to enjoy both an elevated marriage and the company of her young lover. It made Allegra wonder if Lord Crandon, who had been indulgent of Laura so far, would continue to give rein to her wishes in this matter. If so it would be quite uncharacteristic of him in Allegra's opinion, as was his indifference to whatever Laura did now.

"Do you feel so very ill?" Laura asked, displaying true sympathy as she peered worriedly at her sister.

All at once Allegra regretted her unkind thoughts, and she forced a smile to her lips. "Not so very."

"You poor dear. It is so unlike you to take to your bed."

"This is just a temporary indisposition, so you must not concern yourself. I have not as yet been given notice to quit; I'm just a trifle off the hinges this morning."

She had, however, suffered an almost sleepless night, first furiously attempting to fight off the memories of the marquess's harsh kisses and then, in desperation, trying to blot out from her mind the recollection of her own enjoyment of them. Then, when she did manage to fall asleep at last, it was to dream of being pursued by the marquess while Laura chased him, followed by Mr. Marsham and Sir Angus Beane.

When she awoke with a start her head pounded and she was soaked in perspiration. Come the morning small wonder she had not felt well enough to climb out of bed and wanted only to languish beneath the sheets.

Laura sat down at the side of the bed while Mrs. Montescue continued to fuss. "I shall stay with Ally, Mama, if you wish to attend Papa or any other errand. It is such a long time since Ally and I enjoyed a coze together, although I declare it is a pity one of us has to be indisposed to bring it about."

"Your sister hasn't touched a morsel of food this morning," Mrs. Montescue complained, "so I had best set about procuring some for her."

"I really couldn't eat even the tiniest morsel, Mama," Allegra protested.

"You will take some beef tea." Her mother started toward the door, but paused to add, "I have it in mind this summer at Wisby is just not going to be the same without you, Laura. Papa was only saying so this morning, and I was bound to agree with him."

"Don't get into a fret about it, Mama," the girl replied. "You can all come to Crandon Park to stay with *us*."

She cast them both a beatific smile, but Allegra looked horrified at the thought of spending languid summer days under the brooding gaze of Laura's new husband. Husband! The thought gave her a nasty jolt, knowing at that moment that she was bound to find his company even more unbearable when he was Laura's husband.

"I hardly think Lord Crandon would welcome his bride's relatives to Crandon Park—at least not this year when he is still an April gentleman," Mrs. Montescue told her with a smile as she left the room at last.

Laura's good-natured smile faded somewhat then. "Oh, how tedious it will be," she lamented. "I wish Mama had not reminded me of it."

Whereas Allegra would normally tease her sister, now she addressed her more seriously. "All newly married couples enjoy a degree of solitude, Laura. You should be looking forward to it."

"That is all very well," the girl replied, avoiding meeting her sister's searching look, "but I am not enamored with the joys of rusticating, as you know full well."

"Surely it is different when one is newly married. You will relish the solitude in Lord Crandon's company."

"Oh, I do wish you would not go on so about it, Ally." Allegra's eyes opened wide with surprise. "Crandon will wish to ride out every day, which will not suit me at all. No doubt I shall be left to visit the poor or keep Lady Lucrezia out of mischief. That will be better than riding, I daresay, although it is like Lady Lucrezia will accompany him or take me on one of those botanizing expeditions she prates on about."

"Shall you dislike it excessively?" Allegra asked, and she could not help but feel amused at her sister's complaints, for all at once Crandon Park sounded idyllic to her.

"You know full well I will."

274

"Then mayhap you should consider crying off this marriage, for staying at Crandon Park will be expected of you."

Laura looked totally confounded. "Is your attic to let, Ally? Cry off marrying Crandon? I am not such a goosecap. He is the catch of the Season—of any Season. Everyone says so."

Her sister eyed her soberly from the bed. "That is not the sole justification for marriage in my opinion."

"It certainly is mine!" Laura retorted. "I do hope this elevated marriage will not cause envy in you of all people, Allegra."

"Oh, Laura, do you know me so little?" Allegra asked.

To her credit the girl did look abashed then. "I do beg your pardon, dearest. I should not have flown up into the boughs. My accusation was an unworthy one. Even if it was in your nature you could not envy me a man you dislike so heartily." As Allegra began to toy with a loose thread on the counterpane her sister went on, "Do you believe a gentleman can be foxed without showing any sign of it?"

Allegra looked up sharply then, her eyes narrowing. "It is not a matter to which I have addressed much thought."

"Then I beg you to do so now."

"I daresay it is possible although not like. Why do you ask?"

"The other day when I rode in the Park with Geo—Mr. Marsham, do you recall that Crandon arrived just beforehand, expecting me to go with *him*?"

At the recollection Allegra's cheeks grew hot again. She would always remember that day as being one of the rare occasions she and the marquess enjoyed any felicity together.

"Yes, I recall it," she answered in a muted tone.

"Do you think he was foxed?"

Allegra couldn't help but smile. "I don't think so, but I am persuaded his lordship enjoys a bottle as do most other gentlemen."

"I am persuaded he must have been bosky, for I can think of no other explanation."

"Explanation of what, dearest?" Allegra asked, her brow knitted into a frown.

"When Mr. Marsham arrived he declared he had seen Crandon not an hour earlier and had then informed him, out of politeness, his intention of taking me riding in the Park. I cannot, in that

275

event, conceive how he could have forgotten so soon after unless he was foxed."

Allegra stared at her sister blankly for a moment or two before another knock at the door heralded the arrival of Lady Lucrezia, and Allegra was never more glad to see her, not only for her own sake but in order to end the uncomfortable conversation.

"May I come in?" she asked timidly.

"Pray do," Allegra invited. "I am not accustomed to staying abed, and I need diverting constantly. It is an awesome task, I warn you."

As Lady Lucrezia came further into the room she confided, "When your house steward told me of your indisposition, I was afraid you might be horribly ill, although I could not truly conceive of it. You seemed in such high snuff when you were dancing last night."

"It really is only a trifle," Allegra assured her, "but Mama insisted in calling in Dr. Pomfret when he came to see Papa, and he diagnosed a fever, although I am not so convinced."

"You are not a physician," Laura pointed out, "so how could you possibly know?"

"In any event I am obliged to stay abed. If you are able to stay for a while you are very much welcome."

"I was on my way to Oxford Street with Miss Chapstone, when I felt I must call in to see my friends and ascertain that they, too, had a most enjoyable evening at Lord and Lady Broxbourne's. They are cousins of ours, you know."

"It was quite splendid," Laura concurred, but Allegra made no reply.

Laura got to her feet, saying, "Now I am able to leave my sister in such congenial company, I believe I shall go about my own errands for a while."

"I will stay for as long as Miss Montescue wishes," Lady Lucrezia assured her, her eyes wide beneath the brim of her poke bonnet.

Her eyes, so like those of her brother, were always bright and never brooding or filled with mockery, Allegra thought, experiencing the now familiar stab of dismay.

"In that event I shall leave you two to enjoy your coze," Laura

276

said, smiling sweetly as she gave up her seat to her future sister-in-law.

When she had gone the girl sighed with satisfaction. "I do look forward so much to have the most amiable sister-in-law, Miss Montescue. I cannot credit my good fortune."

Allegra managed a faint smile as she asked, "Are you certain you are able to stay? I would not for anything wish to prevent your continuing your shopping expedition."

Lady Lucrezia laughed and held up her hand to stay any further protest. "I have, in fact, little shopping to do, ma'am. 'Tis only that Crandon is at home this morning, and I am very much afraid he is somewhat out of humor today."

"Is that out of the ordinary, my lady?" Allegra could not help but retort.

The girl laughed in her good-natured fashion. "Oh, indeed it is. I have no notion why he is so Friday-faced, but to be plain, Miss Montescue, he is as cross as two sticks this morning, and it seemed only prudent to absent myself for a while in order to allow him to regain his good spirits. However, the alternative is the company of Miss Chapstone who, I own, is a saint, but a trifle dour for my true liking. I have come to enjoy far more diverting company since my arrival in London."

Her manner could not help but rally Allegra's spirits, although she didn't know whether to be surprised or not that Lucrezia's brother remained in something of a pelter this morning.

"Rest assured, my lady," she replied, "you are always welcome at Montescue House whenever you feel you need a refuge."

The offer appeared to dismay the girl somewhat. "Oh, Miss Montescue, I would not for anything wish you to think my brother is often in a taking, for I assure you he has the sweetest disposition of any gentleman I know."

"I would not wish to gainsay you, my lady, for you have the greater knowledge of his nature."

Suddenly Lady Lucrezia dimpled with delight. "How splendid it will be when Crandon is wed and you all come to Crandon Park!"

Such a sentiment, so genuinely expressed, caused Allegra to shudder. However was it going to be possible to escape the spectre of a stay at Crandon Park in the company of that most hateful of men? she asked herself. As much as it was against her spirited nature, Allegra was beginning to suspect the only way out was to become as chronic an invalid as her father. She would not be the first spinster to resort to such means in order to escape an unsatisfactory existence.

"I do hope you will be recovered enough to attend Covent Garden Opera House on Friday evening," Lady Lucrezia was saying.

"We have no plans to go as far as I recall," Allegra replied, experiencing a modicum of relief at that knowledge.

"That is not the fact as I understand it, ma'am. My brother has issued an invitation for you all to share his box."

As Allegra's eyes opened wide with horror at the news, she didn't doubt the fever would linger until after that event.

"You must know Mrs. Siddons is appearing and also Mr. Kemble," the girl went on enthusiastically. "I am all of a fidge to see them, I am bound to confess. Imagine! The greatest actor and actress on the English stage and I am going to be privileged to see them!"

"I don't doubt it will be the most splendid evening, but I am not so sure I will feel well enough to attend."

"Oh, do not say so, for it will be my first visit to the theater since my arrival in London."

"No doubt you will be able to tell me all about it on Saturday. I shall look forward to it. You must strive to recall all you see and hear, for it is bound to be a brilliant social occasion quite apart from the quality of the performance you will see."

"If you are not able to go, you may be sure I will remain here at your side to bear you company."

"Oh, no," Allegra protested with a shaky laugh. "I could not allow you on any account to miss such a splendid diversion."

Lady Lucrezia's eyes flashed with passion. It was easy for Allegra to see why Barnaby had fallen so quickly and completely in love with her.

"I will not be gainsaid, Miss Montescue."

There was something about the jut of her chin that painfully reminded Allegra of the marquess. Even so, her heart was all at once filled with fondness for the girl.

"Since my arrival in London you have been my greatest ally.

278

Miss Laura, naturally, has been kindness itself, though of course she is much occupied by matters pertaining to her wedding, but you have given unstintingly of your time, which is much appreciated, I assure you."

"It has been a pleasure, my lady. I enjoy your company enormously. You always serve to divert me."

"Precisely. That is why I cannot abandon you in your hour of need. Be assured, my dearest friend, if you are unable by virtue of your indisposition to attend the theater on Friday I shall remain here to bear you company. In any event, I could not possibly enjoy it knowing you were confined to your bed and suffering all manner of megrims."

Chagrined, Allegra sank back into the pillows. It was obvious she was not destined to escape the ordeal of being in close contact with Lord Crandon. As Laura intended to marry him in the near future and as Allegra wished to continue her friendship with Lady Lucrezia, she supposed she must grow accustomed to him, as difficult as that was likely to be.

"Let us hope, then, that I am sufficiently recovered, for I would not want for anything to deprive you of your first visit to the theater," Allegra heard herself saying.

"We enjoyed occasional theatricals at Bousefield, which is close to our home, but that is not in the least like Mrs. Siddons and Mr. Kemble. Sometimes itinerant mummers came our way, especially at Christmas time, and that was most enjoyable."

"They do, too, at Wisby," Allegra told her. "When we were children we often put on our own theatricals with Mama, just to divert Papa when he was in a fit of the dismals. It was greatly diverting for all of us, I am bound to admit."

The young girl looked wistful. "That must have been quite wonderful. There were only the two of us, and Crandon is so much older, we were scarce children together. In fact, my first memory of him was as he went away to Eton."

Allegra cast her friend a sympathetic smile as she continued to look wistful. Then the door opened and Laura came back in.

"I am so pleased you are still here, my lady. I wanted to show you and Allegra what I have been preparing for my trousseau."

Lady Lucrezia began to exclaim over Laura's handiwork as

she held out for approval a night-shift of the sheerest lawn. Laura had been engaged in attaching lace to the hem.

"It is quite breathtaking," Lady Lucrezia declared, but for some reason Allegra could not summon up as much enthusiasm, and she looked away.

"I can continue with my sewing while sitting here with you," Laura decided, casting them both a smile. "It is a pity you are not yet come out else you'd be able to regale us with the latest *on dits*."

All at once the younger girl began to look troubled as she got to her feet. "Truly I do not wish to leave, but poor Miss Chapstone is left downstairs to kick her heels."

"You must not concern yourself so much with servants, my lady," Laura told her. "They are always obliged to await your convenience for as long as is necessary."

"I cannot look upon Chappie as a servant, although I suppose that is what she is." She looked more uncertain as she directed her attention to Laura. "I did wish to ask you a most impertinent question, Miss Laura. I do hope you will not take it amiss."

Both sisters looked intrigued, and Laura laughed. "Impertinent, my lady? Surely not?"

The girl bit her lip and toyed nervously with her reticule. "It is of a . . . very personal matter, I fear."

Glancing wryly at Allegra, Laura drew in a deep breath. "Mayhap you'd be best served speaking to Mama."

At this suggestion the girl became agitated. "Oh no, I could not. It is you I must ask."

"I'm persuaded Laura won't mind what you say," Allegra told her, smiling encouragingly.

The girl lowered her eyes. "I just wondered if . . . what you felt . . . oh, this is most disturbing to me!" She looked directly at Laura at last before blurting out, "What is it like when Crandon kisses you?"

Allegra made a strangled noise in her throat, which appeared not to have been noted by the other two.

Her sister's eyes opened wide with shock. "Lady Lucrezia, I must protest! I am truly shocked you should ask that question of me. You should know your brother well enough to be aware he is a consummate gentleman. He would never take such liberties with me before our wedding!"

Throughout Laura's tirade the young girl's face had become suffused with color. "I do beg your pardon, Miss Laura. Indeed, I do. I never intended to outrage your sensibilities." She nodded to Allegra and made haste toward the door. "Good day, ladies."

"That baggage is becoming a trifle too rag-mannered for my liking," Laura declared as soon as the door had closed behind her.

"You were far too hard on her," Allegra accused, finding her voice at last.

"She had no right to quiz me in that disgusting manner. It does not augur well for the future, I fear."

"You must see that she meant no harm and did not deserve such a setdown."

Laura looked indignant. "Tush! It is shabby of her to make mention of such a matter. I shall be obliged to ask Crandon to take her to task. He would not wish her to be such a hoyden."

Allegra sat up in the bed and shook her head frantically. "Oh, I do beg you not to mention it to him. Laura, you must vow you will not make any attempt to put him out of countenance with his sister."

When her sister feigned weakness and sank back into the pillows, Laura's outraged expression gave way to a smile. "Very well, if you wish it. I would not want to make your fever worse, but you must own that there are moments when Lady Lucrezia behaves as if she is still in leading strings."

Allegra closed her eyes with relief. Her sister took up her sewing as she sat down. "Did Lady Lucrezia tell you we are invited to join them in the Crandon box at Covent Garden on Friday evening . . . ?"

Chapter Twelve

*B*ecause Allegra remained confined in her room for as long as was possible, an opportunity to give Barnaby the promised trimming did not present itself until the very evening they were due to go to the theater.

Up until the very last moment she had hoped she would not, after all, be obliged to go to Covent Garden and share a box with Lord Crandon, but Lady Lucrezia remained adamant she would stay with her at Montescue House if Allegra was still too indisposed to attend. Despite the temptation to feign illness she really could not deprive her friend of an opportunity of seeing Mrs. Siddons, especially since the famous actress had recently declared her intention to retire in the very near future.

When Allegra came down the stairs that evening, with as much enthusiasm as must have been displayed by aristocrats on their way to the guillotine, she saw that her brother was waiting in the hall dressed in evening clothes and evidently eager to be gone. On hearing her step he turned on his heel, an engaging smile immediately coming to his lips.

"Ally! You look so fetching this evening I can scarce believe you've been off the hinges for the past few days. Your complexion is quite pink, and what a splendid gown you're wearing!"

"There is nothing wrong with me now," she answered shortly, "but I am bound to say you certainly displayed no eagerness to come and comfort me while I was confined to my bed."

The young man looked wry. "I do beg your pardon most heartily, ma'am, but life at the present is all hurry-scurry. I was persuaded you would understand and forgive me." When her expression remained unyielding he went on, "You're surely not going to give me a setdown for such a trifle."

"Not for that, Barnaby, but I do intend to ring a peal over you for making free with Lady Lucrezia at the Broxbournes' the other evening."

His eyes opened wide and he began to bluster. "Good grief! What can you mean?"

"I believe you know full well. I saw you both in the alcove, although you were too well occupied to note my presence close by."

"Oh Lord!" he declared, his cheeks growing ruddy. "What a case of pickles. I'm really in the suds now."

"Just be thankful it was I who saw you there and not Lady Lucrezia's brother."

"Do not speak to me of such a possibility, I beg of you."

"Even if it had not been Lord Crandon who saw you, it could have been one of any number of people only too happy to stir up the coals and curry favor with his lordship by cutting you up."

"Now you are alarming me, sis!"

She put one hand on his arm. "I do beseech you to take the utmost care, dearest, in the future, for the happiness of you both is very close to my heart. Lord Crandon is not a man to allow you such freedom. I dare not even think on what he would do if he comes to hear of it, for I have seen him deal with others who displease him."

The young man nodded and swallowed noisily. "I know it, Ally, but you've got to understand I did not plan to act in an unchivalrous manner. Lady Lucrezia is much beloved by me. I would not harm her in any way, you may be certain."

"I believe you, Barnaby, but that does not mitigate the wrong you did."

"I know, but you have to understand I couldn't resist her loveliness any longer. It's a result of being so much in love. I lost my reason for the moment."

"A long moment," Allegra reminded him not unkindly, and he looked sheepish.

"That kind of thing happens when a fellow is lost for love. You can understand that, can't you, sis?"

She looked away in dismay, murmuring, "Just do not allow your impulsiveness to spoil your future happiness. It would do neither of you any good."

Barnaby grinned, his good spirits revived. "You may rest

assured I will exercise restraint in the future, however difficult it might be. I was not proud of myself, but I have it in mind Crandon would understand all too well. After all, he is a man in love himself. You cannot gammon me into believing he does not snatch a few kisses from our sister when the opportunity arises, not an out-and-outer like our future brother-in-law."

His words made Allegra feel more wretched than ever. It was fortunate she was not obliged to reply, for just then her brother cried, "Another ravishing creature! What good fortune is mine tonight."

Mrs. Montescue blushed as she came down the last few stairs. "What a bag of moonshine! 'Tis to be hoped you do not fill Lady Lucrezia with such flummery."

The young man's eyes sparkled and there was no sign of his penitence now. "Why else would she have thrown her cap over the windmill, Mama?"

When, a moment later, Laura came down the stairs to join them, the party moved to the waiting carriage. Allegra observed her sister closely during the journey to Covent Garden and believed she had never looked lovelier. There certainly seemed to be no conflict between her feelings for Mr. Marsham and Lord Crandon.

It was then that she began to wonder if she had been foolish to allow her sister's attachment to Mr. Marsham to trouble her. After all, Laura was given the opportunity to choose between them and had seemed firm in her decision to become betrothed to the marquess. She would not be the first debutante to decide upon position rather than love when accepting an offer of marriage. To do otherwise was often construed as eccentricity.

"Every one of us is in high snuff this evening, and yet you are as mute as a fish," Laura told her sister as the carriage began its long crawl to set down outside the theater. "I do trust you are fully recovered from your fever and not about to relapse."

"No, I am perfectly well," Allegra replied, putting aside the thoughts that so often teased her of late.

"As long as you do not wear the willow for Sir Dudley Rymington."

The notion made Allegra laugh. "What a crack-brained notion!"

"I am considerably relieved to hear you say so." Laura smiled slyly then. "Mayhap you are in love at last. You have the look of a moon calf about you."

Again Allegra laughed, the memory of the marquess's kisses uncomfortably vivid in her mind. No amount of effort over the past few days had succeeded in erasing the memory from her mind.

"What taradiddle!" she scoffed.

"The choice before you is not such a great one, so you must endeavor to take the greatest care you are not left on the shelf."

"There are worse fates," her sister countered.

"I cannot conceive of one."

"Mayhap you will before long."

"Ladies! Ladies!" their mother pleaded. "This pulling of caps is most unseemly."

"I find it deuced diverting," Barnaby interpolated and earned a dark look from all three ladies in the carriage.

"Do not tease your sister, Laura," Mrs. Montescue scolded. "She is bound to feel a little less robust than is usual after a bout of fever. That is all that ails her, I am sure."

"Allegra was teasing *me*," the younger girl protested. "She insinuated that marriage to Crandon is worse than being left an old maid."

"Those of us who are fortunate enough to be settled in love are always seeking to make a match for others," Barnaby said, addressing his younger sister.

Mrs. Montescue cast a worried glance at her elder daughter. "When Allegra decides upon a match, I don't doubt she will be only too pleased to tell us, and not one moment before."

Barnaby's eyes sparkled. "I have a notion she will one day surprise us, much as Laura did."

"Why was everyone so surprised when I made such an elevated match?" Laura complained. "Anyone would think it was beyond the bounds of reason, which it patently was not because I am about to marry one of the wealthiest men in England and become a marchioness to boot!" She fixed her sister with a hard look as Allegra stared down at her satin reticule that rested in her lap. "If you do not take steps soon to encourage someone you may be obliged to take any respectable gentleman who offers for you."

"To me social position is not everything," Allegra told her. "Happiness is of far more import to me."

"I dare say you are correct," Laura replied, looking suddenly crestfallen.

The carriage jerked to a standstill, and the moment the steps were let down Barnaby got out and handed the ladies out of the carriage. A great many people were attending the performance and streamed in a colorful throng into the lobby of the theater. The crowds were so great Allegra did not immediately see the marquess standing at the top of the steps, waiting to greet his guests.

When she looked up and saw him he appeared taller and broader than she recalled, but his strength was no illusion. She had felt it in his hands that had held her so firmly, and in his lips when they pressed upon hers with such cruel passion.

At the memory that haunted her with maddening persistence Allegra shivered slightly, and then she looked away, for it seemed his eyes bored into her very soul, challenging her in some way she could not comprehend. There was no expression she could read upon his face, which did not surprise her. Such ill use came naturally to him, and she was convinced that the incident that had affected her reason had not even happened for him.

A moment later his face relaxed into a smile as he greeted first Mrs. Montescue and then Laura, raising each of their hands to his lips in turn. Hovering behind them Allegra soon discovered she was not even now destined to escape his attention and she would be obliged to strive not to let her hatred of him be apparent to her relatives.

His eyes surveyed her with insolence she noted as he raised her hand to his lips. "Miss Montescue," he said as he allowed it to drop, "how glad I am to see you so well recovered from your indisposition. Laura and Lucrezia have both informed me you became quite ill soon after my cousin's assembly. I am, therefore, much honored you have decided to join us this evening."

She nodded briefly as she averted her eyes. His company had always been insufferable to her, but now, as she had suspected, it was intolerable. The evening stretched endlessly before her and she had no notion how she could bear it. Even seeing Sarah Siddons and John Philip Kemble could not make it bearable, she feared.

Mrs. Montescue was smiling benignly as the marquess went on, "We may as well take our seats. Lucrezia is already ensconced in the box. She is determined to quiz everyone as they take their seats."

"It is like she will be prosing on about it for days to come," Laura said in an aside to her sister.

Although the comment was meant only for Allegra's ears, the marquess responded in a sarcastic manner, "My dear, if she does, it is certain you will not oblige yourself to listen."

Laura cast him a resentful glance as Allegra said, "I recall very clearly my first visit to the theater. It was most exciting, so I know exactly how she feels."

Lady Lucrezia did look excited when they entered Lord Crandon's box. Her cheeks were becomingly flushed and her eyes bright, especially when they alighted upon Barnaby. A moment later she averted her eyes and Allegra felt she knew the reason why; she was recalling with embarrassment their kisses. Once again she could sympathize with the girl's feelings.

"I have never been so excited in my life," Lucrezia confessed as the ladies seated themselves at the front of the box.

"You really should contrive to be more sophisticated," Laura acknowledged, fanning herself furiously. "You should recall that you will be making your debut in a few months' time and leave the schoolroom far behind."

In the face of Lady Lucrezia's evident dismay Allegra said loudly enough for all to hear, "I confess to feeling a mite over-excited myself, my lady. Who could not at the prospect of seeing Mrs. Siddons and Mr. Kemble together in the one play?"

The marquess held each lady's chair in turn as they sat down, brushing aside Barnaby's attempt to do so. When Allegra sat down he held hers, too, and she looked up at him in alarm, seeing there was a faint smile on his lips, and she turned away from him quickly once again.

"I'm so glad you are recovered sufficiently to attend, Miss Montescue," Lady Lucrezia went on, having recovered her spirits. "In all truth, I should have excessively disliked to miss this evening."

"You will soon grow heartily tired of seeing Shakespeare's plays," Laura told her, affecting an air of boredom. "They are, after all, not in any way out of the ordinary."

"We must ensure in the future that we only attend pantomimes when Laura is present," the marquess announced, smiling ironically.

Barnaby burst out laughing. "You're right up to the snuff where m'sister's concerned, Crandon."

"Oh, indeed, you needn't doubt it," the marquess agreed.

Laura looked more than a little vexed by his teasing, and Allegra feared she might fly into one of her miffs, but instead she said (as Lady Lucrezia continued to enjoy the spectacle of her peers filling the boxes around the auditorium and enjoyed polite conversation with Barnaby and Mrs. Montescue), "It appears that Sir Angus Beane is back in Town." Allegra cast her sister a worried look as she smiled and went on, "He's sharing Mrs. Radleigh's box across the auditorium. I thought you would be interested."

"You are quite wrong. If he is returned to Town it is nothing to me, I assure you."

Allegra was unable to recall their last encounter without feeling very angry indeed.

"Oh, come now, you cannot blame the poor fellow for a previous disappointment that was none of his doing."

"My dislike of Sir Angus, I assure you, has nothing to do with what passed, or did not pass, between Sir Dudley and me. I beg of you credit me with disliking him for his own sake. There is much to disapprove of in him."

Laura was once again taken aback. "I cannot truly believe it is so, Ally."

"I beg of you do."

Her sister drew a profound sigh. "I was evidently in serious error when I counseled him to persist in his pursuit of you."

"Laura," Allegra gasped, her eyes opening wide with horror, "you utter and complete chucklehead. No wonder that Jack Straw assumes my rebuff to be all modesty, hiding a true affection for him! I am out of all patience with you."

288

"There really is no need to get on your high ropes, Ally. I did it for your sake," Laura whispered.

"Then for my sake allow me to control my own future with whomsoever it eventually lies."

"You must own you have not been oversuccessful so far."

Once again Allegra made a low noise of annoyance, but it was at this point that the theater grew quiet as the performance was announced to begin, and she was left with her irritating thoughts while the others enjoyed the drama onstage.

Chapter Thirteen

The moment the interval commenced, Lady Lucrezia began to exclaim the excellence of the performances. No one present, not even Laura who drew an almost imperceptible sigh, could argue against her, and Allegra noted that both Barnaby and the marquess were eyeing the girl with unashamed indulgence. It occurred to her that if anyone was to treat Lady Lucrezia with the disdain Lord Crandon had displayed toward *her*, he would deal with them with the utmost severity.

A brief discussion ensued as to whether they intended to remain in the box to receive visits from their acquaintances or go to mingle outside in the lobbies.

Immediately Laura declared her interest. "I must take refreshment and ease my legs after sitting still for so long a time," whereupon her sister and brother elected to accompany her.

Throughout the first half, Allegra had felt that the marquess's eyes had been boring into her back, which had been an uncomfortable experience. On one occasion she had glanced behind, only for his brooding gaze to meet her eyes before she looked away again quickly.

Mrs. Montescue decided to remain in the box, and Lady Lucrezia said, "So shall I. After all, I know so few people as yet, it seems pointless for me to go out there. I don't want to be considered a hang-by."

"Not possible, ma'am," Barnaby gallantly informed her.

She flushed slightly as she added, "Apart from all of us I have only espied one other person I am acquainted with," she went on, smiling shyly, "Mrs. Radleigh. She was exceeding kind to Crandon when he came down from Oxford."

Laura drew in a sharp breath. "That piece of overlaced mutton is accommodating to all young bucks new to Town."

Once again the girl looked dismayed. "She has always been condescending toward me."

"Be warned," Laura answered. "She has her oar in everyone's boat, and I am persuaded most *on dits* emanate from her drawing room, whether they are true or not. When I am Lady Crandon you may be certain I shall snub her. She shall not attend any of my diversions."

So saying, she swept out of the box followed by Allegra, who was obliged to walk past the marquess far too closely for comfort. He made no attempt to move out of her way, and as she passed close by him she was obliged almost to touch him.

Barnaby was laughing at what his sister had said, and chided, "How toplofty our little sister has become of late. It is like before long she will be issuing vouchers to Almack's!"

"Anything is possible," Laura replied, glancing mischievously at her sister, but Allegra's thoughts were far away.

By the time she had enjoyed a welcome glass of lemonade and exchanged pleasantries with an acquaintance, both Barnaby and Laura had wandered away. It was just as she looked around eagerly, seeking a sight of them, that she espied Sir Dudley Rymington approaching her through the crowds, and her already depressed spirits took a further downward plunge. She had known all along that this evening could be nothing but a disaster

When he reached her he smiled faintly. "Miss Montescue, is it not the most enjoyable performance?"

She affected a smile. "I am bound to own that it is, sir. I trust that Lady Rymington is enjoying it as well."

The young man was plainly discomforted at the mention of his wife's name. "Indeed she does." He hesitated for a moment before going on, "I . . . caught sight of you as you arrived with your party and determined to seek you out at the first possible moment. Since my return to London I have had few opportunities to have words with you, which is a great sadness to me."

"As an April gentleman no one should be surprised at how busy a life you lead, sir. The hectic pace in Season is like to continue for us both. Now, I beg you to excuse me as I see my brother beckoning and I am in a fidge to rejoin our party."

There was no such sighting of Barnaby, but Allegra made to go past him. As she did so he said in a low, urgent voice, "Miss Montescue, I am bound to say you are the most admirable female I have ever been privileged to encounter."

She froze on the spot for a moment or two and then she turned on her heel to face him, eyeing him for the first time with total dispassion, something she would have once believed impossible.

"I do believe I have heard you say so before, sir, but it is kind of you to repeat it."

Just at that moment Allegra caught sight of her sister once again, now in the company of Mr. Marsham. The couple were standing closely together in a manner Laura never employed when in Lord Crandon's company. They were conversing intently, and Allegra was startled to see Laura so engrossed in whatever he was saying to her.

All at once Allegra's thoughts were bound up in the possibility of the earl catching sight of Laura and Mr. Marsham. He could not possibly fail to interpret their closeness. However indulgent he had been so far toward Laura he could not possibly sanction the intimacy of conversation she could perceive between them now. With such worried thoughts going round in her head she scarcely heeded what Sir Dudley was saying. She certainly took no note of his words, merely nodding her head at regular intervals while viewing Laura and Mr. Marsham over his shoulder.

When she caught sight of the marquess coming in their direction, appearing to be looking for someone, Allegra quickly said, "Sir Dudley, I must beg you to excuse me. We may continue this conversation better at another time. Just now there is a matter of some considerable import I wish to convey to Lord Crandon."

"By all means, Miss Montescue," he replied, but nevertheless appeared disappointed.

Once again she scarcely heeded him as she moved quickly

away at last, determined not to allow the marquess to catch sight of Laura and Mr. Marsham.

"Lord Crandon," she said breathlessly as she approached him. "I wish to have words with you if you can but spare me a few moments before the play recommences."

He looked at her with a dispassion quite unlike she had observed in him the other evening. "Miss Montescue, I am indeed honored," he responded, his voice heavy with irony.

Allegra's cheeks flushed at his sarcasm, and she addressed herself to his carefully folded neckcloth. "I have come to believe, as you so rightly stated a short time ago, it is necessary for us to seek some accord for the sake of our respective families. No purpose can be served by remaining in a state of enmity."

Still she dare not look at him and she pinned her gaze some way past one of his broad shoulders.

"How do you propose we achieve this miracle?" he asked a moment later, and his manner was remarkable for its coldness toward her.

Her cheeks took on a deeper hue. "For myself I am more than willing to forgive your transgressions toward me."

"That is truly magnanimous of you, ma'am," he responded, and never had his sarcasm been more marked.

For once she was obliged to control the customary irritation he aroused in her, for it was imperative he did not move on and see Laura and Mr. Marsham.

She noted that his neckcloth was pristine in its whiteness and folded with a great precision she could not help but admire.

"In view of the fact my sister is to become your wife in the near future, it would be foolhardy to harbor ill feeling toward you, despite what has happened between us."

"But what of your transgressions toward me, Miss Montescue?" he countered, and her eyes opened wide with shock.

His eyes met hers levelly at last as she protested, "My transgressions! Do I hear you correctly, my lord?"

"I believe you do, ma'am."

"What moonshine! What arrogance! Your arrogance and knavery are astounding. It is I who have been ill used by you on more than the one occasion, not to mention your abominable behavior at Lady Broxbourne's the other evening. . . ."

"Most females would give greatly to be kissed by me," he answered.

"How dare you speak to me in such a cavalier manner?" she cried, which did nothing to hide her fury.

"It appears that you are more often to be seen in the company of Miss Allegra Montescue than your bride-to-be, Crandon."

Both Allegra and the marquess turned to see Mrs. Radleigh close by, on the arm of a handsome young buck, known to be her latest *cher ami*.

In an attempt to hide her anger Allegra fanned her cheeks furiously, noting the muscle at the side of the marquess's mouth had tightened somewhat during their exchange, which she felt indicated he was controlling a towering rage much as she was herself doing.

However, when he spoke no one could possibly be aware of it. His self-possession astounded Allegra, whose fury, she was certain, must be clearly etched upon her features for all to recognize.

"My dear Mrs. Radleigh," he responded, bestowing upon her a devastating smile, "am I not the most fortunate of men? Not only do I have the most delightful bride-to-be, but I have the blessed good fortune to be about to acquire as sister-in-law someone equally as ravishing."

It was all too much for Allegra, who determined not to remain to hear more of his moonshine and she quickly excused herself, watched by an amused Mrs. Radleigh whom she heard say, "Crandon, I fear you are always outside of enough to green girls."

By the time he returned to the box the second half of the performance was about to begin, and Allegra kept her attention focused firmly on the stage. Even a brief glance in his direction was likely to cause her anger to burst forth once again.

However, she was obliged to remain feeling uncomfortable through the rest of the evening, conscious more of his unwelcome closeness than the brilliance of the actors upon the stage.

Chapter Fourteen

"*H*ow I wish you could have been with us last night, Papa," Allegra told him, injecting great enthusiasm into her voice as she made an effort to disregard the discomforting part of the evening, which, if she was to be more honest, overrode her enjoyment of the play. "Mrs. Siddons was quite splendid, as you might suppose."

"Ah yes," Mr. Montescue agreed, "Sarah Siddons and Kemble. What a combination. It must have been a sight well worth seeing. The theater was always such a pleasure to me. Yes, I do so wish I had been well enough to attend. Mayhap next time."

"That would be splendid, Papa."

"However, I don't doubt you were all quite content in Lord Crandon's fine box."

Allegra busied herself tucking in her father's blanket and adjusting his shawl before she retreated to a chair some distance from the overwhelming heat of the fire.

"I'd as lief you could have attended," she said truthfully. "Others may fawn at Lord Crandon's feet and regard us as the most fortunate creatures on earth, but I cannot confess to a partiality."

Mr. Montescue chuckled softly. "In those feelings I'm persuaded you are a most uncommon young lady, Allegra. I recall that Crandon had females throwing themselves at his head the moment he came down from Oxford."

Allegra's lips clamped together in a tight, stubborn line, fearing that her family must, after all, grow resigned to the fact she and the marquess would never enjoy a carefree relationship, although as long as Laura did, that was all that really mattered.

In any event she had begun to suspect that the marquess had

been quite deliberately engineering their confrontations for whatever Machiavellian reasons that pleased his twisted mind. It was evident he had planned their ride in Hyde Park, and his kisses were obviously designed to bestow a clear insult upon her.

Allegra frowned as she wondered idly if Laura was at last seeing faults in his character. It could well be the reason why she was so often to be seen enjoying Mr. Marsham's company and looking far more carefree than she ever did with her husband-to-be. The possibility was teasing to her now that her mind had seized upon it.

"I recall seeing Garrick in *Hamlet*," Mr. Montescue was saying wistfully, and Allegra forced herself to attend his words.

"That must have been quite a revelation, Papa. It is said he was the greatest actor who ever lived."

"I daresay that is so, but naturally I was very young when I saw him. It was a long time ago."

"Tush! You cannot consider yourself *old*."

"There are days when I feel ancient, my dear. If only I still possessed my health and strength, I would be more content. It is so vexing to be prey to every distemper that abounds. I am constantly afflicted by pain and agues."

"You must contrive to conserve all your strength for Laura's wedding. You would not wish to miss such an auspicious occasion."

"No, indeed, I would not. Being obliged to pay so heavily for the privilege of seeing my daughter become a marchioness, I intend to be present even if it does become my very last act on this earth. Do you feel a draught, Allegra?"

She smiled at him fondly. "No, Papa, there are no draughts in here despite the chill outside."

Satisfied, he went on. "What was I saying? Oh yes, Laura's wedding. I shall have Dr. Pomfret bleed me beforehand so as to be certain I will be well enough to attend. Mark me when I say I wish to live long enough to attend *your* wedding, my girl."

Allegra felt her cheeks growing red. "Papa, you sound as if you are eager to be rid of me."

"Oh no, far from it, you may be assured. Both your mother and I will miss you sorely when you do make a match. I'd as lief have you bear me company for as long as I have left, but it is only right for you to marry and have a fine establishment of your own. I cannot conceive why you have not made at least as good a match as your sister's. She is a chucklehead, and you are a woman of great worth."

"It is kind of you to say so, but you do not do Laura justice."

"Balderdash! A flibbertigibbet if ever there was one! I hope Crandon knows fully what he is about to take on. I always considered him well up to the rigs, but love often makes fools of the stoutest of hearts."

"Well, you may be assured that I am quite content to stay as I am."

"You always were, unlike your sister, who was less easy to please. What suited her one day did not the next. Now the opposite is true, although I dare say any chit faced with the offer of marrying Lord Crandon would leap at the opportunity. I cannot blame that in her. By the by, where is the baggage? Not taken to her sickbed, has she?"

"I believe she went out to buy some gewgaws." Allegra could not help but laugh. "Her shopping list appears to be endless."

"If only my purse was bottomless," he complained as his daughter eyed him indulgently.

"She will very soon be Lord Crandon's responsibility."

As Allegra spoke she felt unaccountably resentful, which shocked her. Up until now she had been concerned only for her sister being affianced to that dreadful man, but resentful? No doubt it was only because the marriage would bring him into the family fold at last. It was *her* family, but she did not doubt, with her father so often indisposed, the marquess would in his customarily arrogant manner take over as head of their joint families with alacrity.

Allegra shuddered slightly just as her father asked, "Where is your mama? I have not seen her since breakfast. She has not come down with an ague, has she?"

"Mama has gone to attend a card party given by Lady Fossborough," Allegra told him, smiling wryly.

"That is a great relief. Lady Fossborough is an old crony as I recall. She will enjoy a coze and an exchange of the latest *on dits*. It will be a welcome change to looking after a gouty old man."

"You know full well Mama relishes every minute she spends with you."

"Your mother is a remarkable woman, I own, and I am only surprised you did not accompany her. You must know that she values your company above all others."

"I deemed it time to bear you company for a change, Papa." She laughed. "In any event I have no fancy to be quizzed endlessly by Lady Fossborough and her cronies."

"Tattle-baskets, all of 'em," Mr. Montescue declared. "And it will be such a squeeze your mama is bound to contract a chill."

"The weather has taken a decided turn for the worse today," Allegra told him. "It has become unseasonably cold out there but exceeding cozy in here."

"I did perceive a change, Allegra. This morning when I rose I said so to Randall and charged him to stoke up all the fires. I shall be obliged to take the utmost care lest I contract a chill," he added, drawing the blanket and shawl closer about him.

"Yes, you must, but we are most fortunately cozy in here, Papa, where it is warm."

"Your mama tells me that Barnaby is paying court to Crandon's sister."

"As far as I am able to observe, he is in earnest," Allegra replied, which reminded her wretchedly that his relationship with Lady Lucrezia could only strengthen the connection between the two families.

"I am bound to own the cub is not as foolish as I had supposed, and it will, no doubt, keep him from indulging in rakehell ways."

"In comparison to other young men, Barnaby is a paragon of virtue, and as for Lady Lucrezia, she is utterly delightful. You will be enchanted by her when you meet."

"It is evident you favor her ladyship with rather more enthusiasm than you do her brother," Mr. Montescue said wryly, and she was forced to look away from him.

"You concern me, Allegra," he said a moment later, and her head jerked up in alarm.

"Papa?"

"Your happiness and well-being is of the utmost import to me, child. Would that I were stronger and able to care for your needs more."

"You mustn't trouble your head on my account."

"But I do, and recall I have much time to think on matters that tease me. It has occurred to me, very reluctantly I might add, that your profound dislike of your sister's husband-to-be may well stem more from the fear of partiality than a true grievance."

"Papa!" she protested, looking utterly horrified.

"You think because I no longer mix freely in Society I know nothing of what occurs, or indeed of human nature. I do know you, you must grant me that, child."

Allegra contrived to calm her agitation. "I have always considered you to be the wisest of men, Papa, but I assure you, on this occasion you could not be more wrong. Why, I'd as lief set my cap at Sir Angus Beane!"

Mr. Montescue looked far from convinced, but to Allegra's profound relief the conversation could not be prolonged, for her father's faithful valet, Randall, arrived with his master's physic.

It was with considerable relief that she excused herself, and as she closed the door behind her she paused outside to take a deep breath. How could anyone confuse her hatred of the marquess with quite the opposite feeling? She only hoped that her father's state of chronic ill health was not beginning to affect his powers of reasoning.

When she passed through the hall on her way to her room, she saw standing there a large basket of flowers. Because such gifts almost invariably arrived for Laura, Allegra took only a fleeting note of them, but as she passed by, the footman on duty by the door attracted her attention.

"Miss Montescue, the flowers arrived half an hour ago for you."

"For me?" she could not help but ask. "Are you quite certain they are not for Miss Laura?"

"Oh no, ma'am," the lackey assured her. "Your name is written on the attached note quite clearly."

Fearing that the extravagance stemmed from Sir Angus Beane, she snatched the note from the basket and with a fast beating heart broke open the seal without taking note of what it represented. However, the coat of arms at the head of the parchment was immediately recognizable as she unfolded the note. The lion rampant seemed entirely in character.

298

There is no excuse for incivility, she read. *Accept my sincere apologies with this peace offering. Crandon.*

Such curtness could not be construed as regret, she decided, and when she looked up at the lackey her eyes were narrowed with anger. "You may remove this basket to the servants' quarters as soon as you please."

The footman appeared somewhat taken aback at so magnanimous a gesture, but replied in his customarily urbane manner. "As you wish, ma'am."

"Do it immediately," she added, somewhat unnecessarily.

"Yes, ma'am."

"Has Miss Laura returned home yet?" she asked as the footman began to do her bidding.

There was an odd hesitation before he replied, "Not as yet, ma'am."

As she hurried up the stairs, she felt as outraged as if the marquess had abused her again. His arrogance was, she felt, becoming unbearable if he truly believed he could insult her as he wished and then buy her forgiveness with flowers so soon afterward. There would be no reconciliation, Allegra decided, not for her family's sake or her own. He was entirely odious and nothing could possibly improve upon his nature.

For some few minutes she angrily prowled around her room, seeking to calm her agitation. A fire had been lit in the hearth, no doubt on account of the sudden snap of cold weather, but Allegra's anger kept her warm enough. Her cheeks were still burning with the anger the note had instilled in her.

Carriages passed beneath her window constantly, and the rattle of their wheels and the sound of the horse's hooves were clearly heard, punctured frequently by the different cries of the pedlars in the street below.

Allegra stared out of the window at the scene below, longing for the company of some member of her family or a friend who might call, to divert her mind from angry and discomforting thoughts. But it was evident that the snap of cold weather was keeping many indoors.

Eventually, she turned her back on the bleak scene outside, and as she did so she caught sight of a note on the dressing table. Frowning, she went to read it. At first, as she quickly scanned the

299

scrawled hand, she was disbelieving, but then, as she read more carefully what was written, she gasped in dismay.

Dearest Ally,

I beg you to ensure everyone will understand what I am about to do, but I have come to believe I shall never be able to be a satisfactory wife to Crandon, as my true affections are engaged elsewhere, which I believe you have suspected all the while. I am, therefore, going to marry Mr. Marsham. We are obliged to engage in secrecy because I cannot possibly endure Mama's dismay and disappointment, and of more import it is to ensure that my dear Geoffrey does not fall foul of Crandon's temper and natural desire for revenge. I pray you will all forgive me in time and wish me happy. I do not do this lightly.

Your sister, Laura

For some moment Allegra was stunned, unable to think properly or to act, and then, crumpling the note in her hand, she ran down the corridor to her sister's room. A quick survey of Laura's press proved beyond doubt the girl had taken some of her clothes. Her jewel case stood open on the dressing table and Allegra could see that it was all but empty. Only a few small, unimportant pieces remained.

Frantic, now that the reality of the situation was beginning to impress itself upon her, she dashed first one way and then the other until she hurried to pull the bell rope, pacing the floor until the maidservant came hurrying along in answer to the summons.

"Do you know when Miss Laura went out?" Allegra asked breathlessly the moment the abigail appeared.

"I believe it was about an hour ago, ma'am."

"Did you happen to see which carriage she took?"

"I regret I did not, ma'am. Would you have me enquire of the footmen?"

Allegra shook her head. "Do you know if Mr. Barnaby is at home?"

The maid frowned momentarily, and then her face cleared, "Yes, yes, he is, ma'am. I understand he is in the library."

Allegra drew a profound sigh and rushed past the startled

maid, for it was only rarely that Miss Allegra was seen to be in a taking. Now Miss Laura . . .

A few minutes later Allegra burst into the library, causing her brother to look up from his documents in surprise. One glance at his sister's face brought him to his feet.

"Ally, what has put you in such a pelter? It is not Papa, is it?"

"No, it's Laura! Oh, Barnaby, I am totally out of countenance. I do not know what to do!"

His eyes opened wide. "Laura! What has the chit done to cause you such vexation?"

"She has eloped!"

The young man cast his sister a disbelieving look.

"You're bamming me. Why should Crandon, of all people, wish to elope with Laura so close to their wedding day?"

Allegra stamped her foot in vexation. "She has not eloped with Lord Crandon, goosecap! She has eloped with Mr. Marsham."

"Hell and damnation!" the young man cried. "The little sly-boots. Has she taken leave of her senses?"

"Very like she has regained them," Allegra could not help but retort.

Barnaby sank back down in the chair, staring sightlessly ahead of him. "This is a real case of pickles, sis. I don't relish telling Crandon his little bird has flown."

Allegra's eyes opened wide in alarm. "Oh no, Barnaby, he must never know of it. We must make sure that he does not."

Barnaby smiled then, eyeing his sister wryly. "Good grief, Ally, how can he possibly be kept in ignorance? We must also tell Mama without delay, although I don't relish that task either."

Allegra caught hold of his sleeve. "Don't you see, Barnaby? We must bring Laura back before *anyone* else comes to know of it."

"She has chosen a deuced awkward time. There is every indication of snow in the air, and I have arranged to join Carruthers for dinner this evening."

His sister's eyes rolled upward. "I am out of all patience with you! Do you really not understand what this means to our sister? I cannot conceive you are such a gudgeon."

"No need to go name calling, Ally. Laura's made her choice.

Let her fry in her own grease. In any event the tattle-baskets will find something else to prattle on about after a sen'night."

"You really are as dizzy as a goose, Barnaby, if you do not realize the consequences of this escapade. If Lord Crandon finds out he has been bested by someone like Geoffrey Marsham, there will be hell to pay. He is bound to call the poor fellow out, and I do not have to tell you that Mr. Marsham is no match for the Marquess of Crandon. Moreover, it is certain he will ensure our sister will never be able to go out into Society again."

"I own Crandon is not a man who will easily forgive," Barnaby agreed.

"It is quite evident to me she must be stopped and the matter resolved in a manner that ensures that Lord Crandon's excessive pride is not injured. The baggage has even taken his gift of emeralds to fund her elopement!" Allegra paused for breath before adding, "If you cannot consider Laura and the rest of this family, think of yourself. Do you truly believe Lord Crandon will continue to countenance your courtship of his sister after Laura makes him look a ninnyhammer?"

"He wouldn't be so cruel!" Barnaby retorted in shocked tones.

"Are you willing to gamble upon his good nature?" his sister asked, looking scornful.

"What do you suggest we do? Indeed, what can we do? As far as I can see we are in the suds."

"Fetch a carriage around while I pack a cloakbag." When he immediately started toward the door she added, "Contrive to procure a closed carriage if it is at all possible, Barnaby. It will be more comfortable, I fancy, especially when we return home with Laura."

"*If* we do," he answered darkly.

"We cannot afford to fail."

"If speed is of the essence . . ."

"It is!"

"Then we might be obliged to travel in my phaeton."

"Whatever the carriage, you must ensure a fast team is put to."

"Rely upon it," he answered before rushing off.

With scarcely a pause Allegra hurried back upstairs and swiftly packed a cloakbag with a few essentials for their journey. A very short time later, enveloped in a fur-lined cloak and carrying a matching muff she hurried out of the house into a bitterly cold wind. Snow flurried on the wind, but she disregarded it, concerned only that they should catch up with their errant sister with as little delay as possible.

To her relief she was obliged to wait only a short time before a post chaise came charging around the corner. Allegra smiled with satisfaction and did not question how her brother had contrived to obtain a post chaise at such short notice. She was just relieved that he had returned with it with minimum delay.

The moment the chaise came to a halt outside Montescue House, Allegra wrenched open the door and propelled herself inside, whereupon it set off at a furious pace once more. As she sank back into the squabs she drew a great sigh and then stiffened with alarm, for it was a smiling Sir Angus Beane who sat facing her and not her brother.

Now Allegra sat up straight, her mind in a turmoil. "Sir Angus! What are you doing here?"

"Judging by your anxiety to join me I am certain you know full well, my dear."

Agitated now, she explained, "There has been a grave mistake, I fear. I thought you were someone else."

One of his eyebrows rose slightly but he seemed not in the least put out. "Did you by any chance plan to elope with another gentleman?"

"Elope?" she laughed disparagingly. "By no means; and be certain, sir, I do not intend to elope with *you*. Be pleased to return me home immediately."

When he smiled and seemed disinclined to obey she became even more alarmed. "My dear Miss Montescue, I think it is just what you want, but like so many of your gender you tend to enjoy certain contrariness."

Her considerable irritation then began to turn to real fear and she thumped her fist down on the seat. "Stop this carriage this instant and let me down."

"I would be a fool to comply with what I deem to be quite natural maidenly diffidence."

She shook her head in disbelief. "I think you are quite mad, and you will not escape retribution for this outrage."

"Who is there to stop us? Not your father, who is unfortunately an invalid, or Barnaby Montescue, who interests himself only with matters concerning his own pleasure. I dare say I am obliged to consider Crandon." At this her head snapped up. "But I doubt if he will go so far as to pursue us, and once we are wed he will see it is better to let matters be."

"Wed! Oh no, Sir Angus, I will not marry you."

"The way to the border is clear, and I'm persuaded you will be glad to have the honor of being Lady Beane in a very short time."

He tossed a blanket toward her, saying, "Tuck this around you, my dear. We cannot have you catching a chill."

Allegra tossed it contemptuously to one side and then put her head back against the squabs, closing her eyes in despair. If she had not felt so angry and afraid she would have been tempted to laugh at the irony of the situation in which she found herself.

Chapter Fifteen

The racing curricle of the Marquess of Crandon, drawn by a magnificent team of matching grays, thundered to a halt outside Montescue House. The marquess thrust the ribbons at his tiger the moment he climbed down, before striding purposefully into the house.

"Be pleased to inform Miss Allegra that I wish to have words with her," he told the startled house steward who had been observing the frenetic comings and goings with some astonishment.

"I regret to inform you, my lord, that both Miss Allegra and Miss Laura are out."

The marquess's eyes narrowed somewhat. "It must be near the time for her to return for luncheon, is it not?"

"Normally that would be so, my lord."

"The manner of your reply indicates clearly to me that today matters are not as normal," the marquess responded, a note o even greater irritation creeping into his voice. When the house steward appeared reluctant to elaborate the marquess tossed him a coin, saying, "I am in no mood to be kept cooling my heels."

"It seems a rum go, my lord, but there is no doubt that Miss Allegra left a short time ago in a post chaise."

The marquess drew in a sharp breath. "Accompanied, no doubt, by Mr. Barnaby."

"It was initially thought to be so, my lord, but Makepiece, the footman on duty at the time, believed he caught sight of Sir Angus Beane inside the carriage, although it scarce stopped long enough for anyone to be certain."

The house steward hadn't even finished speaking when the marquess turned on his heel and dashed out of the house. The Montescue servants peered bemusedly into the street as he drove off at a furious pace in the direction taken by the post chaise.

"It appears we shall be obliged to put up at the inn we are now approaching," Sir Angus informed Allegra as he withdrew his head from the window. "The horses are having difficulty with the slippery roads, and visibility is getting worse."

Since setting out the snow had begun to fall with increasing intensity, blanketing the road with surprising speed. There was no doubt the further north they traveled the weather would grow progressively worse. It did give Allegra some cause for hope, although she was fully aware that if they could not travel neither could any rescuer, even if anyone knew what had happened to her, which was doubtful. Her heart suddenly filled with despair.

"I suggest we would be best returning to London," she responded, a comment that elicited a smile from Sir Angus.

"I shall not rest easy until we are wed. I have waited an unconscionable time for you, Miss Montescue, and my patience is growing thin."

As the post chaise drew into the courtyard and jerked to a halt, he stepped down, holding out his hand to Allegra, who hesitated to take it but knew she had no choice. Snow swirled round them as he drew her into the inn where the smiling landlord bowed them down a cold dark corridor and then into a parlor with a mercifully large fire.

When Allegra allowed the hood of her cloak to fall back from her head, Sir Angus said, "You look lovely, my dear."

"Do you truly believe you can succeed in marrying me against my will?"

"I don't believe you are as unwilling as you pretend," he countered. "No female would be if the alternative is spinsterhood."

"This is outside of enough!" she cried in exasperation. "The duns must be mounting vigil outside your house to make you so desperate you would snatch an unwilling bride."

"By the time we reach Gretna I vow you will be entirely willing. After all, we could scarce travel the length of the country and return to London unmarried."

She shuddered, and he went on, "I believe I will procure for us some supper."

"I could not eat a morsel."

"I shall insist that you do. Do you think I want a bag of bones for a wife?"

"I think you want any wife who will enable you to pay the duns."

He was halfway across the room when the parlor door flew open, slamming back on its hinges against the wall. Both Allegra and Sir Angus looked aghast to see Lord Crandon framed in the doorway, the capes of his drab driving coat caked with fast-melting snow.

"What in damnation are you doing here?" Sir Angus demanded, but there was a note of fear in the bravura of his voice.

"I have come in pursuit of my bride," the marquess replied, and with no further ado he punched the other man so hard Sir Angus stumbled and fell. It was then that the marquess looked at Allegra. "Has he harmed you?" She shook her head, and before Sir Angus could recover himself, Lord Crandon, watched by a wide-eyed and fearful Allegra, strode over to him. "Consider yourself fortunate Miss Montescue declares herself unmolested, for if she had not you would be about to suffer a far worse fate."

Sir Angus wiped away a trickle of blood from the side of his mouth. "You make too much of this, Crandon."

"You should give thanks I make little of it, and that is only for Miss Montescue's sake. I would not wish her to witness the brutish side of my nature, for I am tempted to make cold meat out of you. Now get up and be off with you before I am like to change my mind."

The other man smiled crookedly as he began to get to his feet. "It might be deuced awkward, Crandon, for I regret to say we shall all be obliged to stay here until the snow clears."

"I have no intention of allowing you, sir, to remain beneath the same roof with Miss Montescue," the marquess insisted, propelling Sir Angus bodily toward the door where the inn servants had assembled to watch the altercation with evident delight. "Your horses are put to, so be gone. There is another inn a mile down the road. I daresay you will be able to reach it, although I cannot vouch for its comfort and cleanliness, but I believe you will prefer it to facing the muzzle of my dueling pistol."

After he had pushed him outside, the marquess closed the parlor door and then turned to Allegra, his anger melting. "Thank God I found you so soon."

"The snow has been a good friend," she agreed, and when he came to her she went unthinkingly into his arms. "He thought I actually wanted to marry him."

"It's over now," he assured her. "He will not trouble you again, you may be sure."

"I have never been so relieved to see anyone," she sighed, reveling in the comfort of his embrace, even though his coat was damp from the snow.

"Even if it is I," he replied, sounding amused.

She looked up then into his face that was so familiar to her, and she acknowledged at last her father had been wiser than she. He had known what she had not.

"You evidently know about Laura and Mr. Marsham."

"Oh, yes. A note was waiting for me when I returned home this afternoon."

"I did not think of that," she admitted as she moved away from him. Then, when there was sufficient distance between them for her to be able to compose herself, she turned to face him again. "I beg of you do not pursue her any further. If you can find it in your heart, show her compassion. Accept that she means you no disrespect, but she is truly enamored of Mr. Marsham and has been since before her debut."

He frowned and shook his head. "I fear your nerves have been

307

overset by your experience. I have no intention of pursuing them. I only wish Laura happy with her Mr. Marsham."

Allegra gasped. "I don't understand. You have come here in pursuit of her. I heard you say so."

"No. I came in pursuit of *you*."

"You said quite clearly that you had come in pursuit of your bride."

"I hope that is what you will be, Allegra."

As he looked at her hopefully she sank down on a settle by the fire. "I think you may be correct, my lord. My nerves must have been overset, for you seem to be saying the oddest things that I cannot properly comprehend."

He laughed, threw off his damp greatcoat, and went to sit by her side. He drew her back into his arms, and when she looked at him he kissed her gently.

"Now, do you comprehend?" he asked. When she shook her head he went on, "Then allow me to explain it to you. Allegra, I love you so much it has made me beside myself with anger often of late. I daresay you have been aware of that, if not the reason for it."

"I cannot quite credit this. Did you not admit to me you inveigled Sir Dudley out of offering for me? You could not have cared for me to do so."

"Is it not obvious? I couldn't bear to see you married to him. He truly wasn't worthy of you." She couldn't help but laugh bemusedly. "I believed if I was able to dissuade him, you might begin to look upon *me* with some degree of favor. When you did not, I was bound to admit I had made a grave error of judgment."

"Do you regard your offer for my sister in the same light?"

"Oh, indeed I do," he answered heavily. "One evening, after enduring your indifference, I became foxed, and it was while I was in my cups I was foolish enough to offer for Laura, believing that by marrying her I would at least be able to be more in *your* company. Needless to say when I awoke the next morning I was horrified at what I had done, not to speak of my sore head!"

"Oh, Brett, what a goosecap I have been," she sighed.

"If we are both buffle-heads at least it means we are well matched."

"Yes," she breathed.

"Does that mean you are no longer averse to my attentions?"

Her answer was to fling her arms around his neck and hug him close. When he kissed her again she thought she might die of happiness, and it was with some difficulty a few minutes later that they parted.

"Your fight with Sir Dudley cannot have had anything to do with me," she ventured, looking doubtful.

The marquess appeared to be slightly abashed. "I regret to say it was entirely to do with you."

"Do you intend to tell me, for I am truly in a fidge to know?"

He smiled wryly. "On his return to London, Rymington had been obliged to endure several weeks of his new wife's company and had come to realize what a ninnyhammer he had been to cast you off so easily. When he heard that *I* was to marry into the Montescue family his temper snapped, and he decided to call me out."

Again she couldn't help but laugh. "How exactly did you dissuade him from offering for me?"

Once more he looked abashed. "We cracked open a few bottles of claret, and I allowed him to drink most of it. Then I suggested very gently that he would never be happy married to a female who could outride him. The very next day when Miss Pelham, as I understand it, insinuated herself into his company, he offered for her. I take it you no longer feel aggrieved at me for my efforts in that direction."

"He cannot have been in earnest if he gave me the go-by so readily, and although you are entirely to blame, I can only be thankful now."

He took her hand and held it tightly in his. "I cannot tell you how relieved I was to receive Laura's note this afternoon. The only way I could conceive of freeing myself of my obligation to her was to ensure she was as much in Mr. Marsham's company as was possible. Never have I gambled so recklessly. It was neck or nothing!"

The observation caused her to laugh delightedly. "I thought you would kill them should you catch them, so I resolved to bring her back."

"On your own?" he asked in some surprise.

"No. With Barnaby. Once I had convinced him of the necessity

309

to go in pursuit. That was not easy, for he was engaged to dine at Brooks's."

"Where the devil is he?"

For the first time Allegra gave that matter some consideration. "He is probably still trying to find a post chaise to convey us. You see, I thought it was Barnaby arriving when I got into Sir Angus's carriage."

He nodded before going on to explain, "As soon as I received your sister's note I gave quick thanks for my deliverance in the Godspeed and went immediately to declare myself to you. Whatever the outcome I wanted no more pretense between us. My pride, all at once, seemed not to matter any longer. You did receive my flowers, I take it."

Allegra nodded, but did not elaborate on her reaction to their arrival. "Mama is going to be quite overset by Laura's elopement."

"She will have the consolation of seeing you married in her stead."

Allegra caught her breath at the vision of becoming his bride. "This is so sudden. My head is in a whirl!"

"We shall not be obliged to wait an unconscionable time. The church is already booked and invitations issued, only it will be you and not Laura who becomes my bride."

"I do love you desperately," she admitted at last.

When the door flew open once again they were clasped in each other's arms, taking advantage of the degree of privacy they could enjoy for a while.

"Devil take it!" Barnaby exclaimed as he stood in the doorway. "What the deuce is the meaning of all this?"

The young man's coat and high-crowned beaver were also covered with melting snow, some of which dripped down his face, which bore a look of total amazement.

The marquess looked at his future brother-in-law with amusement as Barnaby asked belligerently, "I demand an explanation, Crandon. Is it you who made off with m'sister?"

"No, it was Beane. His destination, if you cannot guess, was Gretna Green. Fortunately I was able to come in pursuit very soon afterward."

"You came in pursuit of *Allegra*?" the young man asked incredulously.

"Who else? Your other sister may go to the devil with whomsoever she pleases, for all I care."

Allegra snuggled closer to him, a sight not lost upon her brother who sank down on a seat facing them, shaking his head in disbelief.

"Be pleased to explain, Crandon. I have struggled through the most appalling snowstorm, not knowing what to expect or even which sister I am like to find, so I am a trifle confused, I fear."

The marquess was gracious enough to explain, causing Barnaby's bewilderment to turn slowly to delight. "That is splendid news! You and Allegra! Well done! I am still a trifle bewildered, but you may be certain I could not be more pleased, and not least that Beane received a basting. I wish I had been here to see you give him a facer."

"It is as well that you have arrived," the marquess told him, glancing at Allegra. "It appears we shall be obliged to remain until the weather lifts, and I am anxious to observe all proprieties until we are married. Heaven knows there will be tattle enough if this little escapade becomes known!"

"It was the devil of a job for me to get as far as this," Barnaby admitted, "so it is certain we cannot leave for some time."

"It will at least give Allegra and I an opportunity to be alone together to plan our future," the marquess ventured, injecting a heavy hint into his voice.

For a moment the young man did not respond and then he got to his feet. "Oh, yes, indeed. I believe I shall go and have words with the landlord, who appears to be an amenable kind of fellow. If I am able, I shall procure for us some rooms and order supper. I don't suppose they are prepared, but we shall contrive."

When he had gone, carefully closing the door behind him, the marquess turned to Allegra, saying, "Alone at last. Let us hope it snows for a week."

She laid her head on his broad shoulder, feeling content. "I doubt if it will at this time of the year. However, we can hope. I wonder where Laura and Mr. Marsham are now."

"Miles ahead I shouldn't wonder. They must have left long before it started to snow and had a good head start. I'm persuaded

311

they wished to get as far up the Great North Road as possible before nightfall. At least we shall be spared her tedious prattle for a while."

"You might have been obliged to marry her," Allegra pointed out, "and listen to it for the rest of your life."

"Heaven forfend! Fate could not have been so cruel."

While the two lovers reveled in each other's company in the privacy of the parlor and Barnaby sought out the landlord, a carriage came slowly into the courtyard.

"Thank goodness we have found shelter for the night," Laura Montescue gasped as Mr. Marsham hurried her inside.

The landlord's wife greeted them, scarcely able to believe her good fortune in having so many members of the Quality in the hostelry.

"We require a private parlor," Mr. Marsham told her.

"I regret, sir, we have only the one, and because of the weather it has already been bespoken. However, sir, as the occupants are all gentry like yourselves, they will be glad enough to offer to share it with you."

Laura looked up at her lover, saying with a sigh, "At least we shall have shelter, Geoffrey." When the landlord's wife began to usher them toward the parlor, Laura lamented, "How unfortunate it is that we were obliged to turn back after making such good progress."

"It's not surprising we could not go further," Mr. Marsham explained, "but the foul weather does at least mean no members of your family, or more importantly, Lord Crandon, can have come in pursuit of us."

"Yes," Laura beamed, turning to him as the landlord's wife opened the parlor door, "they will not find us now. Here we can be alone until we are able to continue our journey to Gretna and not set eyes upon any of them until we are married!"